IVY

WILLA NASH

IVY

ISBN: 978-1-957376-06-6

Editing & Proofreading:

Judy Zweifel, Judy's Proofreading

www.judysproofreading.com

Julie Deaton, Deaton Author Services

Elizabeth Nover, Razor Sharp Editing

www.razorsharpediting.com

other titles

calamity montana series

The Bribe

The Bluff

The Brazen

The Bully

The Brawl

holiday brothers series

The Naughty, The Nice and The Nanny

Three Bells, Two Bows and One Brother's Best Friend

A Partridge and a Pregnancy

contents

one

. . .

"THIS CAN'T BE the right house." Cassia glanced at the map on her phone for the tenth time. According to the little blue dot, she'd arrived at her new home. Except this couldn't be the house, because it wasn't *a house*. It was a manor.

Clarence Manor.

The title was etched in one of the pillars at the gated entrance. Beyond the iron bars, a two-story, red brick building stood proudly at the end of a narrow lane. White windows of varying shapes from rectangles to ovals gleamed under the August sun. Round columns bracketed the entrance, and in the center of the lane, water bubbled from a fountain.

There wasn't a chance in hell she was in the right place. People who owned Federalist-style manors didn't rent out rooms for four hundred dollars a month.

"Damn it." Of course she was lost. That was the theme of her life at the moment.

Lost. Weary. Alone.

She'd been driving for nine hours, and all she wanted to do was collapse. To unpack and sleep for the rest of the weekend. Her clothes were rumpled. The makeup she'd swiped on this morning had melted off her face. The air-conditioning in her car had crapped out three hundred miles ago, and even with the windows down, the air was hot and stuffy.

Cassia opened her phone to double-check the text from her landlord-slash-roommate. She reentered the address Ivy had given her into the GPS. Twice. Both times, it landed on the same location.

"I guess I'll try the gate code." Talking to herself had become a habit. She didn't have anyone else to talk to, and the person she needed to speak with was dead.

Stretching an arm through the window, she punched the numbers that Ivy had given her into the keypad. She'd assumed the gate code would be for an apartment complex or a campus neighborhood full of tiny homes like the ones that had surrounded Hughes. But Dad had always warned her that Aston wasn't like other colleges.

The creak of metal rent the air as the iron gates swung open.

"Uh . . . seriously?" So she wasn't lost. She didn't have the energy for a fist pump. Instead, she lifted her foot off the brake and eased down the lane.

Green, manicured lawns stretched beyond the driveway. Elm trees and evergreen shrubs hugged the fence line. With every turn of her tires, she was driving deeper into a different realm. Her fifteen-year-old, rusted Honda Civic was as out of place as the single cloud in the otherwise clear sky.

Cassia had never felt so poor in her life.

She parked in the loop at the front of the house, then did a quick check in the rearview mirror to smooth out her coral hair. The color was new for her, a change from her natural honey blond. But she'd needed change. Hence the hair. Hence the school.

And now the house.

She didn't bother taking a bag as she climbed out of the car. There was a very real chance that Ivy would take one look at her—disheveled and dejected—and revoke her lease agreement. But since she didn't have anywhere else to go, Cassia squared her shoulders and walked up the staircase to the manor's double doors. She should have worn something other than jeans, a vintage Beatles tee and Birkenstocks.

The outfit, combined with the hair, made her look like she belonged at a hippie commune, not a prestigious private university on the outskirts of Boston. Then again, she'd never really fit anywhere. Certainly not at Hughes.

She had no expectations of blending in at Aston either.

With a deep breath expanding her lungs, she pressed the doorbell, her heart racing as she waited.

It swung open and an older man with thick salt-and-pepper hair answered. His black slacks and white button-down shirt were so crisp that they could likely stand on their own. *He* belonged at a manor. "Yes?"

"I, um . . . hi. I think I'm in the wrong place."

"Your name?"

"Cassie Nei—Collins." *Shit.* She forced a smile. "Cassia Collins. I'm a new student, and I rented a room at a house around here. But the directions my roommate gave me were to this place. Is there a garage apartment or something? I wasn't sure where else to park, but I'll move my car. I know it's an eyesore. Maybe just point me in the right direction. Sorry. I'm rambling. I, uh, sorry."

Dad had always told her that her rambling was charming. Others usually gave her a sideways glance.

From the blank stare, Mr. Starch did not think she was charming, but the man opened the door wider and waved her inside.

"Oh, I can wait out here." She held up a hand. "That's okay."

He scanned her head to toe, his lip curling ever so slightly. "Or you can come inside, and I'll have Miss Ivy show you to your room."

Before she could respond, he strode through the foyer, his shoes as polished as the marble floor.

"Holy shit, no way." Ivy. Her new roommate.

A garage apartment was the most likely outcome, but what if . . .

She didn't let herself finish that thought. Cassia no longer believed in luck.

Taking a tentative step across the threshold, she eased the door closed behind her.

"Whoa." Her whisper echoed.

A sweeping staircase curved to the second floor. A crystal chandelier caught the sunlight streaming through the windows and cast small rainbows around the entryway. A floral bouquet made of white roses and lilies sat on an intricate table at her side, their fragrance filling her nose.

Footsteps sounded from the hallway the man had disappeared through and she stood straighter, her breath caught in her throat as a stunning blond strode through the foyer.

The woman's green chiffon sundress billowed behind her. The neckline dipped low in a V and a single diamond glittered at the base of her throat. She could sit for tea with a queen, while Cassia was dressed for an afternoon at a dive bar.

"Hello! You must be Cassia. Welcome." The woman extended her hand with a smile. "I'm Ivy Clarence."

"Hi." She gulped. "It's nice to meet you."

"I'm so glad you're here." Ivy's blue eyes softened. "You found the house okay?"

"Yes. Your directions were perfect." And had Cassia asked for Ivy's last name during their one and only phone call to discuss the rental listing, the manor's name would have made sense.

Her lease agreement was with CM Enterprises. *CM. Clarence Manor?* Yeah, she probably should have read the contract she'd signed. It had just been bumped up her to-do list. But in her rush to leave Hughes behind, she'd skipped details beyond the monthly rental rate and physical address.

"You met Geoff," Ivy said.

"I did. Is this his house?" She wasn't opposed to living

with the older gentleman, but her assumptions had been tripping her up since she'd stopped at the gate.

"No, Geoff's our butler." Ivy giggled. "He takes care of the property. But I promise, you won't hardly know he's here."

A butler. Nine hours of driving and she truly had arrived in an alternate universe.

"I'm sorry." Cassia swallowed a laugh. "I wasn't expecting all of this. You did say four hundred a month, right?" Because that was all she could afford to pay.

Ivy nodded. "Yes, that's correct."

"Okay." The air rushed from her lungs.

Her heavy class load would require her fullest attention if she was going to graduate in the spring. And she *had* to graduate. Her miniscule inheritance would cover a year's rent with just enough cash to spare for cheap food. If she had to get a job, she would, but adding work to the mix, well . . . she'd drown.

"I'll show you to your room," Ivy said. "Then let you get unpacked and settled."

This was the moment Cassia expected to be led to a basement cellar, except Ivy walked toward the sweeping staircase and led her to the second floor.

Even if she had to live in an upstairs storage closet, she'd make do. For four hundred bucks, she'd anticipated a cramped apartment with a shared bathroom. If her room was an actual *closet*, so be it. This was just a short-term situation for her senior year.

Besides, she'd survived the past three months. She could endure a shitty bedroom for a year.

Ivy's heels clicked with each step. Her fingertips skimmed the wooden banister, the light catching on her glossy, green nails. Ivy was undoubtedly the type of girl who got weekly manicures. Meanwhile, Cassia chewed her nails to the nubs.

She tucked her hands into her jeans pockets.

"How was your trip?" Ivy asked over her shoulder. "You came from Pennsylvania, right?"

"Yes. And it was long. It's nice to be here." It was good to be away from Hughes.

The minute she'd driven off campus this morning, it had been like fleeing a storm. Aston was an unknown. New school. New classes. New professors. That was a nerve-racking trio. But Cassia would take this knot in her stomach if it meant she no longer had to stand in the center of a tornado.

"This is quite the house," she said as they reached the landing on the second floor. "You didn't exactly tell me it was this, um . . . fancy."

Ivy shrugged. "I guess it is. To me, it's just home."

What would life be like if a manor was normal? At any moment, a cameraman was going to pop out of his hiding spot and announce that she'd been pranked. She really should have asked more questions.

Cassia's decision to transfer to Aston had been a spur-of-the-moment idea three weeks ago. After months of avoiding the world and wallowing in her grief, she'd crawled out of her solitude for a meeting with her advisor at Hughes. Five minutes on campus, with people giving her strange looks and whispering behind her back, had sent her into a spiral. She'd skipped the meeting, rushed home and made a call.

There were too many memories at Hughes. Too many horrors. Abandoning that life had been her only option.

One, and only one, person at Aston knew about her past. And he'd vowed never to share the ugly truth.

Nearly all of her credits had transferred to Aston. The two classes that hadn't, she'd tacked on to her course schedule. School would be her focus. She'd let it consume her every minute until she forgot the past.

Until people asked her name and Cassia Collins was the automatic response.

Until the ghost of Cassie Neilson had vanished.

"You're this way." Ivy swung an arm toward the hallway at their left. "Please make yourself at home. The parlor on this side of the manor is really cozy on rainy afternoons. The library is fair game, and if you want a fire lit in the hearth, just ask Geoff."

The manor had a parlor and a library. Cassia's jaw hit the shiny hardwood floor.

They passed door after door as they walked the wide hallway. The crown molding and the window trim were hand carved with scrolled details found only in classic buildings.

Ivy turned down another hallway, walking to the last door. "This is your suite. We've got a housekeeper who cleans this side of the house every Friday but if you need anything—"

"Just ask Geoff."

"You're catching on." Ivy winked, then entered the room, spinning a wrist. "What do you think? Is this okay?"

"Uh . . ." *Okay?*

The space was larger than the apartment she'd left in Pennsylvania. The four-poster bed was so massive she'd probably get lost beneath the plush, white duvet. A table in the corner had two wingback chairs. She had her own gas fireplace. The windows overlooked the rear of the house and the gardens beyond.

"This is a dream," she whispered to Ivy. And to herself.

"I'm glad you like it." Ivy pointed to the doors opposite the bed. "En suite on the right. Closet on the left."

"Wow. It's . . . wow." Sweat began beading at her temples. This was too good to be true. Much too good. Good things didn't happen to her these days.

"Would you like some help hauling in your things?" Ivy asked. "Geoff would be happy to carry them upstairs."

Given the way Geoff had looked her up and down, she highly doubted he'd volunteer. "No, thanks. I can grab them. I don't have much."

The contents of her life had fit into the trunk of a Honda. That might have been depressing had she not felt a weight leave her shoulders when she'd sold the rest of her belongings.

A fresh start. A blank slate.

"Want a tour?" Ivy asked. "I kind of love giving them, so please say yes."

"Yes, please. Absolutely."

"Thanks." She laughed and waved for Cassia to follow. When they reached the top of the staircase, she pointed to the hallway that stretched toward the opposite end of the house. "My rooms are that way."

Rooms. Plural. Cassia stifled a laugh. What the hell was she doing here? "All right. Cool."

She was seconds away from a nervous breakdown, but if Ivy noticed, she didn't say a word.

They retreated downstairs and through the foyer, weaving through the manor's maze of hallways until Cassia wasn't sure which way was up or down. Ivy showed her the formal dining room and the informal dining room. They passed the billiards room and another parlor. Then there was the theater and in-home gym.

"Elora's rooms are on the first floor," Ivy said as she turned into the huge kitchen with industrial-grade appliances.

"Elora?"

"Our other roommate. I think she left a little bit ago, but I'm sure she'll come introduce herself later."

"Okay."

"We've lived together since freshman year."

"Ah." So Cassia would be the third wheel. For four hundred dollars and a bathroom of her own, she'd be the tenth wheel. Considering this house could comfortably sleep fifty, having two roommates would be no problem.

A middle-aged woman with a severe gray bob strolled into the kitchen. "Miss Ivy."

"Hello, Francis. Meet Cassia Collins. She'll be living here for the year."

Francis nodded. "Miss Cassia."

"Oh, you can just call me Cassia," she corrected. "I don't need the *Miss*."

"Very well. Cassia." A doorbell chimed in the distance. "That would be the market delivery. If you'll excuse me."

"Francis is our chef," Ivy said as the woman left the room. "She keeps the fridge stocked for breakfast and lunch, then prepares a meal each night."

"Okay. Is there a place where I can stash my groceries so they're out of her way?"

Ivy blinked. "Pardon?"

"My food. I don't want it to be in her way or intrude on her workspace."

"Why would you need to buy food?"

"To eat?" Why was this a question?

Ivy shook her head. "Francis will insist on cooking for you too. It's included with your rent."

For the second time in the span of an hour, Cassia's jaw dropped. "Huh?"

There was no way her rent would cover the space *and* meals. What sort of game was this, take in the poor girl? Her pride prickled, and she wished she could afford it.

Ivy gave her a kind smile, stepping closer. "Here's the truth. We don't really need a roommate to cover expenses."

"No kidding," Cassia deadpanned.

Ivy's smile widened. "Elora and I like having another person here. It makes it a little less lonely. Our last roommate left on short notice, which is why the room came open. But if I put out an ad for free rent, who knows the type of person we'd get. And I guess I figured that if someone was paying a little, it would make the place feel more like their own."

"I do want to pay." Even if her measly rent only covered the cost of floor wax, she'd been raised to contribute.

"Then this is perfect." Ivy clapped her hands. "Besides, I like you already, and it's too late to get a new place before classes start Monday. So lucky for me, you're stuck with us."

"Trapped in a fancy manor. I suppose I can make do." Cassia laughed and the knot in her gut loosened, just a little.

Ivy's watch dinged and she glanced at the screen. "Shoot.

I'm due at a nail appointment in fifteen minutes. Are you going to be okay?"

"Of course. Thank you so much for renting me the room." Whatever Ivy's reasons, Cassia was grateful for a home, even if it was only temporary.

"You're welcome. See you later?"

"I'll be here."

"Okay." She waved. "Bye."

Cassia waited until Ivy had walked out of the kitchen before drawing in a long breath. On her exhale, she laughed. "Oh my God. How is this happening?"

She got turned around twice before finding the foyer. Her hand was outstretched for the front door's handle when it pushed open and Geoff walked in with one of her suitcases in his hand.

"Oh, shoot. You didn't need to do that. But thank you." She snatched it from his grip. "You don't have to help. I can handle it."

"It's my pleasure." His voice was as tight as his smile as he turned and strode for the car again.

"Uh . . ." She rushed past him to the trunk of the Honda, loading up as many bags as she could strap over her shoulders. Her lungs burned by the time she had them in her room, passing Geoff with the last load.

"If that's all, you may park your vehicle in the lot behind the house," he said, setting down the last suitcase.

"Sure." Her chest heaved as she nodded. "Thank you."

He spun on a heel and left.

If Geoff's cold shoulder was the worst of her problems, she'd manage fine.

Cassia rushed to her car and followed the driveway around the manor to where six garage bays were closed. She parked outside, locking the doors on the Honda—her dad's Honda—wishing it weren't so out of place. Then she hurried to her bedroom, working quickly to unpack.

Besides her clothes and toiletries, all she'd brought were a laptop, three books and a handful of photos. After she hung her last sweater on a wooden hanger, she took a step back to survey the enormous walk-in closet. It had been built for a designer wardrobe, with shelves and drawers and rods for miles. All she had to offer it were thrift-store finds and discount jeans.

A wash of sadness filled her, but she shoved it aside and zipped her empty suitcases, stashing them in a corner before retreating to the bedroom.

One step through the closet's door and she froze.

A woman sat on the bed. Her black hair hung in sleek, shiny panels to her waist. She had to be Cassia's age but the freckles across the bridge of her nose and petite frame made her seem younger. Except there was nothing youthful about her dark eyes. They gave her an edge. So did the blank look on her pretty face.

Cassia had never seen an expression so entirely void.

"Uh, hi? Who are you?"

"Elora." She spoke the word like it was obvious.

"Oh, of course." Cassia relaxed and waved. "Nice to meet you. I'm Cassia."

Elora stood, walking closer. Her strapless black top was tucked into a pair of slim black pants. On her feet were six-inch heels that lifted her to Cassia's height of five nine. "So you're the new candidate."

"Excuse me?"

"The candidate. For the trials."

"Trials?" *What the fuck is this girl on?* "You mean like at school? Tests? Do you call them trials at Aston?"

Elora shook her head. "No."

Cassia waited, expecting more of an explanation, but Elora offered none. Just that same empty expression.

"Well . . . this has been fun." She forced a smile. "But I'd better finish unpacking. I'm sure we'll see each other later. Have a good afternoon."

There was a sharpness to her tone. Not the best way to

speak to a new roommate, but she was exhausted and had no desire to play this strange little game.

The corner of Elora's mouth turned up. "I think I like you."

And I think you're insane. "Super."

"You might be the one who makes it, Cassia."

"Make what? The trials? Is that your thing? Like a hazing to live here?"

"Oh, not mine. Ivy's. Didn't she tell you? You're the new toy."

Cassia's head began spinning. "W-what?"

"Word of advice," Elora said. "She's used to getting her way. Don't let her win. It'll be much more entertaining if you put up a fight."

Without another word, Elora crossed the room, her strides full of grace and poise. The sound of her heels on the hardwood was no match for the pounding of Cassia's heart.

Trials? Ivy's toy?

No way. Ivy had seemed so sincere and sweet. This had to be a joke. Dread churned in her veins. That knot in her gut twisted tighter than ever.

So why did she have this feeling that she'd just traded one hell for another?

two

. . .

"MISS ELORA." Geoff knocked on her office door.

She glanced up from her laptop as he hovered by the threshold. "Yes?"

"You have a delivery." One swift nod and he was gone, disappearing to wherever it was that Geoff disappeared to. He avoided them all, but in particular, he avoided Elora.

She appreciated that about Geoff. And she liked Francis for the same reason. Both strived to blend into the walls, and if they did cross paths, they gave her a wide berth.

Elora shut her laptop, not wanting to risk that anyone would see her emails. Yes, Geoff kept to himself and seldom came into her rooms, but she still didn't trust him. After all, he worked for Ivy. And Elora had learned a long time ago not to trust her best friend.

She strode down the hallways, in no rush as she made her way to the foyer. She knew what was waiting at the door.

The delivery guy was wearing a beanie and holding a vase of white roses. A beanie? In August? The temperature was in the triple digits. Her father's favorite floral shop must have been desperate if they'd hired this idiot.

"Hey." He jerked his chin, not even trying to disguise his

perusal as he looked her up and down. He was probably her age, early twenties. The cocky grin that stretched across his mouth was as ridiculous as his hat. "These must be for you."

Elora stopped three feet away and nodded to the table against the wall.

He blinked.

She blinked back.

"Oh, right. These are heavy." He rushed to set down the vase. "So, uh—"

She walked to the table, lifted the bouquet and, without a word, retreated to her office. The beanie-wearing dumbass could show himself out.

Her side of the house was utterly still. There weren't many people who enjoyed silence. They found it uncomfortable. But she enjoyed the quiet. If she had something to say, she said it. Otherwise, she was content to keep her mouth shut and watch the weak squirm. She also enjoyed making people wriggle from time to time.

After setting the roses on her desk, she plucked the card from the flowers, pulling the note from its envelope.

LOVE YOU - DAD

He spoke in shouty caps, unlike Elora, who preferred one-word answers whenever possible.

The scent of the roses lured her in until her nose brushed the silky petals. The peonies he'd sent last week had wilted, so she'd had them tossed out yesterday. Somehow, Dad always knew how long her flowers would last. Or maybe his sixth sense was knowing when his daughter needed a fresh arrangement to brighten her day.

After another long inhale, she resumed her chair and cracked her laptop open again, scanning the email she'd spent an hour drafting. Her finger hovered over the touchpad, ready to hit send.

Depending on the outcome, there was a chance she'd need to swap roles with her dad and send something to brighten his day for a change. Flowers wouldn't be enough.

Maybe she'd help him drink a bottle of his favorite Macallan single malt.

Her finger tapped send. The sound was like the slam of a gavel. Then came a whoosh as the email burst through cyberspace.

God, I could use a drink.

Maybe this theory of hers was nothing. Maybe her paranoia had reached new bounds. Maybe her mother had fucked her up so thoroughly that she suspected everyone was lying.

Or maybe she was simply pragmatic.

Nearly every person in her life *was* a liar and a cheat.

Elora slammed the laptop closed and squeezed her eyes shut. It was done. Now all she could do was wait for the investigator to do his job.

She shot out of her chair and strode from the office, retreating to her suite and closing the door. Her heels sank into the plush carpet as she passed through the sitting room, then plopped on the end of her bed.

School started Monday. This summer had been nothing but a string of endless days with nothing to do but let her fears swallow her whole. Monday seemed like an eternity away.

If she'd had the courage, she would have sent that email months ago. It had taken the entire summer to work up the nerve.

She pulled her phone from her pocket and sent Dad a quick thank-you text for the flowers, then opened Instagram. The top photo in her feed was of her brother playing basketball. Elora smiled for the first time all day.

Lucas was thirteen, and their eight-year age difference meant that she'd been partly a sister and partly a parent. Maybe another girl would have resented being the one to care for him after school, but she adored her brother. It had been no hardship to help Lucas with his homework because their mother had been too stoned to function and their dad had often worked late.

They relied on each other. Lucas was the best and most

important person in her life. If not for her mother, she might have lived at home for college just to stay close to her brother.

She hit the heart on his photo, then closed the app. She didn't care to see anyone else's photos. Well, there was one person, but he didn't believe in social media. The idea of him taking a selfie was enough to make even Elora Maldonado laugh.

The door to her bedroom burst open and Ivy swept inside. "Did you see her?"

"Knock," Elora clipped.

Ivy flicked her wrist. "Next time."

Liar. She would never knock. This was Ivy's house. And Elora was merely a guest, even though she'd lived here for three years.

If Elora didn't love her suite so much, she'd move out simply to see Ivy's reaction.

Clarence Manor had been in Ivy's family for five generations, and the day Ivy had been accepted to Aston was the day she'd claimed it as her own. The two of them had been friends since kindergarten at Aston Prep. Elora had considered pledging a sorority their freshman year, but Ivy had convinced her to live at the manor instead.

It had been for the best.

Ivy created just as much drama as a sorority house, and Elora would have suffocated living with that many women.

Being roommates with Ivy was risky, but she was a known quantity. And Elora was a Maldonado. Her father had taught her long ago to hug her enemies close.

Not that Ivy was necessarily her enemy. But grenades were built to detonate. There was always the chance that the pin would shake loose and *boom*. Decimation.

Ivy Clarence made a beautiful bomb.

"Well?" Ivy walked to the bench seat at the window, glancing outside to the garden. "Did you see her?"

"Cassia. She has a name."

"Whatever."

"Yes, I met her. I like her hair." And Elora liked the promise of Cassia's spirit.

"That coral is an *interesting* shade." Most would think that was an insult. But they didn't know Ivy. Her compliments were always disguised as critiques.

"Why don't you leave this one alone? We can enjoy a peaceful senior year."

Ivy scoffed. "That's no fun. Besides, I think *Cassia* might be different than the others. I guess we'll find out."

The glint in Ivy's eyes used to give Elora a little thrill. Like when the lights in the theater dimmed before a compelling show. But after three years of the same game, that devilish look only made her tired.

Three years of watching Ivy test and torment their temporary roommates had grown old. Maybe because the ending had always been the same.

Ivy's greatest pleasure came from pushing people. From seeing how far they'd let her shove. Usually, it was out the front door.

"Are we friends because I don't put up with your bullshit?" Elora asked.

"Yes." Ivy spoke with no hesitation.

Maybe Cassia would be different. Elora had seen a spark in the woman's hazel eyes this afternoon. A steel that none of her predecessors had possessed.

"I think she'll last a month." Ivy toyed with a lock of her shiny blond hair. "Want to bet on it?"

"No."

Her lips thinned. "You're irritable today."

Elora arched an eyebrow.

"Okay, you're irritable every day," Ivy corrected. "But especially today."

Because Elora had more important things to consume her life than harassing their newest roommate.

"What are you doing tonight?" Ivy asked, inspecting her nails. She'd swapped last week's sage green for sea-foam.

Green, in any shade, was Ivy's signature. She'd no doubt ruined the color for many.

"Nothing," Elora answered. "I want to stay home."

"Great. We're going to the club. Leave at nine." As quickly as she'd swept into the room, Ivy was gone.

Then Elora let herself smile.

Ivy thrived on being in control. She made the rules and set the pace. It was almost too easy to manipulate her. To make her think that going to the club tonight was actually her idea.

Nine o'clock was hours away, but when Elora went to the club, she always looked her best. She had her reasons. So by the time darkness had fallen beyond the windows and Ivy had returned to her room—again without a knock—Elora stood in front of her mirror, the hours primping well spent.

"You look . . ." Ivy's gaze narrowed at Elora's outfit. "Beige isn't really your color."

In Ivy speak, that meant she looked hot. Too hot. "Afraid I'll get the first look when we walk through the club's door?"

Ivy smirked. "Yes."

"Deal with it."

"Fair enough. You can have the first look." Ivy ran a hand down the bodice of her emerald, satin minidress. Green really was her color. "I'll take the rest."

Fine by me. Elora didn't desire attention from the masses. No, she was dressed to catch a specific gaze.

Her corset top was only a couple of shades darker than her skin. It hugged her torso and accentuated her small breasts. She'd paired it with a black leather pencil skirt and her favorite Jimmy Choo stilettos.

She swept her clutch from the bed, tucking it under an arm, then strode past Ivy. They fell into step as they walked through the foyer. Outside in the loop, Ivy's town car was waiting, her driver standing stoically beside the open rear door.

Ivy acknowledged him with a nod before sliding into the back seat. Elora did the same. This driver was new as of last week. Jason? Jaxon? If he lasted through the fall, she'd ask his name.

While Ivy was fiercely loyal to Geoff and Francis, her drivers were expendable. If they drove too fast or swerved recklessly, she fired them in a snap.

Elora couldn't blame her. After everything that had happened to her friend, she understood Ivy's motives.

The driver—*Jaron?*—didn't ask for their destination, but simply climbed behind the wheel and pulled away from the manor.

Elora glanced to the second-floor windows. "You didn't invite Cassia?"

"I did. She declined." The irritation in Ivy's voice was as clear as the town car's windshield.

Score another point for Cassia. People rarely turned Ivy down.

She typically put on the sweet and bubbly act during the first week of a new roommate's stay. Then she'd flip the switch and reveal her true colors. Maybe that was why Elora had warned Cassia. Because she was tired of the on and off.

Ivy had chased away six women since freshman year. Elora hadn't been sad to see any of them go, especially the first, but their house had a reputation now. Anyone who'd been at Aston long enough knew to pass up Ivy's classified ads.

But Cassia was fresh blood. She'd learn soon enough.

Ivy smoothed the skirt of her dress and adjusted the thin straps. The neckline draped low, revealing plenty of cleavage. The skirt was asymmetrical and rose high on one thigh, nearly to her hip.

Elora had taunted her earlier, but the truth was, Ivy turned heads. It wasn't only the blond hair, blue eyes and beautiful face that captured attention. It was her energy. Everything about Ivy oozed wealth and power. And beneath the stunning exterior was an undercurrent of the unattainable.

Ivy was out of reach. Untouchable. And she made sure that the world knew it too.

The ride to the club was silent except for the whir of the

car's tires on the pavement. When they arrived, the driver stopped beside the entrance in a space reserved for exclusive patrons. He rushed out of the car to open their door, offering a hand as they stepped out.

A line had already formed against the club's exterior wall. Scantily clad women shifted their weight from heel to heel as they waited. They might stand a chance at getting in tonight since they'd probably been here for an hour. But as the line grew, their chances dimmed.

The men in line were fooling themselves if they thought they'd be admitted. Yet they came, nearly every night, and waited nonetheless.

Treason was the most exclusive club in the area. Most of the people inside were affiliated with Aston's elite. To enter without waiting meant you had a personal connection.

Elora didn't need Ivy to get in, but she let her roommate lead the way to the velvet ropes. No one asked for their names. No one asked for their IDs. They simply walked past the bouncers dressed in black suits, never slowing their pace as the doors swung open.

Faces turned their way as they stepped inside the darkened club, like a spotlight had been cast in their direction. The crowd clustered beyond the entrance parted, making room for them to pass.

Treason was one large room broken into a series of smaller spaces. The sunken dance floor, encircled by a steel railing, took up the center of the club. A DJ was perched in a loft overlooking the moving bodies. The bar ran the length of the nearest wall.

Seven bartenders, each dressed in black, wouldn't struggle to fill orders yet, but by midnight, they'd be slammed. Behind them, mirrored shelves teeming with liquor bottles stretched to the ceiling.

The club was cloaked in dim light, the color tinted by the blue, purple and white strobe lights above the dance floor. The bass pounded, the vibration sinking into Elora's skin and rattling her bones.

Freestanding tables filled the open spaces, and though it was early, nearly all had been claimed. People, both standing and seated, stared when Ivy and Elora passed by. Conversations halted.

Elora looked past them. *Through* them.

Years ago, she'd loved Treason, but lately, it had lost its shine. Now there was only one reason she came to the club.

And it wasn't to appease Ivy.

"Hey." A man's hand shot out, catching her elbow.

She stopped, eyeing her arm and his fingers. Then she leveled him with a glare that could melt flesh.

That glare was all it took for him to recoil, holding up his hands. "Sorry, I, uh . . . thought you were someone else."

She was two steps away when she heard him call, "Bitch."

Why did that sting?

It wasn't the first time she'd been called a bitch. It wouldn't be the last. But she refused to let the hurt show. She wore her cold expression like a suit of armor.

Elora followed Ivy straight through the crowd, people shuffling out of their path. Treason not only catered to the elite, but it segregated them as well. Three tiers of VIP lounges took up the far wall.

The first was for those who'd paid to rent a space for a bachelor party or special event. Their time in the limelight was only for the duration of the occasion. The second tier was for celebrities and those who had the fattest wallets. Then there was the third tier, the space reserved for the owner himself.

Ivy walked toward the staircase that would lead them to the third.

The bouncer at the entrance stood taller as they approached, adjusting the lapels on his jacket. "Miss Clarence."

She ignored him.

Elora wasn't the only guarded woman who lived in Clarence Manor.

They stepped into the private lounge, taking in the space. It was busier tonight than it had been in months. The couches and tables were full of people laughing, flirting and gossiping. Most of them were older, each with a personal connection to the owner, and she recognized a few faces. A waitress wearing a short skirt toted a tray full of drinks from the lounge's private bar.

And in the center of it all, there he was.

He sat on the largest couch with a tumbler of amber liquid in hand as he surveyed his club.

A king on his throne.

Zain.

Ivy spotted him and weaved through the crowd, taking up the space at his side. She dropped a chaste kiss to his stubbled cheek, then raised a hand to signal the waitress.

Elora walked to the bar. "Champagne."

"Of course." The bartender reached for a crystal flute.

With her glass in hand, she took a long sip, letting the bubbles burst on her tongue. This was why she came to Treason. Not for the music. Not for the crowd. Not for the dancing.

She came for him.

What would Ivy say if she knew Elora was fucking her older brother?

three

. . .

IVY CLARENCE WAS BORED out of her damn mind.

"Want to get out of here?" the random man at her side asked. His voice was low and his mouth much too close to her cheek. *Who was this guy?*

She turned slowly, narrowing her eyes until he shied away. "No."

I hate people.

"Come on, baby." His hand came to her knee, his thumb caressing a circle on her skin. His thigh pressed against hers. Over the past thirty minutes, he'd inched closer and closer. "Let's have a little fun."

Fun? He was about to learn that their definitions of *fun* were very different.

It was her turn to invade his personal space. She leaned over, speaking so closely to his mouth that their lips brushed. But she planted a hand on his shoulder, stopping him from closing the distance. "If you want to walk out of here with your cock attached, remove your hand from my leg. When I want you to touch me, I'll tell you when and where."

He snatched his hand away from her knee and put three

inches between them on the couch. "Sorry. I thought you were into it."

She flicked her wrist. "You've been dismissed."

The man blinked. Maybe his shock was warranted. He'd been sitting at her side for a while now, prattling on about his latest business investment and the millions he was projected to earn this year. *Blah. Blah. Blah.* She hadn't engaged in the conversation, but she hadn't ignored him either.

He sprang off the couch and weaved through Zain's lounge, fading into the crush.

In the hours she'd been at Treason, every available seat had been filled with a body. The dance floor was packed, and the lines at the bar were ten deep.

Zain should be happy. Business was better than good.

Treason was pure gold.

Her brother had excused himself hours ago. The epitome of ambition and drive, Zain had claimed there was work to be done. Another club owner would likely be here in the lounge, reveling in his success on a busy Saturday night. But Zain was no doubt locked in his office. Either he was fucking one of his admirers or he was crunching numbers. Ivy was ninety-nine percent sure it was the latter.

Zain was as boring and predictable as the club scene.

Where was Elora?

If that bitch had gone home already, Ivy was going to revoke her best friend status.

"Another champagne, Miss Clarence?" The waitress bent low but still had to shout in order to be heard over the punishing music.

Ivy shook her head, mouthing, "No."

As the waitress shifted to the next cluster, Ivy glanced around the space, searching for anyone worth her time. As always, she came up empty.

The DJ had done the midnight drink special announcement just minutes ago. With two hours until closing, the party was only getting started. Yet the idea of spending another minute here, let alone hours, made Ivy yawn.

She stood, smoothed down the skirt of her dress and walked toward the railing. There was a reason that when Zain did come out of hiding, he preferred his private lounge. From this perch, she could survey the entire club, from the entrance to the dance floor to the bar. There were no corners in which people could hide from her gaze. Zain even paid attendants to keep watch in the restrooms.

The only real privacy at Treason was her brother's office.

Ivy brushed her fingertips against the rail's cold steel. It glinted as the strobe lights flashed bright colors. The ocean of bodies on the dance floor moved to the DJ's unrelenting beat. It was like watching waves ebb and flow.

She yawned again.

Fuck it. Ivy took one step toward the exit, ready to go home—if Elora was still here, she'd have to find her own ride—except she paused when a commotion at the entrance caught her eye.

A group of guys strode inside. Unlike every man in Zain's lounge, none of the newcomers wore suit jackets. No slacks or polished shoes. She recognized them from Aston. They were the Sigmas—she never could remember all three letters of their fraternity's name.

Like all groups and organizations on campus, the Sigmas had a reputation. They were the elite fraternity, and only the wealthiest were admitted into their fold. To pledge meant having the right last name.

Michael Bamford wasn't just a Sigma.

He was *the* Sigma.

He commanded attention as he strode through the crowd on his way to the dance floor. He jerked up his chin and shook a few hands. His white T-shirt strained across his broad chest, the cotton molding to his muscled biceps. His loose jeans clung to his narrow hips and draped to his worn Converse.

His dirty-blond hair was trapped beneath a faded Red Sox hat.

Tonight, Michael looked nothing like the sophisticated man who strode across Aston's campus like he owned the place. The last time Ivy had seen him without a designer button-down shirt, tailored pants and Italian loafers, he hadn't been wearing much of anything.

Neither had she.

Well, well, well.

Maybe there was a reason to stay at Treason after all.

The corner of her mouth turned up as he stepped onto the dance floor. The sea parted, making space for Michael and his crew. His fraternity brothers encircled him, not one daring to dance until he made the first move.

And God, what a move it was.

A swirl of his hips made Ivy's mouth go dry. Then he spun his hat backward and sank into the music. That man was erotic on the dance floor. He wasn't too bad in the bedroom either.

Ivy gripped the railing, her gaze transfixed as he danced. He was as much a part of the music as the melody and rhythm, his moves like flowing water. His footwork was complex. His style unique. That athletic, strong body was a trap, and at the moment, Ivy was caught in his snare.

An arm brushed against hers as a man took the space beside her at the railing. "You're Ivy Clarence."

She paid him no attention. Every shred of her focus was on Michael.

The man snapped his fingers in front of her face, forcing her to blink and glance his way.

She huffed. "Go away."

"Tate."

"Did I ask for your name?"

"No, but you'll take it." He grinned. "I'm a friend of your brother's."

She circled a wrist at the busy lounge. "You and the rest of these people."

"Yeah, but Zain and I are actually friends."

Liar. She'd never seen Tate before, and Zain was selective. She was like her brother in that regard. As a Clarence, friendships were difficult. She never knew if someone was genuinely interested in her opinions or out to boost their social circle.

Testing people, their allegiance and their fortitude, had become Ivy's favorite hobby.

The only friend who'd ever passed was Elora.

"Go away, *Tate*." She turned her gaze to the dance floor once more.

Tate bent until his forearms rested on the top rail. "You go to Aston."

"Are you asking or telling?"

His grin widened. "I graduated with Zain."

"Congratulations," she muttered.

"What are you studying?"

Persistent, wasn't he? "Social sciences," she lied. Her major was history. "I'm fascinated with the behavior of people. Especially those who can't take a hint. Goodbye."

He chuckled and stood tall, holding out a hand. "Dance with me."

Ivy opened her mouth to reject him, but Michael was on that dance floor. He hadn't noticed her when he'd come in with his crew. And she definitely wanted him to notice. So she placed her hand in Tate's, surprised at how naturally his long fingers fit against her knuckles, and let him escort her down the staircase.

When they reached the dance floor, Tate eased through the mass of gyrating bodies. The closer he got toward Michael's group, the closer Ivy huddled to his back, their hands still intertwined.

Then Tate stopped and spun her into his arms. His chocolate-brown eyes locked with hers as he banded an arm around her back, pinning her close.

She gasped. This man, this Tate, was one of the most handsome men she'd seen in her life. His dark hair was just a little too long. His nose had a bump at the bridge and his chin had a slight dent in the center. Bold features that shouldn't have blended, but together, his face was perfection.

The hard strength of his chest surprised her. She hadn't paid enough attention to just how tall he was either. This close, he towered above her as his expensive, spicy cologne chased away the stench of sweat and alcohol.

Tate took her hand and placed it on his shoulder. His white button-down was smooth beneath her palm. The top two buttons of the shirt were undone, revealing a sliver of tanned skin. The cuffs were rolled up his sinewed forearms. And his dark-wash jeans were rough against her bare legs.

He put her exactly where he wanted her, and only then did he move. He rocked his hips to hers, setting the pace. Building the tension. There was no doubt who was in the lead.

Tate was a talented dancer, but he was no Michael.

Her eyes drifted over Tate's shoulder to her obsession. Michael's gaze was waiting.

She held back a victorious smile and clung to Tate, her eyes locked with Michael's. Tate might have her in his arms, but Michael and Ivy had been doing this dance for years.

Michael shifted, making space for a woman to enter his circle. Not just any woman. Allison Winston.

Ivy's lip curled. If she had an enemy—a worthy opponent—it was Allison. As ruthless and vicious as Ivy herself, the two didn't cross paths often these days. The last time had been at Treason, on this very dance floor. Allison had been hanging all over Michael that night too.

Bitch. Last year, Ivy had asked Zain to ban Allison from his club. But her brother the businessman had refused. Beautiful women meant rich men flocked, and unfortunately, Allison was not lacking in beauty. Her sleek brown hair was especially glossy beneath the nightclub's lights.

The moment Allison shifted in front of Michael, their

connection was broken. He settled his hands on her hips and any chance Ivy had of making him jealous evaporated.

Fucking Allison.

Michael was the only man in the world who didn't fall at her feet. There were times when he barely acknowledged her existence. That only made her crave him more.

If Ivy wasn't careful, her daddy issues would begin to show.

Tate spun her in a circle, forcing her to look away from Michael, then bent, his lips caressing the shell of her ear. "Didn't work."

She tensed. "What?"

"Your ploy. I know exactly why you followed me to the dance floor. You're using me to make him jealous, except it didn't work."

"You don't know that."

He leaned away, his dark eyes sparkling. "Baby, maybe these games work on guys your age. But they won't work on me."

"Then why are you dancing with me?" she hissed.

"You're not the only one who likes to play." His gravelly voice sent a shiver down her spine.

Why did that intrigue her? Ivy was rarely intrigued, especially by men.

Tate's hand at her hip drifted lower. It was on the side of her asymmetrical skirt that rode up her thigh. His fingertips brushed the sensitive flesh just below her hip bone. Another inch and he'd learn that she wasn't wearing panties.

But she didn't stop him. The touch. The dance. As the heat from his body seeped through the satin fabric of her dress, they danced, their movements never slowing. With every circle of his hips, she rolled hers in tandem. With every beat of the music, a pulse bloomed between her legs.

Who was this man, this *friend* of her brother's? How had she never seen him before?

Tate's body was as solid as granite, muscular but not bulky.

He was tall, inches over six feet, but not lanky. Given that Ivy was in heels, the line of his chiseled jaw was just close enough to trace with her tongue.

A curl of desire tightened her core. His eyes stayed locked on hers, the rest of the dance floor fading to a blur. This man was seducing her.

And damn if she wasn't letting him.

Somehow, since the moment he'd snapped his fingers in front of her face, he'd put her under a spell. He'd stolen control, and she hadn't batted an eyelash in resistance.

That realization was a bucket of ice water tossed over her head. She stiffened and pushed out of his arms.

He let her go and that sharp jaw clenched. Then the flash of irritation melted away as seamlessly as the DJ mixed one track with the next. His sexy, confident smile made her breath hitch.

In all her time at Treason, she'd never laid eyes on Tate. His face was not one she'd forget.

Who was he? How exactly did he know Zain?

Before she could ask, he reached out and traced the line of her nose. Then he was gone, striding past her and across the dance floor like it was empty.

Her heart raced. Someone bumped into her and she nearly toppled because her legs were so unsteady. She risked a glance over her shoulder.

Once more, Michael's gaze was waiting. Allison clung to his shoulders, doing her best to grind against his thigh. He seemed . . . bored.

But did he push Allison away? Did he come to Ivy?

No. He never did.

The music, the heat, the blinking lights were suddenly too much. A headache throbbed at her temples. She forced her feet forward, pushing her way to the exit. The moment she burst outside, the cool night air filled her lungs, and she could breathe again.

"Are you ready for your car, Miss Clarence?" one of the bouncers asked.

She managed a shaky nod.

"Is everything all ri—"

The glare she sent him silenced the rest of his question. "Call my driver."

He nodded, dug his phone from the breast pocket of his jacket and dialed as she rattled off the number.

She squared her shoulders, pushed a lock of sweaty hair away from her face and stepped to the curb.

Jaxon, her latest chauffeur, appeared within a minute. The bouncer opened the car's rear door, and the moment she was seated and buckled, they drove toward the manor. The city lights streaked by her window as they sped through the night. Every few minutes, she leaned forward to check the speedometer.

So far, Jaxon had always driven at or below the limit. Maybe he'd last longer than a month for a change.

When the car's wheels had stopped at the manor, she didn't wait for him to open her door. She retreated to the safety of her home, breathing in its familiar scent as she kicked off her heels. The floor cooled her soles as she padded up the stairs.

She was about to retreat to her bedroom when she paused in the hallway.

Ivy didn't enjoy control.

She required it.

She could not, would not, let anyone hold power over her again. Tate had rattled her tonight. So had Michael. She was off-balance and needed something to tilt the scales back in her direction.

She knew exactly where to find it.

Ivy bent, returning her heels to her feet, then marched toward Cassia's suite. Her roommate hadn't locked her bedroom door. She'd learn to soon enough. Or if she was like

Elora, she'd leave it open because she secretly wanted the company.

The bedroom was dark, the curtains drawn. Ivy flicked on the light, bathing the room in a soft, golden glow. Cassia didn't so much as stir.

"Wake up." Ivy clapped, walking to the foot of the bed.

Cassia gasped as she jolted to a seat. "W-what? What's wrong?"

"I need ten dollars." Normally, Ivy would wait longer before tormenting the new girl, but tonight, she was desperate for power. A hit of her favorite drug.

"Huh?" Cassia squinted as she pushed the coral hair from her face.

"Ten dollars. I want you to give me ten dollars."

Cassia blinked. "For what?"

"For whatever I want." Ivy crossed her arms. "Get up and get me ten dollars."

"Is this one of your trials?"

"I see Elora has been talking." Ivy's bravado deflated but she rallied. "Money. Now."

"Take it out of my rent. Or not. I don't care. I'm just here for school." Cassia's shoulders sagged as she reached behind her, hugging a pillow to her chest. Then she collapsed into the mattress. "Shut the door on your way out."

Ivy's mouth fell open. *What. The. Hell?*

This had been one of her more common trials. An easy test. Every roommate before Cassia had rushed out of bed and dug through their purse for cash. Most hadn't even asked why she needed the money when she had a small fortune at her disposal.

This rejection was . . . unsettling.

She waited and waited, but Cassia didn't move. Finally, Ivy walked to the door, stopping for one last look at the bed. Cassia's hair was splayed over her face, and she was sound asleep, drooling on that pillow.

The walk to her own bedroom felt like a walk of shame.

She'd failed. With Cassia. With Michael.

Ivy didn't fail.

She went to her phone on the nightstand. She'd left it behind tonight because she had no need for it or money in her brother's club. He protected her at Treason, and if he was working, he'd delegate the duty to an employee.

There were no missed calls. No texts, not even from Elora.

She unlocked the screen and pulled up Michael's name.

Don't fuck Allison

The minute the text was delivered, she regretted typing those three words. She regretted their vulnerability. She regretted their desperation.

Ivy stared at the screen for ten minutes, waiting for his reply. When it didn't come, she peeled off her dress and took a scalding shower. Then she forced herself to stay awake until three, her phone clutched to her chest. Before she finally drifted off to sleep, she realized Michael wasn't going to text her back.

He never did.

four

. . .

CASSIA COLLINS LOVED SCHOOL. Cassie Neilson had loved it too, but she hadn't needed it like Cassia. The distraction. The challenge. The focus. Ten days into her senior year at Aston and she was living for every minute spent on campus—which was a lot, considering how many classes she was balancing.

School was her escape. Her coping mechanism. If her brain was overloaded with economics, it wouldn't have room to dwell on the past.

If she didn't know firsthand what the life of a professor entailed, she might have considered getting her PhD to teach. But when she looked into the future, she saw more than classrooms and coeds. That, and she had no money for an advanced degree.

Her stomach growled as she strode across Aston's immaculate campus. She'd missed breakfast. Ivy and Elora had been in the dining room this morning, and since avoiding her roommates had become her second favorite pastime, she'd snuck out the door and skipped her regular stop in the kitchen.

She had an hour break after her next class, and she'd hit up the day-old discount rack at the bakery in the student union. She'd eat a muffin for lunch and update her growing to-do list.

"Study for the quiz in Money and Banking. Review notes from the Labor Econ lecture. What else?" she muttered. "What am I missing?"

"Join a team for the group project in 410," said a deep voice.

She jumped, pressing a hand to her racing heart. "You scared me."

"Sorry." The guy at her side held out a hand, the corner of his mouth turned up. "Michael Bamford."

"Cassia Collins." She returned his shake, mentally giving herself a high-five for not stuttering her name.

"We've got a few classes together. Health Economics. Macro Theory. And 410." *Intro to Econometrics.* Michael winced. "I just replayed that and realize how much I sound like a stalker."

"You're good." She laughed, color rising in her cheeks.

Holy fuck, this guy was hot. Tall. Built. Dirty-blond hair. Gray-blue eyes the color of the ocean before a storm. Why was he talking to her?

"There aren't many of us in the senior-year econ program," he said. "A group of us study together. The professors encourage it too. Interested?"

Was this really happening?

She'd been at Hughes for three years and not once had someone invited her to join a study group. She'd only collaborated on team projects when it had been part of an assignment. Even then, she'd typically ended up doing most of the work herself.

"Uh . . . sure?" It came out as a question. Mostly because her brain was going into lockdown. Michael was the first classmate she'd spoken to since the semester had started. And now he was inviting her into a study group? What was the catch? There had to be a catch.

Just ten days ago she'd walked into Clarence Manor and

had a *too good to be true* feeling. Turns out, that feeling had been right. Ivy's middle-of-the-night drama about wanting ten dollars had set Cassia on edge.

"Don't worry." Michael chuckled. "We don't bite."

She'd be the judge of that. Months ago, she would have chided herself for such cynicism. She called it realism now.

As they walked, Michael jerked up his chin at nearly everyone they passed. She'd been too startled at first, but as they continued toward the Economics building, she began to sense this energy around him. This confidence.

He moved with an easy swagger. It was the walk of a man who could have anything he wanted. Clothes. Cars. Property.

Women.

With every step, she felt more and more out of place at his side.

Michael wore a pair of light-gray slacks, the material smooth and no doubt expensive. His button-down shirt was a pale blue. The watch on his wrist probably cost more than her Honda.

They had to look ridiculous together. Cassia was dressed in a black tee and a pair of denim shorts that had once been jeans until she'd cut them off midthigh. The tangled frays skimmed the tops of her knees.

She dropped her chin, eyes focused on the sidewalk. The curtain of her coral hair swung in front of her face.

It was the color that forced her to straighten. To hold her chin high. Cassie Neilson would have hidden from the world. She would have done her best to remain invisible and locked in her shell.

But she was Cassia Collins now.

So she looked forward just in time to see the man walking their way. And damn it, she should have kept her eyes on the ground.

He was reading something on his phone, and for a split second, she thought he might walk by and she'd go unnoticed.

But Cassia had never been lucky.

The man tucked his phone away and glanced up. His eyes landed on Michael first. He nodded. "Morning, Michael."

"Hey, Dean Neilson."

Then the dean's eyes swung her way. His eyes widened and he opened his mouth, like he was going to say hello, but she gave him a slight headshake. His mouth pursed in a thin line as he strode past them, going the opposite direction.

Cassia had to force herself not to look back.

She'd made her uncle swear to keep their relationship a secret. He'd helped her get into Aston, but that was where their interactions had to stop. No good would come from people learning her truths, including her real name.

Michael hadn't noticed, had he? He was already nodding to someone else, but that didn't mean he'd missed the awkward moment. Or maybe she was fucking losing it.

Ding, ding, ding. Correct.

The air was sticky and humid. She dragged in a breath, her heart racing. The late-August sun was brutal this morning, but it was panic, not the heat, that caused the color to drain from her face.

"How are you liking classes?" Michael asked, his voice distant and muted beneath the roar of her pulse.

"All good." She drew in a long breath, holding it until her lungs burned. The pain settled her and grounded her mind.

Bumping into her uncle was bound to happen from time to time. Eventually, they'd learn to ignore each other. Or she'd find new routes around campus.

It was fine. Everything was fine.

They turned a corner to Bamford Hall, where over half of her classes were held.

"Wait." Her footsteps slowed. "You said your last name is Bamford?"

Michael's gaze followed hers to the sign outside the building, then he shrugged. "My family has been attending Aston for generations."

"Ah." She nodded. Not just attending. Her mind couldn't

fathom the amount of money it would take to have an Aston building dedicated in your name.

Michael kept going for the doors, stopping when he realized Cassia had fallen behind. "Coming?"

"I'm going to refill my water bottle." She pointed to an outdoor drinking fountain, the silver bowl gleaming beneath the sun.

"See you inside." Michael smiled and once more her cheeks grew hot.

He was really, *really* handsome. And way out of her league. She wasn't even interested in guys, not after her last romantic disaster. But still, her heart fluttered.

"There's nothing wrong in looking, right?" she asked herself as she walked to the fountain. She dug her metal water bottle out of her backpack, which she'd stuffed with textbooks, folders and notepads this morning. The water was lukewarm, but since she'd skipped getting ice this morning, along with breakfast, it would have to do.

She had the cap in one hand, ready to twist it on with the other, as she turned and collided with a wall.

Water sloshed out of the overfull bottle and directly onto a chest.

Cassia turned up her chin, horror soaking through her like the water on the guy's white shirt. "Oh. My. God. I'm so sorry. I didn't realize anyone was behind me or I would have been more careful. Gah."

She scrambled for her backpack again, pulling it forward to dig for the hoodie stuffed at the bottom.

"It's all good." The guy swiped at his shirt, the water continuing to spread along with the humiliation through her veins. "It's only water. And in this heat, I'll be dry in ten minutes."

"No. Here." She tugged out the hoodie, dragging a textbook with it. The book clattered to the sidewalk. *Damn.* Cassia tossed him the sweatshirt, then dropped to collect her book.

The corners were dented. They'd probably ding her for that when she tried to sell it back at the end of the term.

Unless . . . maybe Aston didn't buy back textbooks. She was counting on some money back.

She shoved that concern aside, a worry for another day, and stood. Then she forced herself to look at the stranger she'd soaked. The air rushed from her lungs. *Oh, whoa.* Aston had done a hell of a job recruiting handsome men.

He wore a crooked grin with his wet shirt. His light-brown hair had a natural wave, the strands a little long on top. His face was perfectly symmetrical with a straight nose, soft lips and dazzling blue eyes.

Not the grayish blue of Michael's. This man's gaze was a piercing blue, like a cloudless sky on a hot summer day.

"Beautiful eyes," she murmured.

That crooked grin turned into a megawatt smile full of straight, white teeth.

She might have swooned, except sheer mortification chased away any other reaction. "That was supposed to stay in my head."

"I'm glad it didn't." He chuckled. "I like your hair."

"Thanks." Her cheeks were probably the same coral shade. "I, um . . . I think I'd better get to class before I say or do anything else to embarrass myself. Sorry about the water. Really sorry."

"Don't worry about it." He handed her the hoodie, then winked.

Not many men could pull off a wink. In her experience, it usually came across as creepy. But this guy, he could wink at her every day and twice on Sundays. She swallowed hard, stuffing her things into her bag, then unglued her feet and sidestepped him.

He turned as she walked past. "See you around."

"Uh, yes?" She gave him a finger wave. It was awkward. But she was awkward, so . . . that was on point.

Cassia rushed toward the building, disappearing inside.

The air-conditioning cooled her flaming face as she strode toward the lecture room.

Two hot-guy encounters in one day. It was like the universe was torturing her. How long had it been since she'd actually found a man attractive? Six months? A year?

School. She was here for school. Nothing more. It had to be her focus.

Michael was already seated with a group of people. There was an empty desk in his cluster. He pointed to it, waving for her to join them, but she gestured to the chair in the front row where she'd been sitting since the first day of class.

Her ex had told her once that she was clingy. It was one of many reasons he'd ended their two-year relationship. The irony of that situation was stifling.

But his words and his actions had left a mark. The wound was so deep she wasn't sure it would ever fully heal. And though Michael was just a classmate, she didn't want to overstep.

Maybe she'd join his study group. But she was comfortable in her front-row seat. And when the professor began his presentation, the rest of the room melted away.

School was her focus. It had to be her only focus.

After the class was over, Michael jerked up his chin on his way out of the room.

She smiled, packed her bag and walked outside, sweat instantly beading on her brow. The temperature had climbed fast while she'd been in class. She stopped by the student union over her break for that day-old muffin, then went to her last two classes for the day.

No one else spoke to her. She told herself it was easier that way. To sit alone. To eat alone. To walk alone.

Cassia wasn't at Aston to make friends. She was here to learn. And once she had her degree, she could start her life.

Her real life. She'd pack that life with friends and laughter and . . . hope. Maybe she'd be Cassie again. Or maybe she'd come to love Cassia.

With her classes finished for the day, she meandered across campus toward home. Her backpack seemed heavier, like it had grown in weight over the course of the day even though she hadn't added anything but items to her task list.

Clarence Manor was only five blocks from the edge of campus, allowing Cassia to save the expense of a parking pass.

She'd made a few calls after scouring the classified ads. There wasn't much else available to rent, but she'd spoken to a girl yesterday with an empty bedroom in her apartment. The girl had asked if Cassia was allergic to cats.

Yes. Yes, I am.

Staying at Ivy's was likely a mistake. She was only setting herself up for disaster. But for the past ten days, she'd avoided her roommates. Could she do it for a year? Maybe, if she spent all of her time on campus. It would be hard for Ivy to perform a *trial* if they didn't clash.

Besides, the ten-dollar test hadn't been that bad. Awkward. Annoying. But survivable.

She'd endured far worse than a bratty roommate.

And as far as roommates went, Ivy wasn't even the worst. That honor belonged to the girl Cassia had dormed with her freshman year at Hughes. The girl who'd only showered weekly and thought garlic was its own food group.

Life in a manor with a butler, chef and housekeeper was cake, right? Add to that, she was within walking distance to the most beautiful campus she'd ever seen. In only a week, the grounds at Aston had captured her heart.

Red brick buildings greeted her at every turn. Ivy cloaked half of them, the vines curling up walls to add a hint of age and mystery. The history here was as plentiful as the lush green lawns that filled the space in between sidewalks.

She'd gotten turned around a few times since her first day of classes. With so many similar buildings, it had been easy to get lost. But today, she hadn't had to reference the campus map in her backpack once.

Cassia trudged home, in no rush to return to the manor

where roommates awaited. Maybe she could trouble Francis with making her another early dinner before locking herself in her suite and spending the rest of the night on homework.

She could do this. She could live here for a year.

When the going gets tough . . .

Her father's favorite motivational phrase rang through her ears. It hurt to remember.

The gates were open when she reached the manor. A silver Bentley was parked in the loop.

"Guests. Great," she muttered. Hopefully whoever was visiting was in a parlor or sitting room or one of the other unnecessary spaces filled with expensive, unused furniture.

She tiptoed through the front door, holding her breath as she tried not to make a sound. Cassia was easing the door closed when a throat cleared.

"Sneaking in?" A rugged, male voice swept through the foyer.

Damn. "No. I live here." She turned to face the guest and her jaw dropped. "You?"

"Me." The guy from the water fountain gave her that crooked grin as he sat on the staircase. His elbows were balanced on his knees. "Are you following me?"

"You're in my house. Shouldn't I be asking *you* that question?"

He chuckled and stood, crossing the distance. "We skipped introductions earlier."

"You mean when I spilled water all over you. Sorry. Again."

"It's fine." He patted his shirt. "See? All dry."

"Good." She held out her hand. "Cassia Collins."

But before he could tell her his name, the click of heels sent the hair on Cassia's neck spiking up.

Ivy came strutting down the staircase wearing dark-green slacks and a silky cream blouse with barely there straps. She'd probably gone to class in that ensemble. Did the girl own jeans?

"I see you two have met," Ivy said.

"Uh . . ." Cassia took her hand from the guy's grip and inched away. Shit. They hadn't exactly been flirting, but if this was Ivy's boyfriend, then she wanted to cease all contact. Immediately.

"Edwin," he said, his blue eyes sparkling like he could read her thoughts. "I'm Ivy's brother. We're twins, though I'm the more handsome sibling."

Ivy scoffed. "In your dreams. We're going to be late."

Edwin smiled, his eyes locked with Cassia's. "Nice to meet you. I'm sure we'll see each other again."

Brother. This was Ivy's twin brother? He seemed so normal. And Ivy was, well . . . not.

She studied his face, and the similarities jumped out at her. The straight nose. The full lips. The blue eyes.

"Edwin," Ivy snapped.

He shot his sister a glare but stepped past Cassia and walked out the door.

Ivy tsked her tongue as Edwin jogged down the staircase to his Bentley. "You've been avoiding us, *roomie*."

Cassia was so tired, but she forced a tight smile, then took a step, ready to retreat to the safety of her room.

But before she could scurry away, Ivy caught her elbow. "We have rules in this house."

"And I'm sure you'll enlighten me as to those rules. Just make it fast. I have homework."

Ivy's nostrils flared. "We'll keep it simple for today. My brothers are off-limits. Break that rule, and I'll evict you faster than you can blink."

"I literally just met the guy."

"Then it shouldn't be a problem. I'd hate for you to be homeless."

Not homeless. Just living with cats. For seven hundred dollars a month.

"I signed a lease." Cassia jerked her arm free. "One year, remember?"

"Do you actually think one flimsy document is going to keep me from evicting you?"

Cassia's stomach churned, but she raised her chin. "Evict me and you'll hear from my attorney."

Ivy scoffed. "You don't have an attorney. And you don't have the money to afford one."

How did she know that? "I can afford Aston, can't I?"

"No, you can afford *rent*." Of course Ivy would call her bluff. "Thank goodness for financial aid, right?"

Cassia trembled. The spark in Ivy's eyes made her heart race. How the fuck did this girl know about her financial situation? Yes, Cassia had confirmed the monthly rental rate a few times. But she'd never once mentioned financial aid.

"Wondering how I know that?" Ivy inched closer, standing tall, especially in those heels. "Oh, I know a lot about you. I know that according to the bank statement you provided the financial aid office, you have barely a cent beyond what's needed to cover your rent."

"You saw my bank statement?" The room was spinning.

"Just a little research. *Cassie.*" Ivy sneered, victory etched on her beautiful face. "Go ahead. Find a lawyer. Maybe there *is* an ambulance chaser out there who wants to help you take down a Clarence. It will be my utmost amusement to see you try."

Without another word, Ivy breezed past her for the door.

The rumble of the Bentley's engine was a dull murmur compared to the pounding of Cassia's heart.

Cassie.

Ivy had called her Cassie.

Her backpack slipped from her shoulder, dropping with a thud to the floor. The noise sent Cassia flying into action, sprinting for the staircase. Her breath was ragged as she flew into her room, running for the closet.

She knew. Ivy knew. Maybe. Maybe she only knew a small piece. But if Ivy had gotten information from the financial aid office, it was only a matter of time before Cassia's secrets were exposed. Like the fact that Cassia Collins's bank account was just a month old. That it was as new as her legal name.

Cassia knew what it was like to be manipulated. To be tricked. To be played the fool. Last time, she'd come home to a dead body. She refused to relive that again. And if Ivy knew . . .

Forget this manor. Forget Ivy Clarence.

She started packing her shitty clothes into her shitty suitcases.

She'd take her chances with the cats.

five

. . .

"I'M DISAPPOINTED." Elora strode into Cassia's walk-in closet as her roommate frantically tore clothes off hangers.

Cassia jumped. "You startled me."

Elora bent to the open suitcase on the floor and plucked out a cotton tee, returning it to a hanger.

"Hey, don't—"

She silenced her roommate with a frown. "You're letting her win."

"I'm—"

"A pushover?"

Cassia's hands fisted on her hips. "This is not going to work for me."

"What's not going to work?" Elora picked up a pair of distressed boyfriend jeans, folding them in half. "You're living in a suite most girls in your situation would kill for. You've got one of the finest chefs along the East Coast ready to whip up meals whenever you desire. You don't have to clean. You don't have to do laundry. What exactly isn't working for you?"

"Ivy." Cassia's lip curled. "She's a bitch."

"I warned you about that from the start. Get over it."

"I'm leaving." She snatched the jeans from Elora's hands.

"Over a scuffle in the foyer? And here I was, thinking you had a thick skin. So very disappointing."

Elora had come home from class today using the rear entrance after parking in her garage. The acoustics in the house were rather fabulous for eavesdropping. From the hallway, she'd heard the entire conversation between Cassia and Ivy.

After Cassia had bolted upstairs, Elora had almost retreated to her room. But curiosity had made her go to the second floor.

"Why do you care?" Cassia asked.

Elora answered by walking out of the closet and perching on the edge of the bed.

As expected, Cassia followed. "It's not like you need my rent to chip in for internet."

"I don't care," Elora said. If Cassia left the manor, life would go on. "But I think *you* might. I think deep down, you hate that Ivy is winning."

Cassia deflated in front of her eyes, trudging to the chair in the corner. She didn't sit in the seat so much as curl into it, hugging her knees to her chest and shifting so far against the high back it looked as if she was trying to disappear into the jacquard upholstery.

"What's your story?" Elora asked. Because oh, there was a story. She knew enough people with secrets to recognize when a person was hiding something juicy.

"I'm broke," Cassia said.

"That's not your story."

She met Elora's gaze. "No, but it's a part of it."

Cassia's fate was none of her business. She hadn't given any of the other roommates this much of her time or attention. Why Cassia? What was it about this one that intrigued her so much?

Whatever it was, she found herself helping. Again.

"There's a girl who works in the financial aid office," Elora said. "There aren't many scholarships offered at Aston, but there are some. Typically they come with the requirement that the student has a work-study job. Ivy knows the girl and uses her for information."

"That's illegal."

"No, it's leverage." Sooner or later, Cassia would need to learn that Aston wasn't like the rest of the world. "Our sophomore year, Ivy went to a party. She caught the girl attempting to steal some of the host's jewelry. And instead of turning her in, Ivy did what Ivy does best. She blackmailed her. Ivy's silence for information."

Cassia straightened. "Like my bank statement."

Elora nodded. "Ivy is an illusion. Remember that. She's specific about what she says and what she doesn't. She'll let you infer that she knows everything when, in reality, she doesn't. But most of the time, it's enough. Either people will spill the truth. Or they'll run. Regardless, she wins."

"Why are you friends with her?"

Elora lifted a shoulder. "Your definition of friendship is much different than mine."

"Apparently," she muttered.

The truth was, Ivy wasn't the only person living in Clarence Manor who loved having leverage. Elora knew everything there was to know about Ivy. And if Ivy ever turned on her, Elora's revenge would be sweet and swift.

"I won't do this again." Elora stood and smoothed down the front of her ecru romper. "The next time you decide to move out, I'll wave goodbye. So don't be a fool, Cassia. You're broke. This is dirt-cheap rent at Aston. Unless of course you want to live in that rust pile of a car."

Cassia sighed. "No."

They both knew Elora was right.

"Wait," Cassia called as Elora walked for the door.

She turned, arching her eyebrows.

"*Why* are you doing this? Why convince me to stay?"

"Because Ivy is my best friend, and she likes to have a toy."

"So you want her to mess with me? Is this some sick sort of entertainment for you?"

"Yes." Elora gave her a wicked grin. "I want you to ruffle her precious feathers. And while you do, I'll be sitting in the front row."

Cassia gave her a sideways glance. "That's, um . . . a little warped."

"You have no idea." With that parting comment, she left her roommate to put her clothes away.

Back in her office, Elora's inbox was empty. Just like it had been when she'd checked two hours ago. She hadn't expected answers overnight, but waiting over the past ten days had been agony.

School hadn't provided a necessary distraction. The beginning of the semester hadn't been as hectic as she'd hoped for. Her business management classes were interesting but not time consuming. Her professors seemed to be easing into the year rather than slamming their students with assignments.

The only time she'd felt any relief from the chaos in her head had been her night with Zain. But she'd fucked that up too, hadn't she?

Just the thought of him made her insides swirl. Desire mixed with regret and guilt. She hadn't meant to piss him off. She'd just been honest.

They needed to talk. To clear the air after their argument. But she'd been giving him space to cool off. Was ten days enough?

It will have to be. She stood from her chair, dashed to her bedroom for car keys and a purse, then rushed to the garage and climbed in her car.

This much turmoil was going to make her head explode. If all she could do was wait for her investigator to do his job, then she could at least end this distance with Zain.

The drive to Treason was tortuous. Her heart rate seemed to triple in speed the closer she got to the club. Zain had been so angry. So . . . hurt. His reaction had taken her completely off guard, but he had to have calmed down. Thought it through.

And he might not realize it, but she was doing him a favor.

Before she was ready, she arrived at the club, parking in the small lot behind the building reserved for employees. She eased her black BMW into the space next to Zain's Aston Martin. Then she steeled her spine and walked to the rear entrance, punching in the code he'd given her years ago to unlock the door.

It was strange to come to Treason while the sun was shining overhead. This wasn't Elora's first trip before nightfall, but she hadn't made daytime visits a habit either. She couldn't afford to make Zain a habit.

She eased the club's door closed behind her, not letting it slam. With the lights on, the industrial design was more obvious than it was at night, when neon lights stole the focus. From the steel railings to the concrete floors to the exposed ductwork in the ceilings, Treason was a monochromatic dream of stark lines and clean architecture.

The scent of bleach clung to the air from where a man mopped the dance floor. The clink of bottles and a woman's laugh echoed through the open spaces.

Tommie was behind the bar, pulling hot glasses from a steaming dishwasher. Her blond hair was up in a messy knot. The tank top molded to her figure had *Treason* printed across her voluptuous breasts. As she set the last glass down, she leaned her elbows on the bar, smiling at the man seated on a stool across from her. She flashed him ample cleavage to appreciate.

The two of them made a picture so perfect Elora paused, watching from a distance.

Tommie's blinding smile and luscious curves. His broad shoulders shaking with laughter, that deep, carefree sound he rarely gifted Elora.

Had he fucked her already? Had Zain taken Tommie on the couch in his office after Elora had left the other night?

The image of them together made Elora's heart ache but she shoved the pain away. A move she'd been perfecting for years. She tucked her jealous feelings into the darkest corners of her soul and assumed her face of indifference.

They'd decided from the beginning no rules. No expectations. No questions.

No commitments.

Elora caught Tommie's attention as she approached. The bartender stood tall, her smile dropping as her gaze flicked toward Zain. They shared a look, then Tommie frowned before retreating to the opposite end of the bar.

Zain didn't turn as Elora slid onto the stool beside his. "We're closed."

"Even for me?" She traced his profile with her gaze, from the furrow of his forehead down the straight line of his nose to his stubbled chin.

"What are you doing here?" His voice was low, the baritone as smooth and rich as his most expensive bottle of scotch.

"I came to see if you were still mad at me."

He turned her way, those bright blue eyes flaring. Then he was off his seat, his long legs eating up the distance to the staircase that led to his office.

Still mad. "Damn." She sighed and followed. Maybe she should have waited twenty days, not ten.

Years ago, Elora might have thought Zain was walking away from her. But she'd learned that he was simply taking the conversation elsewhere. Zain didn't do personal discussions in public spaces.

When she reached his office, she closed the door behind her. Unlike the club, his office was warm, with rich tones of leather and wood. The rows of bookshelves behind his desk gave it the impression of a library. The caramel couches were plush and oversized to accommodate a man of his size.

He stood in the center of the space, his long legs braced, his fists on his narrow hips.

"Don't be mad." She crossed the distance between them,

her hands wrapping around his waist to dive into the pockets of his jeans. She rose up on her toes, hoping for a kiss, but he was six three, and unless he bent to meet her, there was no way she'd reach his mouth.

Zain's jaw clenched, then he stepped out of her arms. "No."

"You're telling me no? Over a stupid fight. You never tell me no."

"I am today." He dragged a hand over his face, the stubble scraping against his palm. "I'm tired."

"Of me?"

"Of the twisted little affairs. Of the bullshit that reminds me of my parents. Of the casual scene and the petty games."

Her heart sank into her Valentino sneakers. "It was just dinner."

"Exactly." He crossed his arms over his chest, his tattooed biceps straining the fabric of his T-shirt. "It was just a fucking dinner, Elora."

The Saturday she'd come with Ivy to Treason, it hadn't taken more than fifteen minutes for Zain to excuse himself from his sister's company. He'd greeted a few of his guests, pausing to shake hands on his way to his office.

By the time Elora had finished her first glass of champagne and slipped away to join him, he'd already stripped off his shirt. They'd fucked hard and fast on his desk, then had taken their time on the couch for round two.

Both pieces of furniture mocked her this afternoon. She'd never seen him like this before. So crestfallen. So resolute. But she knew Zain well enough to know that when he made a decision, he didn't waver.

No. This wasn't happening. Was he going to end this? Had they already had their last night? She hadn't savored it. She hadn't committed every second to memory.

That Saturday, after they'd showered together in the office's luxury bathroom, Elora had expected the night to be over, but as she'd started for the door, Zain had stopped her. And he'd asked her on a dinner date.

When she'd refused, reminding him that they weren't the dating sort, he'd gotten angry and stormed out, leaving her alone. She'd waited for an hour but he hadn't returned, so she'd finally called a car and left through the rear employee entrance.

The same one she'd walked through today.

Her code had worked. Maybe he'd just been waiting to end it before he changed the number.

"We agreed," she said. "From the beginning."

"Yeah." He nodded. "I know. But it's not enough anymore."

Sex wasn't enough. *She* wasn't enough.

They'd been sleeping together for three years. It had started one night her freshman year. Coming to Treason at eighteen had been a rush. She and Ivy had come through the rear entrance that night too, joining the fray as the youngest in the club.

Zain had allowed it as long as they'd promised to stay in his lounge, and if they wanted to dance, then a bouncer would always be close by.

Ivy had gone to the dance floor while Elora had stayed in the lounge.

Even though she'd been friends with Ivy for what felt like her entire life, Elora hadn't known Zain from their youth. Being nine years older, he'd been long gone from the Clarence home by the time Elora had been old enough to notice boys. He'd simply been a face in framed photos.

But that night freshman year, one look at him in person and she'd been mesmerized. After three years, she was still under his spell. He was even more breathtaking now, after all this time.

Zain and Elora had both agreed it would be best to keep their relationship a secret. After all, it was only sex. There'd been no point in dragging Ivy or their families into the equation.

Maybe if he'd asked her on dinner dates from the start, she would have been able to accept.

But now . . . it was too late.

She was just waiting on the piece of paper to confirm it, but in her heart, Elora knew the truth.

He was tired of the twisted affairs? That was all she had to offer. One fucked-up situation followed by the next. Because when it came to the Clarence and Maldonado families, fucked up was an understatement.

"I'm thirty years old, El." Zain's shoulders sagged as he raked a hand through his hair. "I've spent night after night at this club, watching the same scene play out over and over again. I'm tired. I want more."

More. A simple, terrifying four-letter word. She couldn't give him more.

This son of a bitch. They'd agreed. Years ago, they'd agreed. Fuck him for changing the rules. Fuck him for making her fall in love.

No man compared to Zain. No man had ever captured her attention. Maybe they'd agreed no rules, no expectations, but she hadn't even thought about another man. Why would she need one?

She had him.

And now she'd lost him.

Her heart cracked. Her throat closed as she tried to breathe past the sting in her nose. *Fuck him.* She turned, shoulders pinned, and walked to the door.

"Elora."

She paused, her hand on the knob, and looked over her shoulder. She knew by the look on his handsome face what was coming.

"We're done with this."

God, she was stupid. There had never been another outcome. From the start, they'd been destined to burn. She just hadn't known it then. She hadn't seen what had been right in front of her face.

The sky-blue eyes. The straight nose. The full lips. The shape of his face. Zain looked like his dad. So did Edwin. So did Ivy.

Apparently all of David Clarence's children resembled their father.

She should have seen it coming.

Elora raised her chin. He might have broken her heart, but Zain didn't even know he held it in his hands. She had never let him see just how much she cared. She'd never dropped her guard, even for him.

"Are you expecting me to argue?" she asked, her voice steady. She'd break later, when she was alone.

He flinched. She hated herself for that flinch. "I guess not."

Without another word, she left his office. She didn't hurry to the main floor. She didn't rush through the club for the exit. Every step was measured. She was a depiction of cool and collected.

Zain's eyes were on her as she crossed the parking lot to her car. The windows from his office were the only ones at Treason. The last time she'd visited the club during the day, he'd watched her leave. She'd glanced over her shoulder and blown him a kiss.

Not today.

Today, she moved with purpose, like a woman walking away from a mistake.

The vibration of her engine shook her composure as she drove away. She made it three blocks before there were so many tears swimming in her eyes that she could barely see. Elora jerked her BMW into an empty parking lot, then buried her face in her hands and cried.

Fuck him.

Fuck those twisted little affairs.

six

. . .

WHENEVER IVY WALKED across Aston's campus, she felt at peace. It was the same feeling she got when stepping inside a museum or wandering through Boston Common. Old places gave her a sense of belonging.

Students walked across the courtyard with their eyes glued to smart phones. Six-wheeled robots rolled over Aston's sidewalks to deliver food-service items. A drone buzzed in the air overhead. But even with its modern comforts and technologies, the campus was brimming with history.

And history was the only subject that Ivy had ever enjoyed.

It was only because of expensive math and science tutors that she'd passed her required core curriculum classes in her early years at Aston. Much to her father's dismay, business and marketing weren't her forte.

She was content with a tattered book that smelled like aged paper and being consumed with an old story. On the outside, she was the perfect socialite. A woman satisfied when she was the center of attention. The appearance, like everything else in Ivy's life, was as fake as her nails.

Not many people knew that her favorite place to unwind

was the manor's library. Or that on the weekends, she'd sneak away and spend a few hours at the Harvard Art Museums. That Ivy League school had never been her destiny, not with her family's legacy tying her to Aston, but that had never stopped her from enjoying Harvard's campus and culture.

Ivy's backpack was heavy today, the strap digging into her shoulder. While Elora's classes were almost entirely digital, history professors loved the tradition of books. She tended to agree. She had an hour before her next class, so she walked toward the student union. Hopefully she'd find an empty table and get to skim the newest addition to her bag.

They were only into the second week of the semester, but so far, her favorite class was a study on mapmaking in global history. The coursework started in the 1600s and would carry to present day as the term progressed. They'd discuss cartographic images and how they'd shaped modern states. They'd dive into maritime exploration and colonial conquests. Nothing sounded better than grabbing an iced latte, finding a quiet corner and spending a few minutes studying the map print that her professor had handed out in lecture today.

But the moment she pushed through the doors of the student union building, she knew her map would have to wait.

Michael stood in the lobby, talking with a few of his fraternity brothers. The Sigmas always seemed to travel in packs.

Gone were his jeans and T-shirt from the night she'd seen him at Treason. Today, he wore slacks and a button-down shirt, the ensemble she recognized from this year's Louis Vuitton spring-summer collection.

He looked polished and powerful. He commanded attention, much like he did on the dance floor.

Except he was about done commanding hers.

He hadn't replied to the text she'd sent him the weekend before school had started. Part of her was glad because she knew it had reeked of desperation. But her ego, which hated to be ignored, was thoroughly irritated.

She strode past their group, not sparing them a glance, until a hand wrapped around her forearm.

"You're not even going to acknowledge me?" Michael stepped close, the scent of his Versace cologne filling her nose.

She arched an eyebrow, taking a play from Elora's handbook and not saying a word.

"Come on, Ivy. What did you want me to do at the club? You were all over that guy."

Tate. She'd thought about the sexy stranger more than she liked. More than she should have, considering he'd danced with her once and their interaction had been infused with insults. Why couldn't she get his face out of her head? She had questions, mostly for Zain, but she hadn't had the courage to ask her brother about Tate.

Eventually, he'd be forgotten. If there was anything she'd learned from her years studying history, it was that memory was fleeting. A select few were remembered or memorialized. Everyone else was forgotten within two hundred years.

She'd forget Tate—*whatever his last name*—soon enough. It was just taking longer than expected.

"I'm bored, Michael." She feigned a yawn and slipped her arm free of his grasp.

He inched even closer until his tall body was flush against hers. "Then let's do something *not* boring. Tonight."

She was about to congratulate herself on a victory when one of his fraternity brothers nudged his arm.

"There's your girl, Michael." The guy jerked his chin over Ivy's head.

If his *girl* was Allison, she'd castrate the bastard. She followed Michael's gaze as it shifted across the lobby and landed on a head of coral hair.

"Cassia?" She scoffed. Ivy had to give her roommate credit. She'd aimed her sights at the stars if she was after Michael. And she'd also just signed her eviction notice.

"How do you know her?" Michael asked.

"She's our new roommate." Ivy took a step away, looking him up and down. "How do you know her?"

"She's in the econ program. I'm meeting her today so I can introduce her to our study group."

"Oh," Ivy muttered.

Michael lifted a hand, waving Cassia over.

She had a slight smile on her face as she crossed the room. There was a flush to her cheeks, probably because she was walking toward one of the handsomest, most notorious men on campus. But the lightness in her expression disappeared the moment she recognized Ivy at Michael's side.

Their confrontation at home yesterday afternoon had been entertaining. And informative. There'd been such fear on Cassia's face. And fear meant she was hiding more than a dwindling bank account.

Ivy's first call this morning had been to her private investigator. Whatever secrets Cassia Collins was hiding, Ivy wanted the dirt.

Cassia's footsteps slowed as she approached, her shoulders stiff. She gave Michael a tight smile. "Hi."

"Hey. Thanks for meeting me."

"Sure." She turned to Ivy with a look of absolute scorn. "Ivy."

Interesting. Had Ivy underestimated Cassia? She'd honestly expected to return home after her dinner with Edwin last night to find her roommate packing. Instead, all had been quiet in Cassia's end of the manor. Her rusted car had been parked in the same spot next to the garage this morning.

A challenge. Ivy hadn't had a decent challenge for a while. Her schoolwork was interesting but not strenuous. A smirk tugged at Ivy's mouth before she strode away.

"Ivy," Michael called.

She glanced back.

"Tonight?"

Ivy's attention moved from his blue eyes to Cassia's hazel gaze. "See you at home."

The briefest hint of fear crept across Cassia's face.

I win.

But she was too quick to celebrate. Michael shot her a frown and put his hand on Cassia's shoulder. "Ivy thrives on being a bitch. Don't let her bully you."

Cassia barked a laugh. "So I've learned."

Asshole. But Ivy smiled despite the name-calling. It wasn't the first time. It wouldn't be the last.

You mustn't let them see you upset.

Her mother had taught her that lesson the day Ivy had come home from primary school in tears because one of her friends had called her a brat on the playground.

You're better than them.

Another valuable tip from Mom.

Michael was one of the few who'd dared to speak to Ivy that way. He'd never been intimidated by her. He didn't need anything from her. And because Ivy was totally fucked in the head, she wanted him anyway. Maybe she wanted him because he was a prick.

But if Cassia thought Michael was an upstanding guy, she was going to be sorely disappointed. He might pretend to be kind and attentive, but he was a Bamford. As ruthless and uncaring as his father.

It was why his father and her father were best friends.

Michael used people. He and Ivy had that in common.

She skipped the iced latte and time with her map, fuming as she left the student union. Not only had Michael embarrassed her, but he'd done it in front of Cassia, a woman who was already causing her grief.

Cassia hadn't reacted to her threats or demands at all like Ivy had expected. And what the hell was this thing with Michael? Did Cassia have a crush on him? Did she think she actually stood a chance?

Ivy was so annoyed that not even her next class could hold her attention. The minute her professor dismissed the lecture, an hour spent examining the rise and fall of the Soviet Union, she texted Jaxon for a ride home.

With her backpack discarded on the floor in the entryway —Geoff would haul it upstairs—she marched for Elora's office. The door was open, so she walked inside without a knock. "Cassia has to go."

"I disagree." Elora kept her eyes on the screen of her laptop.

"Don't tell me you actually like her."

"I like her."

Ivy planted her hands on her hips. "Please."

"She's lived here for what, eleven days?" Elora asked. "Why don't you try a different tactic this time? Maybe try not to be a bitch."

That was the second time today someone had called her a bitch. Yes, it was true, but hearing it was wearing thin.

"Did she tell you anything?" Ivy asked. "About her past or why she's come to Aston for her senior year?"

Elora finally graced her with eye contact. "So you *were* bluffing yesterday. You don't know anything about her."

Ivy shrugged. "For now."

"Whatever." Elora flicked her wrist. "I'm busy."

Ivy frowned. Dark circles sagged beneath Elora's eyes. "What's wrong?"

Elora didn't answer. She turned her attention back to her screen as her fingers clicked on the keyboard.

"Elora."

"Go away, Ivy."

What the hell was wrong with everyone today? Normally, Elora would listen to her rant about their roommates. She'd never participate in the fun, but she wouldn't condemn Ivy for it either. Why Cassia? Why was she so goddamn special? First Michael, now Elora.

"Fine." Ivy strode from Elora's office and stormed upstairs, going immediately for Cassia's bedroom.

The door was unlocked. A mistake on Cassia's part.

The previous roommates had moved in so much stuff. From clothes to pictures to books. But not Cassia. There were hardly any personal items on the nightstand or table. According to Geoff, it had only taken two trips to haul in her belongings.

Ivy flipped on the light in the closet, surveying the mostly empty space. Cassia's bargain-brand suitcases were tucked in a corner. An idea sparked as Ivy ran her fingers along a bare shelf.

If Cassia wanted to stay, she could stay.

But Ivy wasn't going to make it easy.

She began hauling clothes off their hangers, stuffing them into the suitcases. She cleared the rods first, then moved to the column of built-in drawers. She emptied the first, then opened the second, working quickly because she wanted it done before Cassia came home from campus.

But when she reached the third drawer, Ivy paused. Instead of more tees, bras and panties, this drawer held a handful of framed photos.

Why wouldn't Cassia put them up on display? Why hide them?

She lifted out a frame, inspecting the picture. Cassia was dressed in a black graduation gown and hat. Her hair was blond and her features slightly younger. High school. Cassia had her arm linked with an older man's, her head resting on his shoulder.

The resemblance between them was as clear as the frame's glass. The oval face. The pert nose. The tapered chin. This had to be her father. The affection between them was also crystal clear. Cassia leaned on him like he was a pillar of the earth, unwavering and unmovable.

Jealousy slapped Ivy across the cheek. What would it be like to count on your father? To love your dad?

Ivy lifted out another picture, then another until the drawer was empty and frames pooled around her knees. They were all of Cassia and the same man, except for one.

The picture that her roommate had buried at the bottom of the drawer, the only unframed photo, was of Cassia laughing with a younger man. Their hands were linked and the guy had her knuckles pressed to his heart.

A boyfriend? An ex-boyfriend?

If this guy was important, Ivy's investigator would find out. She collected the photos and loaded them in a separate suitcase, using Cassia's sweaters to protect them from being broken—Ivy wasn't a complete monster. Then she began carting the luggage downstairs.

She left the bathroom and the nightstands beside Cassia's bed untouched. After all, this was just a trial. She wasn't really evicting Cassia. If Cassia left, it would be by her own choice, not from Ivy's insistence.

Not a single one of the six roommates they'd had at Clarence Manor had been evicted.

Ivy had yet to break any rules in their lease agreements.

Maybe if Cassia passed this test, Ivy would back off. Maybe not.

It took her three trips to the foyer, but by the time Cassia was walking through the iron gates, Ivy had created a neat stack beside the front door. Then she climbed the stairs, leaning on the banister that overlooked the entryway, ready for the show.

Cassia walked inside, her cheeks flushed from the heat. She nearly passed her own things, but then did a double take and stopped. Her backpack slid off her shoulder as she bent and partially unzipped a suitcase, finding her clothes inside.

Ivy's heart raced. Her breath was stuck in her throat. Cassia's shoulders fell in defeat and a pang of guilt twisted Ivy's insides.

God, she really was a bitch.

Why was she doing this? The trials had been necessary at first, but if Ivy was being honest with herself, they'd lost their luster a long time ago. Ivy opened her mouth, about to say something she never said—*sorry*—but then Cassia stood tall and picked up a suitcase.

She didn't realize Ivy was watching until she was halfway up the staircase. Cassia's feet faltered on a step, but she kept climbing to the landing. "Why are you like this?"

"To make sure you're worthy," Ivy said. It was the truth.

"Then let me save you some hassle. I'm not." Cassia set down her suitcase. "I'm not worthy of this fancy house. Of Francis's gourmet meals. Of a butler or housekeeper. I'm not worthy. Happy? I've done nothing to earn this. But I've also done nothing to earn your hate. So back the fuck off, because I'm not leaving."

Ivy was taken aback. Such honesty and tenacity. Both were uncommon, especially within these walls.

"Our freshman year, a girl moved into your room," Ivy said. "Her name was Nicole. Elora and I had known her for years. She'd gone to Aston Prep with us."

"Okay," Cassia drawled. "Your point?"

Ivy wasn't sure why she was telling Cassia this story, but she continued. "Without telling us, Nicole pledged a sorority, even though she'd committed to living here. It wouldn't have been an issue. She could have just moved out. But instead, she fucked with Elora."

Cassia gave her a sideways glance. "What did she do?"

"For Nicole to be initiated into the sorority, she had to prove her allegiance. They asked her to destroy Elora's room and take a picture of the evidence. Elora had almost pledged the same house but changed her mind. The sorority sisters took it as an insult and this was their revenge. So Nicole did their bidding and trashed Elora's room. In the process, she broke a tea set. It was a set that had belonged to Elora's grandmother. She'd given it to Elora the Christmas before she died."

Ivy had seen Elora cry once and only once. Over that tea set. It had sent Ivy over the edge. "Nicole got what was coming to her."

Because instead of kicking Nicole out, Ivy had pretended to buy the bullshit lie that a group of vandals had broken in through Elora's unlocked window. And then Ivy had made Nicole's life hell.

She'd kept her close for months, learning every one of Nicole's secrets. Then she'd spread them around campus like wildfire.

The sorority had dropped Nicole when they'd found out she'd screwed one of the other members' boyfriends. Aston had started an investigation into her academic scores after the dean's office had received an anonymous tip that Nicole was paying another student to write her English 101 essays. And one afternoon, Nicole had come home to a similar situation as Cassia. Except her bags had been outside and the locks on the doors had been changed.

If she had just looked under the flowerpot, she would have found her new key.

Again, not an eviction.

Nicole had left Aston shortly thereafter.

"So you're putting me through these 'trials' to make sure I don't mess with Elora?" Cassia asked.

"Maybe," Ivy answered honestly. Why did she keep doing it? Habit? Initially, it had been a way to ensure the girls here weren't out to use either Ivy or Elora. The five after Nicole had failed epically. So it had become a way to exert control, to test character. But whose character was failing now?

"Well, you have nothing to worry about," Cassia said, picking up her suitcase. "I like Elora. You, on the other hand, I could do without."

Ivy didn't move as Cassia pushed past her, walking to her room.

"Oh, and, Ivy?"

Ivy turned.

"Touch my things again, and I'll burn your pretty manor to the ground. You're not the only person in this house capable of being cruel."

A threat? None of the six other roommates had threatened her. No wonder Elora liked Cassia.

Ivy laughed as she walked to her rooms. “Oh, this is going to be fun.”

Number seven might be the winner.

seven

. . .

"CASSIA." Professor Weston handed over her paper. An *A*, written in red Sharpie, was circled in the upper right-hand corner. "Well done."

"Thank you." Her cheeks warmed.

With the last of the papers returned, he resumed his perch on the edge of his desk. "With the exception of one score, there's room for considerable improvement. Plan to rewrite your paper taking into account my notes. Due Friday."

It was Wednesday. *Ouch.* Stifled groans filled the classroom.

Cassia stood, joining the shuffle as the class was dismissed. She stuffed her textbook and paper into her backpack, zipping her pencil into a pocket, as a tall figure stopped at her side.

"You're going to destroy our curve, aren't you?" Michael teased.

"Sorry, not sorry." She smiled. After another week of school, Cassia had been noticing her own smile, probably because it had been so infrequent lately. She'd also noticed that it usually appeared when Michael was around.

"I'm just glad you're in our study group," he said. "You can teach us your secrets."

The secret was that she'd taken a similar macroeconomics

theory class at Hughes. Her former professor had been brutal compared to Professor Weston, so while some of the advanced concepts were new to her classmates, most of what they'd tackled so far was a repeat.

Not that she'd ever tell an elite Aston professor that they were lacking in curricular rigor. The professors' egos were as inflated as most students'.

Michael held the door for her as they left Bamford Hall. Global trade policy didn't boggle her mind, but it was still surreal that she'd somehow become friends with the guy whose name was on the building.

"What are you up to?" he asked as they strode across the commons.

"I'm done with class for today, but I need to spend a few hours going through that worksheet for 410."

"I haven't started mine either. Want to work on it together?"

"Sure."

Michael checked his phone. "I've got a meeting at the house in an hour. How about we meet up after that?"

"Okay. The library?"

"Aren't you done on campus for the day?"

"Yeah, but I can stick around."

"I'll just come to your place. We can study there."

"Oh, um . . ." Her footsteps stuttered on the sidewalk. She was uncomfortable staying at the manor, let alone inviting over a friend. They were friends, right?

Over the past week, Michael had become this constant in her routine. They'd walked to shared classes together. They'd studied together nearly every day. Yesterday, they'd eaten lunch at the student union. But she still hadn't figured out how to relax when he was around. She blamed it on his good looks and natural charisma. On his quick wit and intelligence.

He was close to perfect.

And the last man she'd thought was perfect had ruined her damn life.

"You're worried about Ivy," he guessed.

"Yup." Another constant in her routine was hiding in her bedroom.

Though she had become a regular in Francis's kitchen. That woman was a genius when it came to food. And Cassia had learned that if she ate at four thirty or five o'clock, she could avoid her roommates. The same held true in the morning, which meant she'd basically become a senior citizen, going to bed by eight so she could rise before dawn.

"You could come to the fraternity," Michael said.

She cringed. A house full of college guys? That sounded worse than another confrontation with Ivy. "You're sure you don't want to just meet at the library?"

Michael smirked. "You're sure you don't want to just come to the Sigma house?"

That was a hard no. "Okay, fine. We can study at my place."

"Good. Ivy will leave us alone. And if she doesn't, I'll deal with her."

Easy for him to say. He didn't have to sleep under her roof.

Ivy hadn't sought Cassia out this week. Maybe it was because of Cassia's outlandish threat. More likely, Ivy was plotting her retaliation.

What had she been thinking, threatening Ivy? That girl was not only insanely rich, but she was just plain insane. Cassia had the sinking feeling that she'd poked a hornet's nest and was about to get swarmed. But if Michael wanted to act as the buffer for a night, so be it.

"See you later." Michael held up a hand and waved, then took the next turn in the sidewalk, heading toward the opposite end of campus.

Cassia took her own turn on the familiar route home. As always, her steps weren't rushed, but today, her slow pace wasn't just to avoid the manor. Today, she savored the weather and a break from the sweltering heat.

Over the past week, the early September air had begun to

cool. Soon, the leaves would begin to turn and Cassia couldn't wait for a new season. Summer reminded her too much of lazy afternoons spent with Josh.

Cassia had always preferred autumn. She had that in common with her father. But Josh loved summer.

A weight settled on her shoulders and it had nothing to do with the books in her bag. She'd worked hard not to think about Josh since she'd come to Aston. School had helped keep her mind occupied. But with every passing day, as she'd settled into her schedule, there were more free moments in her headspace.

Frustrating and upsetting as they'd been, Ivy's antics had given Cassia something to fret over. Something other than her past.

Maybe she'd walk through the manor's door today and find her things repacked. Maybe Ivy had redecorated her room. Or maybe, to Elora's point, Cassia had set her boundaries and Ivy would leave her alone.

How absurd was it that she hoped not?

"God, I am screwed up." She laughed at herself. "Maybe insane is a prerequisite for living in Clarence Manor."

The house was quiet when she walked through the door. There was a fresh bouquet of flowers on the foyer's table and she let herself sniff the pale pink blooms before trudging upstairs to her room. Not redecorated. Everything was just as she'd left it that morning.

Cassia spent an hour reviewing her notes from yesterday's Health Economics class, feeling prepared for their upcoming quiz. She'd just pulled out her Macro worksheet when Geoff knocked on the door. "Yes?"

"You have a guest."

"Thanks, Geoff." She collected her things before rushing down the hallway.

Geoff had already vanished. Given how quickly he could appear and disappear, Cassia wouldn't be surprised if he could walk through walls.

Michael looked at home as he stood in the entryway. Unlike her, he belonged in a manor.

"Hey," she said as she reached the bottom stair.

"Hey. Where do you want to study?"

Why hadn't she figured this out already? Part of her wanted to offer up her bedroom, but considering there wasn't much space on her little table, they'd be crowded.

"How about the library?" He was already walking toward the staircase.

"You've been here before?" she asked as she followed.

"Couple times."

Cassia opened her mouth to ask why, but she clamped it shut. She wasn't sure she actually wanted to know.

Michael swept into the library and walked straight for the table situated beneath the floor-to-ceiling windows. He pulled out a textbook and their assigned worksheet from his bag, then took a seat. All while Cassia stood at the door, wondering why he looked so comfortable in this room.

"Ivy and I had a chemistry class together freshman year," he said, like he could hear her thoughts. "We used to study here."

"Ah." She crossed the room and took the chair beside his, opening her book to the chapter she'd dogeared in class. Then she picked up her pencil, the graphite tip hovering over the worksheet, and began with question number one.

It took them two hours to work through the assignment. Before today, all she and Michael had done together was study with his group at Aston's four-floor library. This was the first graded task that they'd worked on together and Cassia had feared that she'd end up doing all the work while Michael simply agreed and copied her answers. That was how all of her group work had gone at Hughes. But he'd contributed just as much as she had to this worksheet.

"How bad will your rewrites be on Weston's paper?" she asked him as he tucked his completed worksheet away.

"Not bad. I got a B minus. But his notes make sense. I know where I went wrong."

"I, um . . . if you get stuck, just holler." They'd swapped phone numbers last week but he had yet to call or text. No one called or texted Cassia. Probably because not many people had her actual number.

Just Ivy from their early rental conversations. Her uncle for emergency use only. And now Michael.

Three people. Just three.

Cassia refused to let herself feel sad about her number of contacts. She'd had countless numbers in her last phone, and when she'd needed someone, anyone, to call, she'd been alone.

She'd take three people over three hundred, even if one of them was Ivy.

Michael zipped up his bag. "All right. I'd better get out of here. Get some dinner."

"I'll walk you out."

"It's all good. I know my way to the door. See you in class tomorrow?"

"Yep." She smiled and waited for him to leave, then she picked up her own things and carried them to her bedroom.

It was nearly six and her stomach growled.

She'd drop off her books, then hurry to the kitchen for whatever Francis had made for dinner. With any luck, she'd miss Ivy. Though maybe she'd bump into Elora. Maybe Elora would be her fourth contact.

Cassia hadn't seen her roommate since the day Elora had convinced her not to leave last week. They didn't need to be best friends, but acquaintances would work, right? Allies at least?

She pushed through her bedroom door and gasped. A man sat in one of her wingback chairs.

His light-brown hair was finger combed. His T-shirt strained across his broad chest. He was just as handsome as he'd been the day she'd spilled water all over him.

"Oh."

"About time." Edwin looked up from his phone. "I thought you two were going to work all night."

"W-what are you doing?" Why had she stammered? From surprise? Or the fact that she'd forgotten that he was simply that good looking?

"Waiting for you. What are you studying?"

"Economics. Why are you in my room?"

"I thought we had a connection. Something special."

"Huh?" Was he drunk?

Edwin smiled, revealing a dimple in his stubbled cheek. Cassia had always liked dimples. "I'm teasing. Ivy told me about what happened between you."

"You mean how she committed a gross invasion of my privacy? Sort of like finding you in my room without permission?"

He chuckled. "Yep."

"Okay," she drawled. "So are you here to exact her revenge? Or congratulate me on surviving an encounter with Satan's mistress?"

"Congratulations." His blue eyes sparkled as his smile widened. Two dimples. He had two dimples. *Damn.* "Definitely congratulations."

Cassia set her books down on her bed and studied his face. "But you're her brother."

"Exactly."

"Why is it that everyone who knows Ivy is proud of me for not liking her?"

Edwin laughed again, the deep, rich sound sending a shudder down her spine. "Once you get to know Ivy better, you'll be able to answer that question yourself."

Unlikely. At this point, she was only hoping to last through graduation, then with any luck, she'd forget Ivy existed. Though she suspected it would be harder to forget Edwin's face. "Okay, back to the beginning. Why are you in my room?"

He steepled his fingers in front of his chin as he stared at her. "What's your story?"

It was the very question Elora had asked her in this very room. "I don't have one."

"Oh, I don't believe that for a second. But I get it. You don't trust me."

"Of course not." She scoffed. "I've met your sister."

"Touché." He leaned deeper into the chair. "Maybe you will someday."

Trust him enough to share her secrets?

Never.

"My library? Really?" Ivy asked Michael as he strode across the foyer.

He turned to face her, a smirk playing on his face. "It's your favorite room."

Yes, it was her favorite. Though he liked it too. The last time he'd been over, they'd fucked on the table where he'd been studying with Cassia.

When she'd come out of her room earlier and heard voices in the library, she'd recognized his immediately. Cassia hadn't noticed when Ivy had stood in the doorway, watching them pore over a textbook. But Michael had noticed. He'd kept his eyes locked on Ivy's as he'd inched his chair closer to her roommate's.

"What are you doing with her?" Ivy stopped in front of Michael, dragging in his cologne. She missed having it on her skin.

"Studying," he said. "Thought that was obvious."

She arched her eyebrows. "We both know you don't need a study partner. What's the real reason you're being nice to her?"

"Can't I be nice?"

"You're not nice, Michael." Ivy lifted a hand to run her

fingertips down the front of his shirt, touching every button. "Neither am I."

When she reached his belt, she dragged the pad of her index finger across the buckle. He'd worn jeans today and they sat low on his hips. She dropped her hand to his thigh, feeling the muscles bunch as her palm caressed the denim.

"Ivy." He caught her wrist before she could put that palm over his zipper.

"If you want me to stop, all you have to do is say the word."

He kept his eyes locked with hers. Then he released her wrist.

Ivy smiled inwardly as she cupped his growing bulge. "What are you doing with Cassia?"

Instead of answering, Michael slammed his mouth onto hers, swallowing her gasp as his backpack crashed to the floor at their feet. Then his hands were on her face, holding her to his lips as he shuffled her toward the wall.

Her back collided with the table and she scrambled to sit on the surface, shoving Geoff's latest bouquet aside. Ivy's legs wrapped around Michael's ass as his tongue swept into her mouth.

Yes. She sank into his kiss as he pressed his arousal into her core. Too long. It had been too long. The only things separating them were his jeans and the thin leggings she'd pulled on earlier.

She'd planned to spend an hour in the gym downstairs before dinner, a long workout to burn off some of her pent-up energy. But when she'd heard Michael in the library with Cassia, well . . . maybe she'd get a different workout in tonight.

"Ivy," he moaned, tearing his lips away to suck on her neck.

Her hands threaded through his hair, mussing the combed strands. Her legs pulled him closer as the pulse in her core vibrated through her body. "More."

Michael's hand came to her breast, her nipple pebbling beneath her thin top and sports bra. He cupped her, roughly, just the way he knew she wanted it. Needed it. Because rough was the only way she could get off.

Because she truly was as fucked up as most people thought.

A throat cleared from the hallway.

Michael tore his lips away as they both looked to the source of the noise.

Geoff was frowning his disapproval, probably because she'd touched his precious flowers. He turned on a heel and walked away.

Mood killer.

Michael took a step back, his chest heaving as he wiped a hand over his mouth.

Ivy climbed off the table and brushed a lock of hair that had escaped her ponytail out of her face. Then she straightened the floral arrangement and met Michael's gaze. "Are you using Cassia to make me jealous?"

Because damn him, it was working.

"No."

She believed him. "What's your game?"

He dragged a hand through his hair, his usual composure cracking just a bit. The only time he let down his guard was when he had an erection. "She's new. Sits in the front row. Already has the professors raving."

Ah. So *he* was jealous. Interesting.

"No one transfers to Aston their senior year," he said. "It's only allowed for special circumstances."

"You want to know her story."

"Yeah." He stepped closer, their height difference more noticeable today since she was without heels. "And so do you."

"Maybe I already know everything."

He bent down, his lips brushing hers. "You don't know shit. And it's making you mad."

Damn him for being right.

He stepped away, bending to pick up his backpack. "Guess we'll see who figures her out first."

Ivy followed him to the door, standing at the threshold as he climbed into his charcoal Maserati. It wasn't until he was past the gate that she let herself touch her swollen lips.

Why did it feel like he'd won that round? Asshole. Now she was just as frustrated as ever. They'd drawn battle lines years ago. Fighting was part of their foreplay.

But there was no way she'd let him win the war.

She closed the door and turned her eyes toward Cassia's room.

Game on.

eight

. . .

NEVER AGAIN. Until Elora had answers, she was never coming to dinner at her parents' house again. Her fork scraped across her plate, pushing the food. Her stomach was in too much of a knot to eat.

She glanced up, watching Lucas as he shoved a huge bite in his mouth, his cheeks bulging like a chipmunk as he attempted to chew. Elora smiled. He'd done it to make her smile and she wouldn't let him down. Yet.

"Lucas," their mother chastised.

He shrugged an apology.

Since she'd talked to him last, he'd gotten his hair done. The sides were buzzed short, but the top, which was normally as straight as her own, was a mop of dark curls. Apparently this was the current trend and every boy on his football and basketball teams had a perm. She'd teased him about it mercilessly when she'd arrived earlier.

But his new style didn't mask the features she couldn't stop noticing.

His eyes were blue, like Dad's. But the shade was different. Too different.

Lucas swallowed his bite and caught her staring. "You're acting weird tonight."

Elora pushed more food around on her plate.

"Are you feeling all right, button?" her dad asked from his seat at the dining room table.

"Fine. I had a late lunch on campus," she lied.

"When you knew you were coming here." Her mother's tone was full of censure but her face was blank.

Elora was the carbon copy of her mother. The person she despised most was the person who greeted her in the mirror each morning. The person who'd taught her that empty stare.

Luckily for Lucas, the only commonality between him and Mom was their hair color.

"How are classes going?" Dad asked.

"Good."

"Think you'll graduate?" Lucas gave her a smirk.

"It's still early in the semester, but most likely." He loved to rib her about her grades even though he knew she'd never gotten less than an A in her life.

Elora Maldonado's personal life might be a failure, but academically, she was a star.

"How is school going?" she asked Lucas.

His gaze flicked between his parents before dropping once more to his plate. "Meh."

"We've got a little work to do in math." Dad put his hand on Lucas's shoulder. "But we've got a new tutor starting on Monday."

Elora opened her mouth, ready to volunteer to help, then stopped. She was struggling to make it through this once-a-month, Friday-night dinner and she hadn't been home since the last. If Lucas needed help with math, she'd have to visit daily, and there was no way she could do it.

"How is football?" Elora asked.

"Good." That brought a smile to his face. "Coach is going to let me play quarterback at our game tomorrow. You're still coming to watch, right?"

"Yes." She nodded. Elora hadn't missed a game, from the time he'd started in second grade all through middle school.

" 'Kay." He grinned and forked another huge bite, his nose scrunching to make her laugh.

Lucas was the joy in this house. His sweet nature had yet to be tainted. These monthly dinners had been his idea after Elora had moved out after high school. She worried about him alone here. Stuck with their mother.

He'd be starting high school next year. Aston Prep had a way of ruining people. Would he become jaded like Elora? Would they steal his light?

If only she could keep him in a bubble. If only she could get him out of this goddamn house.

"You're staring at me again." He stuck out his tongue. "Stop being weird."

"Sorry. It's just . . . that hair." Another lie that slid easily over her tongue. Another talent she'd inherited from her mother.

"It's awesome." Lucas ran a hand over his curls.

"Maybe I should do it to mine." Dad fluffed his short, brown hair.

"I'm sure the nanny would love it," her mother muttered. "And your assistant."

The table went still.

Mom always jumped at the opportunity to throw Dad's affairs around like candy at a parade. Ironic, wasn't it? Meanwhile Dad had never uttered a word of accusation. Maybe because he knew it wasn't appropriate family-dinner conversation. Or maybe because he'd lived in as much denial as Elora.

Never again.

His phone rang, cutting the awkward silence. Dad held up a hand, stood from his chair and had it pressed to his ear as he left the room.

Mom didn't even bother with a farewell as she stood and walked out, her glass of wine firmly in her grasp.

"Maybe we could, like, meet for lunch or something,"

Lucas said. "Friday nights are sort of busy now, you know, with friends and stuff."

Or he was getting old enough to hate their family dynamic too. "I'd like that. How about after your game tomorrow?"

"Okay. Cool."

They shared a look, one full of apology. Him, for asking her to come. Her, for seeing the truth.

"What are you doing tonight?" she asked.

Lucas shrugged. "Probably playing video games or something. You?"

Drinking. There would be a lot of drinking. "Not much."

They both stood, leaving the dishes for the staff to clear. Lucas walked her to the door, hugging her goodbye as she ruffled his curly hair.

She waited until she was in her car and off her parents' estate before she let herself take a full breath. It had been weeks since she'd sent that email. How long would it take for answers?

Ivy would know. But she wasn't about to bring her friend into this. Not yet. Eventually, it would be unavoidable, but for now, it was Elora's burden.

The trip home took an hour with traffic, and as she parked in her garage stall, a wave of exhaustion crashed over her shoulders. But she couldn't bring herself to go inside. There was nothing waiting for her. Ivy's car was gone. On a Friday night, her friend was probably at Treason.

Normally, that's where Elora would go too. She'd have a drink and lose herself in Zain. But that was over now. She hadn't heard from him since he'd broken it off ten days ago—she'd been counting.

Keeping him out of her mind had taken considerable effort. Maybe that was why she was so tired. Because regrets were heavier than secrets.

God, she missed him. There was this Zain-sized hole in her heart.

He was the only man who'd never pushed her to talk just

for the sake of filling the silent moments. He was the only person who looked past her empty expression. He was the only one she'd let into her tender heart.

And still, she hadn't been enough.

She reversed out of her garage.

Instead of focusing her energy on schoolwork or shopping or hours on the treadmill, she was going to soothe the pain with vodka.

She drove to another one of Aston's popular hangouts, fifteen minutes from the manor. Club 27 wasn't as exclusive or expensive as Treason, but the line to get in was just as long. Elora parked, knowing she wouldn't be driving herself home, and walked to the entrance, her keys tucked in her clutch.

The ripped jeans she'd worn to dinner had made her mother cringe. Her cropped top hugged her breasts and showcased the pale skin of her torso. Her Louis Vuitton heels were embellished with metal studs. Not exactly club attire, but tonight wasn't about fashion or slinky dresses. Tonight was about alcohol.

The bouncers at the entrance waved her inside without hesitation. Ivy might lead the way at Treason, but when it came to Club 27, Elora was the favorite. She went straight to the bar, sliding onto one of the last available seats.

In an hour, the place would be packed. In an hour, she hoped to be oblivious to the world.

She ordered a martini from the bartender, and after that first blissful sip, she spun on her stool to survey the club. Music pounded through the speakers. Lights flashed across the busy dance floor. Elora recognized a few faces from Aston.

And a face that shouldn't be here sitting three tables away.

Zain.

Elora's heart dropped.

There was a woman on his lap. Her blond hair fell in waves to her waist. She had curves. She smiled effortlessly as she threw her head back and laughed. One look and Elora knew this woman was everything she wasn't.

Zain's arm was wrapped around the woman's hip, his fingers splayed on her skintight dress. There was a smile on Zain's face too. Elora couldn't remember the last time she'd made him smile.

He held the woman in place on his knee as he spoke to the other man at their table. *Tate.* He was a friend of Zain's from college. Elora had met Tate last spring during a night at Treason when she'd gone to the club without Ivy.

Tate hadn't asked about her relationship with Zain. Or why she'd come to Zain's office instead of partying with the other twentysomethings at the club. He'd simply poured her a drink and invited her into the conversation.

The three of them had stayed up late talking about Tate's plans to move back to the area from Las Vegas until Elora had fallen asleep on Zain's couch as the friends had reminisced about their days at Aston.

Elora liked Tate. Or she had, until he laughed at something the woman on Zain's lap said. *Traitor.*

She pressed a hand to her chest as she stared at Zain. An ache so consuming, so destructive, spread through her chest that she struggled to breathe.

He looked beautiful tonight. Happy. He was in a button-down shirt, the white glowing beneath the club's blacklights. The sleeves were cuffed at his wrists, hiding the tattoos Elora had always loved to trace while he was asleep.

Had this blond already taken her place? Probably. That was what he'd wanted, wasn't it? A woman who'd sit on his lap. Someone who wouldn't hide her feelings because they terrified her. A lover. A girlfriend. A wife.

It was Tate who spotted Elora staring. His smile fell as he leaned closer to speak in Zain's ear.

Zain's eyes shot her way. His shoulders stiffened.

Elora lifted her martini glass, giving him a salute. Then she took another sip before setting her drink on the bar and walking out the door. *So much for getting drunk.*

At least she wouldn't have to find a ride home. Hopelessness spread through her veins as she returned to her car. Couldn't he have waited a little longer? Couldn't he have pretended to be heartbroken? Couldn't he have taken a date to his own fucking club?

By the time Elora walked through her bedroom at home, she was numb.

She kicked off her shoes and padded quietly through the manor for the largest parlor, where Geoff always made sure to keep the bar cart stocked. She poured herself a glass of tequila, draining it in a gulp. She winced, savoring the burn as it warmed her insides, then headed to her bedroom.

Why couldn't he have stayed at Treason? Elora had spent ten days picturing him with Tommie the bartender. Why Club 27? He knew she went there from time to time.

Was this his plan? To hurt her the way she'd hurt him? Well . . . it was unnecessary. She was plenty capable of punishing herself.

She trudged to the bench in her window, her limbs loosening as the tequila seeped into her bloodstream. She curled into the seat, pressing her temple to the cold glass as she stared into the night, and let hot tears streak down her face.

Fuck him. Fuck Zain Clarence and his pretty blond. Fuck these feelings.

What was the point? To end up like her parents, in a hateful marriage overflowing with lies and betrayals?

Fuck love.

Elora stood and tore off her clothes, leaving them in a trail on the floor as she climbed into her bed. The tears wouldn't stop. Why wouldn't they stop?

Stop. Please stop. The hurt was so much she buried her face in the pillow and screamed.

No one cared.

No one was there to listen.

No one ever was.

Elora jerked awake as a weight settled on the mattress. The room was cast in muted moonlight from the window, enough to make out his chiseled features. But she didn't need to see her visitor. Her favorite cologne, the one she'd bought him at Christmas, gave him away.

"Is that woman who you want?" Her voice was raw from screaming earlier.

Zain threaded a lock of her hair between his fingers.

"Will she go on dinner dates with you?"

He didn't answer that question either as he went to work freeing the buttons on his shirt.

"Will she let you buy her jewelry?" Beneath the covers, Elora curled her legs into her chest in an attempt to hide how badly she began to shake. "Will she meet your parents?"

"She already knows my parents."

Elora squeezed her eyes shut, willing the tears away. Luckily, she must have shed them all earlier. Her pillow was still damp.

"You know my parents too, El."

She hated his parents. But that wasn't the point.

Elora didn't know David and Helena because Zain had brought her home and introduced her to them as his. She knew the Clarences because of Ivy.

And because when she was sixteen, she'd bumped into Zain's mother coming out of her father's office. Helena had been straightening the hem of her dress. When she'd looked to her father, his lips had been stained red from her lipstick.

Twisted little affairs.

Zain stood, toeing off his shoes. Then the clink of his belt unbuckling filled the room before his jeans plopped on the floor. He pulled at the hem of her bedding, the cool air raising goose bumps on her naked flesh. And then he chased away the cold by settling his perfect, strong body on top of hers.

Elora had no choice but to let go of her legs, rolling to face him and stretching her toes toward his. "Did you fuck her?"

His hands bracketed her face, their noses almost touching. "Shut up."

Zain dropped a single kiss to her mouth, tasting like mint and gin.

She tore her lips away. "Answer me. Did you fuck her?"

If he was going to shatter the remains of her heart, he might as well be thorough.

"No," he growled, taking her lips once more. This kiss wasn't sweet or endearing. His mouth was firm and his tongue shoved between her teeth, taking what he wanted. Then he broke away, his cock insistent against her wet folds. "But I'm about to fuck you."

Elora wished she had the strength to resist him. But that ship had sailed years ago, so she rolled onto her back and spread her legs wider, making room for him in the cradle of her hips. Then she moaned as he thrust inside, filling her completely as she stretched around his length.

"Zain," she whimpered, her nails digging into the corded muscles of his back. They fit together like puzzle pieces. Her edges weren't so jagged when he held her close.

"Damn you, Elora." He pulled out and slammed inside once more, her body melting as the root of his cock pressed against her clit. "Damn you."

"You should have stayed at Treason." She tilted her hips, sending him deeper. "You should have stayed away."

"I can't." He spoke through gritted teeth. "Damn you."

She let him curse her. She closed her eyes and let him fuck her. And because this time had to be the last, for her heart's sake, she memorized every stroke.

Her hands explored the planes of his chest as he pistoned his hips, setting a claiming rhythm. Her fingertips dipped into the curves of his abs. She traced the muscles down his spine and palmed the globes of his perfect ass.

Then she held his gaze, drowning in those blue pools. One more time.

He kissed her again, tangling his tongue with hers. He

groaned, their bodies moving together in this perfect dance. Or it would have been perfect if not for the edge of self-loathing. She was so weak.

"Fuck," he hissed as her inner walls began to flutter. "You feel so fucking good."

"Harder."

Zain didn't disappoint. He worked his body like magic, bringing them together until she writhed beneath him. The scent of sweat and sex clung to the air as his mouth captured hers.

No man would ever compare. No man would ever make her feel this much. Zain had ruined her.

She tore her mouth away as her toes curled. "Zain."

"Come, babe. Come on my cock."

The tension built, higher and higher with each roll of his hips, until she broke. Elora pulsed around him as white spots burst behind her eyes. She flew, forgetting the pain and heartache. Nothing mattered except that he was here. That he was hers.

"Elora." Her name in that throaty rasp drew out her orgasm as he poured inside her, his body trembling with his own release.

She watched the ecstasy consume his features. The furrow of his brow. The part in his lips. The tension in his jaw. Perfection. He was her perfection.

Zain collapsed on top of her after a final stroke, wrapping her in his arms as he rolled, positioning her over his chest. His heart thundered beneath her cheek as they worked to regain their breath. Then he pushed the hair away from her temples, his eyes narrowing as he studied her face. Even with the room dark, the softness in his expression said that he saw the puffiness in her eyes.

He pulled her forehead to his lips, dropping a kiss, then he curled her closer, like he'd hold her through the night.

But she wiggled out of his embrace, moving to sit on the edge of the bed.

She'd hate herself the moment he was gone, but he couldn't stay. If he stayed tonight, she'd want him tomorrow night. And the night after that. And the night after that.

For her sake, and his, he couldn't stay. So she swept up his jeans and tossed them across the bed.

"Never again," she whispered. On unsteady legs, she walked to the bathroom, locking herself inside to hide her silent tears as she turned on the shower.

She didn't hear Zain leave.

But when she emerged, dripping wet, he was gone.

nine

. . .

FOR THE PAST THREE DAYS, whenever Cassia walked into her room, her eyes shot straight to the chair. *Edwin's chair.* Funny how he'd spent less than thirty minutes in that seat but now it was his.

She plopped on the edge of her bed, sighing as she glanced toward the stack of textbooks on her table. After a long week of classes and her Saturday spent studying, her mind was officially mush. Her dinner break in the kitchen hadn't revived her like she'd hoped.

Francis had made salmon en croute and the leftovers had been just as delicious tonight as yesterday's meal. Cassia had never eaten the dish before, but that was becoming a regular occurrence. Her days of choosing between Taco Bell and Chick-fil-A were over for a while.

Maybe tomorrow she'd venture away from the manor and hit up McDonald's, not because she missed fast food but for a little remembrance of her old life. She'd come to Aston to forget about Cassie Neilson, and so far, it was working. The extreme hours spent on schoolwork had given her little time to dwell on the past.

But tonight, she longed for a taste of her former life. A hint of the familiar, even if it was only a double cheeseburger and large fries.

"I can't study anymore." Cassia fell into the mattress, her eyes crossing as she stared at the ceiling. While she was mentally exhausted, physically, she needed an outlet. "I could go for a run."

Her groan filled the room. She hadn't braved the home gym at the manor yet. When Ivy had shown her the space during their initial home tour, she'd considered the treadmill. Once upon a time, Cassie had loved to run. But the gym was far from her room and, therefore, in enemy territory.

Like studying excessively, avoiding Ivy had worked. Why change what wasn't broken?

She shifted, propping up on an elbow as she looked to Edwin's chair again.

Why had he come in here? Their conversation had been surprisingly normal. He'd teased her during his short visit. He'd congratulated her for standing up to Ivy. Then they'd just . . . talked. Edwin had asked her about classes and her major. He'd told her he was studying business management. He'd tipped her off to the hidden vending machine on the third floor at Aston's library where every item was just a quarter.

Why couldn't he have stopped there? Why had he asked for her story?

Maybe it had been simple curiosity. Maybe her paranoia had reached new heights. Or maybe . . .

Had Edwin visited the other roommates who'd lived in this room? Had they kept secrets of their own?

Whatever his reason for coming into her room, she wasn't about to drop her guard. It could all be part of Ivy's plot to run her out of the manor. Edwin could be wielding his handsome face and devastating smile to lure Cassia into a trap.

She shoved off the bed and crossed the room to the cabinet against the wall, opening the doors to reveal the television. She'd pulled the remote from her nightstand, ready to lose herself in a mindless movie, when a knock came at the door.

She tensed. It wasn't Ivy—she had yet to knock—so it was likely Geoff. The butler always made her feel like an intruder. "Yes?"

The door opened and Elora strode inside.

"Oh." Cassia relaxed. "Hi."

Her roommate walked to the TV cabinet and closed the doors. "I'm going to a club."

"Good for you?" Cassia gave her a sideways look.

"You're coming with me."

"Is that an invitation or an order?"

Elora shrugged.

On her first night here, Ivy had invited Cassia to a club. She'd declined, too tired to endure loud music and drunk idiots after the drive from Hughes. Hours later, Ivy had revealed her true colors and Cassia had realized she'd dodged a bullet.

Why would Elora want Cassia to go with her to a club?

"Get dressed." Another order as Elora took in Cassia's joggers and ratty tee.

"I think I'd better pass."

Elora frowned. "To what? Watch TV all night?"

Boring. Elora didn't need to say the word because it rang loud and clear.

Cassia used to be fun, hadn't she? Or had she always been this . . . predictable. Boring. It was just a club. And Elora wasn't Ivy. What was the worst that could happen? "I don't have anything to wear."

Elora was wearing a black cropped top. The one-shoulder shirt exposed an arm and most of her midriff. She'd paired it with sleek black pants, and with her dark hair straightened into silky panels, she was as beautiful as any supermodel Cassia had seen in magazines.

Cassia, on the other hand, hadn't washed her hair in two days.

"Do you own makeup?" Elora asked as she walked into the closet.

"Yes."

At Hughes, she would have died before leaving the house without makeup. These days, a swipe of mascara was all she bothered to apply. She wasn't at Aston to impress anyone. And while makeup had been her own indulgence, it had lost its appeal.

Most of the makeup in her bathroom had been a gift from her father. Maybe she'd avoided it because she didn't want to run out. Or maybe it, like so much else, had been tainted by lies and deceit.

Elora came out of the closet with Cassia's oversized Led Zeppelin T-shirt that she used as a nightshirt. "I thought I told you to put on makeup."

"That's my pajama shirt," Cassia said.

"Makeup." Elora snapped her fingers. "And do . . . anything with that hair."

Cassia frowned but climbed off the bed. Call it desperation, but she had nothing else to do tonight and the idea of being social, of acting like a normal college student, was too tempting to resist. Even if this was a trap. Even if this was a mistake.

She'd regret it tomorrow.

Doing her makeup was like walking down a familiar path, one she'd missed since coming to Aston. The gold striations in her hazel eyes popped after she swiped on bronze eyeshadow. Her cheeks were no longer pale and hollow thanks to her favorite blush. And after putting on her lipstick, she looked like . . . herself. For the first time in months, she knew the woman staring back through the mirror.

She was a blend of Cassia and Cassie. Maybe she'd start calling herself Cass.

Another name that didn't really fit.

"Red lipstick." Elora leaned against the bathroom's doorframe and crossed her arms over her chest. "Good choice."

Red had always been Cassia's favorite lip color. "My hair is a mess."

"Swap the ponytail for a messy topknot. It will go with your outfit."

"Okay—wait. What outfit?"

Elora crooked her finger for Cassia to follow.

They walked into the bedroom and on the bed were the remnants of her favorite denim cutoffs. Only they would no longer hit her midthigh. While Cassia had been in the bathroom, Elora had found scissors and her shorts were now, well . . . booty shorts.

"I liked those," Cassia said.

"I made them better." Elora tossed her the shorts and her pajama shirt. "Put those on. What size shoe do you wear?"

"Eight."

"Excellent." Elora shooed her into the bathroom once more to change and do her hair.

Cassia obeyed, curiosity getting the best of her judgment. What club? How many people would be there? Why had Elora taken such an interest in her? Would Ivy be going too?

As she dressed, her heart rate quickened, both with nerves and excitement. The shirt hit her legs at almost exactly the same place as the shorts, and unless she pulled it up, it looked like she was wearing nothing beneath the top. The only evidence of the denim shorts was the frayed edges Elora had pulled after sawing them off.

"Should I tie the hem of my shirt or something?" Cassia asked as she rejoined Elora in the bedroom. "It looks like I'm wearing the shortest dress on earth."

"That's the point. We're going to a club, not church. Grab your phone and ID."

"Why do you want me to go with you? Is this a trick?"

"I'm not like Ivy."

"Then why?" Cassia asked again.

"Because."

"That's not an answer."

Elora sighed, clearly losing interest in this exchange. "Suit yourself. You look hot. So you can waste that look on your television. Or you can come dancing and have a few drinks with people your own age."

Dancing. Drinks. *Fun.* God, it was tempting. How long had it been since Cassia had done anything fun?

"Do I need money?" Cassia asked.

Elora's smile was victorious. "Not where we're going."

Cassia grabbed her phone and ID, tucking them into a shorts pocket, then she walked toward the closet. "Which shoes?"

"None of yours. Let's go."

She followed Elora downstairs in bare feet. When they walked into Elora's rooms, Cassia spun in a slow turn, doing her best not to gawk. The space was gorgeous. Much like her roommate, the bedroom was brimming with grace and elegance, from the grand armoire to the massive bed to the crystal chandelier.

Elora's first roommate had trashed this room? The bitch.

A framed photo of Elora and a boy sat on a nightstand. A brother?

Before she could move in for a closer look, Elora came out of her closet with a pair of boots. "Put these on."

"I can just wear something of my own." The red soles of those boots meant they likely cost a fortune.

Elora raised an eyebrow in silent disagreement.

"Fine." Cassia took the boots, the black suede so smooth she couldn't resist running her hand up and down the shaft. She slid them on, pulling them up and over her knees. Then she glanced at herself in the floor mirror in a corner.

"Wow." She looked young and stylish and . . . sexy. The

messy hair somehow complemented the T-shirt, and the boots gave her outfit an edge.

"Sometimes I even amaze myself."

Cassia smiled at Elora through the mirror. "Careful. I'm starting to like you."

"An unintended consequence of me not wanting to go to the club alone."

Was she joking? The slight smile around Elora's eyes said she was probably teasing, but Cassia had never met someone who could hide nearly all emotion from their face.

"Where is Ivy?" Cassia asked.

"Gone. Once a month, she spends a weekend at a spa in the city."

"Ah." Cassia did a mental fist pump.

"I'm driving." Elora turned and walked out of the room, not waiting for Cassia to catch up.

They left the manor for a garage so clean that Cassia wouldn't be afraid to eat off the concrete floor. Elora's black BMW gleamed under the florescent lights. When Cassia slid into the passenger seat, the smooth leather seemed to mold around her body.

Cassia did her best to calm her heart as Elora drove away from the manor. "This is the nicest car I've ever been in," she admitted.

Elora didn't respond, not that Cassia was expecting a comment. She'd quickly learned that Elora only spoke when necessary. Except the silence only ratcheted her nerves up. She tucked her hands beneath her legs to keep them from fidgeting.

"Where are we going?" she asked. "Which club?"

"Treason."

Cassia nodded, though she'd never heard of it before.

Treason. It was just a name but it sounded expensive and exclusive.

The drive seemed to take forever, the minutes crawling by

on the car's display screen. She was already sweating and they hadn't even started dancing.

Why had she agreed to this? Going to a nightclub with Elora was against everything she'd planned. This year at Aston was about school. Period. There was no time to party. Yes, she liked her outfit, but there was no way she'd fit in at some swanky club. She wasn't a good dancer in tennis shoes. Add in these heels and she was probably going to fall on her face.

Cassia opened her mouth, ready to ask Elora to turn this car around, but then they slowed and pulled into a parking lot crowded with cars.

A row close to the building was marked for VIPs. It came as no surprise when Elora parked in a reserved space.

Before Cassia was ready, they were crossing the parking lot and rounding the corner of the building. The line of people waiting to get in ran the length of the club. Cassia slowed at the end of the line but Elora kept walking toward the doors.

Everyone in line was staring. The urge to duck her chin was overwhelming, but she stayed strong and kept her gaze focused on Elora's black hair.

Red lipstick. She was in red lipstick. Strange how something so trivial gave her just that little boost of confidence. Step after step, they moved for the roped entrance.

A bouncer spotted Elora and sprang into action, moving to open the door and wave her inside.

Cassia made sure to stick close, following her roommate into the club. Then they were shrouded in muted light and electric music.

She slowed her steps, trying to take it all in, but she wasn't sure where to look first. The dance floor. The bar. The lounges. Face after face after face. She hadn't realized she'd stopped walking until a hand gripped hers.

She glanced to her fingers, then up to Elora.

Cassia expected to find irritation on Elora's face for holding up the party, but her roommate's eyes were gentle.

She wanted to hug Elora for it. Instead, she gripped the woman's hand tighter and followed Elora through the crush.

People made a path for them as they walked, giving Cassia the freedom to soak it all in. She was so busy looking around, she nearly collided with Elora when her roommate stopped beside the railing that circled the dance floor.

"I'll get champagne," Elora said, nearly shouting over the music. "Hold our place."

"Okay." Cassia nodded and gripped the steel railing with both hands, using it to steady herself. Then she took the few minutes alone to really examine the club.

Her hunch from earlier proved to be true. Treason oozed money and power, not just from the high-end ambience, but from the patrons too. Most of the men in the lounges were in tailored, three-piece suits. Most of the women were dripping in jewels.

She might have felt completely out of place except for the people on the dance floor. Nearly everyone moving to the DJ's mix was around her age. There were a couple of girls in shorts and tank tops, their outfits casual yet sexy, like hers. Some of the guys were wearing jeans.

In the center of the floor, a cluster of guys were garnering a lot of attention. They were all good dancers, especially the one in the middle. The guy could freaking move. And damn, those hips were talented. His back was to her, but as he spun, she stood straighter, doing a double take.

Michael. He was nearly unrecognizable in his backward baseball hat, baggy jeans and T-shirt. It was odd to see him . . . unbuttoned. Almost like he had two faces and she was seeing the opposite side of the coin.

She was so busy studying him, watching him dance, that she didn't notice when a tall figure took the space beside her.

A glass of champagne appeared in front of her face.

"No, thank—oh." A single glance and her pulse spiked, just like it had when she'd found him in her bedroom.

"Oh," Edwin mimicked. "One of these days, maybe you'll greet me with a *hello*."

"Maybe if you stop startling me, you'll get that hello." She took the flute, glancing past him, searching for her roommate.

"If you're looking for Elora, she left you in my charge."

"W-what?" Seriously? They'd been here for a whole ten minutes and already she'd been ditched.

"She said something came up, but she didn't want to make you leave."

"And instead of telling me herself, she sent you."

"I volunteered."

"Right," she drawled. Damn. She should have stayed in her room.

Of course this was a setup. Why? Why would Elora drag her out here only to leave?

Cassia brought the champagne to her lips but hesitated before taking a sip. They wouldn't drug her, would they?

"You really don't trust me, do you?" Edwin sighed. "I don't roofie women, Cassia."

"I'm—sorry." She couldn't deny that was where her mind had gone. He'd read her perfectly.

It was the wounded look on his handsome face that made her take a risk and sip the drink. She'd had enough cheap champagne to know this glass was out of her price range. She took another sip, savoring the dry bubbles, as she turned her attention to the dance floor again.

Looking anywhere but at Edwin seemed safer. Cassia didn't want him to see the flush of her cheeks. To notice that her breaths were short.

She'd grown comfortable around Michael but Edwin was a different kind of attractive. The dangerous kind.

As he inched closer, bending to drop his forearms to the railing, her heart rate doubled. Cassia snuck a glance at his profile. The sharp contours of his jaw sent a flutter to her lower belly.

This was insanity. Not once in her life had she had this sort of physical reaction to a man. Not even Josh.

"Did you come here looking for him?" Edwin asked.

She followed his gaze to Michael. "No."

"Well, if you ever need to find him, just look in Ivy's bedroom."

Cassia blinked, letting that statement sink in. Michael and Ivy? It should have surprised her but . . . it didn't. Why didn't it? Probably because the idea of Michael and Ivy made sense. They both had money. They both had prestige. They'd gone to school together for years. They fit. Except, unlike Ivy, Michael wasn't an asshole.

"It's not like that," she told Edwin. "We're friends."

"Friends. You trust Michael but not me?"

"You and I aren't friends," she said. "And I don't trust anyone." Especially friends.

"That's smart." Edwin smiled and *damn it.* Her breath hitched. Again. He heard it too. His breathtaking smile stretched wider.

Yep. Definitely in trouble.

He nudged her elbow with his. "I like the red lipstick. You look beautiful."

There was warmth in his tone. Honesty. That sort of comment should have made her heart soar. A sexy-as-hell guy thought she was beautiful. Instead, she shied away to study his face. Was he fucking with her?

"It's just a compliment. You can believe it," Edwin said, proving once more he was in her head.

"No, I can't."

"Why?"

Because she was totally messed up. "There are a lot of reasons."

"Give me one."

She went for the obvious. "You're Ivy's brother."

"I'm not my sister." That sharp jaw clenched as he stood tall. "See you around, Cassia."

The smart thing to do was let him walk. But before he could take a step and disappear into the crowd, she touched his elbow.

Edwin turned.

"Sorry," she said. "Thank you for the compliment. This just . . . it feels like a game and I don't know the rules."

The irritation on his expression vanished and he stepped close. The club's lights flashed. The bass pounded. But in that moment, as he towered over her, she slipped into his bubble and let the rest of the club become a haze.

"You're irritatingly beautiful," he said, so quietly that the deep caress barely touched her ears over the music.

"No, I'm not."

"You don't even see it."

"See what?"

He circled a hand around the room. "The looks. You walked into this club and every woman envies you. Every man wants to fuck you, including me. You're the most beautiful woman in Treason."

Cassia gasped. That wasn't just another compliment. That was a statement.

The lust in his eyes was unmistakable. His gaze was locked on the red of her lips as he shifted even closer. "Why can't I stop thinking about you?"

Was he going to kiss her? Did she want him to kiss her?

Yes. The confession almost escaped as she closed her eyes and dragged in the heady scent of his cologne.

"You can trust me, Cassie."

Her eyes snapped open. Every muscle in her body tensed. Why would he say that? Why would he call her Cassie?

She forced her feet to move, one step backward. Then another.

The confusion on his face seemed genuine, but she'd learned her lesson about men's faces. They could be just as deceitful as their words.

She flew past Edwin, leaving her champagne flute on the

nearest table as she retreated for the corner where she'd spotted the restrooms earlier.

The smile she gave the attendant was shaky before she locked herself in a stall. Then she dug out her phone, leaning against the steel partition as her fingers flew across the screen, typing a text to one of her three contacts.

Have you told anyone about me?

His reply was instant.

You asked me not to.

But that wasn't really an answer to her question, was it?

ten

. . .

GUILT PRICKED Elora as she watched Cassia and Edwin from a distance.

She'd hoped he'd be here tonight. She'd hoped Michael would be too. Because had she not bumped into Edwin, she would have asked Michael to watch over Cassia.

It was a shitty thing to do, pawning off her roommate. But Elora needed the house empty tonight.

She checked the time on her phone. There was still an hour to kill before her meeting. *A damn hour.* Convincing Cassia to come tonight hadn't taken as long as she'd expected.

Elora should burn that hour waiting at the manor or driving around. She was only three sips into her flute of champagne, the glass she'd ordered along with the one she'd sent to Cassia via Edwin.

Lingering at Treason was dangerous, yet she stayed beside the bar. She'd told Edwin she was leaving, but walking to the door was proving difficult.

And it had everything to do with the man seated in the owner's lounge.

Zain wasn't secluded in his office tonight. He wasn't away at another club. He sat in his favorite seat, arms stretched over the back of a lounge couch, as he surveyed Treason. Tate sat at his side, the two of them drinking amber liquid from crystal tumblers.

If Zain had spotted Elora, he hadn't acknowledged her presence. It was for the best. She'd purposefully pushed him away last night. After he'd fucked her wildly, she'd told him never again.

They were over.

This sick, cruel cycle their parents had started must stop.

But that hadn't stopped her from choosing Treason tonight. She could lie and tell herself it was because she'd suspected Edwin would be here—he liked Treason just as much as Ivy did. Except Elora was weak. She'd wanted to see if Zain had found his way back to his blond.

So far, she was nowhere in sight. Maybe she was on her way. Would Zain whisk her away for a tryst on his office couch? The champagne in Elora's stomach churned. She forced her eyes away, turning her back to Zain's lounge.

She checked the time again, wishing the numbers would change faster. Then she focused on her roommate.

Elora really did like Cassia. The more time they spent together, the more she imagined they could become friends. Not that Elora had the first clue how to have a normal friendship.

Cassia had secrets. But what Elora liked about her most was that she didn't deny them. Cassia didn't pretend to be an open book.

It was refreshing.

Her parents had more secrets than Treason had shot glasses, but they pretended. Everyone pretended.

Including Elora.

Edwin smiled as he talked to Cassia and a bit of worry for abandoning her roommate vanished. She'd be fine. Edwin would make sure Cassia was safe tonight and that she had a ride home.

Tomorrow, Elora would apologize. Maybe she'd gift Cassia

those boots. Though Elora had kept them in her closet for months, she had yet to wear them. And they made Cassia's toned legs look a mile long. She had curves Elora could only dream of.

After a last sip, she set her flute on the bar and made her way toward the door.

Don't look back. Don't look.

She might have walked out the door but a couple came rushing off the dance floor, nearly colliding with her as they hurried to the bar. Their hands were linked as they smiled and laughed. The guy slowed to drop a kiss to the girl's mouth.

What would it be like to have that obvious, obnoxious sort of love? The kind she saw on campus from time to time when couples would cuddle at the base of a tree or share a kiss before class. The kind of love she'd only witnessed from afar.

Her feet slowed. Her resolve fizzled. She twisted, stealing a last glance toward Zain.

He was smiling at Tate, the friends carrying on their own conversation as people milled about his lounge. He looked happy tonight. Relaxed. Was it because of Tate? Or was that lightness because, after three years of hiding, Zain was free from Elora?

Like he felt her stare, his gaze darted toward the door. The moment he spotted her, his smile dropped.

Her heart broke all over again at the hate in his eyes. God, this fucking hurt. She swallowed the lump in her throat.

He hated her.

She loved him.

Not that she'd ever let it show.

She rushed for the door, her footsteps going faster and faster, her lungs craving fresh air. This had to be her last trip to Treason. Maybe not forever but for a while. Watching him fall in love with the right woman would be excruciating. Until her heart mended, she didn't have the strength.

And tonight, she had an appointment.

The drive home was a blur of streetlights and trembling

limbs. Soon, she'd have answers. Soon, the guessing would be over.

The manor was dark as she eased into the garage. Saturday was the only day of the week when Francis wasn't here to cook. Saturdays were also Geoff's only day off. And since this was Ivy's spa weekend in the city and Cassia was occupied at Treason, the manor was Elora's.

She went inside, skipping her rooms, and walked straight for the foyer, where she flipped on the lights and paced. With every click of her heels on the polished floor, her heart climbed closer to her throat. Until finally a flash of headlights burst through the windows.

Elora raced to the door and ripped it open, watching as the gray sedan eased into the loop.

The man behind the wheel parked and stood, adjusting the brim of his newsboy cap as he tipped his head up to inspect the manor.

She felt as if she was going to burst with questions but Elora forced herself to stand at the threshold and wait for him to finish his perusal and join her at the door.

"Elora Maldonado." He dipped his head, like a bow, before holding out a hand. The answers to her questions were in the envelope tucked under his arm. "Sal Testa."

"Nice to meet you." She shook his hand, hoping that he couldn't feel it shake. "Please. Come inside."

He followed her into the foyer, once more taking his time to study his surroundings. Maybe that was the investigator in him. Or maybe he was naturally nosy. "Beautiful home."

"Thank you." She swallowed hard. "You said in your email that you've concluded your investigation."

Sal nodded. "I have."

Elora had been waiting weeks for this meeting. When Sal had called her this morning, the timing couldn't have been more perfect. He'd asked to meet next week and she'd insisted on it being tonight.

All she'd had to do was ensure Cassia was out of the

house. She wanted the freedom to ask questions without fear that someone would overhear.

"Shall we sit?" he asked.

"Will this take long?" She held her hands clasped in front of her to keep herself from ripping that envelope from his grasp.

"No. But . . . it might be better if we sit."

Meaning she wasn't going to like what he was about to tell her. "This is fine."

Sal sighed as he withdrew the envelope, opening the top flap. Then he slid out two pieces of white paper, handing her the sheet from the top.

"How did you get this?" Elora asked, keeping her gaze from the page. Now that she had the truth, she wasn't sure if she had the guts to accept it.

"I have my ways."

Those *ways* were likely illegal, but Elora wasn't using this to gain money or win a lawsuit. She was searching for answers. And the truth was in her hands.

With a deep breath filling her lungs, she read the letter. And her heart broke all over again.

Elora had kept a sliver of hope that this theory was in her head. That she'd concocted this ridiculous idea because of her trust issues.

Except it wasn't outrageous. It was real.

Lucas, her vivacious, sweet and loving brother, was only her half brother.

His father wasn't Lawrence Maldonado.

Lucas's father was David Clarence.

He was Ivy's half brother. He was Edwin's half brother.

And he was Zain's.

Twisted little affairs.

Her parents had been having them for years.

Was that her destiny with Ivy? Their mothers had started as friends, until resentment and jealousy had consumed their relationship. Now all that remained of their friendship were secrets and affairs with each other's husbands.

"I'm sorry," Sal said.

Elora tore her eyes from the letter and cleared the lump from her throat. "It was expected. Thank you for your discretion."

He gave that slight bow again.

She didn't ask Sal how he'd gotten DNA samples from David or Lucas, but considering how much she'd paid him—both for the investigation and his confidentiality—she didn't care.

So why hadn't Sal left yet? He'd delivered the bad news. But he shifted from foot to foot, glancing down at the other paper in his hand.

"I'm thorough in my work," he said.

The hairs on the back of her neck stood on end. "What?"

He hesitated before handing over the next page, but as he finally extended it, she yanked it from his grasp, scanning it from top to bottom.

She read it once. Twice. Three times. On the fourth, the world began to tilt. She felt her legs falter before she staggered to the side.

Sal's arms reached out, catching her before she could fall. "Whoa. Easy."

She leaned into him, giving herself a few seconds to let the pain spread. To let the misery consume her mind. To let loose an agonizing scream inside her head.

Then Elora shoved the despair away. She'd soak in it later when she was alone in the dark.

"I'm all right." She stood and glanced at the papers in her hand.

Two letters.

All it took to destroy a family were two medical letters.

Two letters to steal the good from her life.

She crumpled them both in her fist. "Who else knows about this?"

eleven

. . .

THE ONLY THING Ivy liked about Club 27 was their Ramos gin fizz. The complicated cocktail was time intensive and difficult to make, but a bartender at this club had it nailed.

Zain was sure he'd hired the best mixologists in Boston at Treason, but the brunette behind this club's bar had slipped through his fingers.

Ivy took a sip, humming at the perfect flavor, then raised the glass in salute to the bartender before spinning in her seat to survey the crowd.

Club 27 was definitely not her preferred place to be on a Saturday night. The club wasn't as big as Treason, nor its circulation system as sophisticated, so the air was sweltering. The bouncers had let too many people inside, testing the occupancy limit. The wait for drinks was fifteen minutes, and the dance floor was jammed.

She recognized plenty of the faces from Aston, but she'd only come for one.

Michael was the only person on the dance floor who actually had space to move. His fraternity brothers had created a circle around him so he could show off. And oh, what a fantastic show it was. Ivy was certain she'd never tire of seeing that man dance.

Damn, but he could move. It was like sex and sin. Dancing was Michael's personal brand of foreplay. A dull pulse was blooming between her legs, and she'd only been watching him for minutes.

Ivy had known Michael would be at Club 27 tonight.

While she'd been wrapped in seaweed at the spa last weekend, Elora had gone to Treason with Cassia of all people. Elora had been acting strange all week, but they'd had breakfast together this morning, and when Ivy had asked what was wrong, Elora had insisted she was fine. Then, as they'd eaten their oatmeal, Elora had mentioned seeing Michael at Treason last weekend.

Over the years, Ivy had learned his habits. He rarely frequented the same club two weekends in a row.

She took another sip of her drink, content to watch him for a while. He was in his standard club attire of a backward baseball cap and baggy jeans. But instead of a T-shirt straining across his chest, he wore a white tank, showcasing the definition in his arms.

Arms she hoped to have wrapped around her later tonight.

Michael hadn't spotted her yet. When he did, would he come to her? Or would she go to him?

It was all just another step to their own dance. It had been a while since they'd played between her sheets.

Tonight.

With any luck, she'd score a couple of orgasms and possibly some information on Cassia.

Had Michael learned anything about her roommate? Or was he waiting, like Ivy, for a private investigator to deliver a report?

Ivy would be damned if she let Michael win this game.

Cassia was hers.

"Hey, sexy."

For a moment, Ivy didn't realize the man was speaking to her. She turned, leaning away from the guy at her side.

He had a short and stocky build, so even seated, they were eye level. There was something sleezy in his gaze as he looked her up and down.

She'd give him five points for confidence but deduct a hundred for sheer idiocy. "Go away."

"You're hot." His hand went to her shoulder, the sweat from his palm sticky on her skin. *Pig.* His breath reeked of alcohol and cigarettes.

"Do *not* touch me." She glared at his fingers until he removed them. Fucking men. Just because she was in a strappy, short dress did not give him permission to feel her up. She instantly wanted to shower away his touch.

"I've seen you in here before," he said, clearly not getting the hint.

"Disappear, little cockroach." She raised her cocktail to her lips, but even after she swallowed a sip, he was still there.

He opened his mouth to say something else but was cut off by a tall, strong body stepping between them, forcing the douchebag away.

"Careful." Michael swung an arm around Ivy's shoulders. "She'll squish you under the heel of her three-thousand-dollar shoe."

The guy puffed up his chest, trying to add six inches to his frame. "We were talking."

"And now you're leaving," Ivy said.

She didn't have to watch the asshole retreat. Michael shifted, blocking the guy from her line of sight.

"Thanks." She raised her drink.

The creep, while irritating, had at least been useful. Michael was the type who liked to rescue a damsel in distress, and that encounter had just forced his hand.

"Welcome." He grinned, lifting the glass from her grip to take a drink. "Not bad."

"It's the best."

Instead of returning it to her, he stretched to set it on the bar. Then he took her hand and tugged her off her stool. "Dance with me."

Yes, please. She smiled as he led her to the dance floor, returning to that free space his brothers had guarded for him.

Michael pulled her flush against his body, banding an arm around her lower back. Then he rolled his hips so fast that Ivy had no choice but to grab his shoulders and hang on tight.

It wasn't the first time they'd danced together. There was nothing different about the way he moved or touched. But something was . . . off.

Michael set the pace and the rhythm while she racked her brain trying to figure out what was weird about this dance compared to its predecessors.

He smelled the same. His hat was the same. His expression was the same. What was wrong?

Michael slackened his hold on her waist, putting a sliver of space between them. It forced her to drop her arms to her sides. He positioned a thigh close to her legs, expecting her to grind against it.

Michael expected her to be spellbound.

And she wanted to be claimed.

Claimed on the dance floor the way Tate had claimed her at Treason.

Damn that man. It had been weeks since that night and he still kept popping into her mind. And now the bastard had ruined dancing with Michael.

Tate had positioned her exactly where he'd wanted her that night. He'd been in control, and he'd made her crave more. Instead of standing on one end of the dance floor, expecting her to walk to him, he'd beckoned. He'd ensnared her. Wholly.

"Relax." Michael moved in closer, bending until his nose brushed hers.

Then his lips were on hers and his tongue sliding past her

teeth. He tasted like his favorite cinnamon gum and her favorite cocktail.

Ivy kissed him but it felt . . . automatic. Wasn't this supposed to be foreplay? She'd been more turned on when she'd been seated at the bar. Before fucking *Tate* had invaded her thoughts.

Maybe Michael sensed that her head wasn't in it because he broke away with a slight furrow to his forehead. Then he took a whole step away before doing some fancy moves that she had no hope of attempting herself.

His fraternity brothers hollered and cheered, joining the fray.

Another woman, like that whore Allison Winston, would have fought for Michael's attention. Hell, normally Ivy would have fought for it too. Instead, all she wanted was another gin fizz and to reclaim her stool.

Actually, if she was being honest with herself, she wanted to finish the book she'd started on her spa trip last weekend.

Huh. What was wrong with her tonight? She was in a funk. She could go home and toy with Cassia, but even that seemed uninteresting.

Michael didn't notice as she slipped away, shuffling off the dance floor.

The stool she'd had earlier was taken. Her drink had been cleared away, not that she would have touched it now.

She could stay, order another drink and let a buzz push this mood away. But the exit was so much more appealing. She changed directions, fishing her key fob from her bra where she'd tucked it next to her credit card.

Last weekend on the way home from the spa, Jaxon had raced through a yellow light. The moment she'd set foot in the manor's driveway, he'd been fired. Geoff had presented her a list of replacement drivers but she hadn't browsed through their files yet.

So she'd driven herself to the club, knowing that if push

came to shove, she could call someone for a ride home. Sober and disappointed, she could drive herself.

"Heading home, miss?" a bouncer asked as she stepped outside.

"Yes." She hadn't been inside long, but the line of people waiting to get in had been cleared. Either people had been let inside or the bouncers had told them there'd be no more admittance.

"I'll escort you—" Before he could finish his sentence, the doors to the club burst open. A very drunk woman stumbled toward the street, bending to vomit on the sidewalk.

Ivy gagged as the bouncer rushed to the other woman's side, catching her before she could faceplant in her own puke. "Fucking Club 27."

With an eye roll, she left the mess behind and walked toward the adjacent parking lot. She was almost to her car when a warm hand touched her shoulder blade. She flinched, spinning around.

Somehow, the creep from earlier had snuck up on her. Ivy's body tensed, her hands fisting.

"What?"

"What?" he repeated, invading her space.

She was forced to retreat until her back slammed against her car. He kept on pushing.

"Don't—"

"Shut the fuck up." His breath blew hot and rank in her face as he grabbed her breast. Hard. "Not so hot now, are you?"

"Get off me." She struggled, pushing at his shoulders and shaking to work his hand free. But he had her pinned. Ivy opened her mouth to scream when a crack split the air and blinding pain exploded across her cheek.

She cried out and would have dropped to her knees if he hadn't had her shoved against her Mercedes.

"Think about that the next time you decide to be a bitch," he spat.

Ivy's head spun, her eye instantly throbbing like it was about to burst. "Fuck you."

He raised his hand, but before he could strike her again, his body was ripped away from hers.

She looked up, expecting the club's bouncer. Instead, her jaw dropped.

Tate.

Four fast and brutal punches were all it took until the creep collapsed in an unconscious heap on the pavement.

Tate rushed to her, taking her chin in a gentle hold as he tilted up the side of her face. "Fuck."

"I'm okay." Her voice trembled. Her eyes blurred with tears. Goddamn it, that hurt like a son of a bitch. And she knew better than to leave alone, even if it was early.

"The hell you are." His fingertips barely touched her skin as he smoothed her cheek. "You need ice."

"Yeah." Ivy knew how to treat a slapped cheek. "What are you doing here?"

"Was with a friend. Saw you leave alone. Wanted to make sure you got to your car okay."

Too late.

Given the guilt on his face, he'd had the same thought.

Fuck, it hurt. Her face. Her heart. Emotion started to claw at her throat. Memories—nightmares—came rushing back from the dark corners of her mind.

Oh God, it hurt. Ivy stood taller, forcing Tate away as she twisted to open her car door. "I have to go."

"Ivy—"

"It's fine. I'm all right," she muttered over her shoulder.

His jaw was clenched and his dark eyes full of concern.

She could stay here. She could let him hold her. But as soon as he wrapped her in those strong arms, she'd crumble. She couldn't afford to break, not again. So she slid into her car.

"Let me drive you home." Tate caught the door before she could close it.

"It's not that bad." A lie she'd practiced many times. She tugged harder on the door. "Please, Tate. Let me go."

"Ivy." He frowned but dropped his hand.

She was about to shut him out but stopped. "Thank you."

Tate gave her a single nod just as the bouncer rushed toward the car. "You go. I'll deal with this."

She blew out a shaky breath and slammed the door, the sound like a hammer to her already pounding skull. Then she hit the locks before starting the engine.

Breathe. Breathe, Ivy. Breathe.

Ivy's old mantra. How many times had she breathed through this pain? The deep inhale steadied her muscles and kept the tears at bay as she eased out of the parking lot. She gripped the steering wheel so fiercely that her fingers ached by the time she made it to the manor.

Her legs were unsteady as she walked inside. Her face throbbed and her eye was already swelling. She swung by the kitchen, grateful that Francis and Geoff were both gone, and made herself an ice pack. Then she toed off her heels and trudged toward the staircase.

"Hey."

No. Fucking hell. "What are you doing here?" Ivy ducked her chin, letting her hair drape across her face. The last thing she needed tonight was for her brother to see the red mark on her cheek.

"Technically, this is my house too," he said with a smirk. He loved to tease, but they both knew this was Ivy's home. "I had a meeting with Dad yesterday and missed a class, so Elora said she'd leave notes for me."

Edwin, unlike Ivy, was making their father proud by studying business so he could assume his rightful place within the Clarence empire.

"You didn't have anything else to do at eleven o'clock on a Saturday night but study?" Her heart hammered in her chest as she tried to make casual conversation. If she rushed him out the door, he'd suspect something was wrong.

He shrugged. "I was out but wasn't feeling it tonight."

"Same." She held her breath. *Go, Edwin. Just leave.*

"Elora left the notes on her desk. Thought I'd swing by tonight, save myself a trip tomorrow. But now that you're home, want to do something?"

"I think I'm going to go to bed. Night." She did her best to walk straight as the pain in her head blossomed. She was almost to the stairs. *Home free.*

"Hold up."

Damn. She kept moving. "See you later."

"Why do you have an ice pack?"

"My knee hurts." She shouldn't have bothered with the lie.

"Ivy." Edwin rushed to catch up, gripping her arm and forcing her to stop. Then he shifted in front of her and his gasp shot straight through her heart.

Shit.

"What the fuck?" he roared.

She held up her hands, trying to calm him down. "It's nothing."

"You said that once, and I believed you then. What happened?"

"I was at Club 27. There was a guy who got a little rough."

"A little rough?" Edwin gaped. "You got fucking hit, Ivy."

"It was just a slap."

His nostrils flared, then he was gone, marching for the door.

"Don't!" She raced to catch him. If Edwin got involved, this would only get uglier. "He got the hell beat out of him already, okay?"

He scoffed. "By who?"

"Tate." She swallowed hard. "He's a friend of Zain's. He was at the club too and saw it."

Edwin studied her, searching for the lie.

"It's true," she said. "I met Tate at Treason. He recognized me tonight. Took care of the asshole who slapped me. End of story. Now it's over."

"I'm calling Zain." Edwin dug out his phone from his jeans pocket and held up a finger when Ivy opened her mouth.

Since there was no point in hiding it anymore, she pressed the ice pack to her face while Edwin called their older brother.

"Do you have a friend named Tate?" Edwin asked Zain. At least she wasn't the only sibling who hadn't heard of Tate before. But given Zain's muted *yes*, Tate had been telling the truth from the start. "Text me his number."

Ivy sighed. As they waited for Zain's text, the silence was painful. Everything was painful. And she was barely keeping her feet. "I'm going upstairs. Don't do anything stupid."

Edwin frowned. "I'll sleep in the guest suite in case you need anything. After I talk to *Tate*."

She trudged upstairs, each step more painful than the last. When she reached her rooms, she climbed into bed, not bothering to undress.

She felt dirty. She felt foolish. She felt used. She felt . . .

A sob escaped, followed by another. Then another. The tears could no longer be contained. They streamed down her face, soaking her pillow, as she curled into a ball.

Breathe.

This was a fluke. The entire night had gone wrong. It wasn't the same as before. It wasn't the same.

He was dead.

He's dead.

Ivy had made sure of it.

twelve

. . .

CASSIA READ the same paragraph in her textbook for the third time. Not a word was sinking in. The sentences blended together, and the lines on the graph in the corner seemed to wiggle like radio waves.

"Ugh." She rubbed her temples. "I'm not getting sick. I'm not getting sick."

She was most definitely sick. Her head was fuzzy, and she shivered for the hundredth time. Zipping her coat up to her chin, Cassia wrapped her arms around her waist and narrowed her gaze at the page. *One more hour.* If she could just focus for one more hour on this chapter, she'd call it quits and walk home from the library. Then, over the weekend, she'd catch up on sleep and her to-do list.

She popped a piece of candy into her mouth, hoping the sugar would give her a boost of energy. Considering she'd nearly finished the box of fruity chews and her exhaustion only seemed to be getting worse, she doubted anything but an early bedtime would help.

"I wondered when I'd find you here." A deep voice startled her, making her spin around in her chair.

"Damn it," she hissed, slapping a hand to her chest.

"Sorry." Edwin held up his hands. "Though I think I preferred it when you greeted me with *oh* instead of *damn it*."

"You startled me."

"So if I don't startle you, you'll actually say hello?"

"Hello."

He grinned. "Hi, Red."

Red. Maybe it was the way he said the nickname—intentionally, almost intimately—but another shiver rolled over her shoulders and it had nothing to do with the bug she'd caught.

It had been a month since she'd seen Edwin at Treason. In that month, he hadn't gotten any less handsome. Or dangerous. A wicked smirk tugged at his soft lips as he walked to her table and pulled out the chair across from hers.

This was her first visit to the third floor of Aston's library. Edwin had mentioned it the night she'd found him in her wingback chair. She'd avoided the nook simply because it had been his tip, but by the time her classes had ended today, she'd been beyond weary. She'd come to the library to study but her usual table on the second floor had been taken.

Cassia had been hungry and the idea of only spending a quarter on a snack had been too appealing to resist, so she'd climbed to the third floor, deciding the risk was worth it. After all, a guy like Edwin Clarence wouldn't be studying late on a Friday afternoon.

When was she going to learn that her assumptions were wrong at least fifty percent of the time?

"I see you found my secret vending machine." He nodded to the green and yellow candy box in front of her. "Mike and Ikes. Those are one of my favorites."

"Mine too." She ate another candy as her heart skipped. What the hell was it about him that always made her so jittery? Maybe it was the blue eyes. Or the fresh cologne that invaded her nose. She ate another piece of candy, fighting the urge to drag in a breath.

"How have you been?" he asked, leaning his sinewy forearms on the table. The sweater he wore had a slight V-neck that made the bump of his Adam's apple stand out as he spoke.

Cassia had never wanted to lick a throat so badly in her life.

Gah. What the hell was wrong with her? Clearly she wasn't in her right mind this afternoon. She couldn't focus on school but she could fantasize about Edwin's neck? *Get it together.* She shook her head, closing her eyes for a couple of heartbeats.

"Cassia?"

Right. He'd asked her a question. "Fine. Busy. You?"

"Fine." The corner of his mouth lifted higher, revealing one of those incredible dimples.

She wouldn't mind licking that too.

Fuck.

"You've been avoiding me," he said.

"Yep." There was no point in denying it.

She'd seen his car outside the manor from time to time and made sure to stay locked inside her bedroom until the Bentley had disappeared from the loop. A couple of weeks ago, she'd seen him walking on campus, and she'd turned and gone the other way to avoid crossing paths.

At Treason, Edwin had said he'd wanted to fuck her. Did he still? If he kept staring at her like she was as delicious as her candy, she might break. That was why he was so dangerous. That was why avoiding him was key.

Because she might let him take her to bed.

"If you're avoiding me, why'd you come here?" he asked.

"I only had a quarter and wanted a snack." She shrugged. "It's quiet. And I didn't take you for a guy who studies on Friday afternoons."

"That's because you don't know me, Cassia."

"No, I don't."

He drummed his fingers on the table. "You say that like you *won't* get to know me."

"I'm just here for school." No friends. No drama. No men,

especially Edwin, who captured her attention whenever he was in the room.

Graduation was the goal. It was the only point in being at Aston. If she wasn't in class or sleeping, she was in the library. And she hadn't seen Edwin once. Why today?

"I figured you'd be at Treason or something," she said as she turned her attention to her textbook.

"It's too early for the club. And I had a craving." The way he said *craving* made her eyes snap to his, and the intensity in those azure pools sent a rush of heat to her core.

She swallowed hard, dropping her chin. That night at Treason, she'd made a huge mistake by looking at him too long. It was like staring at the sun. If you stared too long, you went blind.

Cassia couldn't afford to be blinded by Edwin.

Though she would give him credit for being a gentleman at the nightclub. After she'd emerged from Treason's bathroom, Edwin had been waiting. She'd told him she wanted to leave, and he'd immediately called her a ride. A shiny black town car had whisked her back to the manor, where she'd vowed never to be tempted by fun or her roommates again.

The next morning, Elora had come to Cassia's room with an apology. Apparently something had happened with her little brother, so she'd had to bolt from the club. As a peace offering, she'd tried to gift Cassia those knee-high suede boots.

Cassia had declined.

While she'd appreciated Elora's apology, she didn't want to be indebted to anyone, especially the other occupants of Clarence Manor.

They weren't friends.

And Edwin wasn't her friend either.

He stood from his chair, walking to the vending machine. "What are you going to do with the manor to yourself for the weekend?"

What she always did. "Study. I have—wait. Huh?" She

paused, replaying his question. "I have the manor to myself this weekend?"

Edwin dropped a quarter into the slot and punched the button for another box of Mike and Ikes. He collected it from the dispenser, then returned to his seat. "Ivy and Elora didn't tell you?"

"I haven't talked to them." Purposefully. She didn't trust Ivy, and though she believed Elora's apology, she hadn't spent time with her either. Besides, she was buried under a mountain of schoolwork and didn't have time for casual conversations about weekend plans.

"They're going to Martha's Vineyard for the weekend," he told her. "Zain, my older brother, has a house on the beach."

"Ah." Cassia ignored the twinge of jealousy and rejection. Even if they'd invited her, would she have ever gone on a vacation with Ivy and Elora? Nope. That was asking for trouble. But it hurt all the same to be forgotten.

Maybe someday she'd have friends.

Good friends, unlike those from Hughes. She hadn't heard a peep from anyone in her former life, not that they had her new phone number. Still, she checked her old email from time to time and the inbox was only full of spam.

If she made friends, Cassia wanted the type she could rely on. Friends who'd text simply to say hello. Friends who would check on her when she felt like shit. Maybe it was this headache or this general icky feeling, but today, she felt more alone than ever since coming to Aston.

"I've never been to Martha's Vineyard," she said.

"It's beautiful."

She hummed, eating the last piece of her candy.

"How long are you studying? Mind if I join you for a bit? I promise to be quiet."

"Sure." She didn't have the energy to brush him off or find a new study spot. Or maybe she didn't want to see him walk away quite yet.

It took twice as long as it should have for her to read the

chapter in her textbook. She wanted to blame it on feeling like crap, but it was Edwin.

True to his word, he stayed quiet, concentrating on his own studies. Every time he turned the page of his book, his scent wafted to her side of the table and she went a little dizzy. Whenever his eyebrows knitted together in concentration, he pulled his bottom lip between his teeth. What would it feel like to have her lip between those teeth instead?

Edwin raked his fingers through the light-brown strands of his hair to keep the slight waves off his forehead. Her fingers itched to find out if they were as soft as they appeared.

The way his jaw flexed and clenched as he ate his box of candy was both distracting and sensual. Did he realize he was driving her out of her mind? Forget economics, all she could think about was kissing him. He'd be a good kisser, wouldn't he? *Duh.*

Maybe she should have let him kiss her at Treason. How long had it been since she'd been kissed? Oh to feel his hands on her skin, just once. To bury her nose in the crook of his neck and drag in that delicious scent until she was drunk on Edwin Clarence.

"You're not studying."

She blinked, tearing her eyes away from his throat. "Oh. I'm, uh . . . all done," she lied.

" 'Kay." He slammed his book closed. "I'll walk you out."

Out. Out was good. She didn't protest, putting her things away. It was time to go back to avoiding Edwin. She stood and swayed on her feet. Was that because of him? Had he really made her knees weak? *Seriously, Cassia?*

"Whoa." Edwin rounded the table, taking her elbow.

"I'm okay," she said when she had her balance. Except as she took a step, her body was sluggish and her head foggy. Okay, not just Edwin's presence making her wobble. She was sick.

Shit. She didn't have time to be sick.

"Don't take this the wrong way," he said. "But you don't look so good."

"I don't feel so good," she admitted. "I think I just need to get some sleep."

"Come on." He kept his hand locked on her arm as he escorted her down the staircase to the first floor. Then he held the door open for her, letting her step into the October afternoon.

The scent of leaves clung to the breeze. The crisp air made her tremble. She turned, ready to disappear down the sidewalk that would lead her to the manor, but Edwin's hand caught hers.

"This way." He jerked his chin in the opposite direction. "I'll drive you home."

She was too tired to argue—or wiggle her hand free from his grasp—so she followed him to the closest parking lot, where his fancy car waited.

The silver Bentley was as pristine on the inside as it was on the exterior, and it had that new-car smell.

Up until now, Elora's car was the nicest she'd ever been inside, but Edwin's had it beat. It oozed luxury. After starting the engine, he clicked a button that warmed her seat, and she melted into the black leather.

"This is like being wrapped in a warm hug," she murmured as he reversed out of his parking space. "It's been a long time since I had a hug."

The last hug she remembered had been from her uncle. It had been uncomfortable and short. Her body had been stiff. His had been strained. Then again, they'd been standing next to an open grave in a cemetery. They also hadn't seen each other in years, so awkward had been a given.

Cassia closed her eyes as the rumble of the engine and the whir of the tires drowned out the rest of the world. Then a hand on her shoulder caused her to flinch awake. The manor was outside her window. "Oh."

"There's that word again." Edwin chuckled. "You fell asleep."

She sighed. "Sorry."

"It's okay. Are you going to be all right?"

"I'll be fine." She opened her door, hauling out her backpack. Without the strength to heft a strap over her shoulder, she just held it at her side. "Thanks for the ride."

"Have a good weekend."

"You too." She gave him a weak smile, then hiked the steps, the last of her energy waning as she opened the door to the manor. Her feet shuffled more than stepped as she crossed the foyer to the staircase. She was about to climb again when her backpack slipped from her fingers. *Thud*. "Ugh."

She bent to pick it up but that bottom stair was so inviting, she dropped to a seat instead. "Just sit for a minute."

Normally, she rushed to her room to avoid Ivy and Elora. But they were gone, weren't they?

There'd be no trials today, not that there had been any hint of trouble with her roommate. Maybe Ivy had already forgotten about her.

Was Geoff around? Or had he taken the night off since Ivy was gone? What about Francis? If the chef was gone, hopefully there were enough ingredients in the pantry and fridge to make some soup. Though knowing Francis, she'd probably loaded the fridge before leaving so the girls wouldn't have to worry about weekend meals.

Francis, one of Ivy's paid employees, was more maternal than her own mother. Even if all Francis did was prepare meals, that was more than she'd ever gotten from Jessa Neilson. When was the last time Cassia had let her mother sneak into her mind? Years. She'd blocked out Jessa for years.

"Because she's a bitch. But I do love Francis." Her voice filled the quiet space. Was that why she talked to herself? Because her world was too quiet? *Huh.*

"Oh God, this sucks." She groaned and leaned forward, letting her head fall into her hands.

Could it just be stress? Maybe after a long night's sleep, she'd feel better. But first, she had to make it up the stairs. Given her current state, she might as well be scaling Mount Everest.

Should she go to the doctor? Probably. Except there was no one to drive her. Her roommates were away enjoying a beach vacation at Martha's Vineyard. It always seemed like they were gone, leaving Cassia in the house. "Alone."

Always alone.

She slid off the bottom stair to curl up on the floor. She'd rest for a minute, then go to her bedroom. Her body began to shake, so she hugged her knees into her chest.

Doctor. She should definitely go see a doctor. *Get up, Cassia.*

She passed out instead.

Alone.

thirteen

. . .

ELORA STOOD on the sidewalk in front of the cottage with a suitcase at her side and her feet frozen to the concrete.

The cottage looked exactly like it had the last time she'd visited Martha's Vineyard. Cedar shakes, grayed from years beneath the sun, covered the exterior walls. White-paned windows reflected the afternoon's blue sky. The scents of salt and sand carried on the breeze as the sound of waves crashing echoed from the beach.

The driver who'd shuttled them from the airstrip to the house had left minutes ago with the promise to return Sunday. She should have begged him to take her anywhere but here.

"What are you doing?" Ivy asked, standing in the open front door with her hands braced on her hips.

Past the lawn, the sea was endless. A flock of gulls squawked as they flew overhead. *Take me with you.*

"Elora," Ivy called.

Why the hell had she agreed to this weekend? There was no way she'd be able to stay at the cottage. With a long sigh, she bent to retrieve her luggage. "Coming."

The prospect of a weekend away—from Aston, from the manor, from her life—had been so tempting that when Ivy had burst into her office on Monday and pitched the idea, she'd agreed immediately.

A weekend at the cottage. Just the two of them.

She had to give Ivy credit, her friend had noticed that something had been off over the past month, so she'd pitched this trip as a weekend getaway. Ivy had asked no less than three times on the short flight over if Elora was okay.

No. No, she was not okay.

Ivy turned from the door and disappeared into the house. Should Elora tell her this weekend? It had been a month since she'd met Sal Testa and those two letters had changed her life. At some point, she couldn't keep hiding. She couldn't keep this secret inside any longer. And Ivy deserved to know she had a half brother.

That they shared a half brother.

Elora stepped over the threshold and was slaughtered with memories of her last trip here. Her heart splattered on the gray-washed wood floors.

She'd come to the cottage with Zain last spring. Before the chaos of finals, he'd invited her away for a weekend of sex. They'd fucked on the white couch in the living room. They'd thoroughly debauched his bedroom. Elora had spent her mornings with his cock in her mouth and her nights with his tongue in her pussy.

If it had only been sex, maybe she could have compartmentalized the memories. Except that weekend had been so much more.

The two of them had cooked meals together in the kitchen—Zain teaching her little techniques because she was a hopeless chef. They'd relaxed on the beach, reading books and talking about nothing. She'd slept in his bed, curled into his side, their naked limbs tangled.

It had been the best weekend of her life.

Had he brought the blond here yet? In the month since she'd gone to Treason, had he forgotten Elora?

"I put my stuff in one of the bedrooms upstairs," Ivy said,

emerging from the hallway. "Do you want to stay up there too?"

"Sure." Elora swallowed hard. There wasn't a bedroom in this house she hadn't been with Zain in, so it didn't matter where she slept. They were all tainted.

Ivy stepped past Elora, closing the door that she'd left open. The click was like a nail in a coffin.

Why was she here? Didn't she have enough problems without adding reminders of a broken heart to the mix?

The scent of cleaning supplies lingered in the air from the crew who'd likely swept through this morning. But if she closed her eyes, she could smell Zain's cologne. She could picture him on the deck out back, his hair disheveled, a cup of coffee in his hand as he checked the morning news.

"Hey." Ivy's arm slipped around Elora's shoulder. "Maybe we can order in dinner. Lie low. Talk."

Talk. On the short flight to the island, Elora had faked a nap in the passenger seat to avoid conversation. She doubted that would work over dinner. "I'm fine."

"You're not. Don't forget who you're talking to. Something is wrong, and I'm worried about you."

Tears welled in Elora's eyes and she blinked furiously, wishing them away. With every passing day, it became harder and harder to keep her composure. This was why she'd been avoiding Lucas and her father.

She was terrified that with one look, she'd break and the truth would come spilling out. It was hard enough hiding the truth from Ivy.

"I need to send in an essay." Ivy sighed and let Elora go. "I forgot to do it before we left. I'll do that and give you a few to get settled. Then we can decide on dinner."

Elora nodded, waiting until Ivy was upstairs. Then she left her suitcase in the entryway, crossing through the living room for the french doors that opened to the deck.

The *cottage* was a six-bedroom, five-thousand-square-foot

Chilmark home on four waterfront acres. It was Zain's personal safe haven.

Elora was invading his sanctuary but it was too late to leave now, so she made her way across the path between the grass tufts and descended the small wooden staircase that led to the beach. Hopefully he'd forgive her for intruding. Though she didn't expect his forgiveness for her other countless mistakes.

Large gray rocks dotted the coastline, their bases sunk deep into the sand. She stopped in the middle of the beach, sinking down to the ground and pulling her knees into her chest. Strands of hair blew into her face as she stared across the water stretching to the horizon.

Maybe if she stayed here, in this exact spot where her problems seemed so small compared to the vastness of the world, she'd be able to make sense of this new reality.

Her phone buzzed in her pocket but she didn't bother checking. It was probably Lucas with another angry text about her missing another of his football games. He had a right to be pissed. She'd been lying to him for a month.

Elora had declined the majority of her father's calls too, blaming it on a hectic senior year at Aston. Time was running out. Sooner rather than later, they'd come to her if she kept avoiding them.

A weekend away from Boston had just been another excuse to keep her distance.

Who did she tell first? Her father? Zain? Ivy?

How would her friend react to the news? Elora would strangle Ivy if she was horrible to Lucas. But knowing Ivy and how she loved her brothers, she'd probably welcome him into the Clarence fold with open arms.

Would Lucas want to change his name? Would he resent Elora for opening this can of worms?

Elora had always known her family was fucked up, but this . . .

A tear streaked down her cheek, the drop hot compared to the cool ocean air. She didn't bother wiping it away.

Her phone vibrated again, and when it didn't stop at a single buzz, she dug it out. An incoming call from her dad.

No, not her dad.

Lawrence Maldonado didn't have children.

Her entire body ached so much she wanted to scream. She wanted to hop on the plane that had brought them to the island and fly to a distant corner of the planet and forget her own fucking name.

She wanted to slice open her veins and drain the blood from her body until nothing from her mother remained. Her hair. Her skin. Her heart. Elora's DNA was nothing but betrayal. And her mother was nothing but a traitorous whore.

Her chin quivered as the phone call went to voicemail. Dad would leave her a message. He'd been leaving her messages for weeks. With each, the concern in his voice grew louder and louder.

She was running out of time.

Would he disown her? Would her father forget her too, like Zain?

The tears fell in a steady stream as a familiar numbness crept through her limbs. Why? Why couldn't she have left this alone? Every minute, every second of the past month, she'd regretted hiring Sal Testa.

Elora let herself cry for a few minutes, then wiped her cheeks dry. How many tears had she cried this month? A thousand? A million? She'd probably cry a river before this was through.

With one last look at the sun lowering in the distance, she forced herself to her feet, retreating toward the cottage. She'd just stepped inside when a familiar male voice echoed from the kitchen. Her heart dropped.

No.

Coming here had been hard enough with memories of

Zain. Facing him in reality would be excruciating, especially if he'd brought a woman.

Dragging in a fortifying breath, Elora squared her shoulders and blanked her expression. Then she strode into the kitchen, prepared to find Zain and the blond.

She was half right.

Zain stood next to the island, his hands braced on the counter. His friend Tate was seated on a stool. Not a blond in sight, unless you counted Ivy.

"These two are crashing our weekend," her friend huffed.

"This is my house." Zain shot Ivy a scowl. "And you didn't tell me you'd be here."

Ivy shrugged. "It was a last-minute trip. We needed a break."

His gaze darted to Elora, his eyes narrowing on her face. He frowned as he raked a hand through his silky hair, then his brilliant blue eyes shifted toward the door. "We'll go."

"Come on, Z." Tate stood from his stool, rounding the island for the refrigerator. He opened it and pulled out two bottles of beer, setting one in front of Zain. "This house is big enough for us to all stay. Besides, we need to talk about what happened at Club 27."

"No, we do not," Ivy snapped.

What had happened at Club 27? Before Elora could ask, Ivy marched out of the room. Her heels pounded on the staircase, then moments later, a bedroom door slammed shut.

"This ought to be an interesting weekend." Tate twisted off the cap to his beer, then raised the bottle in salute. "Hi, Elora."

"Hi, Tate." She spoke the words but was looking at Zain.

He was still staring at the door.

Was someone else joining them? Or was he, like Elora, wishing to be anywhere else?

Without a word, she turned and walked out of the room, finding her suitcase in the entryway. *Why am I here?* She was a moment from walking out the door when Tate appeared, lifting the suitcase from her hand.

"I'll carry this upstairs for you," he said, stealing her bag before she could escape.

Her shoulders fell as she followed him wordlessly to the second floor.

"He'll come around." Tate left her suitcase in the bedroom at the end of one hallway, then he winked at her before retreating downstairs.

Elora left her suitcase on the plush carpet and walked to Ivy's room, not bothering to knock. Her friend was standing at the window, staring at the ocean and fading sun. "What happened at Club 27?"

"I had a little mishap there the other weekend." Ivy flicked her wrist. "It's nothing."

"What mishap?"

Her roommate turned, arching an eyebrow. "I'll answer that question when you tell me what's bothering you."

Elora clamped her mouth shut.

"That's what I thought." Ivy pursed her lips, then turned to the glass again.

Elora opened her mouth, ready to confess it all and ease just a little of this burden, but the truth was lodged in her throat. She couldn't tell Ivy before she told her father.

Painful as it would be, the news had to come from her.

He might not be her father, but he would always be her dad.

If he still wanted her.

Elora closed Ivy's door, then returned to her own room, needing a few moments alone to breathe. No doubt the makeup she'd put on this morning before her Friday classes had been cried off, so she'd need to fix it before dinner.

Except the moment she stepped into her bedroom, she found Zain waiting.

His arms were crossed over his broad chest. His hard expression hadn't softened and his jaw was clenched. But

God, he looked good. All she wished for were those strong arms wrapped around her body and his gravelly voice in her ear, promising it would be okay.

"You've been crying," he said.

"Yes, I have." There was no point in lying. Her eyes probably looked as puffy as they felt.

"Because of me?"

"No." She stepped into the room, easing the door closed behind her. Then she raised her chin. "What are you doing here?"

"Why do I have to keep reminding you and my sister that this is my house? Is that why you came? To fuck with my head?"

If her presence here was bothering him, then maybe he hadn't entirely forgotten Elora. She ignored the tiny thrill that raced through her veins, refusing to let herself hope that he'd missed her.

"I didn't know you were going to be here," she said. "That's not why I came. Ivy said it would only be the two of us. And I wanted to get away from the city."

"Yeah," he muttered. "Me too."

She sighed. "Do you want me to leave? I can fly back tomorrow morning."

"Like Tate said, this house is big enough for us to avoid each other. So that's what I'll do because I can't be around you right now."

Elora was too raw to hide her flinch. She dropped her gaze to her feet, already calculating a lie for Ivy. There was no way she'd be able to stay and keep herself together.

"El."

Her nickname in his voice, laced with worry. Fuck, she was going to cry again. "What?"

"You've been crying."

"So?"

"You don't cry very often."

"No." She met his gaze, her own blurred with tears. "But

today I do."

He dropped his arms and took one step, like maybe she'd get her wish and he'd hold her. But then he stopped and dragged a hand over his face. "Want to tell me what's wrong?"

Yes. "No."

"Figured." He scoffed. "Always shutting people out. Especially me."

She couldn't tell him. Not yet. And if he stayed in this room, she'd break. So Elora did what she had to do to get him the hell away. "We're all good at something, Zain. I shut people out. You're a great fuck. Nothing more."

His nostrils flared, and in a flash, he was in her space, his hands on her arms. "Goddamn you. Don't use that crude little mouth to shove me away."

This was the problem. They'd been together too long and he'd learned too many of her tricks. "You like my crude little mouth."

She reached between them, her hand dragging up the denim of his jeans until she reached his swelling cock. She palmed his erection, pressing in as she rubbed. "Yeah, you like it."

He hissed, tilting into her touch. "Be careful what you start, Elora."

"Or what?"

Zain's hands lifted from her arms to frame her face, forcing her to meet his eyes. "Or you'll hate yourself when I walk away."

If not for his grip, she might have fallen to her knees.

Zain would walk away.

And Elora would hate herself.

Damn, but he knew her too well. For all she tried to hide, she'd dropped her guard too many times around this man. Elora liked to think she was in control, but Zain owned her.

The hole in her heart was shaped like Zain Clarence, with blue eyes, high cheekbones and a chiseled jaw. With a magnificent mind and a magnetic touch.

God, she wanted him to fuck her. Right now. Rough and long until all her troubles vanished. There was only one person who could make her forget.

She lifted on her toes, wanting his mouth and not caring that a kiss was a mistake.

Zain's body tensed, like he was using every muscle to hold himself back. "Don't."

"Please." She felt his restraint break. Then his lips were crashing down on hers. She moaned as his tongue tangled with hers.

Zain was her favorite taste.

Their kiss was frantic, like lovers reunited. Except there was a bitter edge to his lips because they both knew nothing had changed. So she banded her arms around his back to keep him from pulling away.

His arousal pressed into her belly as he tore his lips away, dropping them to her neck to suck on her pulse. Her eyes drifted closed as she melted in his arms, holding on to this moment for just one more second. One more heartbeat. One more—

Zain was gone in a flash, leaving her on shaky legs as he strode to the windows, giving Elora his back.

He was walking away, as he'd promised.

The fucking tears came rushing back. She was so damn sick of crying and being weak. It would all go away once she confessed. It would all go away once the truth was in the open.

Once there were no more secrets.

If there was a person besides her father to tell, it was Zain.

Zain, who she trusted more than any person alive.

She had to tell him. She had to get it off her chest.

Elora had opened her mouth, unsure of where to even start, when the door behind her burst open.

Ivy flew into the room, drawing up short when she spotted Zain at the window. Her eyes flicked between the two of them, and then she crossed her arms over her chest. "What the hell is going on?"

fourteen

. . .

"WHAT THE HELL IS GOING ON?" Ivy asked.

Zain's hands were fisted at his sides, like he was seconds from punching a hole in the wall.

Elora's face was pale and she'd been crying. She'd looked upset when she'd come into the kitchen to find Zain and Tate waiting. But this was beyond upset, and Elora didn't cry.

Whatever was bothering Elora had been bothering her for weeks. This entire trip was Ivy's plan to get her friend to confide in her. Except as she stared between her brother and her best friend, Ivy realized that maybe she didn't need Elora's confession.

Maybe she'd just figured it out.

Elora and Zain.

Click. The mental puzzle pieces snapped together, and Ivy stifled a laugh. Of course. Elora and Zain. How had she missed this? But now that she saw it, everything made sense.

Most of the nights they went to Treason, Elora would vanish. So would Zain. Elora never went on dates, and she'd shown zero interest in any of the guys at Aston.

Zain, one of the most eligible bachelors in Boston, was rarely seen with a woman on his arm. Ivy had thought the

Saturday nights he'd spent in his office were because of his dedication to business. But he'd been hiding Elora, hadn't he?

How long had this been going on?

Before she could ask, Zain crossed his arms over his chest, his expression murderous. "We were just talking about Club 27."

Liar. "There's nothing to discuss."

"What happened at Club 27?" Elora asked.

Ivy waved it off. "Like I said, a little mishap."

"A guy cornered you against your car and hit you, Ivy," Zain barked.

"What?" Elora gasped. "When was this?"

"A few weeks ago." Ivy inspected her manicure, feigning indifference.

This was not a topic she wanted to discuss, which was why she hadn't told Elora after it had happened. Instead, she'd hid in her room for a day to ensure the worst of the swelling had gone down, then she'd used her arsenal of expensive makeup products to hide the remaining evidence.

Thankfully, Edwin hadn't brought it up again, and besides a call from Zain to make sure she was okay, she'd managed to avoid the subject altogether.

"As far as I'm concerned, it's over, and I won't be talking about it again," Ivy said. Ignoring and deflecting had worked the last time she'd been in this position, so that was what she'd do again. "The asshole got what was coming to him," she told Elora. "He smacked me, and Tate beat the hell out of him. End of story."

"Tate." Elora pointed to the floor. "That Tate?"

She nodded. "He happened to be there."

"It's not the end of the story, Ivy." Zain shook his head. "You need to stay away from Club 27. Both of you. It's not safe."

"Whatever. I'm done with this topic." She spun and walked out of the room, heading for the stairs. Footsteps followed, her brother on her heels. "So. You and Elora?"

His jaw ticked. "Drop it, Ivy."

Not happening. She wanted answers.

Ivy reached the bottom stair and headed for the kitchen, needing a glass of wine. There was a bottle of chardonnay in the refrigerator, so she searched for the electric opener and poured herself a glass.

All while her brother glowered at her from a stool at the island.

"This is good," she said after her first sip. "Want some?"

"No."

"Your beer?" She pointed to the bottle he'd left on the counter.

"No."

"You're grumpy."

"That's what happens when I walk through the door of my house to find intruders."

She rolled her eyes. "You said I was always welcome. Besides, you should be happy I brought Elora. Is that why you came? Did she tell you we were coming out?"

"Stop." He held up a hand, then pinched the bridge of his nose. "Please."

"How long have you been sleeping with my best friend?"

"Ivy." The warning in his tone sounded eerily like their father. "Not another word. Am I understood?"

She took a long gulp of her wine. "What did you do to make her cry?"

"Ivy." He smacked a hand on the counter, then shot off his stool. "It's none of your fucking business, and I won't tell you again. Leave it alone. And don't pester Elora about it either, got me?"

The older he got, the more Zain reminded her of Dad. "I got you," she muttered, like a child who'd just been scolded.

This was the problem with her relationship with Zain. He was nine years older and in many respects was more like an uncle than a brother.

Zain and Ivy didn't have inside jokes from their childhood.

They hadn't bonded through shared teachers at school or mutual friends. By the time she'd been in fifth grade, he'd moved out of the house and been going to Aston.

Plus, being a girl meant they had very little in common. While he'd meet Edwin at a bar to watch a football or basketball game, the only shared interest she had with Zain was Treason.

And, apparently, Elora.

"She's my best friend," Ivy said. "If you break her heart—"

"Fuck this." He stormed out of the room before she could deliver her threat.

Her brother vanished down the hallway that led to the primary suite only to emerge seconds later with a duffel bag in one hand. Her jaw dropped as he whipped the front door open and stepped outside.

The slam of the door closing echoed through the cottage.

"Did Zain just leave?" Tate asked as he walked into the kitchen.

"Uh . . ." Her eyes stayed locked on the door. Was Ivy really so bad that her brother couldn't stand a weekend under the same roof with her? Not including her trips to Treason, she could count on one hand the weekends they'd spent together.

Three trips to Aspen for family ski weekends with their parents. Zain and Edwin had hit the slopes together while Ivy had opted for the spa. The only time she'd talked to her brother on those vacations had been over a tense family dinner.

The other two weekends had been at her parents' estate outside the city when Ivy had been in middle school. Zain had come home from Aston on a rare weekend, and once again, he'd spent most of his time with Edwin.

By the time she'd been in high school, the only times he'd visit home were for Thanksgiving, Christmas and her and Edwin's birthday. Zain would stay for the meal, then leave.

Ivy didn't know his favorite color. She didn't know if he liked red wine or white. She didn't know if he had any food allergies or what his tattoos meant.

It wasn't supposed to be this way.

Zain was her older brother, and she wanted him to be excited to spend time together. She wanted him to know why she loved the color green and that he wasn't the only Clarence kid who got sick and tired of their parents' bullshit. But they wouldn't be making any headway toward a sibling friendship this weekend, would they?

"I'm guessing he's not coming back," Tate said.

She sighed. "Doubt it."

"Shit." Tate huffed and walked to the cabinets, opening and closing doors until he found his own wineglass. Then the glug of the bottle filled the room as he poured.

Ivy shook herself out of her stupor, looking away from the door and to the ceiling.

She was only part of the reason Zain had run from the cottage. Elora was the other. Still, his rejection pricked and she eased the sting with wine, draining her glass and holding it out for Tate to refill.

He obliged, then sipped his own. "You shouldn't have left the club alone that night."

Fantastic. Not only was she here at the cottage with a sulking, emotional Elora—a version of her friend she didn't recognize—but now that Zain had left, she was trapped with Tate.

Tate, who was trying to fill Zain's shoes in her brother's absence. Tate, who was annoyingly attractive in his jeans and fitted Henley.

"I'm aware of my mistake. Spare me the lecture."

He scowled. Men shouldn't look so handsome when they were irritated.

The buttons at his shirt's collar were open, revealing the hollow of his throat. The fitted cotton showcased the sexy line of his collarbones and his broad, muscled shoulders. His dark hair curled at the nape, and she had the strangest urge to wrap a piece around her fingers.

Tate's perusal was as shameless as her own. She'd worn a pair of boyfriend jeans and a flowy sweater that draped over a shoulder. His gaze roamed her bare skin until those chocolate pools drifted to her lips.

His tongue darted out, wetting his lower lip as he stared at Ivy without hesitation. There was no shyness, like from the guys on campus. No games, like each time she sparred with Michael. No subtlety.

Tate stared at Ivy the way a man stared at a woman he desired. A woman he had every intention of claiming.

Her heart raced. The temperature in the kitchen spiked. He sipped his wine but those eyes never wavered. His attention was fixed solely on her.

It was Ivy who broke first, dropping her gaze to her own glass before taking another healthy chug. The bastard was unnerving her again, just like the night she'd met him at Treason.

If Elora was going to hide in her bedroom upstairs and Ivy was going to be stuck with Tate, she was going to get very, very drunk. So she finished her glass of wine, then stretched her arm for another refill.

It only took two bottles of wine to accomplish her mission. By the time the doorbell rang with food delivery from a local Italian restaurant, she was blissfully buzzed.

"Here." Tate set a bowl of mascarpone pesto pasta on the coffee table. "Eat that."

"I don't have a fork."

He held out the utensil like he'd conjured it from thin air. "I'm going to take a plate up to Elora."

Her friend had yet to emerge from the bedroom. "Aww. That's sweet."

Tate chuckled. "You told me five minutes ago that I was a prick."

"Because you cut me off." She nodded to the glass of

water he'd brought in lieu of a replenished wineglass on his last trip to the kitchen.

"Eat." He smirked, then disappeared.

She collected the bowl, setting it on her lap as she sat cross-legged on the couch. Somewhere between bottles one and two, Ivy and Tate had moved from the kitchen to the living room.

While she'd lazed on one end of the couch, he'd sat on the opposite end with an ankle casually draped over his knee as he'd listened to her talk and watched her drink. His own glass sat on the end table, half full of the cabernet she'd chosen after the chardonnay.

Ivy twirled noodles around her fork, popping it in her mouth. As she chewed, she realized that she was no longer against the armrest. Somehow, as they'd chatted about Aston and her classes, she'd inched closer and closer to his end of the couch.

She couldn't bring herself to leave the center cushion, so she ate her meal, waiting until his footsteps returned and he resumed his seat.

Tate's arm stretched along the back of the couch and his fingertips brushed the ends of her hair. "Elora said to tell you good night."

"She's not coming down?"

He shook his head. "No."

Ivy sighed. "Did you know about them? Elora and Zain?"

"Yes. Though from the sounds of it, not many did."

"Did?"

"There's a reason Elora is locked in her bedroom and Zain flew back to Boston."

Click. Another piece to the puzzle. "They broke up."

Tate shrugged, reaching for his wine. "I don't know the details. I didn't ask."

Ivy slumped, poking at her food. "I asked and still don't know the details. She's been acting strange but won't tell me what's wrong."

"She seems like a private person."

"She is. But the reason she won't tell me is because she doesn't trust me." The alcohol had loosened her tongue.

Tate lifted the bowl from her lap and stole the fork from her hand, taking his own bite.

Sober Ivy would have glared at him for swiping her meal. Drunk Ivy studied the flex of his jaw as he chewed, jealous of that damn fork for getting past his lips.

"That's my dinner." Her protest lacked reprimand.

He shrugged, eating another bite. "You can have some of mine."

"Fine." She slid deeper into the couch, leaning against the back, wishing his arm were still there.

Tate stretched toward the coffee table, handing her the glass of water. "Drink that."

She obeyed as he ate another bite. Then he swapped out her water for the bowl.

"Eat." He nodded at the pasta.

"You're so bossy."

"If you think that's bossy"—he leaned closer, his gaze falling to her lips—"you haven't seen anything yet."

Her breath hitched.

Tate's hand found hers, but instead of taking the fork from her, he forced her fingers to grip it tighter. "Eat, Ivy."

Then he was gone, leaving her alone on the couch with her pulse throbbing between her legs as he went to the kitchen.

As he dished out his own meal, she wondered how she'd fallen under his spell again. Should she move away and sit somewhere else? Maybe he'd eat alone in the kitchen.

But he returned to her side, the heat from his sculpted body radiating to hers as he sank into his seat with his own dinner. "Why do you think Elora doesn't trust you?"

She lifted a shoulder. "Because she doesn't. No one does."

"Why?"

"I don't know," she lied.

Tate stabbed a bite of the meal he'd ordered, penne pomodoro, studying her as he chewed. Like he could see the lie in the air.

She knew exactly why people didn't trust her. She didn't allow it. Just like she didn't trust others. Ivy couldn't even say that Elora was an exception. Though her friend knew of her past, Ivy had always kept Elora at a distance.

Her bitchy attitude was her defense. A defense she'd perfected since Kristopher.

Ivy had been a different person before Kristopher. Before they'd broken each other.

"Maybe it's daddy issues," she teased. She'd had too much to drink, and if he kept looking at her like that, so intently, she might actually tell him the truth. And the last person she wanted to talk about tonight, or any night, was Kristopher.

"Daddy issues." Tate quirked an eyebrow.

"Have you met them? My parents?"

He nodded. "Once. In college."

"Sorry."

Tate laughed and took another bite, a smile on his soft lips.

"My father is a manwhore and my mother is a pill addict," she told him. "Though Mom is equally whorish, but she's better about hiding it than he is. They are awful people, but they have money, which means they get to continue to be awful people."

Ivy regretted her words the moment they were out. She hadn't been that brutally honest in, well . . . years. Especially not about her family. They were flawed, but they were hers.

"Hey." He nudged her elbow with his. "I know about your parents."

"I don't talk about them. Not like that."

"I won't say anything."

She believed him. "Why are you so easy to talk to?"

"Because you're drunk."

No, it wasn't the wine. She'd been around Michael countless times after a couple bottles of wine and she'd never spoken like this to him.

"Tate?" she whispered.

"Ivy."

She met his stunning gaze. "I don't want to be like my parents."

He set his bowl aside, collected hers and stacked them together. Then he shifted to face her, hooking a finger under her chin. "Then don't be."

"Maybe it's too late."

His thumb stroked a line on her jaw. "Why do you say that?"

"Zain didn't tell you about me?"

"No."

For that, she loved her big brother. Because they might not be close, but he would always protect her, right? Like Edwin. Her twin always tried to compensate for their parents' shortcomings. For the signs her mother and father had missed or ignored.

"Do you think there are some sins you can't overcome?" she asked.

Tate's thumb stilled. "What are you talking about?"

About the fact that she'd killed a man.

"Hypothetically," she lied.

His hand fell away from her chin to thread through the hair at her temple. "I don't know, baby."

"I hate being called baby." She leaned into his palm. Though when it came from his lips, she didn't mind at all.

"Tough." His voice was rich and deep and so damn close. "I like calling you baby."

She studied his face, memorizing the details she wanted in her dreams tonight. The bridge of his nose. The shape of his lips. The bump of his Adam's apple. The stubble on his face. Never in her life had Ivy seen a more beautiful man.

"Ivy." Tate's voice sounded pained. "Don't look at me like that if you don't want me to kiss you."

"What if I want you to kiss me?"

He leaned in, his mouth a whisper from her own.

She closed her eyes, her breath caught in her throat as her heart thundered. *Kiss me.*

Then the couch shook. Her eyes snapped open. Tate was on his feet, the dishes clanking as he picked them up from the table.

"That's it?" Ivy's mouth fell open. Was he freaking kidding?

Tate stared down at her, his expression hard and his body taut. A low growl came from his chest. If the bulge behind his zipper was anything to go by, he wasn't entirely unaffected. "Yeah, that's it. When you have a clear head, come find me. Ask me that question again."

Without another word, he came to the back of the couch, pausing to bend over her head. His lips brushed her forehead, then he was striding for the kitchen.

She listened to him wash the dishes and put the leftover food away.

And when the door to his bedroom closed, she flopped on the couch, her eyes aimed at the ceiling as a smile spread across her face.

Tomorrow.

She'd ask him to kiss her tomorrow.

Except in the morning, after she woke on the couch covered in a velvet throw, she searched the house.

Tate was gone.

fifteen

. . .

CASSIA WAS HAVING the best dream of her life. There was a mega-hot guy whispering in her ear and he smelled so freaking good. Dream hottie had leaned in, ready to kiss her, when her eyes cracked open and she was blinded by a ray of sunshine from her bedroom window instead.

Damn. Why did good dreams always end in the middle?

She squinted toward the light, her eyelids heavy. She felt half awake and half asleep. It reminded her of the time she'd jumped off the high dive at a local pool when she was eight. After plunging beneath the surface, she'd had to claw and pull her way to fresh air.

What time was it? She remembered sitting at the library with Edwin on Friday. She remembered him giving her a ride home. She remembered making it inside the manor and feeling so tired that she'd stopped on the staircase to catch her breath.

The softness of her pillows cradled her head. When had she come upstairs?

She sighed and pushed herself up on an elbow. Her coral hair was stuck to her face, so she tucked it behind her ears.

The color was fading. Last month, she'd found a similar

shade at the drug store and had dyed it in her bathroom. She needed to do it again, but not today. Today, she was going to hit her Saturday task list, then rest.

Though she felt better than she had at the library, her body felt stiff and her head groggy, like she could sleep for another hour or two.

"Hey."

Cassia yelped and shot up straight. Her eyes landed on the man in her wingback chair.

Edwin's chair.

With Edwin in it.

"W-what are you doing here?" She clutched her chest, trying to slow her racing heart.

"How are you feeling?"

"Um . . . better?" She searched her nightstand for her phone but it was nowhere in sight. "What time is it?"

He yawned and dragged a hand through his disheveled hair before reaching for his own phone on the table. "It's ten."

Ten. No wonder her head was so foggy. She'd slept for fifteen or sixteen hours. "Why are you here?"

Edwin shrugged. "You were sick."

"How long have you been here?"

"Awhile."

She gave him a sideways glance. If it was ten, then . . . "Uh, did you watch me sleep all night? I can't decide if that's sweet or strange."

"It's, uh, Sunday, actually."

Cassia blinked. "Huh?"

"Yeah. You've been out since Friday night. I crashed in the guest bedroom but came in a while ago to check on you."

There was a lot to digest in that statement but her brain was stuck on Sunday. It was Sunday. She'd slept an entire day away.

"Shit." She flung the covers from her body and stood in a flurry. Except her legs buckled and her head spun at the sudden movement.

"Easy." Edwin flew out of his chair, catching her before she could crash to the floor. His strong arms banded around her waist, keeping her on her feet as she sagged against his chest.

Her head throbbed, her vision full of white spots. Maybe she wasn't as rested as she'd thought.

"Sit back down," Edwin ordered, that deep voice as warm and soothing as the fresh, clean scent of his long-sleeved T-shirt.

That was the smell of her dream guy. She'd heard that voice in her dream too, murmuring words she couldn't remember. Maybe it hadn't been a dream at all.

"You stayed with me," she whispered, tilting her gaze to his face. They'd never been this close, and in her bare feet, he towered over her.

His jaw had more stubble than it had in the library on Friday. There were faint circles beneath his blue eyes. "Like I said. You were sick. And I didn't want you to be here alone."

Alone. Because her roommates were gone. Geoff and Francis didn't work on Saturdays.

"Oh." She tested the strength in her legs, loosening her grip on Edwin's arms. He let her go, his hands at the ready to catch her as she shuffled back to bed, plopping on its edge.

Cassia glanced at her knees. Her bare knees. She was wearing a pair of pink and red striped pajama shorts and a matching button-down top. The set had been a Valentine's Day gift last year from Josh.

She hated these pajamas. She hadn't worn them in months. But when she'd packed up her life at Hughes, she hadn't been able to throw them away either.

"You changed my clothes," she said. On Friday, she'd been in a pair of jeans and a black sweater.

"About that." Edwin rubbed the back of his neck, then returned to the chair, sitting with his elbows braced on his knees. "It was innocent. I swear. After I dropped you off, I went home but started worrying. So I stopped by the store and picked up some soup, thought I'd bring it over for dinner. I found you asleep on the floor by the stairs."

"Hell." Cassia groaned. So the reason she didn't remember anything after that was because she'd basically blacked out.

"I carried you upstairs. Put you in bed. Thought you'd wake up at some point. I hung around, watched a couple movies in the theater room. Checked on you after midnight and you had a fever. So I called a doctor. She came over, made sure it wasn't serious. Told me it was just a virus that needed to run its course and to watch closely that your temperature didn't get any higher."

"You have a doctor who makes house calls?" Why did that not surprise her?

He shrugged. "Dr. Harp is a friend of the family. She's Ivy's doctor."

"Okay," Cassia drawled. "And when exactly did you undress me?"

"I promise I didn't look." He held up his hands. "Much."

Cassia sagged. Maybe if it had been someone else, she would have felt violated. But for some reason, the idea of Edwin caring for her was endearing. Besides, she could feel the underwire of her bra. If he had seen anything, it would have been like seeing her in a swim suit.

"You're not mad?" he asked. "Figured you'd be mad."

"I probably should be. I must still be delirious."

He chuckled. "You need to eat something."

"Yeah." But the idea of trekking to the kitchen seemed as daunting as running a marathon.

"Be right back." Edwin strode from the room and disappeared down the hall.

Cassia drew in a long breath, summoning enough energy to stand. It took her a moment to find her balance, then she shuffled to the bathroom. As much as she needed a shower, her energy was zapped by the time she'd splashed water on her face and brushed her teeth.

She was just making her way back to bed when Edwin came into the room with a tray.

A frown marred his handsome features when he saw her walking. "You should have waited for me."

"I'm all right." She climbed beneath her covers, feeling a new wave of exhaustion roll through her muscles.

Edwin set the tray down on the table, then came to the bed, helping her prop up against some pillows. That fresh scent caught her nose again.

"You smell good." The whisper had been meant to stay inside her head. *Ugh.*

He grinned, flashing her a dimple as he tucked the blankets around her hips. "You told me."

"I did? When?"

"Late last night. Probably around midnight. I came in to check on you and you told me I smelled like a first kiss."

Heat spread across her cheeks. *Oh. My. God.* "Sorry."

"Don't be. I don't know what a first kiss smells like but I'm taking it as a compliment."

A first kiss smelled like a man. Like clean soap with spicy undertones. Like temptation and anticipation. When Cassia closed her eyes, when she thought of the scent she wanted to inhale before a man's lips touched hers, it was Edwin's.

As she sank into her pillows, he retrieved the tray and brought it to her lap. There was a warm blueberry muffin on a small plate beside a glass of orange juice and a cup of steaming tea. In a bowl, her favorite peach yogurt was topped with homemade granola. "Did you make this?"

"Francis," he said. "She's in the kitchen making you soup."

"Oh." Her heart warmed as she tore off another piece of muffin. Before she'd passed out on the staircase, she'd had this endless, empty feeling. Hopelessness, and the realization that she was truly on her own.

But maybe she wasn't as alone as she'd thought.

"Why did you stay with me?" Cassia asked as Edwin returned to his chair.

"I couldn't let you die, Red."

She smiled as she rolled her eyes. "I wasn't dying."

"No, but you were sick. Ivy and Elora were gone. They won't be home for another couple of hours. I didn't want you here by yourself."

"That's—" *Wow.* She hadn't been overly kind to Edwin, yet here he was. He'd even called a doctor. Emotion clogged her throat, so she took a sip of tea, trying to free the lump.

"I'm not the monster you think I am, Cassia."

"I don't think you're a monster."

"You sure about that?"

"I'm sure." She nodded. "Thank you for staying with me."

"Welcome."

The last time she'd been sick had been at Hughes. Her sophomore year, she'd caught the flu and her dad had kept watch, never leaving her side.

She'd never once in her life been sick when he hadn't been there to help her through it. Colds. Flus. Scraped knees and a jammed middle finger thanks to her one and only season of fourth-grade basketball.

It should have been Dad in that chair. He should have been the person to help his sick daughter.

She ate another bite of muffin, keeping her gaze on the tray because tears pricked at her eyes. Since she'd come to Aston, she'd done a damn good job of shoving her feelings aside to concentrate on school. Except today . . .

Today, she had no strength to shove.

"I miss my dad." Her whisper filled the room.

She missed him now that he was gone. She was furious that he'd left her. Cassia risked a glance at Edwin, finding his gaze waiting.

"Is he—"

Dead. She held up a hand, not wanting him to say the word. "Yes."

"I'm sorry."

"Me too." The silence between them stretched, and the longer it continued, the more she needed Edwin to leave. She'd revealed more to him in one sentence than she had to any other person in the nearly two months she'd been at Aston. "You don't have to stick around."

"I'm not going anywhere until you're on your feet."

That was not the answer she wanted to hear. "I'll be fine."

"Of course you will." He picked up the paperback she hadn't noticed on the table at his side, opening it to a folded page.

"My father was a professor. History. If he'd seen you folding a page like that, he'd have given you a stern lecture on treating books with respect."

Edwin chuckled. "That sounds a lot like Ivy. Did you know she's studying history?"

Cassia shook her head, taking another bite of her breakfast. Her father and her roommate had more in common than books and history. They both hoarded secrets too.

Her father's secrets had been his death.

Edwin seemed content to read, so Cassia focused on her breakfast. When she moved to set the tray aside, he put his book down and carted off the empty dishes to the kitchen while she snuggled deeper into her pillows, turning on her cheek to stare at his chair.

Then he was back again, picking up his book.

"You don't have to stay."

"So you've said." He opened his book, crossing an ankle over his knee.

"Why?"

"Why, what?"

"I'm no longer unconscious. I'll be fine. Why are you staying?"

Edwin leaned forward, his attention wholly fixed on her. The intensity in his eyes, the seriousness on his face made her heartbeat spike. "Because I think about you more than I should."

"Oh."

"Oh," he mimicked. "So here we are."

She studied his face as he lifted the book once more. "What are you reading?"

"A thriller." He looked at her from over the edge, the corner of his mouth turning up. "I like to be intrigued."

Why did she have a feeling he wasn't talking about the book?

"I really shouldn't trust you," she murmured.

"Probably not. But you're delirious, remember?"

Definitely delirious. The smart thing to do would be to insist he leave. To shower and attempt to study since she'd lost an entire day already. Yet she closed her eyes and let the flip of his pages lull her to sleep.

And when she woke from her nap, Edwin was still in his chair.

sixteen

. . .

ELORA'S FINGERS hovered over the keyboard as she stared at her laptop's screen. *Yes. No.* Her reply to Sal Testa only had to be a single word, yet she wasn't sure which to type.

The night her investigator had delivered her brother's paternity results—and her own—she'd paid him in cash, assuming it was the end of their transaction. Except Sal's name had graced her inbox an hour ago.

Not only was he a skilled PI, but Sal was clearly a savvy businessman. Elora had specifically asked him to identify Lucas's father, informing him that it was likely David Clarence. The second letter he'd delivered about her own paternity had been unexpected and unwelcome. Yet there was no unreading those words.

Lawrence Maldonado was not her biological father.

But had Sal identified this mystery sperm donor? No. He'd stopped short, planting just enough uncertainty in her mind to secure him another job.

Wisely, he'd waited a month before contacting her again. He'd given Elora time to let the truth marinate. Then he'd pounced, his email asking if she'd like to engage his services again to find her biological father.

Did she really want the truth? *Yes. No.* The more she uncovered, the more her world changed.

At least she wasn't related to David. That was the only detail Sal had given her. With absolute certainty, Elora was in no way related to any member of the Clarence family. The idea that she might have been related to Zain . . .

Her insides roiled. It was unthinkable.

For the past month she'd been so focused on how to tell her father about Lucas, about herself, that she hadn't thought about much else. This was her chance. But should she ask more questions when she was terrified of the answers?

Yes. No.

Sal's email couldn't have been more perfectly timed.

Elora and Ivy had spent the weekend at the cottage. After both Zain and Tate had left Martha's Vineyard, the girls' getaway had actually been relaxing. Ivy had asked if Elora wanted to talk—she had declined. Elora had asked Ivy if she wanted to talk about the son of a bitch who'd slapped her—another decline. So from there, the two of them had pretended like nothing was wrong, in either of their lives.

They'd hired a masseuse to visit the house yesterday. They'd spent a couple of hours on the beach. They'd enjoyed each other's company for a quiet Saturday, talking about nothing and gossiping about school. And today, shortly after lunch, their driver had returned to shuttle them to the airport for the short Sunday flight home.

Sal's email had popped up at exactly the moment Elora had sat behind her desk, almost like he'd known she was home.

Yes or no.

Her family was soon to be in upheaval. Things with Zain were . . . over. As painful as it was, the fact that he'd rather leave the cottage than endure a weekend with her, kiss or no kiss, had just cemented the inevitable. They were over.

And it was her fault. She'd pushed him away because,

well . . . she was still working through the reasoning in her head.

How much could her heart take?

What if her biological father was a monster? What if he was as awful as her mother? Elora wasn't sure she could handle the truth.

She closed her eyes, rested her hands on the keyboard and let her fingers decide. She hit send before changing her mind, then stood from her chair and ran from her office.

Elora hurried to the garage, her heart hammering as she started her car. There was only one way out of this mess. There was only one path to the light. It would get bloody before the end. But damn it, this had to end. The secrets had to stop. So she aimed her wheels down the familiar route that would lead her to her parents' home.

She was three minutes into her trip when her phone rang. Lucas's name flashed on the console's screen. Everything in her brother's life was about to change. She longed for just one last normal conversation, so for the first time in a month, she answered. "Hey."

"Hey?" He scoffed. "That's all you have to say to me? *Hey*. What the hell, Elora?"

"I'm sorry. I suck as a sister."

"Yeah. You do." There was a long silence. "What did I do? Why are you mad at me?"

Fuck. Her chest cracked at the hurt in his voice. "You didn't do anything wrong. And I'm not mad at you. It's just been a busy few weeks. I've been going through some stuff and haven't dealt with it very well."

"With like school or whatever? Dad said your senior year at Aston is hard."

"It is hard," she lied. Her classes had been time consuming but not nearly as brutal as they had been her junior year.

"School sucks for me too."

"Why? What's going on?"

He blew out a long breath, then his latest woes came out in a stream of word vomit, from his struggles in math to his essay on the American Revolution due tomorrow.

Elora soaked it all in, wanting nothing more than to rewind time and slap the curiosity out of herself. "How's football?"

"Good. I decided I like it better than basketball."

She giggled. "Yeah, and as soon as basketball starts, you'll decide you like it better than football."

"Probably." He laughed. "I missed you at my games. I like trying to find you in the crowd."

"I missed it too."

"Next weekend. Can you come?"

"Yes." She agreed without hesitation. Except if she kept driving, she'd be home in no time. And depending on how Dad handled the news, if he decided to share with Lucas, her brother's world would implode. He might have no interest in football again.

Elora's foot hovered over the brake. She couldn't do this. Not yet.

"Are you driving?" he asked.

"Yes, I was running an errand." She slowed at the next street, veering into the turn lane. Then she flipped an illegal U-turn.

Not yet.

"I have to study today," Lucas said. "Dad's working for a while but then he said he'd help me with my essay. We might go out to dinner too. Wanna come?"

"I wish I could," she said. "But I just got back and I've got a lot of work to do."

"Yeah," he muttered. "You could go to Martha's Vineyard and not come see me."

"It was a study weekend." Another lie.

"Just teasing." The smile in his voice put one on her face. "I'll see you at my game."

"I'll be there." No matter what it took, she'd find the

courage to go. If Lucas was about to lose a father, she wouldn't make him lose a sister too. "Text me later."

"Will you actually reply?"

"Yes." She sighed. "I'm sorry. Forgive me?"

"Duh. Bye."

"Bye." Elora ended the call, feeling no lighter and no less conflicted. But the determination she'd had just minutes ago to end this secrecy was gone and she found herself driving aimlessly, not wanting to return to the manor.

There was nothing for her there but knots in her gut and a lonely room.

That loneliness pushed her to East Boston, to an industrial area along the waterfront by Chelsea Creek, where a developer had been converting old buildings into stylish residences and retail shops. The area was hip and growing in popularity, with its kitschy stores, trendy restaurants and handful of craft breweries. While commercial businesses occupied the ground floors of the buildings, the upper levels had been converted to residential properties, mostly studios and penthouse suites.

Elora eased in front of a familiar brick building, taking one of the empty spaces in front of a tattoo parlor. Then she stared at the door. Would he let her inside? She'd just stepped out of her BMW when a man came walking down the street.

His jacket hid the tattoos covering his arms, but a tribal pattern snaked up the dark skin of his neck, revealing a bit of his own artwork. When he spotted her, he grinned and jerked up his chin. "Hey, Elora."

"Hi, Axel." A blush creeped into her cheeks. Zain was the most beautiful man she'd ever laid eyes on, but Axel was a close second.

"You okay?" he asked as he got closer, taking her in.

"Great," she lied.

Elora looked nothing like herself today.

No makeup. Hair unwashed and in a knot. She'd woken up in Martha's Vineyard this morning, in Zain's cottage, and had zero energy to do anything with herself, so she'd put on a pair of leggings and a bulky sweatshirt. It was one of Zain's she'd hidden from Ivy for years and had only worn to sleep. But now that Ivy knew about them, there was no point in hiding it, so she'd worn it on the trip home.

"Heading up?" Axel asked, digging keys from his jacket and fitting them into the door's lock.

She nodded, following him inside. "Thanks."

"Welcome. Tell him hi. He's been busy lately. Haven't seen him in a while."

"Okay." She waited until he unlocked the interior door to his tattoo parlor before she took a fortifying breath and climbed the concrete stairs to the second floor.

Her breath was lodged in her throat as she raised her hand to knock. The moment her knuckles touched the steel door, she regretted coming. He'd only send her away.

As the deadbolt flipped, her stomach dropped. Zain opened the door, and her mouth went dry. He wore nothing but a white towel wrapped around his narrow hips. The tattoos Axel had inked on Zain's skin over the years were on full display. His hair was damp and a few stray water droplets cascaded down the broad plane of his chest.

He didn't greet her or wave her inside. He stood and waited for her to speak.

"Are you alone?" she asked, hating the tremble in her voice.

"Yeah."

Her entire body seemed to sag. "Axel let me up."

"What are you doing here, Elora?"

"You flew home from the cottage."

Zain crossed his arms over his chest, accentuating the incredible strength and definition in his arms. Was he doing it to rattle her? He knew she'd always loved the cut muscles that sculpted his incredible body. At night, whenever they'd lain in bed, she'd spent hours tracing the dips between his shoulders and biceps and triceps.

"I'm sorry about the weekend," she said. "I didn't know you were planning on going."

"So you said."

Elora dropped her gaze to his bare feet. He wasn't going to let her in, not that she deserved it. She was standing here and still wasn't sure why. Maybe because her refuge had become Zain. Because she was so goddamn tired and the only person in the world she wanted to see was him.

"You look like shit," he said.

Elora lifted a shoulder.

"And that's my sweatshirt."

Please, don't make me give it back. "I know."

Zain dragged a hand over his jaw. "I sound like a fucking broken record, especially knowing that you're not going to tell me, but what's wrong?"

"I have a secret." The moment she spoke, tears flooded her eyes. "And it's eating me alive."

He stood straighter. "Want to tell me?"

"Yes. No." She wrapped her arms around her waist, trying to physically hold the rest inside. "I'm scared it will ruin everything."

"Are you pregnant?"

She shook her head. "No."

Something flashed across his gaze—disappointment?—but it vanished as quickly as it had appeared. Zain stepped out of the threshold, waving her into his penthouse. "Come in. Give me a minute to get dressed."

As he retreated down the hallway, her eyes were glued to the dimples that sat just above his ass. He ducked into the bathroom as she stepped into the loft, drawing in the comforting scent of his home and the smell of his soap lingering in the air.

Zain's home had tall ceilings with exposed ductwork. The floors were a warm wood that complemented the brick walls. For a man who had millions to his name, his home was simple.

Elegant and classy, but the loft wasn't much bigger than Elora's suites at Clarence Manor.

The open concept meant she could stand next to the door and survey the living room and kitchen. Zain's bed rested on a platform to her right, the white bedding smooth and the pillows fluffed against the black iron headboard.

Had he invited another woman into his bed? Had he fucked that blond? Had Tommie the bartender finally scored a night with her boss?

She pressed her fingertips to her temples, willing those questions away.

"Headache?" Zain came striding down the hallway dressed in jeans and a black T-shirt with Treason's logo on the breast pocket. He'd pulled on a pair of scuffed, black motorcycle boots. "Want something for it?"

"I'm all right."

" 'Kay. Let's go." He jerked his chin for her to follow him through the loft.

They walked past the bed and beside his large bathroom with the adjoining closet. The bathroom was the only room in the loft with a door and walls. Then they moved through the area he used for an in-home office toward the door that led down the rear stairwell.

His boots thudded on the stairs, echoing off the walls, as they returned to the first floor, this time at the rear of the building. Elora had been to Zain's plenty of times, but she usually came up through the front entrance, like today, because she'd parked on the street.

At the base of the stairs were three doors. One led to the alleyway exit. Another to a private gym Zain had built for himself. And the third to a huge, immaculate garage where he kept his three cars and a Harley.

He opened the door to the garage.

Inside, on a row of hooks, were two leather jackets. He handed one to Elora, and she brought the brown leather to her nose, inhaling the scent of wind and Zain's cologne before shrugging it on. Even with her baggy sweatshirt, the coat was a tent on her petite frame.

Zain pulled on the other jacket, then handed her a helmet. As she was tightening the strap beneath her chin, he hit a button to open one of the three garage doors that led to the alley. He had turned to the bike when Elora cleared her throat. “What?”

She pointed to the other helmet resting on the shelf. “Please?”

“Fine.” He frowned but put it on his head, then strode to the bike, his easy swagger something else she’d loved about him.

The man moved as if he owned the world.

He settled on the seat, waiting for her to slide in behind him. Elora immediately wrapped her arms around his waist and pressed the insides of her thighs to his, closing her eyes as she savored the hardness of his body.

Zain’s stress relief came from riding his motorcycle. It was something he’d told her he preferred to do alone. Yet he’d taken her out twice in their years together. For Elora, he’d bent his rules.

Each ride had been an experience she wouldn’t forget. And Zain always seemed to bring her along when she was at her lowest.

The first ride had been during her sophomore year, shortly after her grandmother had died. The second, her junior year, after her childhood dog had gotten sick and her parents had been forced to put him to sleep.

Zain started the engine, the loud rumble bouncing off the garage walls.

She peered beyond his shoulder as he eased into the alley and rolled to the juncture with the main street, where he stopped to look both ways.

“Axel said you’ve been busy,” she said.

“I have been.” He pointed down the block to where a

dumpster sat in front of one of the last unrenovated buildings. "Started on that remodel two weeks ago."

"It's the last one, right?"

"Yeah." He nodded. That developer who'd taken over this area, who'd invested millions into this two-block radius?

Zain.

When they'd met, he'd just purchased these buildings. It had taken him over five years to secure them all, but he'd been unwavering in his negotiations and unyielding in his desire to have both complete blocks so that when he did his remodel, the esthetic would be cohesive.

Elora had watched as he'd transformed his own building first, making a space for his friend and tattoo artist Axel below the penthouse suite. Then she'd witnessed Zain transform the other buildings, luring other businesses and residents to the area.

She had no ownership in the project, but her chest swelled as they headed down the street. "I'm proud of you."

Elora had spoken so quietly he couldn't have heard. But then his hand came to her knee, giving it a squeeze, before it returned to the handlebar and they left his neighborhood behind.

The wind whipped against her cheeks. The air was cool and crisp, yet the afternoon sunshine kept her from freezing. That, and Zain's warmth.

She pressed her chin to his spine, banded her arms tighter around his torso, and for an hour, let herself think.

About her parents. About the unknown. About her relationship with Zain.

He wanted commitment. He wanted love. Zain had wanted to end the twisted little affairs. Would he care that Lucas was his half brother? What were Zain and Elora as a couple if not twisted and tangled?

His father had had a child with her mother.

Her father had been sleeping with his mother for years.

They were more of the same. A Maldonado and a Clarence.

Would she turn into her mother? Would she become that bitter, jaded person? And that one day, when it happened, when the resemblance went beyond the mirror, would Zain hate her?

And Lucas—sweet, innocent Lucas—would he be caught in the crosshairs?

He was a Maldonado. He was a Clarence.

She felt lost on his behalf.

So after the first hour, she closed her eyes, she held on to Zain, and she shoved the thoughts aside. She forgot it all until the bike slowed and she realized they were at his building. The late afternoon sun was setting, casting a golden glow over the pitched roofline.

He eased into the garage, shutting off the Harley, but he didn't move to stand. He didn't urge her away. He put his arms over hers, holding her for a long moment, until finally, the ride was over.

Elora swung her legs off the seat, stripping off his jacket and the helmet. The sweatshirt was going home to the manor and her closet.

Zain stood in front of her, his own helmet on the bike's seat, and tucked a lock of hair behind her ear. Then a finger touched the freckles on her nose. "Ready to talk?"

"I want to tell you but . . ." She closed her eyes. "I'm scared."

"Of what? What are you so damn afraid of, El? Talk to me."

She was terrified that he'd send her away. It hurt enough that she was the one to walk. But if he truly ended it, if he looked at her like she was less, it would crush the last pieces of her heart.

Elora wasn't ready to tell him about Lucas. Not yet. So she steeled her spine and told him the safer secret. "I don't know who my father is."

Zain tensed, his eyes narrowing on her face. "What are you talking about?"

"Lawrence Maldonado is not my biological father."

It was a relief to speak those words. To set the truth about herself free. To kill a secret.

Now she only had to find the courage to slaughter the other one.

seventeen

. . .

"NICE WORK, MISS CLARENCE." Professor Smith returned the cartography project she'd been working on all week.

"Thank you." Ivy's hands itched to open the portfolio's flap and check her actual grade, but she resisted, keeping her palms flat on the surface.

Professor Smith rarely delivered praise. Maybe that was why he was her favorite. He expected perfection from his students and set the bar extremely high. But a compliment given was one she'd earned, and damn, it felt good.

This project had consumed her life all week since she'd returned from Martha's Vineyard. It had given her a mental outlet to keep her brain occupied and not on Tate.

"That's all for today," Professor Smith announced to the classroom. "Monday we'll begin a study on the Astor Armada drawings, examining the maps themselves as well as reviewing the defeat of the Spanish Armada. Enjoy the weekend."

As the room bustled with noise, people stowing books and papers, she snuck a glance at her grade. *A.* Cause to celebrate.

Ivy quickly collected her things, and the moment she

walked outside of the hall, stepping into a courtyard shaded by autumn trees, she pulled out her phone and called Edwin.

He answered on the second ring. "Hey."

"Hi. What are you doing?"

"Studying in the library."

"On a Friday?"

Edwin was a good student but he wasn't the type to hit the books on a Friday. When his classes were over, he was usually ready to kick off the weekend. Her twin didn't go to Treason as often as she did, but he was always up for a good time.

"I'm done with class for today. Blow off studying. Let's go do something." Ivy hadn't spent much time with Edwin lately. Partly because she'd been busy with school. And partly because she'd been avoiding him.

The incident at Club 27 was history and not the kind she wanted to examine. So avoiding her brother had been necessary to avoid a conversation. But enough time had passed and she missed him.

"Lunch?" she offered.

"Nah," he muttered.

She frowned. "Nah? That's it?"

"I'm busy." Edwin sighed. "And I'm not hungry."

"Okay, fine." She opened her mouth to propose dinner instead, but then the line went quiet. She pulled it away from her ear to find that he'd hung up on her. "What the hell? Rude."

Was he still mad at her? It wasn't like she'd *wanted* some creep to slap her.

Ivy debated calling Edwin back as she made her way to the parking lot, but she knew her brother. If he was in a bad mood, he needed time and space. So she went to lunch alone, stopping at a small café that served a delicious kale salad. She read a book on her phone as she ate in silence, then paid the bill and returned to her car, calling Elora. Maybe her friend would be up for a celebration.

"Hi," Elora answered.

"I'm going shopping."

"Have fun."

Ivy rolled her eyes. "Come with me."

"I can't."

"Why?" Ivy had memorized Elora's schedule the first week of school. She was done with classes for the day.

"Because I don't want to."

Ouch. What was wrong with everyone today? Elora hadn't confided in Ivy during their time at the cottage, but she'd asked if Ivy was angry about her sleeping with Zain. Maybe if it had been a random roommate Ivy would have been pissed, but Elora was her best friend. Her only real friend.

Elora had always been the exception.

And after they'd cleared the air, they'd enjoyed the weekend together. At least, Ivy had enjoyed it. And she'd hoped that if she was just a constant presence, Elora would eventually confide in her.

Instead, she was getting blown off.

"Let's go out tonight," Ivy said, except there was no one on the line to hear her. The chime of the disconnected call hit right as Ivy finished her sentence.

So was everyone mad at her? She hadn't even done anything horrible lately. She'd left Cassia alone, hadn't she?

As much as Ivy wanted answers, she hadn't pushed her private investigator to make Cassia's case a priority. Her PI had emailed her two weeks ago saying that he'd been pulled into an urgent matter and had offered to send Ivy's request to a colleague. Instead, Ivy had told him that it could wait until he had time.

She'd used Sal Testa enough to know he was worth both the cost and a wait.

Michael hadn't been around lately either, so he must have grown bored with Cassia. Or maybe Ivy had grown bored with Michael. She hadn't seen him in weeks, not since that night at Club 27.

Had it really been over a month? Strange that she hadn't

really missed the little game she'd been playing with Michael for years.

Everything felt . . . off. Ever since the beginning of the semester, she'd been out of balance.

Hoping that retail therapy would help, Ivy went to her favorite boutique and spent an hour shopping. When she arrived at the manor, hauling in her bags, she ducked into the kitchen, eager to find Francis and ask for a latte. But a note on the counter said that her chef had left early for the weekend and reheating instructions for dinner were on the meal in the fridge.

Ivy carted her new outfits upstairs into her closet, already planning which one she'd wear to Treason tonight, and called Zain.

"Hey," he answered.

"Hi. I was thinking of coming to the club tonight. Maybe we could hang out for a while."

"Not tonight." The clink of glasses echoed in the background.

He offered no explanation as to why he couldn't spend time with her and shifted the phone from his mouth, talking to someone else before returning. "I have to go, Ivy."

For the third time, before she could say goodbye, she was listening to dead air.

Ivy huffed.

Apparently both of her brothers were still angry and annoyed with her. *Great.*

She moved to her bed, lying on the plush comforter and staring up at the canopy that draped over the four-poster frame. The air smelled like furniture polish and clean linen from the housekeeping staff.

There were hours to kill before Treason opened, but a restless energy crept into her limbs, making her squirm. Ivy pushed off the bed and strode the length of the manor, finding Cassia's bedroom door open.

Her roommate was perched in a wingback chair, bent over a table and the textbooks scattered on its surface.

"Of course you come in the one day I forget to close my door." Cassia didn't look up from her work as she spoke. "I'm busy, Ivy."

"You and everyone else," Ivy muttered. "What are you doing?"

"What does it look like?" Cassia reached for the pack of candy resting next to a yellow highlighter and peeled the box's top open.

"I'm going out tonight."

"Want a sticker?" Cassia ate a piece of candy, finally looking up.

Ivy's nostrils flared. "I'm inviting you along."

Cassia's chewing slowed, her eyes narrowing. "Why?"

"Because I'm feeling generous today." And lonely.

"Hard pass."

"It's not a trick, if that's what you're worried about. As it turns out, messing with you hasn't been much fun."

Cassia sat straighter. "No more trials?"

"Elora likes you." Ivy shrugged. "For whatever reason."

"That's not really an answer."

Ivy flicked her wrist. "I'm going to leave around nine and go to Treason. If you'd like to join me, it's an open invitation."

For a moment, she thought Cassia would accept. There was a glimmer of longing on her face, like she wanted a night of fun. But then she shook her head, hunching over her work once more. "No, thanks."

Disappointment churned Ivy's stomach as she trudged to her bedroom. What was wrong with everyone today? What was wrong with her? She must really be desperate to invite Cassia.

All she wanted to do was celebrate another week of school completed. To cut loose and have a little fun before graduation.

She flopped on her mattress once more. She'd pulled out

her phone, ready to burn an hour on social media, when it buzzed in her hand. Her father's name flashed on the screen. Dread coated her insides as she sat up and pressed it to her ear. "Hi, Dad."

"Ivy."

"Yes?" She tensed.

His tone meant he was not going to improve her day. Hopefully Edwin and Zain hadn't told him about the incident at Club 27. Though she doubted even if he knew, he'd care. "I just received an interesting phone call from Human Resources."

Her heart began thumping hard. "Oh?"

"Do not play dumb with me, young lady."

Her lip curled. Those fucking tattletales in Human Resources.

Last year, Dad had been pushing hard for her to consider a job with Clarence Holdings. After she'd declined twenty times, he'd begun to get irritated, so he'd made her a deal. If she took an internship for six months in any department, he would give her Clarence Manor after she graduated from Aston.

Dad knew each of his children's weaknesses and had no problem exploiting them. Ivy wanted this manor. It was hers by heart but not by law, so she'd agreed. She'd spent half of her junior year working in Human Resources.

She'd loathed that fucking internship. She'd hated the mundane tasks. She'd despised her coworkers. But she'd stuck it out.

Maybe her father had assumed she'd find some secret love for employee benefits planning. Maybe he'd assumed she'd love the idea of hiring—or firing—people. He'd promised her a full-time position once she had her diploma from Aston.

Ivy had no intention of working for her father, but she wasn't stupid. She didn't trust David Clarence one iota. So she'd stayed tight-lipped about her career plans, letting him make his assumptions until the manor was officially in her name. Then she'd tell him to fuck right off.

She should have known that someone in his ranks would nark on her.

A coveted opening at the Smithsonian Institution in Washington, DC had come up two weeks ago. Ivy had scrambled to put together a résumé and cover letter, knowing it was a long shot but taking it anyway.

The application had required her employment history. If they'd called Clarence Holdings, that meant she'd made it through the initial vetting process, right? Her hopes soared that she might get the job of her dreams.

Dad had a special way of sinking her dreams.

"I thought I made myself clear," he said. "Upon graduation, you and Edwin are expected to join the family business."

She opened her mouth, ready to tell him to shove his expectations up his ass, when she glanced around her bedroom.

The manor, the clothes, her car, Geoff and Francis, it was all funded by her father.

Zain had broken free from his expectations because he'd walked away from David Clarence's money. Her oldest brother had taken the trust fund set up by their grandfather and used those millions to create Treason. From there, he'd gotten into real estate development.

But Ivy's grandfather was just as shrewd as his son. After Zain had pulled that stunt, Grandfather had changed the terms on her and Edwin's trusts. Their father had followed suit, doing the same.

Her inheritance wouldn't be under her control until her thirtieth birthday.

Ivy was rich beyond most people's wildest dreams. And she couldn't touch a goddamn cent unless she was granted permission.

"It's the Smithsonian," she said, pleading with him to understand. "This is a once-in-a-lifetime opportunity. They probably won't even pick me, Dad. But please, let me at least try."

"No."

Rage surged in her chest, her body vibrating with anger and resentment. But she swallowed it down, fisted her hands and forced the fury from her voice. "I understand."

Ivy would not be withdrawing her application from the Smithsonian. If by some miracle they hired her, then she'd evaluate her options. Even if that meant saying goodbye to this manor. It was only a house.

"You haven't been home in weeks. Your mother would appreciate a visit."

Liar. Mom was probably screwing her newest personal trainer while Dad banged his secretary. Neither wanted impromptu visits from their children. "Okay."

"Glad we could clear this up."

She flipped her middle finger into the air, plastering on a phony smile. "Have a nice weekend."

He hung up on her too.

"Gah." She flew off the bed, pacing the length of her room until the red eased from her vision. Then she stormed into her closet, ripping through her shopping bags for the dark-green dress she'd bought earlier.

Frustration fueled her movements as she went to her bathroom to apply more makeup and pin up her hair.

Ivy could be free of David Clarence's chains. All she had to do was walk away from his money.

She hated him for putting her in this position.

She hated herself for being too weak to let the riches go.

Disappointment seeped into her bones as she walked out of her room, dressed for a night at the club before the club was even open. But she went to her car and climbed behind the wheel. Maybe Zain would sympathize with her tonight. Maybe he could give her some tips on how to outsmart their father.

She drove, fully intending to head to Treason, but as she

waited at a stoplight, a bar sign from down the block caught her eye. The light turned green, and instead of blowing past the bar, her foot touched the brake and she turned into the lot, parking between two other cars.

Control was slipping from her grasp and she didn't have a clue how to pull it back. Maybe it was useless. Ivy had been under a man's thumb since the day she'd been born.

Maybe the only option was accepting her circumstances.

Accepting her fate as a puppet.

And if that was the case, she was going to need a stiff drink.

Autumn's days were short and the evening light was already fading at six o'clock. But Ivy was grateful for the early hour so that she didn't have to walk in darkness to the bar's door. She stepped inside, the atmosphere moody and rich. In the center of the space was a grand piano. A man dressed in head-to-toe black sat at the bench seat, his fingers gliding across the keys as he played.

"What can I get you?" the bartender asked.

"Drunk," she answered, taking a stool.

Three glasses of champagne later, she felt no better about her future than she had when she'd arrived. But the pianist was enchanting and the alcohol had helped a bit of her frustration ebb.

"Who cares if I don't work at the Smithsonian, right?" she asked the bartender.

"Yeah." He leaned his elbows on the bar, a little deeper in than he had the last time. Inch by inch, he'd crossed too close. "Museums are overrated."

"Museums are glorious." She huffed, reaching for her clutch. Maybe she could have forgiven the intrusion into her personal space, but that last comment was her cue to leave.

She texted Geoff, requesting a ride and someone to collect her car. Geoff replied instantly, promising to be there in fifteen minutes with her newest driver in tow. Ivy waited, finishing her champagne, then placed cash on the bar for the museum hater and slid from her stool, taking an equal amount of money to the piano man's tip jar.

Her ride and Geoff arrived at the bar, exactly fifteen minutes after her initial text.

"Are you returning home?" Geoff asked as she handed him her keys.

"Not yet."

"Be careful," he ordered.

Geoff hadn't asked about the incident at Club 27 but the manor's walls might as well have been his ears. Somehow, he knew what had happened. And the concern in her butler's gaze nearly brought her to tears.

Geoff cared. Why couldn't her father?

"Thank you." She smiled at him, then slipped into the other car, waiting for the driver to get behind the wheel.

"Where to, Miss Clarence?"

"Club 27."

It was time to seize control.

Starting with that fucking club.

"I'll text you when I'm ready to leave," she told the driver after he'd parked next to the entrance. "I'll see myself out."

Ivy stood on the sidewalk, waiting for the driver to leave, but she didn't walk toward the club's door. She turned and strode for the parking lot, walking to the exact place where she'd been that night. To the place where that motherfucker had slapped her.

Her pulse throbbed behind her temples and sweat beaded on her brow, but she forced herself to stand there. To revisit the scene of the crime.

Just like she had years ago.

Breathe. Breathe, Ivy. Breathe.

He couldn't get to her anymore. He couldn't hurt her again.

It took a few minutes for her body to relax, for her lungs to fill completely, but then she stood taller, straightening her spine.

A sleezy asshole was not going to take her confidence. She smiled to herself as she returned to the club, this time passing the bouncers and going inside.

She went straight to the bar, the light crowd making it easy to find a seat and signal a bartender.

"What are you drinking?" the bartender asked.

"Tequila. Top shelf." After all, she'd wanted to celebrate tonight. Might as well do it with a few shots. She'd save the bartender from making her a gin fizz that she'd have only gulped instead of savoring.

Within the hour, her buzz was gone and Ivy was blissfully drunk. A flirty smile graced her lips as she talked to the man who'd taken the seat beside her own.

"Let's do another round." The guy waved the bartender over. "Whiskey neat for me. And another tequila for this gorgeous lady."

She didn't hold it against him that he'd forgotten her name. She'd forgotten his too.

No sooner had the bartender placed her shot glass down than a tall, broad figure slid beside her, filling the space between her stool and the next.

Ivy recognized Tate by his cologne and she fought the hitch in her breath. "You again."

"What are you doing here, baby?"

"Don't call me baby." He'd lost that right after he'd ditched her last weekend at the cottage. Ivy reached for her shot but Tate's palm covered the small glass. "Do you mind?"

He looked over her head to the man who'd just bought her this drink. "Go away."

The guy didn't even put up an argument. *Wimp.*

Ivy's eyes wandered up Tate's chest, a curl of desire pooling in her lower belly. His white button-down shirt was tailored to perfection, showcasing those shoulders and flat stomach. The sleeves strained at the bulk of his biceps.

He leaned in close, bending to speak into her ear. His lips

brushed the shell, sending a wave of tingles across her skin. "Stop drinking. *Baby*."

"Why? Worried I'll go home with someone else?"

"Because I won't fuck you if you're drunk."

She gulped. "Is that why you left last weekend?"

He leaned away, his chocolate gaze swirling with lust. "You're my friend's sister. If I had stayed, I would have fucked you in Zain's house, and I needed to talk to him first. There are boundaries."

Ivy knew all about boundaries.

And how much men liked to cross them.

Most would have jumped at the chance for a weekend of sex. Not Tate. She hadn't known many honorable men in her life, but damn if it wasn't sexy.

"Did you talk to Zain?" she asked, her heart climbing into her throat. What would her brother say to the idea of his friend and sister?

"I did."

"And?"

"He threatened to kill me if I hurt you."

Warmth spread through her veins as a smile stretched across her mouth. Maybe Ivy annoyed her big brothers, but they looked out for her.

"Good." Ivy placed her hand on his chest, standing from her seat and teetering slightly. She found her footing and rose up on her toes, expecting him to lean in and give her the kiss she'd wanted so desperately at the cottage.

But Tate frowned, shying away. "How much have you had to drink?"

"What are you, my babysitter? I'm drunk. I'm not unconscious. Don't pretend to be a saint."

"No, Ivy." He shook his head, his jaw clenching. "Not tonight."

Another rejection. Another person trying to steal her control. God, she couldn't even fuck the guy she wanted to screw.

“Then leave me alone.” Ivy spun toward the bar, wrapped her hand around his wrist and lifted it off her shot glass. Then, before he could stop her, she poured the tequila down her throat. It barely burned.

“Fuck,” he muttered.

“Not tonight, remember?” she quipped, shoving past him, her knees wobbly. But she regained her balance once more and leveled him with a glare. “Good luck with those boundaries.”

Ivy sensed him behind her as she walked for the exit.

She knew he’d keep watch until she was in her car. So she held it together, using every breath to keep her emotions in check. They raged inside of her, pounding fists against her ribs to be set free. Hurt. Anger. Disappointment.

Everyone wanted something from Ivy. Money. Status. Her father wanted her to be someone else. They wanted the façade. They wanted the rich, beautiful bitch.

She’d thought last weekend that maybe Tate had wanted her. The real Ivy Clarence.

Who was she kidding?

There was no real Ivy.

That Ivy was dead, killed in a car crash years ago. With Kristopher.

eighteen

. . .

"HEADS, I'm buying. Tails, candy is on you today." Edwin flipped a quarter into the air, catching it and slapping it over the back of his hand. Then a cocky smirk spread across his face. "Heads."

"Most people don't smile when they lose," Cassia said.

"What can I say? I like buying you candy. Make sure you stay sweet."

"Oh, Edwin." She scrunched up her nose. "Please tell me that's not how you flirt with women."

"Just you, Red." He winked at her as he stood, striding to the vending machine.

Yes, the flirting was cheesy. But Cassia was loving every second spent with this guy, and it had little to do with that handsome face.

Edwin had this steady nature. This way of making her smile so effortlessly. Cassia wasn't sure she'd ever met a person who seemed so comfortable in his own skin. Or a man who was so unabashedly willing to deliver compliments.

Her face was flushed, something that seemed to be a constant when Edwin was around. And oh, had he been around.

She'd seen him every day this week. He'd sat in her room last Sunday, reading while she'd napped and recovered from whatever bug she'd caught. Finally, after she'd insisted she was on the mend—and in desperate need of a shower—he'd left the manor.

Cassia hadn't expected to see him so soon, but then he'd found her in the library on Monday afternoon. She'd been sitting on the second floor, desperately trying to concentrate and catch up on the work she'd missed while sick. Edwin had packed up her books, without asking, and hauled them to his quiet nook on the third floor, forcing her to follow.

Then he'd bought her a Snickers.

Tuesday, when she'd come to the library, she'd headed straight for the third floor to find him already waiting. He'd flipped that coin, lost the toss and bought her a bag of Skittles.

Wednesday had been Reese's Peanut Butter Cups.

Thursday had been M&M's.

Friday had been Hot Tamales.

And today, Saturday, as the vending machine whirled, she held her breath, waiting to see what he'd choose. Those broad shoulders obscured her view until he turned, holding two boxes of Mike and Ikes.

"I'm feeling sentimental today." He grinned and handed her a box before returning to his chair.

She peeled the top open, trying to hide her smile as she chewed a piece. "So why are you here?"

"Thought that was fairly obvious. To study." His blue eyes danced as he studied—her face. Edwin hadn't brought his backpack today. No textbooks or assignments. He didn't even have a pen.

"You can't distract me." She held up a finger. "I am still behind from last weekend."

"No distractions. Got it." He opened his own box of candy, shaking out a handful, as she turned her attention to her notes.

Next week, she had a quiz in two of her classes. She'd felt

fairly prepared, but in between lectures yesterday, she'd met with Michael and his study group. Michael had mentioned that their professor had a tendency to pull quiz questions from material they'd barely discussed in class and to make sure she spent some time reviewing the chapters he'd glossed over.

Cassia had appreciated Michael's tip since she didn't have his history with the econ professors, but it had twisted her stomach into a knot and had made her feel epically unprepared. She was only a page into the first chapter on her review list when she glanced up to find Edwin's gaze waiting. "What?"

"You dyed your hair."

Was that a good thing or a bad? She couldn't tell from his tone. "It was starting to fade."

"What's your natural color?"

"Blond."

He glanced around like he was checking to make sure no one could hear him. They were alone. Not only was the entire library quiet on a Saturday, but no one ever seemed to find this secluded corner. Almost like Edwin had barred anyone from entering. No matter the day, any time she wandered to this floor, their table was unoccupied.

"Want to know a secret?" Edwin motioned her closer as he leaned his forearms on the table. "This is my natural hair color."

She laughed. "You don't say."

"Shocking, I know. A lot of people assume I get highlights."

Not Cassia. Those streaks in his light-brown waves were the same she used to get in the summer months. They'd fade through the winter, then return with the hot weather.

"I like the coral," he said, stretching an arm over the table to touch an errant strand on her shoulder.

"Thank you." Her heart skipped. "You're distracting me."

"I'm not even sorry."

She blushed as her heart tumbled. This guy was . . . too good to be true? "I really have to study."

"And you can't while I'm here?"

"It's difficult," she admitted. Too often she found herself breaking focus to look in his direction. She'd lose minutes staring at the line of his nose or the shape of his lips. She'd memorized the deep sound of his laughter when she should have been memorizing economic theories.

"Do you trust me yet?" he asked.

She sat straighter. "Is that why you've been coming this week? To earn my trust."

"Yes and no." He shrugged. "Yes, I want you to trust me. No, because even if you never trust me, I'll still keep coming just to buy you candy and see you smile."

Whoosh. The air rushed from her lungs. "I-I don't . . ." *Wow*. "I don't know what to say to that."

"Nothing. You don't have to say anything. Just know that I like you."

"You do?"

"Thought that was fairly obvious too."

"But why?" she blurted. Why would Edwin Clarence like Cassia Collins?

"Go to breakfast with me and I'll tell you."

"It's almost eleven. I already had breakfast."

He chuckled. "Tomorrow."

"Like a date?"

"Yes, a date."

Most men would have invited her to dinner or out for drinks. Breakfast was the tamest meal of the day. Maybe that was why Edwin had suggested it, to keep her from getting spooked.

Too late. Whatever interest he had in her, she was wary. But she was wary of all men at this point. And curiosity was eating her alive.

Maybe if she understood why, she'd get a better idea of his motives.

"Okay," she agreed.

He leaned back in his chair and tossed another piece of candy in his mouth, chewing with a smirk.

"Don't look so smug." She rolled her eyes. "The majority of first dates never lead to a second."

"You just made that statistic up."

"It's probably true though." Cassia bit her bottom lip to hide a smile.

Edwin's eyes shot to her lips, his eyes flaring. Then he growled and shot out of his chair. "I'll text you the details for tomorrow."

"You don't have my phone number."

He winked. "See you tomorrow, Cassia."

Cassia was so captivated by the sight of him walking away, by those jeans molded to the finest ass she'd seen in her life, that it took her a moment to pick up her phone and open the contacts. And there was his name.

Edwin Clarence.

She couldn't even be mad that he'd busted into her phone.

Because she had a fourth contact. And in true Edwin form, the cocky bastard had even starred his name as a favorite.

Cassia's nerves rattled her hands as she opened the door to the restaurant. The scent of bacon grease, black coffee and fresh bread filled her nose. Edwin had texted her yesterday after he'd left the library with an address to this café.

The restaurant was in East Boston, and as she'd been driving over, she'd been sure the GPS had steered her wrong. Until the path between two warehouses had opened up to a block full of red brick buildings.

It was trendy and hip, recently infused with money. And God, it was swank. One day, when Cassia had a job and an income stream, she'd love to live in a restored loft like those on the upper floors of these buildings.

This trip away from Aston and the manor had already been worth it. She felt more like herself after getting behind the wheel of her Honda.

Cassia spotted Edwin at a table against a wall, a smile on his face as he waited for her to spot him.

"You broke into my phone," she said when she reached his table and began stripping off her coat.

Edwin laughed and stood from his chair, pulling out Cassia's. "I promise I didn't snoop. I just added my number."

She believed him. Maybe, despite her best efforts, she was beginning to trust him. Or maybe she didn't care that he'd had her phone, because there wasn't anything to find.

The only contact of concern was her uncle and she'd hidden it under *Grandpa*. The few messages she'd sent him had been immediately deleted, including the text she'd sent from the bathroom at Treason.

Cassia had learned the hard way that those tiny devices were full of secrets.

So she made sure hers would never be her downfall.

"Coffee?" Edwin asked when she was seated, picking up a white carafe. When she nodded, he filled her mug, then topped off his own. "I wasn't sure you'd come."

"Truth? I wasn't sure I'd come either."

"Why did you?"

"Because I don't understand why you asked in the first place."

His gaze trailed down her face, like a hiker mapping a tricky path through a dangerous forest. When it landed on her mouth, it stayed there for a heartbeat before lifting to her eyes. "You intrigue me."

It wasn't the first time he'd said that word. "Why? I'm the definition of *un*-intriguing."

"No, you're not."

She traced the rim of her steaming coffee mug with a

fingertip. Her paranoia began to run wild. Was this all a setup to learn about her past? To garner her secrets and deliver them to Ivy? "Is this a trick?"

"No." There was raw honesty to his voice, edged with irritation. "I don't know your story, Cassia. Maybe you'll tell me one day. Maybe not. That's not what this is about."

"Then what is this about?"

"Tell me this." He leaned forward. "Would you be questioning this if Ivy weren't my sister?"

"Yes."

"So she's not the reason you don't trust me."

"No." Cassia's trust issues were courtesy of the two men she'd loved last.

Edwin sighed and dragged a hand through his hair. "I like you. That's it. That's why I wanted to meet you for breakfast. I think you're beautiful. You're smart. The fact that you don't give a fuck about impressing anyone is incredibly sexy. You're witty and sarcastic and beautiful."

Holy. Damn. Now that was an answer. She was stunned speechless.

"I said beautiful twice because it deserves to be said twice." He reached out and ran a knuckle over her cheek. "I don't date. Not really my thing these days. But here I am. For you."

Edwin Clarence was here for her.

"This is . . ." Mind boggling. Cassia was lost in the dream of his statement, so she took a sip of her coffee. Maybe the caffeine would wake her up, because clearly she was still asleep.

"Tell you what," he said. "Let's flip a coin. Heads, I spend breakfast talking about myself. Tails, you tell me why you came to Aston this year."

Before she could protest—there was no way she was agreeing to this—he dug a coin from his jeans pocket and flicked it in the air. Her heart hammered as he caught it and slapped it on the table.

"Heads." He shrugged, entirely unshocked.

Phew. Cassia had never been so terrified of a coin toss in her life. Thank God it had landed . . .

Wait. In a week of coin tosses, each one had landed on heads. Every time he'd flipped for the vending machine, it had landed heads. He'd bought candy each and every day, even though she'd always come with fifty cents in her backpack.

"Give me that coin." She swiped it from the table before he could stop her. Then she examined both faces. Heads on each. Her jaw dropped. "So this is why you're always winning the coin tosses. You're a cheat."

He chuckled. "Guilty."

And he'd positioned this coin toss so she wouldn't have to delve into her past like any other date.

"My father left me money for school." The confession flew off her tongue. Part of her just wanted Edwin to know. Not the whole story, but enough. Enough to show him that she was trying. "He always wanted me to have the best education. I told you he was a professor, so he knew a lot of people in academia. He said Aston's programs were renowned, so after he . . . I applied for a transfer to do my senior year here."

Edwin's face gentled. "I'm glad you did."

"Me too." For the first time, those words rang true.

Cassia was glad to be here. At Aston. And at breakfast.

Edwin smiled and sipped his coffee, then plucked a menu from the holder next to the salt and pepper shakers. "My brother is the developer for this area. He owns the buildings and this café is a favorite of his. According to Zain, the best meal on the menu is the hash."

"Sounds good." She didn't even bother with the menu. When the waitress arrived, they each ordered the hash. And then true to his word, Edwin talked only about himself.

Another date might have been irritated by the one-sided topic. To Cassia, it was the best conversation she'd had in months.

She had never been one to talk about herself or gloat,

even before her world had exploded at Hughes. After, well . . . maybe someday when she'd made sense of it. It would probably take extensive therapy.

"What will you do after graduation?" she asked. A week of studying together in the library and she'd learned he was in business and had quite a few classes with Elora.

"Work for my father in one of his companies."

"You don't sound excited about that."

He lifted a shoulder, his fork pushing across his empty plate. "It's just a job. Truthfully, I'd like to do something like Zain did here. But I need capital and my father and grandfather have locks on my trust funds until I'm thirty."

"So you'll what, bide your time? That's nine years."

"I'm a patient man, Red." He gave her a wide smile that revealed both dimples, and her heart thumped. Somehow, she knew what he was going to ask before he asked it. And that smile wasn't one she'd be able to turn down. "How about next Sunday? We do this again."

A second date? It went against her better judgment, against the siren in the back of her mind warning her she shouldn't trust him or anyone. But she held up the coin she'd kept on her side of the table during their meal.

"Heads is a yes. Tails is a no."

nineteen

. . .

BLOOD IS JUST BLOOD.

Zain's words had been looping through Elora's mind for a week.

After their ride last weekend, after she'd told him about her father not being her father, he'd been so logical. So calm. So . . . Zain.

Blood is just blood. Zain had told her that Lawrence Maldonado was her father and the source of her DNA didn't really matter. And just like that, a simple declaration, and some of the turmoil had eased.

She should have expected Zain to clear the fog. He had a way of balancing her moods. He was steady. He was nearly infallible. He was everything she needed.

And everything Elora refused to let herself hope for.

Yet hope bloomed inside her foolish heart.

She'd spent the week contemplating his words. And Zain himself. She'd retraced their relationship, from that first night to the last and all the ones in between.

In the beginning, Elora and Zain had stayed a secret to avoid Ivy's scorn or interference. But Ivy knew about them now, and her friend hadn't seemed to care in the slightest. An unexpected turn of events. *A damn miracle.* She wasn't going to complain.

Elora wasn't eighteen any longer, underage and sneaking into Zain's club. There weren't roadblocks keeping them apart.

No, it was fear driving this wedge between them. Fear was the reason she guarded her heart.

Her mother's indifference had burned her too many times. And too often, Elora had worried that she wasn't all that different from Joanna Maldonado.

Elora couldn't even count on her dad's genes as an antidote to her mom's poison.

Blood was just blood.

But if a person lost too much blood, they died.

If Zain rejected her, if he walked away, she'd never recover. Wasn't it better to avoid that inevitable outcome entirely?

Elora would rather live alone than suffer through a messy breakup. Or worse, endure it as Zain found someone better. Her parents had been cheating on each other for years, idly watching as the other took new partners to their respective beds.

If—*when*—Zain found a better woman, Elora would be utterly devastated.

Yet here she was, rash and pathetic and weak, standing at his door on a Sunday evening after he'd just buzzed her upstairs.

Her heart beat so hard she could feel its rhythm in her fingertips and toes. The lock flipped and then there he was, dressed in jeans and a crisp, pale-blue button-down, the color accentuating his eyes.

It was the reason she'd bought him that shirt last Christmas.

"Hi."

"Hi." He leaned against the door's frame, crossing his ankles. "How you holding up?"

"All right." She tucked her hands into the pockets of her leather jacket. "I forgot to say it last weekend, but thank you. For the ride. For listening."

"Welcome." He nodded. "I'm sorry. Don't think I said that either. But I'm sorry this is happening."

A lump formed in her throat. "Me too."

"Your dad loves you, El. That's what counts. Take it from a guy who has a shit father. Sometimes the blood in your veins is a curse, not a blessing."

More logic. More balance. Elora wanted to kiss him for it. Instead, she shied away, putting more distance between them. "I'd better go."

"Yeah, me too." He sighed and stood tall.

"Working today?"

"No, uh . . ." Zain gave her a tight smile. "I have a date."

She flinched.

He saw it.

"Oh. Right." She backed away, nearly tripping over her own feet. Then she raised a hand to wave before spinning toward the stairs.

"Elora," he called, stopping her on the third stair. "Give me a reason to cancel it."

She squeezed her eyes shut. Goddamn, how she wished she didn't love him this much. She wished she weren't terrified he'd leave her one day when he realized he could find someone warm and loving and carefree.

But this was reality. And he needed the woman she was not.

"I can't," she croaked.

Zain didn't say another word. He didn't need to. The sweep and click of the door closing was enough to send Elora racing down the stairs. She flew to her car, desperate to close herself inside the BMW. Then she started the engine, her hands shaking so hard that not even a firm grip on the steering wheel would stop the trembling.

She clenched her teeth so hard her molars ached.

If breaking away from Zain hurt this much now, how much would it hurt after another year? Or two? Or ten?

It had to end. This had to end.

Tears blurred her vision as she reversed away from his building and raced down the street. This pain was her own damn fault. She should have stopped this fling with Zain years ago, when she'd felt herself falling.

So the broken heart was her own fucking punishment. A penance for her stupidity and selfishness. Fuck, she'd been an idiot.

She drove, muscles tense, and let her rage brew. Elora was furious with herself. And she was livid with her mother.

And if Elora had to suffer, then it was time Joanna suffered too.

The trip to her parents' estate was short, the adrenaline making time fly. With her car parked, she stormed through the front door, blowing past the new butler as he attempted to welcome her with a greeting.

"Where is my mother?" she barked.

"In her study, I believe, Miss Maldonado." He had the sense to stare at the wall and avoid direct eye contact.

Elora fisted her hands at her sides as she walked, letting the emotion bubble free. And fuck, it felt good to let loose. To free the monster from its cage.

Her mother was sitting on a cream love seat in her study, typing on her phone. At the sound of Elora barging into her private space, Joanna's mouth pursed into a thin line.

Fuck, Elora hated how much they looked alike. She hated that her mother's plastic surgeon was so talented that she'd barely aged in ten years. During the infrequent times they were seen in public together, Joanna was always thought to be Elora's older sister.

"You're a whore." Elora's body drooped. Her fists unclenched and the breath that whooshed from her lungs was so loud it was like a gust of wind blowing through a thousand trees.

Relief. Sweet relief.

That had been buried too deep for far too long.

"Lovely." Joanna blinked, but that was all the reaction she gave her daughter before turning back to her phone. "I'm busy."

Elora slammed the door closed with as much force as she could summon. The print on the wall rattled. "I want to know who my father is."

Now she had Joanna's attention. Her dark eyes narrowed, her mind visibly spinning. "Are you drunk?"

"Answer me. Now."

Joanna pointed a perfectly manicured finger at her face. "Watch yourself."

"Tell me!" Elora screamed. If she had to bring the roof down, so be it.

"Shh," Mom hissed, tossing her phone aside to stand. She paced the length of the love seat, her shoulders pinned and her strides measured. But the flush in her face gave away her panic. "I don't know what has gotten into you."

"The truth," Elora said. "You can tell me who he is. Or I'll find out myself."

Mom stopped pacing and crossed her arms over her chest. "It doesn't matter."

"Fine." Elora spun for the door, her hand gripping the knob.

"Stop."

Elora froze, twisting her head until her chin was at her shoulder.

"He was a man I knew years ago. It was . . . fleeting. And he died."

The floor tilted beneath Elora's feet. Her mind whirled.

Dead.

Was that why her mother had kept the secret? Had he ever known about Elora? If he was gone, that made this mess simpler. She could go on pretending that Lawrence was her father—because he *was* her father—and forget this had ever happened. So why did she want to cry?

There was no strength in her body but she managed to open the door and walk on shaking legs down the hallway. She passed the foyer, heading toward her father's wing of the mansion.

Elora had no idea what she'd say to him, and at the moment, it didn't matter. All she wanted was a hug from her dad.

Her real dad.

Because her biological father was dead.

She was ten steps away from his office when she heard her brother's laugh. Tiptoeing toward the open door, she peeked inside to find both Dad and Lucas at a table beside the floor-to-ceiling windows. Their heads were bent over Lucas's phone, their faces alight with smiles.

Whatever video they were watching had them both bursting out in laughter, the joy ricocheting off the walls.

She'd made it to Lucas's game the day before. She'd put up a front with both her brother and father, managing to hide her emotions thanks to years of practice. But tonight, she didn't stand a chance.

If she walked in there, with her broken heart, she'd steal their joy. The secrets were too close to the surface, and she didn't trust herself to hold them in, so she backed away. She fled from the house, climbed in her car and drove.

For hours she drove, hoping that with every mile she'd find some peace like she had on the back of Zain's motorcycle last weekend. But as night fell and she sped through the darkness, there was no comfort to be found on the road.

There was nothing.

She felt nothing.

Elora returned to the manor, grateful for the numbness that had spread through her limbs. She was silent as she withdrew to her bedroom. Preferring to stay in the dark, she didn't bother with the lights.

Moonbeams streamed in silver rays through the windows, casting the space in the same shadowy gray that clouded her heart.

Elora made sure to lock her bedroom door, then kicked off her booties and shrugged off her jacket, leaving a trail of clothes on her way to the closet, where she changed into a pair of pajama shorts and Zain's sweatshirt.

She'd just come out of the closet, heading for her window seat, when a flicker of movement on the bed caught her attention. Elora gasped, her body tensing. "You scared me. What are you doing here?"

Zain's legs were stretched long on her bed, his back propped against a stack of pillows. He'd kicked off his shoes. The sleeves of his shirt were rolled up his forearms. He crooked his finger, calling her closer.

Elora's pulse pounded as she walked to the bed, stopping at its side. A rush of heat bloomed, chasing away the numbness from her drive, as he swung his legs over the bed's edge, spreading his thighs wide to make a space for her to stand.

"You fucked up my date."

A smile ghosted her lips. "Not sorry."

Zain grabbed her hips in a flash and tugged her close until their bodies were flush. He was so tall that even on her feet, they were nearly eye to eye. "I said this was over."

Elora leaned in to brush her lips across his. "And I said never again. Guess we're both liars."

They were equally helpless to resist.

A growl rumbled from his chest as she skimmed his bottom lip with her tongue.

"Zain," she whispered. "Fuck me."

"On your knees."

Her core throbbed as she obeyed, dropping to the floor, watching with rapt attention as Zain put his hands on his thighs and nodded to the bulge between his legs.

She bit the inside of her cheek to suppress a smile, then her fingers worked with practiced ease to release the button on his jeans. The zipper's click filled the room as she dragged it down. Zain raised his hips so she could tug at his jeans and free his cock.

She stilled when he sprang free.

No boxer briefs. He'd gone on his date commando? She shot him a glare. "Do I need a condom for this?"

"Worried I fucked someone else?"

"Have you?"

He raised his eyebrows. "Have *you*?"

She took his arousal in her fist, stroking the velvety flesh and using her thumb to swirl the pearly drop at its tip.

"Answer my question," he ordered. "Have you been with someone else?"

"No."

"Thank fuck." Zain threaded his fingers through her hair.

"Have you?"

He shook his head. "I want those pretty lips on my dick."

She took a moment to savor the relief. *Mine*. He was still hers. Maybe for just tonight. But tonight was when she needed him most. And as his erection throbbed, she felt his need in her grasp.

Elora leaned forward, taking him into her mouth. She moaned at his taste and the stretch at her lips.

"Christ," he murmured, leaning back on an elbow as she took him deep.

Elora didn't have much of a gag reflex, and as his crown moved further down her throat, she hummed.

Zain's tremble was her reward. "There's no mouth like yours, babe. God, I've missed it."

She'd missed him too. She'd missed this. Elora loved how he'd lose control when she sucked him off. She loved that she had the power to undo this beautiful, commanding man.

She sucked and licked, dragging her tongue across the sensitive flesh on the underside of his cock. She hummed again as his hold on her hair tightened, the vibration making him impossibly hard. Then he began rocking those hips, fucking her mouth.

"Touch yourself, Elora."

Her core throbbed, aching for more. Keeping one hand on his cock, she slipped the other beneath the waistband of her shorts, dipping them inside her drenched panties.

"Are you wet for me?"

She moaned her answer as her fingertip circled her clit. Round and round until her own climax was just seconds away.

"Do not come. Understood? I want to be inside you when you come."

His jaw was clenched tight. Her entire body pulsed, so desperate for a release, but she slowed the movements with her hand, moving away from her clit and dipping her fingers into her wet folds. Then she sucked Zain again, hollowing out her cheeks.

She worked him tirelessly, until she felt his thigh muscles bunch. Then, before he could pour down her throat, he pulled her away. Her lips were puffy, and when his thumb came to the corner of her mouth, she met his gaze.

"That's my girl," he whispered. "What do you want?"

You. All she'd ever wanted was Zain. "Your mouth."

With a swoop, he plucked her off the floor and tossed her on the bed. He tore off her shorts and the panties from her legs at the same time he kicked away his jeans. Then he fisted the sweatshirt, hauled her up to yank it over her head.

Her hands worked frantically to unbutton his shirt, wanting to feel his skin against hers. The moment it was open, he shrugged it off his shoulders and let it drop.

Zain gripped her the backs of her knees, dragging her toward the edge of the bed. He bent and buried his nose in her pussy, dragging in a long inhale. Then his tongue speared inside her sensitive flesh, causing her back to arch off the mattress.

"So sweet," he murmured, placing a kiss on her clit.

Elora's hands fisted in the bedding as he latched on to her

swollen nub and sucked. God, he could suck. She cried out in ecstasy, not caring if the whole house heard her scream his name.

Zain feasted on her flesh. He devoured her like she was his last meal, bringing her to the edge before easing off. Up and down, up and down. She was about to combust when his mouth disappeared.

She cracked her eyelids open as he hoisted her deeper into the bed. Her knees fell open, and the anticipation of him filling her was so much that she could hardly breathe.

Their eyes locked as he climbed on top of her and gripped his shaft, dragging the tip through her center. "Elora."

"Zain." His name fell from her lips as he thrust forward, stretching her inner walls and making them flutter. She was so sensitive, so aching, that just having him inside her nearly sent her over the edge.

"Look at us," he said. "Watch me sink into your body."

She dropped her gaze to where they were connected, watching as he withdrew, then pressed in deep. Stroke after stroke, the sight of them together, of their perfection, took her higher and higher. She watched until her orgasm detonated and white spots broke across her eyes.

Zain buried his face in her neck as she clenched around him, letting go of his own release on a roar.

They clung to each other, their bodies sticky with sweat.

It was foolish to let him into her bed. But when he tucked them both beneath the sheet, she didn't put up a fight.

Elora was playing with fire. She should have been sorry for being so weak.

But like she'd told him when he'd griped about her ruining his date—

Not sorry.

twenty

. . .

IVY STARED at the mess she'd made on the kitchen counter. Dirty bowls. Spatulas and wooden spoons. Two eggshells. A dusting of flour and sugar.

No matter how hard she worked to clean, Francis would know that someone had invaded her space. Her chef had a sixth sense about other people using the manor's kitchen, and this would likely earn Ivy a frown. *Worth it.*

As the scent of chocolate and vanilla infused the air, she closed her eyes and drew in a long inhale. Francis would also forgive the intrusion because Ivy had made her favorite cookies. This wasn't the first time Ivy had struggled to sleep and found herself in the kitchen after midnight.

The clock on the microwave glowed twelve. Maybe Zain would stop by for a cookie on his way out, assuming he didn't spend the night in Elora's bedroom. His Aston Martin had been parked in the loop when she'd come downstairs earlier.

She ignored the mess and propped a hip against the counter, waiting for the oven's timer to ding. The first batch was baking and she'd be up for another hour to finish the rest. Maybe once the cookies were finished, she'd be able to sleep.

Tomorrow promised to be a hectic day—her professors

loved doling out heavy assignments on Mondays. She should be in bed, except her body was as restless as her mind.

This always happened after a massive hangover. Ivy had spent yesterday in bed, nursing a skull-splitting headache and queasy stomach thanks to her escapades on Friday night. Tequila had seemed like a good idea at the time, but she gagged just thinking about it.

Her Saturday had been wasted, but when she'd woken up this morning, she'd felt a thousand times better and had studied most of the day. Then she'd dressed for bed in her favorite green flannel pajamas and tucked in for an early night. Three hours of tossing and turning later, she'd finally given up on sleep and come to the kitchen.

She picked up her phone, planning to scroll through TikTok for the last minute of the timer, but it buzzed in her hand with a text from an unknown number.

Hey, baby

Ivy stood straight, her heart skipping as she typed out a reply.

I told you to stop calling me baby

He called instead of replying. She debated kicking it to voicemail, making him suffer the way he'd made her suffer—Ivy had also nursed crippling embarrassment yesterday along with her hangover. But when it came to Tate, curiosity was a bitch.

"Yes?" she answered.

His deep laugh on the other end of the line sent tingles down her spine. "Wasn't sure you'd be awake."

"How'd you get my number?" she asked.

"How do you think?"

Zain.

The oven's timer dinged, so she sandwiched the phone between her shoulder and ear to pull on an oven mitt, taking out one pan before sliding in the next.

"What are you doing?" Tate asked.

"Baking cookies."

"Can't sleep?"

She moved the phone to her other ear. "Maybe I always make cookies on Sundays."

"Why can't you sleep?"

Ivy frowned, irritated that he seemed to know her so well already. "Sometimes I just can't."

Tate hummed. "What kind of cookies?"

"Chocolate chip."

"Are you going to open the door if I come over?"

Her pulse quickened. "Why would you come over?"

"For a cookie."

A stronger woman might say no. But yeah, she was going to cave. This man was beginning to consume far too many of her thoughts. As annoyed as she'd been about his rejection on Friday, she was glad one of them had kept a sliver of sense. Because she would have regretted it if he'd taken her to his bed. If he'd treated her like a one-night stand.

"I assume you know where I live," she said.

"I do. And I have the gate code."

Ivy rolled her eyes. "Zain and I are going to have a talk about sharing my private information."

Tate chuckled. "Be there in a few."

The moment he ended the call, Ivy flew into action, preparing another cookie sheet with lumps of dough. Then she rushed to put the kitchen to rights, cleaning so well that even Francis would be proud.

She swapped out the cookies when the timer went off, then raced to the front door as Tate's headlights came down the lane. Her hair was in a knot on top of her head. She wasn't wearing a bra and these pajamas were anything but sexy.

If this had been Michael, she would have left the kitchen alone and spent her moments primping. But something about Tate told her he wouldn't care about the hair or her lack of makeup.

Or maybe that was just Ivy's wishful thinking that a man might want to see *her*.

He parked his Land Rover in the loop, behind Zain's car, and climbed out, his long legs taking the stairs two at a time. Then he stood before her. Every time they met, he seemed taller. And more beautiful. But the scent of spice and soap was just as dizzying as always.

Tate's gaze roved over her body, head to bare toes. His lack of subtlety was one of the things she liked best about his company.

He wanted her. No question.

And she wanted him. She wanted to tear that dove-gray button-down off his broad shoulders and drag his black slacks from his thick thighs.

"You're dressed up," she said.

"I was at a meeting."

"On a Sunday night?"

He shook his head, putting a hand flat on her belly and pushing her inside, closing the door behind him. "My meeting was yesterday in Las Vegas. I stayed the night. Just flew back."

"Ah."

"You ever been?"

"Once. Didn't love it." Ivy had spent most of that trip drunk in a hotel's penthouse suite. She wasn't into gambling and the girls she'd gone with had each found hookups within the first hour of going to a club. She hadn't been in the mood for a random guy, so she'd gone to her room and raided the minibar.

"I'll take you one day," he said. "Change your mind."

A weekend in Vegas with Tate? That would be a trip she wouldn't mind spending in a hotel room. "What makes you think I'd want to go with you?"

He leaned down, his lips brushing the shell of her ear. "Baby."

A single word to call her bluff. God, it was frustrating how quickly he'd figured her out. How her usual games weren't just unnecessary, but complete failures.

She forced herself a step away before she forgot the oven and burned the manor down. "Come on."

Ivy turned and walked to the kitchen, his footsteps sounding in the foyer as he followed.

The timer was seconds away from beeping, so she went to the oven while Tate stood next to the counter, unbuttoning the cuffs of his shirt to roll them up his forearms.

Ivy felt his eyes on her, his attention rapt on her every movement as she took out the cookies, turned off the oven and used her spatula to add the last batch to the cooling rack.

Electricity crackled in the air. The heat between them was an oven of its own. One cookie barely made it to the cooling rack because she could barely keep the spatula steady under his devoted attention.

Ivy couldn't remember a time when the sheer presence of a man had been such a turn-on. Maybe with Michael. But there was something different about Tate. Magnetism. That constant undercurrent of desire. The maturity of a man who knew exactly who he was and what he wanted.

"You had a busy weekend," Ivy said, needing conversation to break the sexual tension. "Club 27 on Friday. Vegas Saturday."

He walked closer and stretched past her, taking a cookie. "I've got a lot happening at the moment."

"Like what?" Did he have another woman he was driving wild?

"Business." He took a bite from the cookie and hummed as he chewed. "Yum."

She shrugged. "They're about the only thing I can make."

"Best cookie I've had in a while." He proved it by devouring the rest and going for a second, eating it just as quickly. "Thanks for this. I haven't eaten since lunch."

"Welcome." She walked to the fridge and took out a jug of

milk, pouring each of them a glass. Then she took her own cookie, tearing off a bite. "What kind of business?"

"I lived in Vegas for seven years. Owned a club. Been working to sell it since I moved back. As of yesterday, it's no longer mine."

"Congratulations." She clinked her glass of milk to his. "Why'd you leave Vegas?"

"It was time," Tate said, going for his third cookie. "I was ready to come home. Be closer to family."

"Then your family must be different than mine. Living across the country seems like a brilliant post-graduation idea." She hadn't heard from the Smithsonian, and with every passing day, she figured her father had killed that dream along with many others.

"All families come with difficulties, but I won't lie. Mine is pretty great."

"What would that be like?" she teased, except it came out more wistfully than she'd intended.

"You've got Zain and Edwin."

She nodded. Yes, she had her brothers, but they were each busy with their own lives. Her relationship with Zain was already thin. Edwin spent less and less time with her, and the time he did spend was usually spent lecturing her about, well . . . drama.

"Now that you sold your club, what are your plans?" she asked, not wanting to dive into the Clarence family dynamics.

"I'm thinking of buying Club 27."

Ivy cocked her head. "Really? Wouldn't that compete with Zain?"

"Don't worry." He touched the tip of her nose. "There are plenty of nightclub goers for us both. He came with me to scope it out a while back. I'll make some changes, fire most of the staff and start fresh, but the current owner is . . . motivated to sell."

"He's broke?"

"Not broke. He's about to go to prison on drug distribution charges."

"What?" Her jaw dropped. "Really?"

"There's a reason I don't like seeing you there alone."

"Now my brother's warning makes sense," she muttered. "Zain could have just told me the truth instead of being so damn cryptic."

"He didn't tell you because he didn't want rumors flying," Tate said. "Last thing I need is to take over a club that everyone is gossiping about. I'd rather clean it up quietly, fly under the radar."

"So Zain just assumed I'd start rumors." Ivy scoffed. "What a vote of confidence from my brother."

"Hey." Tate slid closer, moving to set his glass aside. "I don't think you'll say anything. That's why I'm telling you."

"Thanks." Except the damage was done. Zain didn't trust her. She shouldn't have been surprised or hurt.

"Zain and I go a long way back," Tate said. "He doesn't trust many people."

"He trusts you."

Tate nodded. "Yes, he does."

"I'm his sister."

"You're nine years younger. He was gone by the time you were growing up. What he knows is that you were raised by his parents. People he does know and absolutely does not like or trust."

"You're saying the reason Zain doesn't trust me is because he thinks I'm like our mom and dad."

Tate shrugged. "He doesn't know what to do with you, Ivy."

"He told you that?" she whispered.

"He did. So show him who you are."

Who was she?

She didn't know the answer. Worse, if she tried to find the words, would she like the story that came from her mouth?

"Hey." Tate took her glass, setting it aside. Then he

pushed a lock of hair away from her forehead. "What's that frown for?"

She kept her gaze locked with his. The answer to that question was too complicated, so she asked one of her own. "Why'd you come here tonight? Because we both know it wasn't for a cookie."

"Guess."

"For me."

"Yep." He leaned closer, brushing his lips across hers. Then his tongue dragged across the seam of her lips. "And I know *exactly* what to do with you."

Ivy's entire body was on fire, the heat between her legs unbearable. This man had worked her up in just minutes and he'd barely touched her. "If you walk away this time without kissing me, I swear to make your life a living hell."

He laughed, the rumble only stoking her desire. Tate broke away, his eyes so dark with lust that the chocolate swirls had nearly faded to black. "I'm tempted to leave just to see what you'd do. Got a feeling I'd enjoy your brand of torture. But . . ."

"Tate." Ivy stood on her toes, nipping at his bottom lip. Yet still, he didn't kiss her. She let out a frustrated sigh, about to kick him out of her kitchen.

But then his mouth was on hers, swallowing her gasp.

She melted. Totally. Fucking. Melted.

His taste, mixed with the chocolate from the cookie, consumed her senses and she moaned as he tangled his tongue with hers. Tate's arms banded around her, hauling her to his body so hard it was like touching granite. He put her exactly where he wanted her, just like their first dance.

The heat from his chest seeped through her pajamas and pebbled her nipples, sending a new rush of need to her core. Then he slanted his lips over hers to plunder every corner of her mouth.

Ivy had let men kiss her. She'd allowed it.

But this?

Tate claimed her. She was entirely out of control, and for once, she reveled in the surrender.

This was a man who knew exactly what he wanted and wasn't shy about taking it.

Her hands clung to his sides, gripping the crisp fabric of his shirt. She whimpered when he thrust his hips forward, his arousal like stone against her hip.

God, she was going to come if he kept this up. Fully clothed in flannel pajamas, she was going to orgasm from a kiss alone.

She lifted a leg, wanting to wrap it around his hip and use the friction to relieve her ache, but before she could hook her leg around his, he was gone, tearing his mouth away and stalking to the opposite end of the kitchen.

Ivy blinked, working to clear the fog from her mind. She put one hand on the counter to keep from swaying.

"Woman." Tate dragged a hand over his mouth, stopping next to the fridge. He planted his hands on his waist, dropping his head as his chest heaved.

"Why'd you stop?"

He looked at her, his jaw clenched. "I'm not fucking you tonight."

"I'm getting sick and tired of hearing you tell me all the times you're *not* going to fuck me."

"So am I," he muttered, raking a hand through his dark hair. "But not yet."

"Why?" Ivy crossed her arms over her chest, the high from the kiss fading to anger. "Am I not good enough? Am I too young? Give me a decent reason."

He crossed the room in a flash, forcing her against the counter. "Because I want you to crave me just a fraction of how much I crave you. Because I want you so worked up you can't see straight."

Great answer. "You're very blurry."

He dropped his forehead to hers, then he reached past her

for another cookie, snagging one before striding to the door. "Night, baby."

"That's it?" she called.

Tate raised a hand and kept walking.

Ivy picked up her oven mitt and threw it at his head. She missed. "I'm never making you cookies again."

"Go to bed, Ivy."

"Don't tell me what to do."

Tate's laugh echoed from the hallway.

She grumbled, giving herself a moment to pout, before putting the cookies away. Then she shut off the lights in the kitchen and climbed the stairs to her bedroom.

"That bastard," she muttered, slipping beneath her sheets.

She should have been more aggressive when she'd threatened him. She should have demanded more than just a kiss. Maybe what Tate needed was a taste of what he was missing.

Maybe she'd torture him, just a little.

Ivy stretched for her phone, unlocking the screen and pulling up the camera. She turned on the bedside lamp so that her face was cast in muted light as she propped herself up against her headboard. Then she set the phone against a pillow to her side, making sure it would capture her profile at just the right angle.

The screen showed her face. It showed her torso. It showed the sliver of skin she exposed on her stomach when she pushed the bedding down her lap and slipped her hand inside the waistband of her pajama pants.

The recording wasn't long. All Ivy had to do was think of Tate's tongue in her mouth and she was on the edge of an orgasm. Her finger circled her clit, her movements getting faster and faster as her breath came in jagged hitches. Then she was coming, her eyes squeezing shut as her moan of ecstasy filled the room.

She breathed heavily, waiting for the aftershocks to fade. It wasn't enough. Not nearly enough. But it was all she'd get tonight.

After stopping the video and making a quick trip to the bathroom, Ivy snuggled into her bed, turning off the lamp. A yawn pulled at her mouth as she saved Tate's number into her contacts. Her eyelids were heavy as she burrowed deeper into her pillows. She yawned, ready to text Tate the video, when her phone dinged.

Thinking of you tonight.

Michael. The caption came with a photo of him in his own bed, his shirt off and a smirk on his handsome face. It wasn't the first time he'd texted her late at night for a hookup. But it was the first time she'd wished he were someone else.

She went back to her video, trying to think of a snarky caption for Tate. A sleepy grin stretched across her mouth as she typed. Ivy yawned again, then hit send and tossed her phone aside.

Within seconds, she drifted off to sleep.

The next morning, the first thing she did was reach for her phone, expecting a message from Tate.

Except it wasn't his name on the screen. It was Michael's again.

That's hot.

"What?" She scrolled up, only to find her video. In her rush, she'd sent that video to Michael instead of Tate.

Damn.

twenty-one

. . .

"LAME. I'M SO LAME," Cassia told herself in the mirror, her voice garbled from the toothbrush in her mouth. A senior in college and her Halloween plans included a DIY facial and going to bed by nine. The only costume she'd be wearing was these purple flannel pajama pants and matching tee.

It wasn't much different than any of her other Saturdays since coming to Aston, but tonight, it bothered her more than usual.

But at least she had Sundays.

Sundays had become Cassia's favorite day of the week.

Edwin had given her a standing invitation to a Sunday breakfast at the café in his brother's development. They'd shared three Sunday breakfasts in a row. Tomorrow would make four.

Were they dating? Did studying in the library together count as dates? Was she even ready to date?

Or had he changed his mind?

He'd said that he liked her, but otherwise, he'd given her no indication that he intended to take it further. Three breakfasts without a hug. Without a kiss on the cheek. Without so much as a brush of his hand against hers. Three breakfasts and . . . nothing.

Maybe he'd changed his mind? Maybe whatever allure she'd had early on had finally worn off, and now he saw her for what she really was.

Lame.

But that was a good thing, right? She wasn't ready to date. She wasn't ready for a guy in her life. Not yet. It was too soon.

"It's good, Cassie."

She used her old name more often these days when she talked to herself. It didn't hurt as much to be Cassie.

Time was healing her wounded heart. Or maybe Cassie and Cassia were becoming one and the same. Together, they were stronger. Though at the moment, both wished there was more to a Saturday night than pajamas and skin care.

She spit her toothpaste into the sink and rinsed her mouth, then flipped off the light in the bathroom.

Cassia rose on her toes as she stepped into the bedroom's open space, lifting a leg and spinning in a pirouette. Her muscles strained—her balance was shit. But the rush of the familiar was so comforting that she smiled and did the spin again. Then she reached her arms over her head, stretched toward the ceiling and closed her eyes.

Months. It had been months since she'd danced. Months since she'd *wanted* to dance. But that little twirl had come from deep in her heart, like a butterfly waiting to be set free from its cocoon.

Cassia elongated her body, feeling her spine straighten. Then she bent, her back arching and her arms falling behind her as she gave her heart to the heavens. She could only hold the pose for a brief second before her legs faltered and she had to stand upright.

A giggle escaped her lips. She'd probably hurt herself if she pushed too hard but . . .

"Screw it." She leapt across the room.

Her old ballet instructors would cringe at her technique.

They'd shake their heads at a body gone slack. But the foundation was there. And more importantly, the desire.

Maybe her Saturday wasn't doomed after all.

Cassia rushed to her nightstand, opening her phone and pulling up an old playlist. Then she let the music blare at the highest volume while she danced around her room.

Her arms warmed first, finding their way to wings. Her legs came next as she shut off her brain and let muscle memory take control. This room, with the open floor and plethora of space, was perfect for her to let go of whatever had kept her from enjoying this.

Tonight, she danced for Cassie. For Cassia. She danced because once upon a time, her dad had worried that his daughter hadn't had enough *girl* in her life, so he'd enrolled her in ballet at eight. She'd loved it so much that she'd never stopped. Dancing had become her sanctuary.

Until her dad had died. And everything associated with him had died too.

An ache spread through her heart, grief that she hadn't let herself feel. Her feet stopped. Her arms dropped to her sides. Her chest rose and fell while she tried to regain her breath and shove the pain aside.

Her hands fisted and she closed her eyes before she could cry.

Why? She wanted to scream that question into the night, but no answer would come from the void.

Why?

How could he do this to her? How could he leave her like this? Had she really meant so little to him?

A ding echoed through the room, the music fading for a moment. Cassia ripped her mind away from the past, those unanswered questions, and walked to her phone, her footsteps as heavy as her heart.

Until Edwin's name appeared on the screen.

Front door.

She swept up her phone and raced from the room barefoot. A thrill carried her through the hall and down the staircase. She opened the door to find him outside, then laughed. "Nice costume."

Edwin was wearing a white toga with a wreath of greenery around his head. The fabric cut across his shoulder, showcasing a defined and extremely sexy shoulder.

"Still no hello." He chuckled and stepped inside.

"Hello."

"Better." He grinned. "I come bearing gifts."

"Besides your charming personality?" she teased.

"You love my charm." He leaned in close, his lips caressing her cheek. The kiss took her by surprise, so much so that it took Cassia a moment to realize he'd thrust a bag into her arms. "Go change."

"Huh?"

"Change. We're going out."

"Oh, uh . . ."

"No excuses." He took her shoulders and turned her, giving her a tiny push toward the stairs. "It's Halloween. If I have to suffer through tonight in a costume, so do you."

She held up the bag. "If this is some slutty nurse or teacher or angel costume, you can forget it."

"I know you well enough by now to know you're not the slutty nurse type."

That comment made her footsteps pause.

He did know her, didn't he? And she was getting to know him. They'd talked at length about his long-term plans once he had control over his inheritance. They'd shared the mundane details of daily life, complaining about professors and agonizing over assignments and celebrating test scores.

"I'm nervous to go out," she confessed. "Last time was . . . you were there."

"I was there. But we'll have fun. Promise." He reached for the scrunchie she'd used to tie up her hair and tugged it free.

Between the kiss on the cheek and the hair tie, it was more

than he'd touched her in weeks. Her heart skipped, but Cassia couldn't decide if it was in excitement or panic.

It was too soon for a guy. Wasn't it?

"I won't let you down, Red."

That nickname alone was worth the hassle of dyeing her hair regularly. "Fine."

Cassia made her way to the stairs as Edwin waited in the foyer. The sight of him in that toga sent a flush to her face. His arms were bulkier than she'd realized, since he normally wore hoodies and long-sleeved shirts on campus. But bare, well . . . the sight of him was as delicious as a bowl of Halloween candy.

All it would take was a tug at the shoulder and that costume would fall to the floor. God, he was tempting.

Too tempting.

She tore her eyes away and hustled to her room. It didn't take her long to put on her makeup, adding some red lipstick for courage and a quick curl to her hair. Then she pulled on the costume he'd brought.

Cassia had gone to a toga party once. With Josh. They'd worn bedsheets held together with rubber bands, knots and well-placed duct tape.

Of course Edwin wouldn't bring her a sheet. This consume was perfectly fitted for a woman's body. While his had one shoulder strap, hers had two that formed a low V, the cut dipping between her breasts. The waist was tied with a golden rope, and the skirt had two long slits that ran up her thighs.

He hadn't brought shoes, so she slipped on her favorite Birkenstocks. Leave it to Edwin to pick a costume that made her feel like a Greek goddess—in comfortable shoes.

The sandals would have been reward enough, except as she descended the stairs, Edwin's gaze, full of heat, tracked her every step. "You should wear togas every day."

"We're very matchy."

Edwin met her at the bottom stair, taking the leafy ring

from his head and putting it on hers. "The matching is intentional. That way everyone at the club knows who you belong to."

Her heart skipped at the meaning, but her stomach clenched at that word. *Belong.*

She'd belonged to a man once.

And he'd destroyed her life.

"What did I say?" he asked, his eyebrows coming together.

She waved it off. "Nothing."

"Tell me. You got this look on your face."

"I don't want to belong to anyone but myself," she admitted.

"Fair enough," he said. "Then how about this. We match so everyone at the club will know who *I* belong to."

Whatever unease she'd had a moment ago vanished.

Cassia wanted so badly to trust him. To believe his every word. But she wasn't quite there yet. After everything that had happened at Hughes, maybe she never would be. "So where exactly are we going?"

"Treason."

She groaned.

"Don't worry." He laughed and took her hand. "It'll be fun. And if it's not, I'll bring you home."

"Okay." She followed him to the door, closing it behind them. The cold air bit into her skin, raising bumps.

"Want me to grab you a coat?" he asked.

"I'll be all right."

Edwin opened her door to his Bentley, waiting until she had her dress tucked around her legs before shutting her inside. The scent of his cologne filled her nose as he slid behind the wheel, turning on her seat warmer before they sped through the night.

The trip to Treason was shorter than it had been with Elora. The nerves she'd had the first time were different tonight. Her anxiety was more about Edwin than it was the club itself.

What did he want from her? He had to want something, right?

Except as much as she wanted to know the answer, she couldn't bring herself to ask. Maybe because if he told her the truth, it would end this friendship.

And right now, her friendship with Edwin was keeping her going.

From Sunday breakfast to Sunday breakfast.

"Did you study all day?" he asked.

"Pretty much. I have a test on Monday."

"Alone? Or did you meet with your study group?"

"Alone." Michael had asked if she'd wanted to join them at the library, but she'd opted to study at home because it was more efficient. Her classmates, including Michael, spent a solid hour on small talk and gossip before actually studying. And Michael had been asking more questions lately, curious about her past.

They were the normal get-to-know-your-friend type of questions, but his relationship with Ivy was a red flag. And since she was tired of dodging his overtures, she'd skipped the study group altogether.

"What about you?" Cassia asked.

"I spent my Saturday shopping for matching Halloween costumes." Edwin looked over and winked as he turned into the club's parking lot.

Her heart rate spiked as he drove around the building, parking the Bentley in a reserved space.

"Ready?" he asked.

No. "Yep."

Unlike the time she'd come with Elora, they didn't round the building for the front entrance. Edwin led her to a rear door, stopping at a keypad to punch in a code. The lock clicked. One step inside and they were swallowed by the music.

Edwin stretched a hand behind him, interlocking their fingers as he pulled her deeper into the club. He nodded to the bouncer stationed at the rear entrance, then led the way toward the lounges.

"Want to dance?" Edwin asked. He had to lean back and speak almost directly in her ear so she could hear him over the pounding bass.

"No." Cassia shook her head.

She'd had enough dancing for one night.

He took the staircase to the lounges slowly, stopping every few steps to shake his free hand with someone passing by. And while it was too loud for him to make introductions, his hand never left hers. That, along with the matching costumes, was introduction enough.

Either people would think they were Halloween fuck buddies.

Or they'd assume Edwin and Cassia were a couple.

That label was intimidating. She was managing a friendship, the breakfasts and study sessions. But a couple? It felt rushed. Yet she couldn't pull her hand from his. She didn't even try. She just stood beside Edwin as he smiled and charmed.

"Sorry," he said after getting stopped for the tenth time.

"You're very popular."

"It's Zain." He shrugged. "Everyone wants to know the owner's brother. They think they'll get free drinks or access to his lounge if they kiss my ass."

"That's . . ."

"Annoying? Tell me about it."

"That sucks." She gave him a sad smile. "Sorry."

"You know what I think I like most about you, Red? You don't want anything from me."

No, that wasn't true. At this exact moment, she wanted him to keep hold of her hand.

"Let's go." He jerked his chin up the stairs, tugging her along to the third tier, where a bouncer dressed in head-to-toe black moved aside to let them into the lounge.

It wasn't quite as busy as the rest of the club, but there was still hardly any room to walk. They shuffled together, Cassia hovering close to Edwin's tall frame, as he made his way to the bar.

Everyone was dressed in some sort of costume, and almost every woman was in a skimpy number. When they passed a sexy nurse, Edwin smirked over his shoulder, wagging his eyebrows.

She laughed and rolled her eyes.

Cassia scanned the crowd, clutching Edwin's hand, as she searched for either of her roommates. She hadn't seen Ivy or Elora since Wednesday, a brief encounter as they'd come into the kitchen one morning when she'd been running late to escape the manor before seven.

Eventually, she had to stop hiding from them. She needed to stop letting their schedules dictate hers. But at the moment, it was easier this way.

"Who are you looking for?" Edwin asked.

"Elora and Ivy." She fought a lip curl at his sister's name.

"They're not here. The Sigmas host an annual Halloween party. Ivy and Elora are always on the guest list."

"You don't go?"

"Not this year."

Because of her. Because coming to Treason was one thing but heading to Michael's fraternity was another.

Been there. Done that.

After waiting in the short line, they finally made it to the bar. Edwin was about to order their drinks when a man appeared at their side, clapping him on the shoulder.

Edwin's face lit up. "Hey. Busy night."

"It's fucking great." The man laughed. He was gorgeous and dressed in a tailored black suit.

Cassia looked between the two men, and it clicked.

Brothers. This had to be Zain.

Edwin tugged her closer. "Cassia Collins. Meet my brother, Zain Clarence."

"Nice to meet you," Zain said.

"You too." She smiled, taking in the similarities. Zain was older with lines crinkling his eyes. Where Edwin had this easy-going and smooth way about him, Zain had an intimidating edge. Maybe it was his age. Maybe it was because he owned this club.

Maybe it was because she'd never stood next to two men so utterly breathtaking.

"Are you going to be here for a while?" Zain asked Edwin.

Edwin nodded. "As long as she wants."

"I'm busy tonight." Zain checked his watch. "I've got some people coming that I need to see to. But come find me if you need anything."

"Will do." Edwin nodded.

Zain waved the bartender closer. "Whatever they want tonight. Pull from my shelf."

"Yes, sir," the bartender said as Zain clapped Edwin on the shoulder one more time before disappearing into the crowd.

"Tequila," Edwin ordered. "Clase Azul."

Cassia didn't recognize the brand, but she opened her mouth to object—she'd had tequila once and only once and that experience had been bad enough to remember the liquor's horrible taste.

Except her objection went unspoken as the bartender set out two frosted shot glasses. He filled them with liquid from the most beautiful hand-painted bottle she'd ever seen.

Edwin handed her a shot, her fingertips cooling on the glass. Then with his hand on the small of her back, they inched out of the line to a quiet corner next to the railing.

"Cheers." He clinked the rim of his glass to hers, then tipped it back, swallowing it in a gulp.

She did the same. The tequila was cold too, a surprising contrast to the burn as the alcohol made its way to her belly. And the taste was entirely different than she remembered.

"How expensive was that shot?" she asked.

"Expensive." He chuckled. "Zain's shelf only has the best."

"Ah. Why is it cold?"

Edwin shrugged. "It's better cold."

Cold tequila seemed like a rich person's preference.

Cassia turned her attention toward the club, peering down at the lounges below and the space next to the bar. She was surrounded by rich people. Was that why she'd been so uncomfortable on her last visit to Treason? Except tonight the club wasn't stuffed with women in swanky, designer dresses and men in tailored suits. The Halloween costumes balanced the scales.

Edwin lifted the glass from her hand and set it on a nearby table. Then he adjusted the wreath on her head that had gone crooked when she'd taken her shot. "Having fun?"

"Actually, yeah. I am." This was fun. It was a welcome break to the Saturday nights spent in her room alone. And as the alcohol seeped into her blood, she felt her body relax. She felt herself breathe.

"Mr. Clarence." A waitress appeared with a tray holding two more shots.

"Thanks." Edwin picked them up and handed one over.

"I don't drink that much," Cassia warned.

"This one. Then we'll call it quits."

She nodded and took the shot, once more clinking her glass to his before bringing it to her mouth. She savored the taste this time. Enjoyed it. Memorized it.

Leave it to her taste buds to like what was entirely out of her price range.

Cassia laughed.

"What?" Edwin asked, taking away her glass.

"I was just thinking that my taste buds like what I can't afford."

His blue eyes sparkled as his hands came to her face, his fingers threading through the hair at her temples. "Fuck, but I want to kiss you."

Yes. She wanted it. She'd wanted it for weeks. The doubts, the insecurities, the warnings, the objections . . . they should have been front of mind. Except the only thought in her head was *yes*.

"What do you say, Red?" He leaned in, pulling her so close she had to rise up on her toes. "Gonna let me kiss you?"

"Yes."

It had barely escaped her mouth before his lips were on hers, chilled from their shots. But soon the warmth of his mouth melted into her bones. The people in the lounge, the music and the noise, became a dull rumble in the background as Edwin's kiss erased the world.

He dragged his tongue across her bottom lip, seeking entrance. She opened for him and he didn't hesitate. As his strong body pressed against hers, desire pooled in her core. A hunger she hadn't felt in a long time clawed to be set free. To give in. To feel. To want.

To fuck.

Her heart thumped as his teeth nipped the corner of her lips.

Edwin pulled away before she was ready and the lust in his eyes only made her want him more.

Oh shit, she was in trouble. She'd awoken a beast—her own. And there was no way she'd stop him tonight.

Not until she found out exactly what was beneath his toga.

twenty-two

. . .

ELORA YAWNED. Had the Sigma party always been this dull?

"No yawning!" a guy yelled. He was dressed as a banana. He was the same guy who'd yelled when she'd yawned five minutes ago.

"Ivy." She elbowed her friend in the ribs.

Ivy yawned too. "What?"

Elora quirked an eyebrow.

"Yeah, this is awful," Ivy admitted. "Want to leave?"

"Twenty minutes ago."

Ivy nodded and pointed toward the party room's exit. They started across the space but progress was slow given the number of people crammed down here.

The party room was nothing but an open basement beneath the fraternity's house. The concrete floors were sticky from spilled drinks. The air reeked of sweat. A bar in the corner had been set up with three kegs and a garbage can full of red jungle juice.

Elora wouldn't have taken a cup of that juice for a million dollars.

Even Ivy had abstained from drinking. The only reason

they'd come tonight was to make an appearance. It wasn't easy to secure a spot on the coveted Sigma Halloween party's list and only a fool would waste the invitation.

Or maybe only fools cared to be seen.

Elora was surrounded by faces she didn't recognize, and it had nothing to do with the costumes. Most of the people here seemed to be younger Aston students, like sophomores and juniors who weren't allowed to legally go to a club.

She yawned again, unable to stop.

There were a few familiar faces in the crush, mostly Sigmas and some sorority girls. Across the room, Allison Winston pranced as a Playboy Bunny. The bitch. Elora disliked Allison, but Ivy hated her with a passion. At last year's Sigma party, Ivy had *accidentally* bumped Allison, causing her to spill her drink over her costume.

Elora didn't have the energy for that sort of drama tonight. What she needed was a shower followed by at least eight hours of sleep.

After what felt like an eternity, they finally reached the door to the stairwell. In the corner, a guy dressed as a cowboy had a girl pressed against a wall. The girl's giggle was like nails on a chalkboard, and Elora cringed.

Never again. Even if this wasn't her last year at Aston, she'd never come to the Sigma house again.

Ivy sneered at the cowboy's back. "If I ever tell you I want to come here again, please slap me."

Elora nodded. "Deal."

"What a waste of hair and makeup," Ivy muttered.

They'd spent most of the day getting ready for tonight. A costume makeup artist had come to the manor and spent hours on their faces.

Ivy was dressed in green, as always, her sequined dress shimmering as they made their way upstairs. Her makeup was relatively simple with green around her eyes and forehead. The artist had styled her blond hair in space buns before threading it with ivy vines.

Elora's makeup had taken considerably more time to paint, an exquisite sugar skull design. One of her eyes was outlined in black, detailed with red and white dots. Her other eye was a myriad of reds and golds and whites. The intricate design had taken an hour.

Her lips, stained maroon, had a stitched line that stretched to her cheeks. That same stitching was woven across her forehead and cheeks.

But beyond her face, her costume wasn't much of a costume. Her dress was a strapless black number she'd found in her closet. The same was true for her heels.

Elora just didn't . . . care. About Halloween. About a party. About her appearance.

They reached the landing and followed the maze of hallways toward the front door. Ivy's fingers flew over the screen on her phone as she walked, summoning her driver.

Elora felt the cold breeze from the open door—she was desperate for some fresh air—but before they could escape, a man's voice called from behind them.

"Ivy!"

Damn. They both turned as Michael walked their way.

His steps were unhurried, like he knew they'd wait. He was dressed as Hugh Hefner, from the white sailor's cap to the red velvet robe to the satin black pants and the pipe he held in a hand.

And now Allison Winston's Playboy Bunny costume made sense.

Had Ivy noticed?

Michael was good looking and rich, but Elora had never seen the appeal. His arrogance was stifling and had always rubbed her the wrong way. That, and he was much too friendly with Allison Winston.

Part of her thought that was why Ivy was interested in Michael. Not so much for the guy, but to piss off another girl.

"Hey." He jerked his chin up at Elora, then leaned in to drop a kiss on Ivy's cheek. "You're leaving?"

"Yes," Elora said before Ivy could say otherwise.

Michael pouted. "Stay."

"Don't you have a little bunny to entertain you tonight?" Ivy asked with a saccharine smile. So she *had* seen Allison.

"It's just a costume." He shrugged, then lifted a hand to trail it down her bare arm. "Stay awhile. Twenty minutes. Ten. I'll take whatever I can get."

Elora knew from the sigh Ivy blew out that she was going to stay. But even if Michael convinced Ivy to stay for ten minutes, that was ten minutes too long.

"I'm leaving," Elora told Ivy.

"You can take the car. Just send him back once he drops you off."

Without a word, Elora strode from the house, leaving Ivy in Michael's clutches. Or maybe it was the other way around. She still hadn't figured out their power games.

The town car was waiting in the Sigmas' circular driveway when she stepped outside. The moment she slid into the back seat and closed the door, she breathed in the quiet.

"Ivy is staying here," she told the driver. "You're supposed to come back after dropping me off."

The driver nodded. "Back to the manor, Miss Maldonado?"

"No. To Treason. Please."

"Of course."

Elora liked this driver. He only spoke when absolutely necessary and seemed to prefer driving in silence instead of having the radio on low. That, and he had kind green eyes. His hair was snow white, and for some reason, she pictured him with grandchildren. What was his name? Ryan? Riley? Roy.

"Roy."

His eyes flicked to hers through the rearview mirror before darting back to the road. "Yes, miss?"

"Never run a yellow light. Never go over the speed limit.

Ivy runs through drivers like water through sand. She'll fire you without hesitation if she thinks you're a bad driver."

He pondered her words for a moment, then gave her another nod. "Thank you."

Elora hadn't warned the drivers before, just like she hadn't warned the previous roommates the way she'd warned Cassia. Why him? Why her?

Maybe it had nothing to do with the driver or the roommate and everything to do with the fact that she was entirely drained of energy. She didn't want to learn a new driver's name or meet another roommate.

In the two weeks that had passed since the confrontation with her mother, Elora's emotional fortitude had dipped to an all-time low. Joanna hadn't reached out to her, not that Elora had expected anything from her mother. Certainly not an apology.

So along with her secrets, she carried a mountain of resentment.

The weight was so heavy on her shoulders that by the end of each day, she felt like she'd run a marathon. Each morning, it became harder and harder to get out of her bed—her empty bed.

She hadn't heard from Zain in the past two weeks. Not since the night she'd found him in her room after she'd unapologetically ruined his date. He was likely putting up walls and moving on with his life. Nothing had changed.

They were over.

Going to Treason tonight was a mistake. Elora regretted her decision and they hadn't even arrived. Yet she just . . . needed to see him. She needed to steal a sliver of his strength, like she had two weeks ago, to endure this for a bit longer.

The holidays were approaching. She couldn't ruin Thanksgiving and Christmas for Dad and Lucas. If she could make it through New Year's, then she'd find the right opportunity to discuss this with her father.

Her eyes were heavy, the swaying motion of the car nearly

lulling her to sleep. But then they slowed and she straightened while Roy pulled up to the club's entrance.

"I can open my door," she said.

"Will you be needing a ride home?"

"No, I'll be fine."

He nodded. "Then I'll return to get Miss Clarence."

The line outside the club was rowdy tonight, the chatter loud as she stepped out of the car. There was an extra bouncer stationed at the door. The music seemed deafening tonight, like the beat was pulsing through the walls. Its tempo matched the throb behind Elora's temples.

She had no doubt that if she texted Roy, he'd turn around and pick her up, but she pushed forward, her desire to see Zain overpowering the blooming headache.

Treason was packed to capacity with costume-clad patrons. The club was ablaze with vivacity and all she wanted to do was sleep. Elora was bumped and jostled constantly as she made her way toward the lounges. She was about to head up the stairs for Zain's tier when she glanced up and stopped.

Above, Cassia and Edwin were standing next to the railing in coordinating toga costumes. Edwin bent low to whisper something in Cassia's ear.

Interesting. Not surprising though. Edwin had always preferred the bookworm type, probably because it was so anti–Helena Clarence. Their socialite mother wouldn't be caught dead in a library.

Elora dismissed them and continued her search for Zain.

There. At the railing on the second-tier lounge, dressed in a black suit, talking to a cluster of men also clad in suits rather than costumes. The white shirt beneath Zain's jacket looked neon blue thanks to the club's black lights. So did his teeth when he flashed the group a smile. Zain shook hands, clapping one of the men on the shoulder, then he moved to the next group, giving that same beautiful smile to his guests as he shook more hands.

Zain had come to work tonight. He'd make small talk for

hours, winning over his patrons so they wouldn't bat an eyelash at dropping a few thousand dollars on his top-shelf liquor selections.

Elora yawned.

As tempting as it was to watch Zain in his element, she needed to get off her feet. Her heels were killing her and this headache wasn't going away, so she slipped through the masses and headed toward the staircase that led to Zain's office.

The bouncer stationed at the staircase put up a hand as she approached, then it dropped by his side as recognition dawned. "Oh, sorry. The makeup . . ."

"It's fine." She waved it off. "I'd like to go upstairs."

"I'll have to check with Mr. Clarence."

Elora nodded.

On nights like this, Zain would often take his elite customers to his office for a private drink. It wasn't the first time a bouncer had made her wait, asking for permission first.

So Elora turned, giving him a moment to send Zain a message. At the bar, Tommie mixed a drink. The bartender was wearing a strapless top that barely contained her breasts. On her head were a pair of bunny ears, much like the ones Allison had been wearing.

Figures. She scoffed.

"All good," the bouncer said, shifting out of the way.

By the time she reached the top stair, her feet ached, so she slipped off her shoes, carrying them to Zain's office. With the door closed behind her, the music became a dull rumble and the reprieve to her ears made her body sag.

She padded to the couch, curling up against a toss pillow while digging the phone from her dress's pocket.

A notification from Lucas greeted her when she unlocked the screen. The photo he'd sent was of him and his friends, each dressed as football players with black lines smudged beneath their eyes.

She smiled, typing a reply.

Original costume

A smile ghosted her lips when the three dots appeared instantly on the screen.

Shut it

Elora laughed as she typed her next text. *Be safe tonight*

Same to you

She clutched her phone to her chest and closed her eyes. The thrum of the music resonated through the floor. Zain's scent lingered in the air. The combination was like a lullaby, and sleep claimed her almost instantly.

Until a caress on her cheek made her eyelids flutter open.

Zain crouched beside her, his knuckles tracing the line of her jaw. "Hi."

"Hi." She closed her eyes again, enjoying the tingles across her skin. It was quiet. The music was gone. "What time is it?"

"Three. You missed the party."

"I'm tired of the party."

"Nice makeup."

"Thanks." She smiled, and as his hand stopped moving, she realized she couldn't stay on his couch all night. She shoved up to a seat, tucking a lock of hair out of her face and behind her ear.

Another yawn stretched her mouth. They seemed endless, like no matter how much she slept, she'd never get enough rest.

Zain stood and walked to his desk. "Did you drive?"

"No."

"I'll take you home."

She nodded and stood, feeling a rush of cold on her skin. The couch had been warm and she was already dreading stepping outside. She shivered, wrapping her arms around her waist.

"Here." Zain shrugged off his jacket and put it over her shoulders. "Unlike my sweatshirt, I'll need this back."

"Okay." *We're over. We're over. We are over.* If she didn't keep up that reminder, she'd forget. She couldn't forget.

"Hey." He hooked a finger under her chin, tilting up her face. "You okay?"

"Tired."

He studied her face like he could see beyond the fancy makeup and façade to the fatigue in her soul.

"It was busy tonight," she said.

"Yeah." He rounded his desk, opening a drawer to fish out his keys and wallet. Then he ran a hand over his face, his own exhaustion seeping through.

She met him at the door.

With his hand on the small of her back, he escorted her out, jerking up his chin and waving to his employees as they finished putting the club to bed.

Tommie was behind the bar, the bunny ears she'd been wearing earlier gone. Her smile faltered when she spotted Elora. "Bye, Zain."

"You okay to lock up?"

"No problem. See you next week."

He nodded, steering Elora for the back door.

The bouncer who'd been at the office stairwell was outside, smoking a cigarette. "Night, Zain."

"Night. Would you do me a favor? Tommie's going to stay and lock up. Would you mind waiting until she's done and escorting her to her car?"

"You got it, boss."

"Appreciated." Zain put his arm around Elora's shoulders, hauling her close as they walked to his car in his reserved space. He'd driven his Range Rover tonight.

As soon as she was in the passenger seat, he closed her in and rounded the hood for the driver's seat. "Your place or mine?"

"Yours." Maybe if she let him exhaust her body, if she could sleep on one of his pillows, she'd actually wake up rested.

The drive to his loft was silent. Lights streaked beyond the windows. When Zain eased into the garage, he parked next to his bike but didn't get out. Instead he shifted, draping one arm over the wheel so he could face her. "You came to the club and went straight to my office to sleep. Why?"

Clearly the bouncers had talked if he knew that she hadn't spent a moment in the crowd. Did they always alert him when she came in? Or was that just tonight? "I'm tired. And no matter how many hours I sleep, I can't seem to find any energy."

"Have you talked to your dad?"

She shook her head.

"It's eating at you."

She nodded.

"What do you want, El?"

"Tonight? You."

"And tomorrow?"

Elora didn't have an answer. Because coming up with an answer meant facing her fears. Voicing her fears. And telling him that they shared a half brother.

When she stayed quiet, Zain pinched the bridge of his nose. "I can't . . . If we don't stop, this will just end bloody. For both of us."

"I know." They'd been drifting into the past with their hookups. It had to stop.

Tomorrow.

Tomorrow, she'd put an end to this for good.

But for tonight, she needed to sleep. So she climbed out of his vehicle and followed him upstairs, where she stripped off her dress, washed the makeup from her face and curled into his bed, closing her eyes on another yawn.

Already dreading what she had to do come morning.

twenty-three

. . .

IVY FOLLOWED Michael through the Sigma house. Why hadn't she left with Elora?

The party had spread from the basement and was spilling into the upstairs hallways as they made their way toward Michael's room on the third floor. Two people were fucking—loudly—in a room they passed, the door cracked. In another room, a man was snoring, passed out on his face.

When had this ever been fun? She should have gone to Treason.

As they approached Michael's room, he dug keys from the pocket of his robe to unlock the door, then he waved Ivy in first, closing them inside.

At least with the scent of his cologne she could actually breathe in here.

She surveyed the space, the largest room in the house, reserved for the Sigma president. His bed was against the wall to her left. His desk and a closet took up the wall to the right. Michael's room also had a private bathroom, the shower she'd used on the rare hookup in his fraternity.

As far as sex with Michael went, Ivy had always preferred him to come to the manor. Her bed was bigger, so was her shower, and she didn't need to worry about doing a walk of shame the next morning.

But there'd been times when she'd come to the Sigma house with Michael, slightly intoxicated after leaving Treason. Or drunk, like she'd been at last year's Halloween party.

Maybe that was why tonight was miserable. She was stone-cold sober.

Ivy walked to the desk, propping herself on its edge. "What's up?"

"Nothing." He sat on the leather couch beneath the windows that overlooked the Sigmas' circular drive. His robe fell open as he spread out his arms, his washboard abs on full display. Those silk pants did nothing to hide the bulge beneath and he was clearly going commando.

There was a reason he'd brought her up here, and normally, Ivy would take him up on a night between the sheets.

Except she wasn't feeling much like herself tonight. The party was dull. Drinking and dancing held no appeal. And at the moment, neither did Michael.

If she was being honest, she hadn't felt like herself in weeks.

"You almost left without finding me," Michael said. "Why?"

Ivy shrugged. "I'm not in a party mood."

"What are you in the mood for?" His gaze raked over her dress, traveling down her legs to her green heels.

Ivy crossed her arms over her chest. "Why is Allison here?"

His mouth pursed in a thin line. "I guess she *was* in a party mood."

"If I walk out of this room, will she be in here next?"

His jaw clenched.

"I'll take that as a yes." She scoffed. "Nice."

"What the fuck do you want, Ivy? We never said this was exclusive. You know the score. Don't come in here acting like a jealous girlfriend. If you don't want to stay, fine. I thought this was what you wanted. You're the one who sent me that video."

That goddamn video. She hadn't bothered correcting her mistake. Michael could think that the little show had been intended for him.

"You're right." She sighed. "Do what—and who—you want."

"I always do." The corner of his mouth turned up. "Too bad Cassia didn't come tonight. I invited her, but she seems to have a problem with fraternities."

"I wouldn't know." She feigned indifference as he attempted to bait her.

Ivy had no idea if or why Cassia might dislike fraternities. And she didn't give a shit. Her roommate was boredom personified. According to Geoff, Cassia was hardly at the manor. Although Francis never shut up about Cassia.

You should spend more time with Cassia. She's a darling.

That girl is such a sweetheart. The nicest roommate you've ever had.

Why don't you get to know Cassia? You'd really like her.

The only way Ivy had plans to get to know Cassia was through Sal Testa's investigative report.

"Did you figure out her story yet?" Michael asked. There was a glint in his eyes, like he already had the intel.

Except if there was anything interesting to find, he would have acted on it, right?

Ivy suspected that Cassia was just as lackluster as she seemed. But . . .

Curiosity wormed its way into her mind.

Sal hadn't been in touch with her for weeks, not since telling her he'd had to shelve her job for an urgent matter. It was time she reached out and put pressure on him to make her requests a priority.

She'd paid him enough over the years to take precedence.

"I'm bored with Cassia," Ivy lied. If she gave him any

indication of her interest, it would only spur Michael on. "She's all yours."

"Oh, I don't think she'll be mine. She's set her sights on someone else."

Ivy bit her tongue. Cassia was dating? Who? Maybe one of their economics classmates. "Whatever."

"You have no idea, do you?"

"I don't care, Michael." She stood, flicking a hand to dismiss the subject. "She's nothing to me. I've decided to let her stay at the manor this year, and as soon as graduation is over, she'll be forgotten."

He studied her face, searching for a lie, but Ivy gave him nothing. Her phone dinged in the hidden pocket of her dress, so she fished it out. A text from Tate.

Trick or treat?

The corners of her mouth lifted as she replied *Treat*. Then she was walking for the door.

"Ivy."

She lifted her phone, waving it in the air. "My driver's here. Have fun at your party, Michael. Give Allison my best."

"Nah. But I'll give her *my* best." There was an edge of irritation to his voice.

Michael didn't get rejected often, but it wasn't the first time Ivy had walked away. He'd done the same to her too. The moves and countermoves had always been part of their foreplay.

But as she navigated the hallways, texting her driver as she walked, Ivy was as turned off as the lights in the darkened study nook she passed on her way to the exit.

She pushed past the Sigmas stationed at the door, the unlucky members who'd been chosen to remain sober and monitor the people coming and going. When she stepped outside, the cold night gave her a welcome breath of fresh air.

The black town car was waiting. Roy stood stoically by the back door, opening it as she approached. "Miss Clarence."

"You took Elora home?"

"She wished to go to Treason." To see Zain. "Would you like to join her?"

"No. Take me home, please." She ducked into the car, and her phone dinged with another text from Tate.

Her *treat* was a photo of him dressed in a hoodie with a shadow of stubble dusting his jaw, taking a bite out of a cookie.

Yummy

Ivy's response had nothing to do with that damn cookie, but the man himself.

Want one?

She smiled. Oh, she wanted something from him. Her fingers flew over the keyboard.

Depends. Are you any good in the kitchen?

Find out for yourself

Tate's reply came with an address.

"Roy, change of plan," she said, rattling off their new destination as he put the Sigma house in the rearview mirror.

"Of course, Miss Clarence."

Her excitement ratcheted up with every block he drove.

Tate's place was in Boston's Back Bay, and as they turned down a street lined with brownstones, she felt like a child, giddy with her face practically pressed against the window.

She'd always loved this part of the city. The porch stoops. The white windows with black shutters. The stone's iconic color and the history lining these streets.

The car slowed as a group of teenagers with pillow sacks in their hands passed.

"It'll be slow going," Roy said. "Sorry."

"It's fine." She reached for the door's handle. "It's just at the end of this block. I can walk."

"Uh . . . I'm not too keen on leaving you, miss."

Score a point for Roy. "How about you park in that space up ahead? I'll text you as soon as I get there."

He sent her a frown, but he eased into the only empty

space on the street. Then he shoved the car in park. "I'll walk with you."

She opened her mouth to argue, but he was already turning off the engine and pushing outside, so she hurried to join him.

The sidewalk was chaos. Happy kids laughed and shouted *trick or treat.* Spider-Man flew past her with Superman on his heels. Then came a group of 80's hard rockers, their teased wigs and inflatable guitars brushed against Ivy's arm.

The air was freezing and her dress was too short. They'd only made it halfway down the block before her teeth began to chatter.

"Wear my coat," Roy said.

"I'm all right." She shook her head. "We're almost there."

Besides, maybe Tate would warm her up.

Ivy was so focused on the addresses, making sure she didn't pass Tate's place, that she was startled by a group of men coming her direction. None of them were in costume but looked to have been at a bar, given the glassy eyes and slight sway to their steps. One lifted a flask from his coat pocket, taking a swig.

Ivy aimed her gaze forward, not wanting to make eye contact.

Roy shifted closer, walking behind her in single file as they passed the group.

"Ivy?"

She slowed and turned. One of the guys had stopped. "Benjamin?"

"Thought that was you." He chuckled. "Nice costume."

Roy inched closer as Benjamin walked her direction.

"It's okay," Ivy told her driver and newfound protector. "We go to Aston together."

Benjamin and Ivy had struggled through the same freshman-year statistics course and occasionally bumped into one another at the student union building. His father was a well-known local lawyer and Benjamin was studying to follow in his footsteps.

Ivy had learned from her father that a good lawyer was priceless.

"Haven't seen you on campus this semester. Still a history nerd?" he asked.

She smiled. "Always."

"What are you up to tonight?"

"Just visiting a friend. You?"

"Same." He hooked a thumb toward a building. "How's everything going?"

She shivered as a breeze blew past. "Cold at the moment."

"I'll let you go." He held up a hand to wave. "See you around."

Ivy had turned, about to walk away, when another voice made her blood turn to ice.

"Don't get too close to that one, Ben." Cooper Kennedy stepped out from a parked car and onto the sidewalk, a glare aimed her way.

"You two know each other?" Benjamin asked.

It was Ivy's turn to inch closer to Roy.

"Yeah, we do. Don't we, Ivy?" Cooper sneered.

Fear rendered her speechless.

The last time Ivy had spoken to Cooper, he'd threatened to slit her lying throat the next time he saw her. In his defense, his brother had just died and emotions had been running high. That, and he'd believed Kristopher's bullshit.

How did Benjamin know Cooper? What was Cooper doing in Boston? He'd moved away years ago and only visited at Christmas. She'd paid Sal to keep tabs on Cooper, yet here he was and she'd had no warning.

"Steer clear, my friend." Cooper put his hand on Benjamin's shoulder, pulling him back as he took his own step away. "Touch her and you'll end up dead."

Ivy stood frozen on the sidewalk as they walked away.

They went to a house three down from where she was standing, jogging up the stairs and going inside.

Benjamin didn't look back.

But Cooper did.

One look and her stomach plummeted.

Kids continued to streak past her, racing from door to door to collect candy. Her fingers and ears were numb, yet she couldn't seem to move. She couldn't seem to stop staring at the house Cooper had gone inside.

That wasn't his home, was it? Oh God, he wasn't moving back, was he?

Cooper was arrogant and ruthless. He was a miserable asshole and had no qualms about tormenting his enemies. And Ivy was undoubtedly on his enemy list. Once, she'd held the top spot. Maybe she still did.

She trembled, shaking so hard she teetered on her heels.

"Miss Clarence." Roy put his hand on her elbow. "Who was that? Are you all right?"

Ivy shook her head, still unable to speak. But she managed to unglue her feet from the cement and take a shaky step, followed by another.

She started to move and didn't stop, not until she was jogging down the road to where their car was parked.

Roy kept pace, his shoes clipping in time with hers.

She yanked on the door handle but it was locked. She kept pulling anyway.

"Here." Roy hit the key fob and brushed her hand aside, opening the door.

She practically fell into the back seat, wrapping her arms around her knees and hauling them to her chest. It wasn't until they were blocks away from that neighborhood that she uncurled. Then she dug out her phone to text Tate.

Rain check?

His reply was instant.

Everything okay?

No. No, it was not okay. *Migraine*

The moment she hit send, she opened her email, ready to chastise Sal for this extreme fuckup. But an email from him was waiting in her inbox.

Just heard that Cooper Kennedy flew in tonight. I'll find out what he's doing here.

She rubbed her temples. The headache she'd lied to Tate about was becoming a reality.

And its name was Cooper Kennedy.

twenty-four

. . .

"READY TO GO?" Edwin asked, his lips next to Cassia's ear.

"Yes." She was more than ready to leave the club. Her entire body buzzed, and the ache in her core was agonizing.

They'd been at Treason for hours, flirting and talking and touching. It had been the most delicious foreplay of her life.

Edwin clasped her hand and tugged her through the lounge, his long legs eating up the distance to the stairs as he weaved past people and tables. Cassia had to jog every few steps to keep pace, but she wasn't going to complain. The sooner she could strip him out of that toga, the better.

This night would end with them tangled between sheets.

Sex would change everything.

It always did, and in her experience, not for the better. Yet she didn't care. She wanted Edwin more than her next breath.

His grip tightened as they navigated the stairs, then turned for the rear exit. He jerked up his chin as they passed the bouncer stationed next to the door and stepped into the night. Edwin was pulling the keys to the Bentley from his pocket when a woman's moan filled the air.

"Fuck, yeah. Take my cock," a man gritted out.

Cassia's footsteps stuttered as Edwin slowed, both scanning the parking lot.

Two rows away, directly past the Bentley, a man in a suit had the slutty nurse she'd seen in the lounge bent over the hood of his orange Corvette. His hands gripped her hips as he thrust into her with slapping strokes. He reached for the top of her costume and yanked it away from her breast, the sound of material ripping joining their moans as he pinched her nipple.

"Yes," the woman hissed, pressing her cheek against the car. Her eyes landed on Cassia and a smile spread across her mouth.

Cassia froze, unable to move but unable to look away. Her heart thundered and that ache in her center pulsed.

The man must have noticed his partner's gaze because he turned, his eyes locking on hers too. He licked his lips, never breaking rhythm.

Cassia's breath quickened. A rush of heat pooled in her core as she watched them have sex. It was shocking and dirty. Sexy and rude. They were fucking, out in the open, and she should be ducking her gaze, not watching with rapt attention. Why couldn't she stop watching?

Edwin's hand unthreaded from hers, the movement breaking her trance.

A flush flamed her cheeks as she tore her attention from the couple, embarrassment tempering the lust. God, Edwin must think she was a freak. She squeezed her eyes shut. "Sorry."

Edwin hooked a hand under her jaw, lifting her chin and forcing her eyes open. Then a wicked smile stretched across his mouth. Because instead of putting her in the Bentley and driving her home, he turned her face so she had to watch. "Have you ever watched before?"

"No," she whispered.

"Do you like it?"

"I don't . . ." *Yes*. She gulped. "I don't know."

Edwin moved to stand behind her, letting go of her face so

he could trail his fingertips over the bare skin of her arms. Up and down. Up and down. The tingles he left in his wake only made her desire skyrocket.

At the Corvette, the suited man moved faster, his attention back on the nurse. He flipped up the skirt of her costume, revealing her ass. He palmed her cheeks with both hands, exposing her so they had a better view of his dick disappearing into her body.

This was wrong. So wrong. Wasn't it?

"If they didn't want to be seen, they wouldn't have chosen the parking lot." Edwin's mouth brushed against her ear as he spoke.

"Do you, um . . . like it? Watching, I mean?" *Please say yes.* Cassia didn't want to be alone here.

"I like you." He shifted forward so she could feel his erection press into the crack of her ass.

She sank into the strength of his chest, pressing against him and earning a groan. Then she looked up and over her shoulder, his lips just an inch from her own. "Are you going to take me home?"

"Not yet." His mouth slammed down on hers, stealing her breath as their tongues tangled.

She whimpered, spinning to face him and rising up on her toes. Holy shit, this man could kiss. He nipped and sucked and devoured her.

The couple screwing got louder and louder. The woman cried out as the man grunted, each of them finding their release. And through it all, Edwin kissed her, until she felt like she would come apart.

When he finally tore his mouth away, both of them were panting. He studied her, tucking a lock of hair behind her shoulder, then glanced at the couple. Cassia followed his gaze.

The man had pulled the woman up off the car. His arms were banded around her chest, shielding her breasts, as he buried his face in her neck. She leaned into him with her eyes closed and smiled.

Cassia suddenly felt like she was intruding on an intimate moment, so she turned back to Edwin. "Can we go?"

"Yeah." He nodded, keeping his hand on the small of her back as they walked to the Bentley.

Cassia didn't let herself look up at the couple as Edwin reversed out of his space and sped away from the club.

"You good?" he asked, reaching across the cab to take her hand.

"Yes. That was, um . . ." Cassia couldn't make sense of her reaction. She wasn't a virgin. She wasn't naive or shy. But watching another couple have sex had been a first. An erotic first.

"Close your eyes," Edwin ordered.

She obeyed, relaxing into the leather seat. He probably wanted her to reset her mind, push away the sounds and sights of what she'd seen. But instead, his hand dropped to her leg, finding the slit in her costume. Her breath hitched as he drew circles on the bare skin above her knee.

Inch by inch he worked his way up her thigh, teasing her until her only mental image was of him. By the time they reached the manor, she'd forgotten about the Corvette couple. She'd forgotten about the club and her studies and her fears.

Hell, she'd nearly forgotten her own name.

All she wanted was Edwin.

The moment he parked in the loop and shut off the engine, she flew across the car, this time taking his lips. She swirled her tongue with his, her hands pulling at his face to draw him closer.

But he didn't let her kiss him long. Edwin broke away to rest his forehead to hers. "You sure?"

"Yes."

"Thank fuck." He planted a hand on her belly, nudging her toward the door.

Cassia fumbled with the door's handle before pushing it open and hopping outside.

Edwin was right behind her as she jogged up the stairs and

swept inside the manor. The moment the door closed behind them, he wrapped an arm around her waist and hoisted her up. Her legs wrapped around his hips as he took her mouth once more and headed for the stairs.

If her roommates were home, she didn't give a damn.

He carried her like she weighed nothing, taking her straight to her bedroom where he closed them inside. He didn't bother with the lights as he walked her to the bed and laid her on the mattress.

And finally, she freed that goddamn toga from his chest.

It was too dark to see much, so she let her hands wander, feeling the hardness she'd memorize come morning.

Edwin latched his mouth on her neck, sucking and licking his way down the column of her throat to the hollow of her collarbone. He traced the V in her own costume, down past the swell of her breasts to the skin above her heart.

One of her hands found its way into his hair, the waves just as silky as she'd always expected.

"Fuck, you are beautiful, Red." Edwin peppered kisses over her breasts, leaving the cloth of the costume in place. It was a touch, but not enough. It was sinful torture.

"More." Her hands glided over his shoulders, feeling the heat from his skin and the dips between the muscles of his back. God, he was ripped. She wanted to turn on the lights and spend an hour studying his body the way she pored over her schoolwork.

Tomorrow.

Cassia rocked against him, trying desperately for some friction. Except before she could find even a sliver of relief, he was gone, standing and letting his costume drop off his narrow waist.

Her mouth went dry.

Even in the muted light streaming in from her window, every washboard ab on Edwin's torso was defined. A delicious V disappeared beneath the waistband of his black boxer briefs. She needed his strong arms wrapping her tight as he fucked her senseless.

The image of that couple at Treason snapped into her mind and her heart rate spiked.

She wanted to be fucked, like that man had fucked that woman. Cassia didn't want gentle or timid. She wanted nothing that would remind her of Josh or the two lovers before him.

Cassia was ravenous for Edwin, and not only to satisfy this desire. If there was ever a man who could erase another's touch, it was him. She hadn't realized just how badly she needed to be touched again. To replace the memory of the last man who'd carried her to bed.

"What's that look, Cassia?"

She blinked, shaking herself out of her own head. "Huh?"

Edwin planted his hands beside her, bending close to inspect her face. "That look. I don't like what your face is saying at the moment."

"I just . . ." *Shit.* She was going to scare him away if she couldn't pull herself together. "I haven't been with anyone for a while."

He reached for the wreath on her hair. Somehow, it hadn't fallen off, so he lifted it away. "Nervous?"

"No." She shook her head, hoping he could hear the truth in her voice. "Not even a bit."

"Good." A smile tugged at his lips and he flashed her a dimple.

She leaned forward, doing another thing she'd wanted to do for months. She licked that dimple. Then she licked his Adam's apple. "Fuck me, Edwin."

He growled, reaching for the straps of her costume and peeling them off her arms to expose her breasts. His mouth latched on to a nipple, sucking it so hard her back arched off the bed. She savored the wet heat of his mouth, letting him turn her into a puddle as he gave the same suck to her other breast.

Those soft lips stayed locked on her skin as he tugged at her toga, stripping it from her body along with her panties. Only when she was naked did he stand, taking a step away from the bed so his gaze could trail over her skin.

Not an inch went unnoticed.

It was the sort of inspection that would have made *Cassie* nervous. Cassie would have reached to cover her breasts or shifted to close her legs. But she wasn't Cassie anymore, so she refused to let herself move as he continued his perusal.

Edwin bent for his costume on the floor, pulling out a foil packet from the pocket. His arousal strained against his boxer briefs.

Cassia couldn't tear her eyes away as he pushed the black cotton down his bulky thighs, kicking the boxers free. "You're . . ." *Huge*. She couldn't bring herself to say it.

Edwin gripped the shaft, pumping it with a tight fist, before putting the condom's packet between his teeth and ripping it open. Sheathed, he planted a knee in the bed, settling into the cradle of her hips as his elbows bracketed her head.

His nose traced the line of hers, his hand reaching between them, touching her soaked folds. "So wet and ready for me."

"Edwin," she pleaded. She'd been wet and ready for hours. If he didn't ease this ache soon, she'd scream.

He positioned his cock at her entrance, pressing forward just an inch. Then he stopped.

More torture.

She tilted up her hips, seeking more, but he shook his head.

"Slow."

"Hard," she countered. It only earned her another inch.

"You'll get it hard. But first I want to feel you." He took her hands, lacing their fingers together, as he continued his slow, shallow thrusts. Until finally he went deeper, rocking them together just as he'd promised. Until she wasn't sure where he ended and she began.

"Oh God." She'd never felt so full. The root of his cock rubbed against her clit. Her body stretched around him, pulsing and ready for a release. "I need . . ."

"More." He sealed his mouth over hers as he withdrew. Then he thrust forward. Hard.

She cried out into his mouth, letting him swallow her moans. His hips worked like magic, rolling and thrusting in a rhythm unlike anything she'd felt before. It was like a dance, the timing perfect.

"Fuck, you're tight." He nibbled on her earlobe, then trailed openmouthed kisses down her throat.

She wrapped a leg around his hip, the angle sending him even deeper.

"Next time, we'll play." He leaned up, his gaze locked on hers as he hovered above her. "But you feel so fucking good that I won't last."

Yes. If it was anything like this, oh, she would let him play.

He propped up on one elbow so he could reach between them. She expected him to toy with her clit, but his fingers pressed against her belly, close but not enough. "And next time, I'm going to taste your sweet cunt."

"Yes." She shivered. "More."

He pistoned his hips against hers, his hand between them still not finding her clit. "Ready to come?"

Cassia managed a frantic nod.

His fingers shifted, moving down to her swollen nub. One circle of his middle finger and she was done.

Cassia's orgasm broke on a gasp and her entire body came apart. Pulse after pulse. White spots erupted behind her eyes, and she didn't just see stars.

Edwin brought a whole damn galaxy.

"Fuck," he hissed as she clenched around him. His hips worked harder. Faster. His arms shook as he hammered inside her, chasing his own release. Then he came on a roar.

The aftershocks racked her body for minutes. Blood rushed in her ears until finally her racing heart calmed.

Edwin collapsed at her side, his breath ragged and his heart thundering. "That was . . . damn."

"Yeah." She panted, shoving the hair off her forehead. She was boneless. Her skin was sticky with sweat. She'd be sore between her legs tomorrow and a hot shower was calling. But she didn't have the strength to move.

Edwin shoved up and off the bed, walking to the bathroom to dispose of the condom. The light flipped on and he closed the door. By the time he'd returned, she was nearly asleep. "Up you go, beauty."

"Too tired," she murmured.

He chuckled, tugging down the bedding. "That was fun, Cassia. Thanks."

Thanks? Not exactly what she'd expected to hear, but as she relaxed into her pillows, she was too close to sleep to come up with a snarky reply.

She'd tease him about it in the morning.

Except when she woke the next day, Edwin was long gone.

twenty-five

. . .

THE SUNBEAMS STREAMING through the windows warmed Elora's face, waking her from a dreamless sleep. She blinked, squinting, as she cleared the fog from her head.

This wasn't her bed. Where was she?

Zain's. Halloween. His words in the car.

If we don't stop, this will just end bloody. For both of us.

The decision she'd made last night came rushing back. She closed her eyes, willing herself to sleep for just another ten minutes. Ten more minutes to forget what she had to do this morning.

But sleep was gone and the inevitable was looming. The scent of coffee filled her nose and she turned to her other side. Zain was propped up against his pillows.

His hair was disheveled, not from sex but sleep. His chest was bare, his tattoos on display. He had a steaming mug in one hand and his phone in the other, his thumb scrolling over the screen.

He glanced at her and offered a small smile but kept reading whatever he was reading. Probably an article in the *Wall Street Journal*. It was his favorite morning pastime—

besides sex. So while he sipped his coffee, she curled into her pillow, content to watch.

One last time.

Mornings like this were rare. Elora hadn't slept over at Zain's often, just like he hadn't spent entire nights in her bed at the manor. Mostly because Elora hadn't wanted to field Ivy's questions about the guy sneaking out of her bed or where she'd spent the night.

Looking back, she should have slept here as often as possible, just to get mornings like this.

The dusting of hair on his broad chest begged to be touched. Her fingertips wanted to outline his tattoos. But she kept her hands tucked beneath her cheek, tracing them with her gaze instead.

Her favorite was the black eagle that stretched from his shoulder to his heart. The bird's wings were spread, its talons extended, like it was about to snatch its prey and carry it into the air.

It was his most recent piece, one he'd gotten six months ago. The reason Elora loved that eagle wasn't its symbolism or placement. It was because she'd been there the day Axel had inked it on his skin. She'd sat by Zain's side in the parlor downstairs and watched his body change.

In all their years together, it had been one of the most intimate experiences they'd shared.

He said the eagle represented his freedom. He'd broken the chains tethering him to his family's legacy and forged his own path.

Most men in Zain's position would boast about their last name, but for him, it wasn't a source of pride. He resented his lineage.

He and Elora had that in common.

But Zain did love his siblings. She hoped he'd extend that love to Lucas too when the truth came to light.

And she hoped that when Zain looked in the mirror ten

years from now and saw that tattoo, maybe she wouldn't be entirely forgotten.

Maybe when he slept in this bed, he'd remember her curled into this pillow.

Today, Elora was all about foolish hopes.

Zain drank his coffee and finished reading whatever it was he was reading, then set both the mug and his phone aside. When he shifted his attention to her, it was like she'd been standing in the rain and he had the only umbrella. "Hi."

"Hi."

"You okay?"

She nodded. "Thanks for letting me sleep."

He tucked a lock of hair behind her ear before tracing what she assumed was a purple circle under her eye. She'd been covering those dark circles with concealer for weeks. Then he trailed his finger to her nose, touching each of her freckles.

She closed her eyes, memorizing his touch and sending another foolish hope into the universe. Whenever Zain saw freckles, she wanted him to see her face.

"I have to leave in about an hour for a meeting," he said. "I'll drive you home on the way."

One hour. She was going to spend it wisely.

Elora pushed up, the sheet falling to reveal her naked breasts.

Zain's eyes dropped to her rosy nipples, his hand trailing down her neck to roll one between his fingers.

She leaned into his touch, rising higher until her month hovered over his. "What do you want?"

He answered by crushing his lips against hers and hauling her into his lap.

The tangled sheets fell away as she settled her knees outside his thighs. His cock swelled beneath her. His hand flicked and pinched her nipple as his tongue plundered her mouth, leaving no corner untouched.

Elora was frantic, touching his shoulders and arms and

chest and stomach. Zain's urgency matched her own, both of them determined to make the most of this hour.

There wasn't much foreplay. Neither of them needed it. His shaft pulsed as she rocked against him, letting it fit into her slit and coating it with her wetness. They kissed, rough and wild, until the coil in her center twisted tight, demanding more.

She reached between them, taking him in her grip and fitting him to her entrance. Then she rose up on her knees and took him inside, so deep she knew she'd never feel this full again.

"Fuck, that's good." Zain groaned, his eyes closing as his head fell back against the headboard. That chiseled jaw flexed. His Adam's apple bobbed. He'd never looked so beautiful as he did at that moment, his expression full of lust while his body was tense, fighting for restraint.

Her fingertips touched the eagle tattoo, tracing a feathered wing. Then she skimmed the edges of the Roman numerals blocked across the top of his other shoulder.

XVIII

Eighteen, for his age when he'd outmaneuvered his father and grandfather, finding a loophole in his trust so he could take the money that was rightly his and tell them to both fuck off. Until he'd started Treason, Zain had considered it his greatest success. Because until that point, he'd played their game. He'd followed their rules.

And then he'd walked away.

As she moved, up and down, rolling her hips every time she was seated, she studied his face, watched as his breath quickened. She didn't just love this man. She admired him.

Zain was the king of his own destiny and deserved a worthy queen.

Maybe Elora had the strength to be everything he needed. Maybe. But her fears had a grip on her heart, and when—if—she conquered them, it would be too late.

Her hands continued on their path down his arm,

touching the skull on the underside of his forearm. It was black with wispy edges and had always reminded her of a ghost.

With his back to the pillows, she couldn't see the lion that took up an entire shoulder blade. Or the intricate flames that licked the base of his spine. Those two, plus the *Treason* inked across his calf, were tattoos she'd simply have to remember from their other times together.

"Look at me," she ordered, bringing her hands to his pecs.

He lifted his head, and when he met her gaze, she drowned in those crystal-blue pools.

I love you.

Could he see it? Did he know that she loved him? He was her heart. She loved Zain Clarence with her soul.

She loved him enough to let him go.

His eyes softened, his hand coming up to her face while the other went to her thigh, helping as she moved.

Her muscles burned but she wouldn't stop, not today. Because when he had the next woman riding his cock, she hoped her face would always be in the back of his mind.

"El." His thumb traced her bottom lip, then pushed the finger inside, past her teeth. She licked the pad, then wrapped her mouth around it and sucked.

Zain pulsed inside her, his eyes flaring with heat. His thumb popped free from her mouth and dropped to her clit. The moment he touched her, she ignited.

Her mouth opened, her back arching as she kept riding.

"That's it, El. Fuck me."

A moan escaped her throat as the pleasure built, higher and higher. His hips thrust up, meeting her as she sank onto him.

"Zain." She gasped.

"Come. Now." He pinched her clit and she was done, detonating on his command.

Her entire body quaked, her limbs no longer in her control as the wave crashed over her again and again.

Zain leaned forward, cupping his hand at the back of her head and hauling her mouth to his as he poured inside of her. He half kissed her, half roared against her lips so she could feel the intensity of his release melded with her own.

It was fitting, for the last time to be the best time. To have a climax so powerful and passionate that she would remember it until the end of her days.

As the haze of her orgasm cleared, she leaned into him, her arms wrapping around his shoulders. She hugged him, tucking her face into the crook of his neck.

Zain did the same, holding her so tight it was hard for her to breathe. His nose was buried in her hair, and when he took a long inhale, it sounded pained.

They stayed locked together, bodies connected, until she felt the prick of tears behind her eyes.

It was time to let him go.

So she unwound her arms, forcing him to do the same, and leaned away, cupping her hands on his face to take one last look at him this way.

Mine.

His cock twitched and he took her hips, lifting her free. "I'd better take a shower."

She nodded, waiting for him to walk down the hallway. When she heard the click of the bathroom's door, she sprang from the bed, searching the floor for her dress to tug it on. Her phone was still tucked in a pocket.

But where were her panties? She crouched to look beneath the bed but she couldn't see them, and she didn't have time to search, so she snatched up her heels and rushed to the kitchen.

Elora went straight for the drawers next to the fridge, finding his junk drawer first. She dug past the mail he'd shoved inside looking for a pen. She found one at the same time a square of yellow caught her eye.

She tugged out a single yellow Post-it, clicking the pen open, ready to leave her note. But before she could scribble down her message, ink from the other side of the note made her pause. When she flipped it over, her stomach dropped at the note scrawled in neat handwriting.

I had fun last night. I forgot how much we used to laugh.
I'm so glad you called me.
xoxo
Mira

The blond. Mira was probably Zain's blond from the night she'd seen them at Club 27. The image of them together, of her on his lap and the smile on his face, flashed in her mind.

He'd looked so happy that night. So carefree.

Mira.

Elora loathed that name. But mostly, she hated that Mira was better for Zain. He'd realize that eventually too. Maybe he already had. Maybe this note wasn't from that night, but another. Maybe Mira had slept in his bed and this note had been a morning farewell.

Tears flooded her eyes as Elora gently returned the sticky note back in the drawer, careful not to bend the corners. Then she pulled the top piece of mail from the stack, taking it to the island to write on the white envelope's blank back side.

I wish I could tell you I was in this.
But I'll always remember.
El

The pen dropped from her shaking fingers, clattering on the granite countertop. A single note and she'd shattered her own heart to dust.

Elora backed away before she could rip up the envelope,

then she ran for the door, feeling Zain's come leak down her legs. She wouldn't wash him away, not today.

The stairwell was cold when she stepped outside his loft, the chill seeping into the bare soles of her feet. She pulled out her phone and ordered an Uber. With it on the way, she turned and gave Zain's door one last look.

Then Elora did what was best for him.

And maybe what was best for herself too.

She closed her eyes and whispered, "Bye, Zain."

twenty-six

. . .

"HE'S VISITING HIS MOTHER," Sal told Ivy.

She shifted her phone from one ear to the other. Maybe Sal's voice wouldn't grate on her nerves so harshly on the opposite side. "How long is he staying?"

"His flight leaves next week."

Yep, this conversation was painful no matter how she heard it. Fucking Cooper Kennedy. Since she'd bumped into him last night, her fear had morphed into simmering rage.

She'd tossed some of her fury at Sal when he'd called, giving him a stern lecture about notifying her before Cooper got on a plane to Boston, not after he'd landed. But the remainder of her anger smoldered beneath the surface, making her skin hot and her limbs restless.

"He usually only comes home at Christmas," she said.

"I guess this year he's making an extra trip. But there's no indication he's moving back."

Yet. The knot in Ivy's stomach said this trip of Cooper's was different.

"Watch him," she snapped. "I want to know where he goes and if he comes anywhere near Aston or the manor."

"Done. I'm outside of his mother's house as we speak."

"Good." Clearly Sal's priorities had been reshuffled. "And what about Cassia Collins?"

He sighed. "Still on my list."

"Bump it up."

"I need a couple more weeks."

Ivy's nostrils flared but she stayed silent. There was no need to voice her frustration. It rang loud and clear through the phone.

Sal excelled at his job, but an unhappy client, especially someone like Ivy, might tarnish his reputation. His work might be garnering secrets, but Sal's true love was money. And Ivy had provided him a steady stream of cash over the years. It was something she'd continue to trickle his way, but if he pissed her off, she'd dry that river up faster than a raindrop beneath the desert sun.

"I'll get to it," he said. "Soon."

"Excellent," she said dryly. "Text me with updates on Cooper."

"I will. I'll stay on him until he's gone."

That should have made her feel better. But Ivy wouldn't relax until Cooper was back in San Francisco, where he belonged.

Without another word, she ended the call, setting her phone aside and standing from her desk. Her eyes felt puffy and the coffee she'd been guzzling this morning had given her jitters.

After she'd gotten home last night, she'd spent an hour in a hot shower washing away her costume makeup and trying to chase away the chill in her bones. She hadn't even attempted sleep, knowing it was pointless. So she'd spent the night hours at her computer.

Studying would have been a better use of her time.

Instead, she'd read emails.

Email after email, Ivy had waded through them all until the sun had streamed through her office window and she'd taken a break for coffee.

When Ivy had walked into the kitchen, Francis had taken one look at her and known something was wrong. Francis had shifted from chef mode to mother mode, insisting that Ivy eat and drink a glass of orange juice. Breakfast had sounded as appealing as having her head shaved, but Francis had made Ivy's favorite blueberry muffins.

It churned in Ivy's stomach as she paced the room.

A knock came at the open door.

Geoff frowned when she faced him, but he didn't comment on her appearance. "Tate Ledger is here to see you."

"Oh." Her stomach did a flip, but she couldn't tell if it was a good or bad flip. "Tell him I'll be right down."

"Not necessary." Tate's rugged voice came from behind Geoff.

The butler frowned, clearly irritated that Tate hadn't waited in the foyer like he'd surely been told.

"It's fine." Ivy sighed. Tate wasn't exactly the kind of man who followed orders, and while normally that was a turn-on, today she would have liked a few minutes to freshen up.

Geoff backed away, giving Tate a scowl before disappearing down the hallway.

Tate strolled into her office, his hands in his jeans pockets. His charcoal sweater strained at his biceps and across his chest. His jaw was clean-shaven this morning and his hair combed.

"You got a haircut," she said, disappointment lacing her voice.

"Yesterday." His eyes raked her from head to toe. "You look like shit."

"Aww. Thanks," Ivy deadpanned.

Not that he was wrong. She was wearing a pair of black leggings and an oversized gray sweatshirt. Not a stitch of green in sight except for her shamrock nails. After her shower last night, she'd tied her hair in a sloppy, wet knot. Her eyes were bloodshot, and without makeup, there was no hiding the pastiness of her skin or the circles beneath her eyes.

Tate closed the distance between them, stepping into her space. He raised a hand, his fingertips skimming her pale lips. "What happened last night? Why'd you change your mind?"

"Sorry," she whispered. Oh, she was sorry.

Ivy was sorry she'd convinced Roy to let her walk. She was sorry she hadn't left that Sigma party earlier with Elora. She was sorry she'd stopped to talk to Benjamin. Just five minutes earlier or five minutes later, she would have gotten to Tate's and not known about Cooper until she'd read Sal's email.

"What's going on, baby?"

Cooper Kennedy was not a topic she wanted to discuss, today or any day. That asshole had already taken enough of her headspace.

"Do you call every woman *baby*?" she asked.

"No, just you."

Good. She wanted that endearment for herself. "What are you doing here?"

"I was worried." He reached into her hair, tugging free the tie. Then his hands began to unwind the knot, letting her tresses, some still damp, fall down her back. Tate's hands slid through the strands, his fingertips massaging her scalp.

Her eyes fell shut, the exhaustion from last night bubbling to the surface. It made holding up any type of façade impossible. "Why?"

"Why what?"

She relaxed into his touch. "Why do you worry?"

"Why do you think?"

"I don't know." The people who came into Ivy's life usually wanted something. When they realized they wouldn't get it, they'd vanish as quickly as they'd appeared.

But Tate didn't need her money. He didn't need her last name. If he was after sex, he could have had it weeks ago, yet he'd turned her down. So why was he here, worrying about her?

"You don't want anything from me," she whispered. "Everyone wants something from me."

"Oh, I want something." His lips dropped, touching the corner of her mouth. Except when she rose up on her toes, seeking more, he backed away. "Tell me what's wrong."

"You don't kiss me."

"I just kissed you."

"Not the kiss I want."

He chuckled, his hands in her hair never stopping. "Tell me what's wrong, and I'll give you what you want."

"Promises, promises."

Tate unwound his hands from her hair, causing Ivy's eyes to open. His frown was waiting. In a swift sweep, he lifted her by the hips, making her gasp. Then he took two quick strides to deposit her on the edge of her desk.

Her eyes widened as he leaned into her space, towering above her as he stood between her open knees. Ivy wasn't a fan of being manhandled, but there was something about Tate, something different.

For this guy? She'd let him haul her anywhere.

He arched his eyebrows. "I'm waiting."

"I applied for a job at the Smithsonian in DC and didn't get it." It was one of many shitty emails she'd read this morning, and partially responsible for her mood.

"Sorry," Tate said.

Ivy shrugged. "It was a long shot to begin with."

The email had come through this morning. It was a Sunday, yet clearly someone at the institute was working. The timing was either a blessing or a curse. She'd received it just about the same time she'd finished wading through the other emails.

The emails she'd been rereading as a form of personal torment.

Getting bad news about a job was nothing compared to those, so in a way, having it arrive today had lessened the disappointment. Or maybe it was just worse, like lemon juice on a papercut.

Ivy was too numb to decide.

There wasn't a doubt in her mind that her father had made sure the Smithsonian job went to another candidate. Yes, she likely wouldn't have gotten the job anyway, but David Clarence didn't operate on chance. She'd bet her trust fund that he'd made a call to ensure the outcome was exactly as he desired.

"My father expects me to work for his company," she told Tate. "I don't want to, but it will be easier not to fight him."

"Giving up without a fight? That doesn't sound like you."

She cocked her head to the side. "Why do you say that? You don't know me well enough to know what does and doesn't sound like me."

"I might not know your favorite book or the best memory from your childhood, but I've got a decent read on you, Ivy. You fight me at every turn because it makes it interesting. You crave control, and when I steal it, part of you gets angry and part of you loves it. Not that you'd ever admit that to me or yourself."

Her heart raced as his chocolate eyes bored into hers. She hated giving up control, but she kept letting him steal it. The thief.

"You love your brothers." Tate traced the shell of her ear, making her shiver. "You love your butler and he loves you, enough to stand outside in the hallway to make sure I'm not taking advantage."

At the mention of Geoff, faint footsteps retreated down the hallway.

"You're a brat," Tate said. "You're spoiled. You're selfish."

"Wow," she muttered. "Don't hold back to protect my feelings."

"I won't. Because you're all of those things."

Ivy wanted to argue, but once again, he wasn't wrong.

"You feel trapped, don't you, baby? You feel trapped into

being that person. But that's not who you really are." A smug grin spread across Tate's mouth. "Now. Are you going to tell me that I don't know you?"

His accuracy was deadly.

She rolled her eyes. "Whatever."

How was it that this man had figured her out so quickly? It seemed entirely unfair that she didn't know much about him.

"What was your major in college?" she blurted.

"You're irritated that I know more about you than you do about me."

Damn. "Answer the question."

"Business finance."

Not surprising, considering he'd owned a club in Vegas. "Favorite food?"

"You'll find out tonight at dinner." He leaned in closer, his lips seeking hers. But she planted a hand in his chest, pushing him back.

"Are you asking me out on a date?"

"Wasn't asking." Tate ducked lower, his lips skimming her neck. "Any other questions?"

Lots. Ivy had lots and lots of questions. But as his breath floated against her pulse, his tongue darting out to taste her skin, not a single thought remained in her head other than hoping he'd fuck her on this desk.

"Hmm." He hummed as his lips traced the shape of her jaw.

Her eyes drifted closed. Her mouth parted, waiting for the kiss she'd earned. Except the heat from his body disappeared and his footsteps sounded on the floor.

"Six o'clock."

Ivy's eyes flew open. Her jaw dropped. "That's it? Where the hell is my kiss?"

Tate chuckled, slowing at the door to turn and look at her. "Six o'clock."

"You're such a goddamn tease." And if she was being honest, she loved it. She loved that he never did what she expected. She loved that he'd come in for five minutes and given her something else to think about for the rest of the day.

"Wear green. I like green."

She harrumphed. "I always wear green. It's my favorite color."

"Mine too." He winked, then strode into the hallway.

Ivy held her breath, straining to hear the front door. Then once he was gone, she rushed to her bedroom, straight for the window that overlooked the front of the house.

The arrogant bastard stood next to his car, arms crossed and legs planted wide, his eyes aimed her way. Given the smirk on his face, he'd known she'd run to watch him.

She huffed and marched away from the window, fighting a smile. She lost the battle, and by the time she returned to her desk, her heart was lighter.

As much as she wanted a nap, she woke up her computer to spend a couple hours studying so she could rest this afternoon and get ready for dinner. She'd just opened an assignment for her Modern India class when a ding alerted her to a new email.

The name in her inbox shouldn't have surprised her.

It was a Sunday.

And like every Sunday for the past three years and ten months, she'd received an email from Kristopher's mother.

There was no subject line. There never was.

But the content of the email wasn't much different than its predecessors. the same words that had made her cry, though the first hundred still assaulted her eyes.

Killer. Prison. Grave.

Maybe Ivy did deserve to be in prison. Maybe she was a murderer. Maybe it should have been her in a grave.

The noises in her head came rushing back as she read the message. Her screams. His shouting. Every Sunday, thanks to these emails, she got to relive the worst day of her life. Maybe she should have told someone about these emails years ago, someone who would have made them stop.

But this was part of her penance.

So she read the email, twice.

Her hand hovered over the mouse, ready to drag it into the folder where she kept the others.

"What the fuck is that?"

"Jesus." Ivy jumped in her chair, slapping a hand to her heart as she swiveled. Tate stood directly behind her. His stance wasn't all that different from when he'd been standing outside. Arms crossed, legs planted wide. But there was no smirk on his face.

No, his face was hard as stone.

"What is that?" He jabbed a finger at her screen.

"I thought you left." And she'd been so lost in that email, in the sounds of her past, she hadn't heard him walk in.

"Changed my mind." His glare shifted from the screen to her face. "I was going to have you load up, come to my place for the day, then I'd cook you dinner."

"Oh." Ivy dropped her chin, her frame sagging in the chair.

The damage was done. Strange how she was glad it was Tate who'd seen an email first. And she barely knew the man.

"What the fuck is that email, Ivy?" He braced his hands on his hips, waiting for her answer.

Ivy spun back to the hateful words. For the first time in three years and ten months, instead of keeping the email in her hidden folder, she hit delete.

There was no need to keep it.

There'd be another coming next Sunday.

"That is a secret for another day."

twenty-seven

. . .

WEARING bright red lipstick to a Sunday breakfast was a bit bold, yet Cassia swiped on the color anyway. If Edwin didn't show, she'd need some bold to sit there and eat alone.

She was going to force herself to stay and eat the café's famous hash, simply to spite the man who hadn't bothered to stick around after fucking her last night.

After saying *thanks*.

God, what the hell had she been thinking?

He'd had a condom in his toga pocket. Edwin had expected her to be a sure thing. What if she had turned him down? Would he have used it with another woman? Would he have slept in some other woman's bed?

Jealousy and humiliation slithered beneath her skin, making it hard to look herself in the mirror.

Cassia wasn't a one-night-stand sort of girl. Casual sex made her feel slimy, and the shower she'd taken this morning hadn't rinsed away the embarrassment of feeling used.

"Such an idiot," she muttered.

Had it all been a lie? The kiss. The coin tosses. The hours spent in the library.

Damn it. "Why did I trust him?"

Hadn't she learned her lesson months ago?

She clenched her fists and stood tall. Avoiding her reflection was impossible, and today, despite the coral hair, she looked like Cassie Neilson. Foolish and gullible.

But this time, she wasn't going to hole up in her room with shame as her loyal companion. No, she was going to walk into that café with her shoulders squared and pretend that if—*when*—Edwin wasn't waiting, she was fine. Better than fine, right? She'd earned a fantastic orgasm.

Before she lost her nerve, she marched from the bathroom, snagging her bag from the bed.

The sheets had already been stripped. First thing this morning after putting on some clothes, she'd carted them downstairs to the laundry room. Now she stopped to swap them from the washer to the dryer, then went outside and unlocked her Honda.

Every block she considered turning around. Every mile she drove, this idea seemed like a bigger and bigger mistake. She'd get to the café and her fears would be realized. Edwin had played her.

When was she going to stop falling for these games?

Her heart bounced like a ping-pong ball against her ribs, and by the time she'd eased into a parking space outside the café, she was about to puke. There was no way she'd be eating anything. Yet she pushed out of her car and walked to the restaurant on shaking legs.

After dragging in a long breath, she pulled the door open and aimed her eyes at the usual table.

It was empty.

"Of course it's empty," she scoffed, her hopes shattering all over again. "Such a dumbass."

"Talking to yourself, Red?"

Cassia whirled, and the air rushed out of her lungs. Edwin stood behind her on the sidewalk.

The hood of his sweatshirt was pulled up over his hair,

shielding his ears from the chill in the air. His cheeks were flushed and his eyes were bluer beneath the morning sun.

Edwin took a step, taking the weight of the open door from her hand. Then he put his hand on the small of her back, urging her inside. The moment the door swung closed behind them, he stepped in close. "Hi."

"You left, asshole," she barked.

His eyebrows came together. "How many orgasms does a man have to deliver to earn a *hello*?"

"You don't get a hello because you didn't say goodbye." Her emotions had been spinning on a roulette wheel all morning, and apparently when faced with Edwin, the ball had landed on *fury*.

He frowned and took her arm, walking them to their table, where he pulled down his hood as she ripped off her coat before taking her seat. When the waitress came over, he offered her a polite smile while he ordered their usual coffees.

"Okay." Edwin leaned his elbows on the table. "Why are you pissed?"

"Because you left," she hissed.

"Yes. But I told you I'd meet you at breakfast." He pointed to the table. "Here."

"You did?" She cocked her head to the side. "And did I respond?"

"You hummed."

In the fuzzy edges of her memory, she remembered him saying something in her ear as she'd drifted off to sleep. After the *thanks*. "Oh."

"Oh." He shook his head. "She says *oh*."

"Well . . . you left."

"You also didn't ask me to stay."

"Would you have stayed?"

Edwin nodded. "Yep."

Cassia sighed. "Can we start over?"

"Please."

"Hi."

Edwin's eyes softened as he stretched a hand across the table to cover hers. "Hi."

"I thought maybe I'd been played," she admitted.

"You still don't trust me." It wasn't a question but a statement. "You will. Eventually."

"Trusting people is how you get your heart broken."

"You've got it wrong." Edwin shook his head. "Trusting people is how you mend your broken heart."

If Cassia weren't sitting, she might have fallen on the floor.

Maybe he was right.

Maybe, eventually, she'd believe that too.

His index finger drew circles on the back of her hand. "I wanted to stay last night, but I left because of Ivy."

Cassia stiffened at his sister's name.

"I love my sister," he said. "But she's complicated."

"Meaning she won't like that you and I are . . ." *Together.* Were they together? Or just sleeping together? "Whatever it is we are. She won't like it."

"First, we are not a 'whatever.' Second, no, she won't like it. So instead of her finding out because my car is parked in the loop and you're screaming my name while my cock is buried in your pussy, I thought it would be best to leave before she woke up this morning."

"Uh." The waitress stood next to their table with two coffees. "Did you want to order or . . ."

"Two hash specials," Edwin said. "One orange juice. One apple juice. Thanks."

Cassia blushed as the waitress scurried away. "Oh my God."

Edwin only smirked. "It'll give her something to gossip about in the kitchen."

She buried her face in her hands, but Edwin stretched to tug on her wrist.

"Listen, this will be easier if I tell Ivy we're together," he said. "She doesn't do well with surprises."

Together. He hadn't ditched her. He hadn't used her. That condom he'd had in his pocket had been intended *for her*.

But as far as labeling this relationship . . .

"I need us to stay a whatever," she said.

Edwin had just picked up his coffee and the mug stopped midair. "What?"

"Us." She gestured between the two of them. "I need this to stay a *whatever*. And I need our *whatever* to stay between us."

He set his mug down. "Why?"

"Trust." There was a longer, sordid explanation that would probably have been better. But Cassia wasn't in the place to offer it up. Because it meant telling her story, spilling her secrets.

He studied her as he lifted his mug again, taking a steaming sip. When he set it down, his expression was like granite. "No."

"N-no?"

"No." Edwin leveled her with a stare that made her squirm in her seat. In all of their time together, he'd always been easygoing. Smooth. This was the first time he'd radiated raw power.

It was unnerving, yet erotic.

"I won't be a secret," he said. "I won't play games. I won't fuck around. I have no desire to be a whatever. We don't need a label, but I sure as hell won't pretend you don't mean something. Clear?"

"Uh . . ." She gulped. She'd read books with alpha males. Now she was sharing a meal with one. Her pulse raced and a wave of desire curled between her legs. Who was this Edwin and was he willing to fuck her later?

He leaned forward, his eyes locked on her. "Yes or no, Cassia."

"Yes." The whisper escaped her lips before her brain had formed it.

"Good." He leaned back in his chair, the intensity

vanishing like a puff of smoke in a breeze. "Want to go to dinner tonight? Or do you need to study?"

"Study." She held up a finger. "Wait. So what about Ivy?"

He lifted a shoulder. "I'll tell her."

"Tell her what?"

A smirk spread across his soft lips. "That we're a *whatever*."

"Smartass." She snatched a sweetener packet from its holder and threw it at his head.

He snatched it from the air and put it away. "Such violence."

"I don't like your sister. I don't want her screwing with me—"

"Because I'm screwing you."

She nodded. "Exactly."

Edwin dragged a hand through his hair. "I dated a girl for six years."

"Oh, um . . . okay." That was not what she'd expected him to say. Six years? That was three times longer than her relationship with Josh. "That's a long time."

"We started dating our freshman year in high school. We broke up about as often as we got back together. She was just like Ivy. Thrived on the drama. Maybe I did too. She went to Harvard while I came to Aston. We cheated on each other. We fought all the time. We hurt each other. Deliberately."

Cassia could relate to a fucked-up relationship, though she'd never intentionally hurt Josh. That had been his specialty. "Sorry."

"We had the relationship that my parents have." Edwin gave her a sad smile. "It was toxic. And when I finally ended it for good, I promised myself I wasn't going down that road again. I'm not going to look in the mirror when I'm fifty and see my father staring back."

This wasn't the first time Edwin had mentioned problems with his father. She was glad that she wasn't the only person at this table with parent issues.

"You are unlike any woman I've ever met," he said. "You don't give a damn about my money or my last name."

"I like you despite your last name."

"True." He grinned. "I don't need to rush out of here and inform my sister that we've got something going on. But I won't hide it. Don't ask me to hide you. There are very few real and normal things in my life. Don't steal one from me."

Once again, her chair kept her from falling on the floor. "I can't even argue with that."

"No, you can't." Edwin laughed and the sound made most —not all—of her worries subside.

"Ivy intimidates me," she confessed.

"That's her game."

"Why? Why is she like that but you're, well . . . you? How did you turn out so different?" He was grounded. Confident but not cocky. Genuine. Sweet.

"Who says I'm different from Ivy?" he asked.

She rolled her eyes. "Not funny."

Edwin shifted, digging his phone from a pocket. He swiped through the screen but kept whatever it was he had on there to himself. "When Ivy and I were younger, we spent our Monday afternoons at my grandparents' house visiting my grandmother."

"Were you close?"

Edwin scoffed. "She is a miserable bitch."

"Oh." Cassia jerked.

"Madam Clarence. That's what she makes us call her. She is the by-product of a bad marriage to my grandfather, who is a coldhearted bastard. His first love is money. His second was his mistress, Bridget, who he moved into their guesthouse when I was seven."

Cassia's jaw dropped. "Next to your grandmother?"

He nodded. "Yep."

"Wow. That is cold."

Edwin chuckled. "Grandmother moved out not long after, but Bridget stayed. She never moved out of the guesthouse either or in with my granddad. Mostly because my grandparents never got divorced."

"Really? Even after he cheated?"

"Madam Clarence likes her lifestyle and it's funded by my grandfather. Besides, she's not without her lovers."

"Huh." Rich people were strange.

"Even after Grandmother moved out, our weekly visits never stopped. I'm not sure why but we kept going. But every Monday after school, our nanny would drive us to Grandfather's estate, and since he was never home, we'd spend the afternoons with Bridget. Ivy eventually stopped as we got older, but not me. Even if I only had an hour or two, my Monday afternoons were for Bridget."

There was a softness in his expression when he spoke her name. And pain. Cassia knew where this was going without him having to say it. "You loved her."

"Bridget was like you. Real. Normal. She'd make Ivy and me toasted cheese sandwiches with tomato soup from a can. She'd send us home with candy bars stuffed in our backpacks. And she'd hug us. All the time, she hugged us."

Cassia placed her hand on the table, palm up, ready for his when he needed hers.

"She was like a rainbow. To most people, she probably would have just been this lovely lady. But when you're surrounded with ugly people, the beautiful souls shine a little brighter. My ex, God, Bridget hated her. Thought she was a snake. The day we broke up for good was the day Bridget died."

Cassia's heart lurched. "I'm sorry."

"She wasn't perfect. She was a rich man's mistress, but she loved him. She took him as he was, even if that meant *married* because he wasn't going to divorce my grandmother either."

"Why?"

Edwin shrugged. "Money. Hassle. If Bridget had pushed, maybe he would have pursued a divorce. But Bridget didn't and he had everything he wanted, so why fight?"

Cassia couldn't fathom sharing a man's heart. "How did she die?"

"Breast cancer." He studied his phone. "I used to be like Ivy. The secrets and games. That sort of thing used to piss Bridget off. And if she's watching over me, I want her to be proud."

"She would be." Cassia gave him a soft smile as he handed her his phone. On the screen was a woman with cheery coral hair, the color nearly identical to Cassia's.

"It was your hair," Edwin said. "When I saw you that day at the drinking fountain, I came to stand behind you because your hair reminded me of Bridget's."

Cassia couldn't respond. Her eyes were glued to the photo.

Bridget was beautiful. Her brown eyes sparkled and her smile was framed with laugh lines.

No. It couldn't be her. What were the chances?

"What?" Edwin asked.

Cassia shook her head. "I-I know her."

twenty-eight

. . .

"THIS IS KINKY," Edwin said. "What are your thoughts on ass play?"

"You're done." Cassia stretched for the book in his hand, but he rolled away, holding it over the side of the bed and blocking her from stealing it.

In the two weeks since she'd told him that the woman he'd adored, his Bridget, had been her favorite author, Edwin had spent plenty of time in her bed. She'd resisted giving him her paperbacks, not sure how he'd react to the scandalous, erotic scenes in Bridget's work. But this morning, after he'd come over before dawn to sneak into her room and give her an orgasm, she'd been helpless to resist when he'd asked to read a book.

"I'm equally mortified and impressed that Bridget wrote this."

Cassia giggled, leaning over his bare shoulder to steal the tattered paperback from his hand. Then she made sure all of the pages were smooth before returning it to her nightstand. "I can't believe you didn't know."

"That my pseudo-grandmother wrote trashy romance novels? I can't believe it either. She had this entirely different life." He relaxed into the pillows, staring up at Cassia's ceiling. Then he cringed. "I'm trying really hard not to picture Bridget and my grandfather using anal vibrators."

Cassia burst out laughing, slapping a hand over her mouth. "Sorry."

"Good for her, you know?" Edwin chuckled. "She never had a job and I always assumed it was because he was paying for her life. But she had this entire career. And a successful one at that."

"Very successful."

Bridget was actually Laurel Lewis, a bestselling author of over thirty novels.

And Cassia's favorite.

There hadn't been many things Cassia had brought here from her life at Hughes. But her three favorite paperbacks, their corners dented because of how many times she'd reread the stories, had been carefully packed in a suitcase.

She hadn't had time to read them since she'd started school at Aston, but over the holiday break, she was going to remedy that. Maybe they'd take on a whole new meaning now that she knew the woman who'd penned the stories had been so wonderful to Edwin.

Or maybe Bridget's heart had always shone through her books and that was part of why Cassia loved them.

Part of why when she'd needed a new hair color, she'd picked coral.

Because in the photo on the back cover of her books, Laurel Lewis had coral hair.

Edwin turned onto his side, propping himself up on an elbow. The white sheet covering his lower half slipped closer to his navel, revealing the definition of his abs.

She'd traced the lines at his hip bones this morning with her tongue.

"Do you think he knows?" Edwin asked. "My grandfather?"

"I don't know. You could ask him."

He sighed and shook his head. "If he didn't, then she kept it from him for a reason. I won't ruin her secret."

Cassia turned onto her stomach, hugging the pillow to her naked chest.

Edwin's fingers stroked up and down her spine, tracing letters and invisible patterns on her skin.

Two weeks and they'd found a new pastime beyond studying together in the library. He seemed as obsessed with her body as she was with his.

"What do you have to do today?" he asked.

"Study." The end of the semester was rapidly approaching and the amount of work she had to tackle over the weekend was daunting. Except she couldn't bring herself to leave this bed. "Have you talked to Ivy?"

"Not yet."

That explained why Ivy hadn't burst into her room demanding she vacate the manor immediately. There was a good chance she hadn't learned about Cassia and Edwin. Yet.

"Why?" she asked. He'd been so adamant about not being a secret.

"I like our bubble."

"And she'll burst it?"

"Maybe."

Cassia chewed on her bottom lip. It had been her idea to keep this a secret, but she felt a sense of impending doom, and the longer they stayed quiet, the worse the reaction would be when the truth was revealed.

Someone—probably multiple members of the Clarence family—was going to object to the rich, handsome, world-at-his-fingertips Edwin getting involved with the poor transfer student who was hoping to survive one last semester on less than one thousand six hundred dollars and eighty-two cents.

"Did you park outside?"

He shook his head. "I walked."

"Wait." Cassia lifted her head from the pillow. "You can walk? How far away is it to your house?"

"About four blocks."

"That's it? Four blocks? Where do you live?" And why hadn't they spent their nights in his bedroom instead of hers, where the evil Ivy wasn't under the same roof?

"I bought a place my freshman year. I didn't want to live in the dorms and had no desire to join a fraternity."

"Thank God," she muttered.

"Not a fan of fraternities?"

"Not especially."

"Why?"

"Long story."

In a flash, she was on her back with Edwin looming above her. "What if I want the long story?"

If he stuck around, maybe he'd be the person to hear it first. But she couldn't give Edwin her truths, not yet. First, she had to make sense of it herself. She had to heal enough to relive the past, to examine it. To peel it apart and see where she'd gone wrong.

To see where they'd all gone wrong.

"Why would you buy something when you could live in this manor?"

He cast his eyes to the heavens. "She changes the subject."

Cassia smiled, taking his face in her hands to drag his focus back. "Yes, I am. But you still have to answer me. Why don't you live here?"

There were at least two other bedroom suites that went unused, maybe more, though she hadn't spent enough time exploring to know for sure. She kept to her wing of the house and didn't venture far from her usual path.

"Asking me to move in?" Edwin bent to brush a kiss against her lips. "And here I thought you wanted to take it slow."

Slow? Since they'd started having sex, nothing about this had been slow. Every day felt like a rush to go to class and cram in her studies so she'd have time with Edwin after dark.

"But to answer your question . . ." He moved off her and

onto his side, his fingers once more drawing on her skin, this time above her breasts.

Edwin had taught her the appeal of pillow talk. She'd never been touched this much, like he couldn't keep his hands off her. Most guys she'd been with had climbed out of her bed after they'd had sex. Where Josh was concerned, she should have seen that as a red flag.

Was she missing any red flags with Edwin?

Cassia shoved those worries aside. They'd be there in a few hours when he left.

"This manor has always been Ivy's," he said. "After my grandmother moved out, she came here to avoid my grandfather and Bridget. She didn't stay long. It was too close to Aston and there were *young people* crawling all over the area."

"Those dreaded young people." She rolled her eyes. The more Edwin spoke of his grandmother, the more Cassia disliked the woman.

"She moved to one of their other estates and gave the manor to my father. When I was a kid, my parents weren't getting along well—which was really no different than any other year. But Dad did something when I was in third grade that sent Mom into a rage. She moved here and brought Ivy and me along."

"You lived here?"

He nodded. "This was my bedroom."

Cassia's eyes widened. "This room? My room?"

"Was my room first." Edwin smirked. "Ivy stayed in the same room as she does now. Mom had a suite on the first floor."

"Huh." She dropped into her pillow and stared at the ceiling, picturing a young Edwin in this big room alone. "How long did you stay?"

"A year. Dad convinced Mom to come home. Or maybe he threatened to divorce her if she didn't. I don't know. I learned a long, long time ago not to ask questions about my parents' marriage."

Cassia hadn't asked questions about her father's love life either, not because she dreaded the answers, but because she'd assumed it was nonexistent. Her mother had broken his heart and left him with a daughter to raise. She'd made the assumption that she'd been Dad's whole world.

She really should have asked questions.

Now it was too late.

"That year we spent here, Ivy loved it. Mostly I think she loved being away from our father."

"They don't get along?" Cassia asked.

"Dad is . . . demanding. He loves money about as much as he loves control," Edwin said. "He wants Ivy to be someone she isn't. He throws her mistakes and what he believes are her shortcomings in her face."

Ironic, because Cassia's impression of Ivy wasn't entirely different.

"He dangles carrots he knows she can't resist to manipulate her," Edwin said. "Like he wanted her to work as an intern for his company to get a feel for it. Told her if she did it for six months, he'd deed her the manor after she graduated. We'll see if he really does. I'm not holding my breath."

"So the manor isn't actually hers?"

"Not legally. But every summer, she'd beg our parents to let her come and stay here. It became her sanctuary. And during high school, it was never a question of where she'd live when she came to Aston. This manor is *hers*."

"But if she wants it, she has to play your dad's game."

Edwin touched the tip of her nose. "Exactly."

A hint of compassion for Ivy snuck into Cassia's heart. Which was ridiculous, considering their few encounters. But Ivy had left Cassia alone for months. They coexisted as roommates and nothing more.

Hopefully once Ivy found out that Edwin was spending his nights in Cassia's bed, that wouldn't change.

"That doesn't really answer my question," Cassia said. "You could have lived here too."

"Nah." Edwin shook his head. "I wanted my own space."

"What's your place like?"

He leaned closer, dragging his mouth over the shell of her ear. "You're full of questions today. It's my turn to ask some."

Cassia tried to hide the tension that stiffened her spine. "Okay," she drawled.

"What do you want to do after Aston?" He shifted away with a smirk on his face. Apparently she hadn't hidden that tension after all, and he'd spared her.

"Get a job."

"What job?"

She lifted a shoulder. "Anything in economics. I'm in it for the salary for a few years. I've already started looking."

"Oh, yeah? Where?"

"London. Or Melbourne."

His eyebrows rose. "Really?"

The idea of being an ocean away from her past was entirely too tempting. "What about you?"

"Nice try, Cassia." He rolled, pinning her again. The way this man moved in bed was so fast and sure, she was always taken by surprise. "You don't get to ask questions anymore. Have you ever been to London or Melbourne?"

"No. That kind of trip is out of my current price range."

"Then I'll take you." A trip across the world was nothing for Edwin. "We'll get in my jet and flip a coin to see where we go."

Another man had also promised to take her on whirlwind vacations.

Brakes screeched in her mind.

Cassia squirmed to get out from beneath Edwin, hopping out of bed. She rushed to snatch her pajamas from the floor and tug them on.

"What?" His forehead furrowed. "What's wrong?"

"We can't . . . I can't talk about taking trips together." She pushed the hair out of her face, then flew into the bathroom for a hair tie. By the time she'd returned to the room, Edwin was sitting on the edge of the bed, his bare legs kicked over the side.

"Cassia—"

She held up a hand. "I think you should go."

"Kicking me out already?" He huffed. "Got what you needed from me this morning?"

She crossed her arms over her chest. "Like you didn't get the same."

Edwin stood and stalked her way, his naked body a lethal weapon. It was impossible not to notice the way his cock swung between his legs. "That's it? I mention doing something that's not fucking or studying and you kick me out?"

Cassia gulped. That power she'd felt weeks ago at breakfast, the one that made her shiver, was radiating off his chest. "I can't—"

"What? You can't consider getting out of your own goddamn head?" Edwin stepped even closer, his frame towering over her as he gripped her chin before she could duck it. "You can blame this on my family, that you don't trust my sister and whatever other bullshit you're letting yourself believe, but when I walk out that door, it's on you."

"Don't." *Don't be so right.* She squeezed her eyes shut, either to shut out his words or her own.

"Fuck, but you are frustrating." The sound of his teeth gritting hit her ears a moment before his mouth came down on hers in a hard, closed-mouth kiss.

She shouldn't like his rough touch, but she rose up on her toes, craving more.

Instead, he let her go to step away. His eyes were a storm of lust and anger, and in that moment, she knew he was going to walk.

She'd become the drama he'd sworn off. "I trusted someone and he crushed me."

"Sort of figured that out already."

She swallowed hard. "I can't make the same mistake."

"And I'm a mistake."

"No, I—maybe."

Edwin's nostrils flared.

"I mean no." She tossed her hands in the air. "I don't know. I don't know what to think or how to feel about this."

"You just know how to run when you get spooked." His jaw clenched as he gave her his profile, staring out the window. His parting shot made her want to curl into a ball and cry.

Yes, she knew how to run. And she knew how to push.

She'd been pushing people away for months. She could blame it on a new phone, but part of the reason none of her friends from Hughes had called was because she'd shoved them all from her life long before she'd changed her number. As soon as the rumors had started flying, she'd shut everyone out.

"I'm going to ask you questions." Edwin faced her again and the determination on his face made her breath catch. "I'm going to test each of your limits. You don't know how to think or feel about this? I'll make it crystal fucking clear. I'll push and fight and rip free these truths you're guarding."

"Edwin—"

"But you have to decide. Do you want me? Or are you looking for someone to fuck while you finish school? Because I'll gladly fuck you, Red. But my cock is all you'll get. So what's it going to be, Cassia?"

The growl of her name, the intensity of his expression . . . this was not an Edwin who played games. She didn't want to either. "You."

Relief sliced through the tension in the room. The frustration on Edwin's face melted away as he blew out a long breath. Then he reached out an arm, hauling her into his chest.

She collapsed into him, breathing in the scent of his skin. Soap and sweat and Edwin.

Maybe this was another mistake. Maybe she'd regret this in an hour. But Cassia didn't want shallow sex.

"You never answered my question," he murmured into her hair.

"What question?" Whatever he asked, she'd answer. At least, she'd try.

"What are your thoughts on ass play?"

She laughed, holding him tighter. "I have no experience."

Edwin hooked a finger under her chin, lifting her face away from his chest. Then he bent, running his tongue along her bottom lip. His free hand wrapped around her waist, sliding beneath her pajama pants. His palm dragged over the curve of her ass before his fingers dipped lower, sliding through her slit.

Cassia's breath hitched when he plunged a finger inside, stroking her inner walls.

His cock twitched between them, his arousal hardening against her belly. "You're soaked for me, aren't you, beauty?"

"Yes," she whispered, reaching between them for his cock. She'd just wrapped him in her fist when his fingers toyed with her again, plunging in and out, spreading her wetness through her folds.

She wanted him in her mouth, except before she could drop to her knees, his finger rose, pressing against her back entrance. Cassia gasped.

Did she want that? A thrill shot through her body, just like their first night two weeks ago when they'd watched that other couple have sex outside Treason.

"Someday. Soon." He pressed his finger deeper, her muscles tightening against the intrusion, then he eased off and swirled her juices through her crack. "You like that idea, don't you?"

"I—" She couldn't bring herself to say *yes,* so she nodded.

"Dirty girl," he murmured against her neck as his finger skimmed her clit. "Gonna let me corrupt you, Red?"

"Yes." She arched into his touch, rocking her hips against his hand.

"Take off your—" Before he could finish, the ring of his phone filled the air. "Fuck. Ignore it."

Cassia gripped him harder, stroking him as he fingered her. Except the phone kept ringing, and the moment it stopped, it started again.

Edwin cursed and stormed to the nightstand, pinching the bridge of his nose as he answered. "Now's not a good time. I'll call—what? I can't understand you."

The color drained from his face. "Slow down, Mom. Say that again. What happened to Zain?"

twenty-nine

. . .

ELORA HOVERED over the toilet as her breakfast was flushed away.

She wasn't pregnant. There were three negative pregnancy tests in the trash can to prove it.

No, she was heartsick.

That was the thing to explain the constant queasy state of her stomach over the past two weeks. Since the moment she'd walked out of Zain's building, her body had been rejecting food, as if it were punishing her for the bad decision.

"Ugh." She wiped her mouth and forced herself to stand, shuffling to the sink to brush her teeth. Again.

She'd just rinsed the toothpaste from her lips when the sound of her bedroom door bursting open carried to the bathroom.

"Elora!"

"Knock, Ivy." She didn't have the energy for her friend today.

"Elora!"

There was a panicked edge to Ivy's voice that made Elora stand straighter. She rushed for the door, yanking it open just as Ivy was about to knock. Her friend's hand stopped midair.

Ivy's face was pale. Tears streaked mascara down her cheeks.

"What's wrong?" Elora asked as a sinking feeling wormed into her gut. There were only a few reasons Ivy would be crying. There were only a few people Ivy would cry for.

Either something had happened to Francis, Geoff or Edwin. Or something had happened to Zain.

More tears poured from Ivy's eyes as she slapped a hand over her mouth to muffle a sob.

"Tell me." Elora grabbed Ivy's shoulder, shaking it from her.

Ivy dropped her hand, freeing another sob, then delivered the news that stopped the world from spinning.

"Zain. He was in a motorcycle accident."

Elora's knees ached.

After Ivy had told her about Zain's accident, she'd collapsed to the floor, cracking her knees on the tile.

No sooner had Ivy told her the news than Edwin had come jogging through her bedroom, panicked and searching for his sister.

It was Edwin who'd hauled Elora to her feet. Then he'd driven them to the hospital, where they'd been sitting in a cold waiting room for seven hours.

Elora had chosen a chair in the farthest corner of the room, pressed against a window. Cold air seeped through the glass, and night had fallen outside thanks to the short days of November. Streetlights illuminated the parking lot. An ambulance siren wailed in the distance, the pitch changing as it sped closer and closer to the emergency room.

She couldn't stop shivering. Her teeth chattered. Her feet bounced against the floor, making the pain in her knees worse. What she needed was to stand and walk around, but she was doing her best to blend into the walls.

To go unnoticed as the Clarence family converged on the opposite end of the waiting room.

Edwin had Ivy tucked under his arm. The twins had been leaning on each other since they'd arrived this morning. Zain's mother was so distraught and disheveled, Elora had hardly recognized her at first.

Helena's blond hair was in a knot that had fallen loose and was now hanging crooked. If she'd put makeup on this morning, it had been cried away. And instead of the pressed slacks, cashmere sweaters and pearl necklaces Elora had seen her wear whenever Helena had been sneaking out of her father's office after a fuck, she was in a pair of loose cream sweatpants and a matching zip-up. There was a coffee stain on her sleeve from when Edwin had brought her a cup earlier and Helena's hands had been shaking so badly she'd spilled it on herself.

Then there was David.

Elora hadn't seen him since she'd found out about Lucas's paternity.

Where his wife was a wreck, David looked as if he'd simply had a long day at the office. His necktie had been loosened, so it hung casually around his neck. The top button of his starched white shirt was undone and the sleeves had been rolled up his forearms. His suit jacket was draped over the upholstered back of a chair. But otherwise, he looked like an older version of Zain, minus the tattoos.

Apparently, Elora and her mother had a type.

Emotions warred inside her as she stared at him. She didn't trust herself to speak.

If she opened her mouth, she'd either start sobbing hysterically or the truth would come spewing out. So Elora sat in her chair, hoping the cold would make her numb. It hadn't yet. But it had only been seven hours.

Seven hours.

Zain had been in surgery since they'd arrived. Was that a good sign? Was it bad? Not long after they'd arrived this morning, a police officer had come to meet with David and

Helena. Elora had shamelessly eavesdropped when the cop had shared details of Zain's accident.

He'd taken his motorcycle out for a ride. He must have needed to clear his head. Maybe last night had been a rough one at the club. Or maybe he'd wanted to take advantage of the good roads before the snow came and his bike would be locked up until spring.

Whatever the reason, Zain had been about ten blocks from his neighborhood when a car had run a red light and smashed into the motorcycle.

The car's driver was just a kid. A teenager who'd been late for his shift washing dishes at a nearby diner. He'd walked away without a scratch.

Meanwhile, Zain was fighting for his life.

The trembling in Elora's hands was so noticeable she tucked them beneath her thighs. Then she closed her eyes and prayed.

Please don't take him.

The last time Elora had been to church was for last year's Christmas Eve service. She hadn't prayed since. But tonight, she prayed. She begged. She pleaded for Zain's life.

Because this world—her world—would be dark without his light.

"Hey."

Elora's eyes flew open at Ivy's voice. A tear dropped down her cheek and she brushed it away.

Ivy gave her a sad smile and settled into the seat beside Elora's. Then her friend took her hand, clutching it tight, as they sat in silence.

The clock on the wall ticked too loudly. Every time someone passed the waiting room, Elora sat up straighter, hoping it was news. But another hour passed.

Eight hours.

Nothing good happened if someone was in surgery for eight hours.

Please. Please. Please.

He had so much left to give. So much left he wanted to do with his life.

Zain hadn't hiked Mount Kilimanjaro. He'd just bought a house in Maui, but since it was being renovated, he hadn't stayed there once.

He wanted a few more tattoos. He hadn't decided what to get yet, but he'd chosen the locations. His foot. The underside of his right forearm. And something small across his heart.

He hadn't married the love of his life.

He hadn't made beautiful babies.

Elora's eyes flooded. There was no stopping the tears, so she spent the next hour catching them and praying.

Please don't take him.

"Mr. and Mrs. Clarence." A throat cleared. "I'm Dr. Chen."

Ivy shot out of her seat, rushing to join her parents as a man wearing navy scrubs and a matching cap stepped into the waiting room.

Elora rose from her seat, her breath caught in her throat because she didn't want to miss a word.

"Zain is alive," the doctor said.

Helena cried out, burying her face in her hands.

David put an arm around his wife, hauling her into his side. "Can we see him?"

"Briefly. He's in critical condition. His body has suffered extreme trauma, so we're not out of the woods. But he was wearing his helmet and that probably saved his life."

He'd worn his helmet. Zain hated his helmet, but he'd worn it today. Just like he had on their ride weeks ago.

The doctor went on to list Zain's various injuries, describing the hours they'd spent in surgery. Elora listened but all she heard was that he was alive.

And he'd worn his helmet.

Hours of dread and worry poured from her eyes. A sob worked its way loose, and before the next cry could interrupt the doctor, she slipped from the waiting room.

Her muscles ached. Her body was stiff, but she walked, faster and faster, until she saw a sign for a ladies' restroom. She pushed the door open, the light flipping on from the motion, and she ran into the first stall.

Then she let her emotions rip free from their chains.

She buried her face in her hands and screamed. She cried so hard and so loud that the noise bounced off the tiled walls. Her chest ached and her throat was raw by the time she'd finally pulled herself together enough to stand.

Elora blew her nose on cheap toilet paper and splashed water on her face, risking a glance in the mirror. She looked every bit as miserable as she felt. The sobs had stopped but there'd be no damming the tears, so she wadded up that cheap toilet paper and stuffed it into her pocket.

Only Edwin and Ivy were in the waiting room when she returned.

"Mom and Dad went to see Zain," Ivy said. "We'll go in next."

"Okay." Elora pointed for the hallway. "I think I'll get going."

Ivy scoffed. "No, you're going to see Zain."

"I just . . ." She swallowed the lump in her throat. "I just wanted to know he was okay."

Ivy crossed her arms over her chest. "You can see for yourself."

"I'm not family."

"Do you want to see him or not?"

Elora wanted to see him, if only for a moment. "Yes."

"Then shut up." Ivy took Elora's hand and pulled her to the hallway, just as Helena and David emerged from a set of double doors.

David had his wife tucked into his side, holding her close and whispering something in her ear as they walked.

Helena nodded at whatever it was he said, wrapping her arms around his waist.

Edwin came to stand beside Elora. "Well?" he asked his parents.

"He doesn't look good. Prepare yourself for that," David said. There was a haunting in David's eyes she'd missed earlier. He cared for his children, and tonight, he'd almost lost one.

Elora's heart twisted.

He didn't know about Lucas, did he? David must not know he had another child. Her mother must have spun an impressive lie to all of the men in her life.

"Can we all go in to see him?" Ivy asked.

David nodded. "Just for a few moments. They prefer one person at a time but the nurses will make an exception."

They'd make an exception to any hospital policy for David Clarence. After saving his oldest son's life, this hospital would surely be getting a sizeable donation when the dust settled.

Edwin led the way toward the double doors. He pushed a large button on the wall, and when it buzzed open, he went to the desk in the ICU, bending to speak to the nurse.

She nodded, waving them to follow her.

The rooms had glass panels instead of walls to separate them from the hallway. Most had white curtains drawn, giving patients their privacy, but the beeps and dings of various machines escaped the open doors. The sterile scent burned Elora's nose.

Ivy reached for Elora's hand. They clung to each other with every step.

The nurse peeked into a room, drawing away the curtain. "Just a few minutes, okay?"

"Thank you." Edwin gave her a nod, then slipped past the screen.

Ivy dropped Elora's hand to follow her brother.

She wanted to give them a moment alone, so Elora's feet stayed glued to the sterile white floor. Her heart thumped so hard she felt her pulse in her fingertips. When Ivy let out a gasp, Elora fisted her hands so tightly her nails left crescents in her palms.

She counted her breaths, forcing them in and out, until finally the curtain moved and Edwin and Ivy emerged.

Ivy was burrowed into her brother's side, much like Helena had been with David.

Elora hurried past them, ducking behind the curtain, and her own gasp filled the air.

Zain was lying flat on the bed, his torso covered in bandages. There was a tube coming out of his chest. Another was in his mouth. Both arms were covered in bandages. His bottom half was draped with a white blanket except for one leg that hung suspended from a series of wires.

And his face.

Elora brought a hand to her mouth, her chin quivering.

His eyes and nose were both swollen. His lips were puffy and scraped raw.

As she inched closer, the sutures and incision marks from surgery stood out. The damage to his organs was what had nearly killed him.

The monitor across from her beeped, the lines spiking up and down on the screen with his heartbeat.

Elora focused on the fingers of his left hand. His knuckles were scraped but none seemed broken. Carefully, she touched his hand, and the minute she felt his skin, the tears started falling again.

His hand was too cold.

"I love you." Her voice cracked. "I'll always love you."

She half expected Zain to open his eyes and give her a look like he'd known it all along. That she'd never hidden her love as well as she'd tried.

Instead, his heart monitor flatlined.

thirty

. . .

IVY JERKED AWAKE. The chair she'd fallen asleep in was so uncomfortable her left leg had gone numb. Her father's arm was around her shoulders and he loosened his hold as she sat up straight.

The events from last night came rushing back. The hospital. Zain's room. The monitors' shriek when his heart had stopped beating.

Elora's shattering cry.

Zain had crashed twice last night. Once, while Ivy had been standing with Edwin in the ICU. And again while she'd been in the waiting room, leaning into her father's side, just like she was now. The doctors had revived Zain both times, but the terror of being just feet away while her brother stood on death's doorstep was something Ivy wouldn't soon forget.

"Did the doctor come back?" she asked, looking up at her father. He seemed older today. Haggard. Heartbroken.

"About thirty minutes ago." Dad nodded. "Zain's stable. They're keeping a close eye on him."

There was no hope in his voice. Either the doctor hadn't given him any. Or he was preparing himself—and his daughter—for the worst.

No. Ivy wouldn't let herself fall down that trap. "He'll be okay."

Dad gave her a defeated smile.

She raised her chin. "He'll be okay."

His eyes turned glassy as he leaned forward, elbows to knees, and dropped his face in his hands. When his shoulders began to shake, Ivy wrapped her arms around him, hugging him as she willed her own tears away.

Don't cry. Don't cry.

She wasn't the strong one in the Clarence family. That was Dad's role. Zain's. Edwin's.

But she held her father tight, like she was forcing the strength from her own muscles into his. If this was all she could do today, ensure that her father didn't collapse, then she'd do it. So she closed her eyes and held him fiercely until the shaking in his body stopped and he sniffled, sitting upright.

"Sorry." He cleared his throat, wiped his cheeks.

Never, not once, had Ivy seen her father cry. "It's okay, Dad."

He tucked a lock of hair behind her ear, running his thumb over her jaw. Her skin felt gritty from the salt of her dried tears. "We'll have to make some phone calls today. I need to call your grandparents and give them an update. Get ahold of his manager at Treason. His friends."

Tate.

Shit. She should have called Tate.

Yesterday had passed in such a panicked blur, only a handful of people had been notified of the accident. Maybe Edwin had called people. Ivy wasn't sure. She hadn't touched her phone since her mother had called yesterday morning.

"I'll help," she said. Not that she had any idea of what to say. Ivy wanted to report good news except she didn't have good news to give. *Yet.* But Zain would be okay and then she'd have her good news. "We should probably wait a little longer. Until he wakes up."

There was Dad's defeated smile again. "Okay."

A surge of irritation rippled through Ivy's body. Why was he already giving up on Zain? He was young. He was strong. He'd come through this. Before she could snap at her father, she tore her eyes away and glanced around the waiting room. It was empty. "Where are Mom and Edwin?"

Where was Elora?

"They went for a walk after the doctor stopped in. You were sleeping and they didn't want to wake you."

Exhaustion—physical and mental—had forced her body to shut down.

Her nap couldn't have been for more than an hour, yet she felt jumpy, like she'd slept for days. Adrenaline and fear were her fuel at the moment. Standing, she took three steps, then turned and retraced the short path.

The walls of the waiting room had inched closer overnight, the space smaller than it had been earlier. Sunlight streamed through the windows, the yellow glow of morning too cheerful.

Too familiar.

Dawn and dread. They swirled in the air, taking her back to another hospital on another morning, not so different than this one.

A chill rolled over her shoulders, making her shiver. Ivy wrapped her arms around her waist and paced. Three steps. Turn. Three steps. Turn.

It was something that should have annoyed her dad. Fidgeting. Restlessness. He used to scold her for bouncing her knees beneath the dinner table when she was a kid. But he kept his eyes on the windows in a blank stare.

A throat cleared and she whirled as Edwin and their mother walked into the waiting room. Mom had fixed her hair at some point and it was now braided in a blond rope over her shoulder. But her face was still pale. Her eyes were as haunted as Dad's.

"Hi." Edwin came to Ivy and pulled her into his side. He'd

hugged her more times in the past twenty-four hours than he had in twenty-four months. "Any news?"

Ivy shook her head, leaning into him. They leaned on each other. They had their entire lives. "Nothing."

Mom went to sit beside Dad, taking the space Ivy had vacated. He turned to her, holding her close and kissing her temple.

It was strange to see them cling to each other. Ivy couldn't help but stare. The last time she'd seen them together, appearing like a married couple in love, had been years ago.

In another hospital, on another morning not so different than this one.

That shiver returned.

"You okay?" Edwin asked.

"No." She swallowed hard, forcing away the past. She didn't have time to relive it today. She didn't have the strength. "Where's Elora?"

Edwin pointed toward the hallway. "There's another waiting room down the hallway. She went to lie down."

"Alone?" Ivy stiffened. Elora shouldn't be by herself, not today.

"I just checked on her. She's asleep."

"We can't leave her alone."

Edwin sighed. "Seems like I've missed something, huh? Elora and Zain?"

"Yeah." She lowered her voice to keep it from their parents. Whatever was going on with Elora and Zain was not her announcement to make. All she cared about at the moment was that he'd be here to navigate that path. That he'd be here to love Elora as she loved him.

The echo of that wail in the ICU was stuck in Ivy's head.

She'd never heard such agony as when Elora had cried in Zain's room. Her best friend had a talent for hiding her emotions and feelings, but last night, the walls had fallen down. Maybe they'd broken up, but it couldn't be the end.

Elora deserved Zain. And he deserved her. So he had to wake up. They needed to sort their shit out and stop hiding their relationship from the world.

"He'll be okay," Ivy said, more to herself than Edwin.

"He'll be okay." Edwin held her tighter. "You doing okay? Being here?"

In the hospital.

Of course he'd notice.

"I'm trying not to think about it," she whispered. "Tell me something. Anything."

He nodded toward the chairs next to the window. They shuffled together, out of earshot of their parents, who were still holding on to each other, eyes closed and hands clasped. "What was the last thing you said to Zain?"

She flinched. That was not a distraction. That was just leading her down the path that her father was walking. "I don't know," she snapped. "I don't really want to think like that."

Edwin frowned, dragging a hand over his face. His stubble scraped against his palm as his eyes stayed focused out the window's glass. "He tried to call me last week. I was at the library on campus and didn't answer."

Edwin had probably been sitting in that quiet corner on the library's third floor next to the quarter vending machine. *His* quarter vending machine. The staff always made sure it was stocked with his favorite candy—which he paid for, along with a stipend to compensate them for the work.

It was an indulgence by the campus because the Clarence name went a long way at Aston, especially in the library.

Their junior year, Grandfather had donated ten million dollars to Aston in Bridget's name, requesting it be used to renovate the library. Bridget had loved books, and Grandfather had loved Bridget.

Wonderful. Loving. Beautiful Bridget.

She hadn't shared their name or their blood, but she'd

been the bright spot in the Clarence family. Nothing had been the same since she'd passed. There was a hole in Ivy's heart. Edwin's too. And their grandfather had become a miserable bastard.

Elton Clarence had all the money in the world but he'd been helpless when she'd gotten sick. They'd all been helpless, forced to watch as the cancer had stolen Bridget's light.

Edwin went to the library's third floor to remember Bridget. Not Ivy. She only went if necessary for a class. Mostly, she gathered her books from the history department's private collection. It was there, immersed in the pages of a tattered text, that Ivy remembered Bridget. The grandmother of her heart. The person who'd taught her the joy of escaping reality by diving into a story.

Bridget had also been the person to stand strong during the Clarence family's last congregation in a hospital waiting room. Bridget had never once given up hope, not until the doctors had declared death.

"I wish Bridget were here," Ivy whispered.

"Me too." Edwin's voice was hoarse.

"I hate being here." Her chin began to quiver. "It's too familiar."

Edwin reached for her hand, holding it tight. "I know."

Her muscles began to shake. The trembling started in her fingertips and crawled up her arms before creeping down her spine and into her legs.

On the outside, she stood perfectly still. Her hand was unmoving in Edwin's grip. But her bones rattled. The quivering settled beneath her skin, crawling like insects trailing over her veins.

Ivy wrenched her hand from Edwin's grip, needing to get the fuck out of this waiting room. She spun around, ready to run anywhere, then froze. Dr. Chen walked into the room.

Mom and Dad shot out of their seats, their hands still clutched together as the doctor nodded in greeting.

"How is he?" Dad asked.

"Stable," Dr. Chen said. "I don't have much to report other than he's stable. And right now, that's good news. We're going to give him more time, then reassess this afternoon. But we're on the right path. He's improved considerably from last night. His body is strong. We just need to give it a chance to heal."

The air rushed out of Edwin's lungs. Dad's shoulders relaxed away from his ears and the tension in Mom's face eased.

It was a relief. So why was Ivy still shaking?

"Thank you, Dr. Chen." Dad shook the surgeon's hand.

The moment the doctor was out of the waiting room, Mom dug her phone from her pocket. "We need to tell people what's going on. My parents are waiting for an update. So are yours."

Dad put his hand over hers. "I'll do it. You need to rest. I can stay here and you should go ho—"

"No, David. I can't go home." She shook her head. "I won't go home."

"All right." He kissed her forehead. "We'll both stay."

"I'll get coffee." Edwin's tone said he'd be staying too.

Ivy should want to stay. To be close to her family while they waited. Except the nervous energy was bubbling free. The shaking was setting it loose. She wanted to leave this waiting room and never look back.

Run. Run. Run.

It pounded in her mind with every thundering heartbeat.

What the hell was wrong with her? She hadn't felt like this last night. Why now?

Maybe the weight of it all was becoming too much. Zain's accident. The hospital.

She'd almost lost her brother in a crash.

It was entirely different than Kristopher.

And entirely too similar.

"I, um . . ." Ivy's pulse boomed. Her head began to spin.

The walls kept inching closer and closer, trapping her in this space. "I need to walk or something."

"Let's go to the cafeteria," Edwin offered with a sad smile. Could he see her panic brewing? Could he feel the shaking now too?

"Air." She dragged in a breath through her nostrils. "I need some air. Elora. Will you—"

"I'll check on her."

Without another word, Ivy flew from the room. She hit the hallway, jogging every three steps, as she kept her eyes on the elevator ahead. She was about there, just a few more steps and she could escape, when a chime filled the air and the elevator doors slid open.

Tate stepped out.

Ivy's heart crashed. Her knees buckled.

"Whoa." He caught her before she could fall, hauling her into his chest. "Is it Zain?"

She shook her head, her fingertips digging into his arms as she clung to him. "No. He's stable."

"Thank fuck." He held her tighter, his lips against her hair. "I came as soon as I heard."

"How?" Ivy dragged in his scent, praying that spicy aroma would make the shaking stop. It didn't.

"Edwin. Texted me about thirty minutes ago." Tate took her chin, studying her face. "You're shaking."

She nodded. "I can't stop."

"Come on." He reached behind him, hitting the button for the elevator. The doors slid open instantly and he pulled her inside, never lightening his hold.

She didn't have to tell him what she needed. He took her to the first floor and through the double-door exit, walking her into the chill of the morning, where the cold air burned in her nostrils.

The crisp air should have worked. The shaking should have stopped. But she was still coming out of her skin.

A therapist years ago had told her to watch for panic attacks. Was this one?

"I can't—" She shook her head, pushing out of Tate's hold and hurrying down the sidewalk.

She felt dizzy. She felt drunk. A nurse wearing baby-blue scrubs passed by, giving her an assessing stare, but Ivy kept walking until she reached a crosswalk.

Before she could step onto the road, Tate's hand clamped around hers, tugging her to their left. His long strides forced her to jog but she had enough anxiety in her bones to run a marathon.

Tate didn't say a word as he led her to his Land Rover in the visitors' parking lot. He dug the keys from his jeans pocket and hit the locks, whipping open the rear door.

Ivy dove inside, sliding across the leather seats.

He sat beside her, closing them inside. Then he put his hand on the nape of her neck, pushing her head between her knees. "Breathe."

The air burned as she forced it into her lungs, expanding them to their brink. She held it, counting the seconds. When she hit fifteen, she blew it out in a rush.

"Again," Tate ordered.

This time, she counted to twenty.

It was on the third breath, when she'd made it to twenty-three, that her head began to clear. The spinning stopped.

But the shaking. That goddamn shaking.

She held out her quivering hands. In the waiting room, she'd managed to hold it in. Now it had escaped and she wasn't sure how to shove it back in the bottle.

"I hate hospitals," she whispered. "How am I supposed to go back in there?"

"I'll go with you." Tate's hand stroked up and down her spine while she stared at her hands.

She fisted them. Relaxed them. Fisted them again. They still trembled. "Gah."

"Talk to me."

How was she supposed to explain this? It wasn't just fear for her brother's life. It was the memories. It was that damn waiting room. It was reliving the devastation when a doctor had come out with bad news instead of good.

Ivy had pushed through it yesterday, but today there was no ignoring the past. She needed a distraction. A release.

Tate's cologne infused the cab. With the tinted windows, they were tucked in a safe cocoon. So she took one of her shaking hands and placed it on his thigh.

The moment her palm touched his jeans, the shaking stopped. Relief coursed through her body.

Tate tensed as she slid her hand toward his zipper. "Ivy—"

"Don't tell me no." *Make me forget.* She turned to face him. "Please."

A crease formed between his eyebrows.

"Please," she begged again. She'd get on her knees if necessary.

He growled. "This is not how I wanted this to go."

Before she could plead again, his mouth slammed down on hers, swallowing a gasp.

Ivy had expected a no, so it took her a split second to realize this was the *yes* she'd wanted for weeks.

She opened for him, his tongue making a slow slide against her own. Then he fluttered it against her lips before tangling them together, rough and hard. He plundered where other men might start soft. He tasted like a dream, sweet and smooth with a hint of mint.

God, this man could kiss. Ivy went boneless against him, drowning in his taste and touch.

He sucked on her bottom lip and the shaking in her hands was history. The world outside the car vanished. All that mattered was the craving curling in her lower belly.

Their teeth clashed. Her hands roved over his chest, like she was trying to touch everything before the spell broke.

She cupped his growing bulge, feeling his hardness beneath his jeans. A bolt of desire, stronger than any she'd felt before, zinged through her body. Her core clenched. *More.*

Tate groaned and tore his lips away. A frown marred his handsome features but there was no hiding the pure lust in his dark eyes.

Make me forget.

The words rang so loudly in Ivy's head she could have sworn Tate heard them too.

There was nothing graceful about how they stripped out of their clothes. Hands fumbled between sloppy kisses. Urgency fogged the air, clinging to the windows. There was no time for seduction. No space for foreplay.

Tate gripped her by the hips, lifting and spinning Ivy to settle her over his naked lap. Her knees dug into the seats, her hands finding his pecs and her fingers skating across the dusting of dark hair. Their breaths mingled.

His hand clamped around the back of her neck, hauling her in for a kiss. His cock, covered with a condom, pulsed between them. As his lips moved over hers, that hand on her neck kept her mouth pinned against his as his other hand gripped his shaft, dragging the tip through her slit.

Soaked. She was soaked for this man.

He tugged harder on her neck, and Ivy sank down on his cock. Her eyes flew open at the stretch, his size stealing her breath.

Tate's eyes opened, finding hers, their mouths still latched. His hand came to her hip, gripping her flesh so tightly it was like he wanted to tattoo his fingerprints on her skin. There'd be bruises tomorrow.

She couldn't wait to see them in her mirror.

Ivy relished the sting, rising up to slam down on him again. Her back arched. Her mouth broke from his as a wave of ecstasy rolled down her spine. Her moan filled the cab.

"Fuck, baby," Tate hissed, cupping her breasts in his hands. He rolled her nipples once, giving them a hard pinch that made her pleasure skyrocket. Then his lips were there, sucking her into his mouth.

Her fingers threaded into his hair as she moved, riding him with wanton strokes. Chasing her own release. The smell of sex filled the air, mingling with his heady scent. The sound of slapping skin mixed with the sound of panted breaths as they rocked together.

A groan, deep from Tate's broad chest, made her move faster.

She wanted to close her eyes, to disappear into the feel of fucking Tate, but she memorized his body instead.

His washboard abs were bunched. His chest was strong, his arms ripped with muscle. Later, when they were in bed and she had room to explore, she'd touch every peak. Every dip. Every inch of his skin. For now, she focused on the chiseled cut of his jaw, the clench that came every time she brought them together.

Harder and harder, he thrust up into her as she sank down onto him. Over and over, until a sheen of sweat coated her skin. Ivy's fingertips dug into his chest, her nails leaving red marks. It was seeing those scratches that pushed her to the edge.

Then his finger came to her clit, giving it a swirl.

She was done.

"Tate," she cried as she detonated, leaving this world for the heavens. Her entire being pulsed as wave after wave of her orgasm crashed. Blood rushed in her ears. Her heart felt like it was going to leap out of her chest.

"Oh fuck, that's good." Tate groaned before he threw his head back, his eyes squeezing shut as he was lost to his own release.

Limp and sated, she sagged against him, her nose buried in the crook of his neck. Their chests heaved as the haze from their orgasms cleared. She wanted to burrow beneath his skin, to disappear into his strong body where it was safe. To pretend reality wasn't waiting for them outside.

They stayed connected, draped against each other, until finally his hand skittered up and down her spine. "Now you can tell me what that was about."

"About making me forget."

"Forget what?"

Forget another hospital, on another morning not so different than this one.

"Everything," she whispered.

thirty-one

. . .

CASSIA PAUSED on the staircase at the library. Above the entrance to the third floor was Bridget's name. The satin, silver block letters blended beautifully with the robin's-egg-blue paint of the walls.

"Observant, Cassie," she muttered with a laugh. Weeks she'd been hiking these stairs and not once had she noticed the name.

It wouldn't have made sense to her anyway, not before Edwin.

She reached the landing and plucked her phone from the pocket of her coat, typing out a text as she walked toward her usual quiet corner next to the vending machine. Their usual corner.

How are you?

Yesterday morning, after Edwin had dressed in a flurry and raced out of her bedroom, explaining that Zain had been in a motorcycle accident, Cassia hadn't been sure what to do.

If Edwin were her boyfriend, she might have gone to the hospital to keep him company. Refill coffees and offer hugs. But they were . . .

"Something," she whispered.

They were something. She just didn't have a name for that something yet.

She stared at the screen, scrolling through the texts she'd sent him last night.

Are you okay?

How is Zain?

Can I do anything to help?

Most of his replies had been short. He'd given her a quick text that Zain was in critical condition, but that had been around midnight, and she hadn't heard anything since. Cassia didn't expect much conversation, but she wanted him to know she was there.

Her heart leapt as three dots appeared on the screen.

I'm okay. The doctor just gave us an update. Zain's stable. They're watching him closely but he seemed more hopeful, I guess. I don't know. Maybe I'm just hopeful.

Her fingers flew across the screen as she typed out a reply.

I'm sure he'll be fine

She deleted it. She typed again.

Stable is good

That was deleted too. What the hell did she know about medical terminology?

Hang tight

Delete. Delete. Delete. Everything she wrote seemed shallow. Cassia had only lived through one emergency situation, and when they'd taken her father's body away, it hadn't been to the hospital.

It had been to the morgue.

Finally she landed on a message she didn't hate.

I'm so sorry. I'm hopeful too.

She hit send on her reply, then quickly typed out another.

I know you have a lot going on. If my texts are bothering you, just tell me to stop.

Edwin's reply was instant.

Don't stop

"Okay." She gave the screen a sad smile and walked to the

table, setting her phone on the surface as she shrugged out of her coat to take a seat.

Studying had been futile yesterday. Her mind had been with Edwin, not economics. Every five minutes, she'd gone online to search for news about Zain's accident. There hadn't been any until late last night.

But she couldn't miss another day of studying, so here she was in the library. If only she hadn't loaded so many classes into her schedule. Cassia wanted the ability to take an entire weekend off without putting herself behind. In the beginning, the work overload had been necessary. Except now she had Edwin and their . . . *something*.

"Thought I saw you come up here."

Cassia whirled around in her seat. "Oh my God, Michael. Make a noise. Warn a girl."

"Sorry." He chuckled, holding up his hands. With that confident swagger, he rounded the table and took the other chair. Edwin's chair.

She held back a frown. "What are you working on today?"

"That research paper for 410. You?"

"Same." She unzipped her backpack and hauled out her laptop. "I haven't even started it yet."

"Want to work on it together? I just got here. My stuff's around the corner."

She shrugged. "Sure."

It wasn't a group assignment and her topic was entirely different than his, but someone to keep her accountable, to keep her from checking her phone every few minutes, might help. It was why she'd come to the library on a Sunday morning instead of working in her bedroom. In the hopes of finding a shred of focus.

"Nice." Michael stood. "Be back."

They worked quietly for an hour before Michael groaned and closed the lid on his laptop. "I hate this class."

"But is it as bad as Health Econ?" Cassia giggled.

"Hmm." Michael tapped his chin. "It's a draw."

Their professor in Health was dull and every hour-long lecture felt like a day. Plus the assignments were basic. Boring. Her theory was that their professor wanted them to have busy-work for the sake of wasting paper rather than expending any critical thought.

Cassia pushed her own laptop aside, reaching for her phone, hoping to see something from Edwin. But the screen was blank, so she sent him a quick note.

Thinking about you. Need anything?

How long was he going to wait at the hospital? Was he hungry? Should she take him food or a decent coffee?

"What are you doing tonight?" Michael asked.

"Not much." She returned her phone to the table. "Why? Is the study group meeting?"

"Not until tomorrow. You haven't joined us lately."

"I've been sort of overloaded, so I guess you could say I'm suffering in solitude." It was total bullshit. She'd skipped the study group so she could race through her assignments and spend a few hours each night with Edwin.

Michael's gaze narrowed on her face, like he could see her lie. Irritation flashed through his expression but was gone just as quickly, his charming smile fixed in place. "Well, how about you take a night off from the suffering and go to dinner with me?"

"Oh, uh . . ." *Shit.* Weren't they firmly in the platonic, classmate zone? "Like a date?"

"Yeah." He grinned. "Why not?"

Her phone buzzed, the vibration drawing her attention. And Michael's.

I'm good. Call you later

Cassia swiped Edwin's text notification away but not before Michael had seen the name on the screen.

"Ah." Michael nodded. "You're after Clarence."

She took her phone and set it on her lap, out of sight. "We're just . . ." *Something.*

"Look, Cassia." Michael leaned his arms on the table. "We're friends."

Were they friends? She wasn't sure what a friend was anymore, but if she had to label Michael, *friend* was probably correct.

"So friend to friend," he said, "be careful. Edwin is known for chewing women up and spitting them out."

Wait. What? She sat straighter. "Huh?"

"He dated my cousin for a long time. Took her virginity. Promised he'd be her only one. She would have married him. She loved him. What he did to her"—Michael shook his head—"it broke her. It's taken her years to recover."

This had to be Edwin's ex, the woman Bridget had despised. Michael's cousin was Edwin's ex. Did everyone know everyone around here?

"What do you mean, 'what he did to her'?" Cassia asked. The way Michael spoke was like the demise of that relationship had been solely Edwin's fault.

"He cheated on her so many times she started doing weekly STD tests. He used her when it was convenient. Then after a couple years of being at Aston, he decided he could do better. He tossed her aside."

No. That didn't at all seem like Edwin. Yes, he'd told her that he'd been different. That his relationship with his ex had been toxic. But that venom had flowed both ways.

"He told you about her, didn't he?" Michael asked. "Probably said she cheated too. That she was a liar and a bitch."

"He didn't . . . he didn't call her a bitch," she murmured.

Michael scoffed. "Just watch out, okay? I'd hate to see you devastated like she was."

"We're not . . . it's nothing."

"He has his hooks in you."

Oh, how Cassia hated that expression. *Hooks*. Josh had used it all the time as a joke. *I've got my hooks in you and I'll never let you go.*

The goddamn liar. His hooks had been cast in an entirely different pond.

"Appreciate the warning," she clipped, pulling her laptop closer. The last thing she wanted to do was dive back into her paper, but this was her table. Edwin's table. And she wasn't about to leave.

"You're mad."

"I'm . . ." Cassia sighed. Yes, she was mad. But she couldn't pin all her frustration on him.

Because she was pissed at herself too. For the doubts blossoming in her mind. She wished more than anything she could tell Michael exactly how he was wrong, but the truth was, she couldn't. She hadn't known Edwin long enough. And they'd only shared a single conversation about his ex.

As much as she wanted to defend him, she simply didn't have the ammunition.

"I'm not just speaking for my cousin," Michael said. "I've got my own experience with the Clarence family."

"You mean Ivy."

"Yeah." He nodded. "It's no secret we've been on and off for years. Every time I thought we were together, I'd learn otherwise. She takes what she wants. She uses people until she's had her fill. Then you're nothing. People are expendable."

"Edwin and Ivy are different people." The argument sounded solid in her ears, yet there was a crack in her confidence. One she hoped Michael would miss.

"Maybe," he said. "Maybe not. I've known them both for a long, long time."

"Maybe." She waved off the topic, settling her hands over her keyboard.

"I'm not trying to be an asshole. I'm just being honest."

"I know." She typed a word. Deleted it. Typed another. Damn it. Now Michael had screwed up her focus too. She dug through her backpack for a quarter, finding one at the bottom of her smallest pocket. Then she stood and stomped to the vending machine.

The Mike and Ike boxes were gone.

Her lip curled as she punched in the code for Starbursts.

Behind her, Michael collected his things.

"I'm going to take off," he said.

Thank God. "Okay."

"Don't sound so relieved." Michael chuckled. "I was just trying to help."

"Yeah." *Damn.* "Sorry. I just wasn't expecting this to be our conversation today."

"Just think about my warning, all right? Ivy plays with people. So does her brother."

She nodded. "Fair enough."

"Good luck on your paper. See you in class tomorrow?"

"I'll be there." She forced a smile and a wave as he walked past her, disappearing around the corner. Then her body sagged, resting against the vending machine.

Why would Michael warn her about Edwin if it wasn't true? Was it just a jealousy thing? Maybe Michael had known she was going to turn him down for a date and this was his way of deflecting. Or maybe he'd been sincere.

A different warning sprang to mind, a warning she'd heard years ago on a drunken night at a fraternity party when a guy had told her to be careful. That Josh was not what he seemed.

Cassia hadn't listened back then.

And it had cost her everything.

It had cost her a life.

Maybe she should listen to Michael. Maybe she needed to slow down this *something* with Edwin. But why? Except everything was different this time around.

Cassia had nothing to lose. Not even her heart.

She'd lost it at Hughes.

thirty-two

. . .

ELORA STARED at herself in the hospital's bathroom mirror, a ghost in the reflection. Her dark-brown eyes had lost their luster. Her skin had a gray tinge. Her lips were an odd, pale mix of pink and blue and purple.

Using her fingers, she combed her hair, tucking it behind her ears and pulling twin panels down her front. She washed her hands, wishing the water were warmer. Then on a sigh, she retreated to the hallway.

She'd fallen asleep in an empty waiting room earlier, wishing when she'd closed her eyes that when she opened them, this nightmare would have passed. Instead, the stench of the hospital, sterile and plastic, had greeted her when she'd startled awake.

Elora shivered as she trudged across the floor. Her toes were numb in her shoes. In the rush to leave the manor yesterday morning, after Edwin had picked her up off her bathroom floor, she hadn't thought to put on socks. The sweatshirt she was wearing was too thin and her leggings offered no insulation. It had been warmer in the waiting room where she'd taken her short nap, but she didn't want to be too far from the Clarences.

So she returned to the waiting room where she'd sat last night, where she'd mentally and emotionally shut down after Zain's crash. Her footsteps were heavy but she forced herself to pick up her feet, to walk in silence, back to the chair next to the chilly window.

Edwin, sitting beside Helena with his gaze on his phone, looked up as she entered. Thankfully, David had gone somewhere else.

Zain's parents hadn't acknowledged Elora once. Not that she'd expected a smile or a hello. They were in their own heads, like she was, and pleasantries were unnecessary. After all, she hadn't approached them either. She might be Ivy's friend and roommate, but she was also a Maldonado.

Those twisted little affairs were wrapped up in her name. Her face reminded them of their sins.

Edwin came to sit beside her, leaning close to keep his voice low. "Want some coffee?"

"No, thanks." Too much coffee had made her jittery and her stomach ache. "Where's Ivy?"

"I think she needed to get some air. Being here, at a hospital . . ."

"Memories." *Nightmares*.

"Yeah." Edwin put his arm around her shoulders. "You okay?"

She sank into the comfort he was offering. A comfort so similar to Zain's she would have cried if there were any tears left. "Has the doctor come back?"

"Not yet." Edwin had come to find her in the other waiting room to pass on the doctor's last update. Zain was stable. He needed time.

Elora needed Zain.

So she'd wait. She'd linger on the fringe of this waiting room, clinging to hope.

"I might take a walk later. Want to come?" Edwin asked.

"Sure."

"You're cold."

Frozen. She was stuck in Zain's room, hearing the shrill alarms of his monitors. "A little."

"I don't think we'll hear anything for a while. You could drive my car to the manor. Change clothes. Get Francis to make you something hot. Come back in an hour or two."

"I'm all right." Elora's phone was in her pocket, and if it got too bad, she'd call Geoff and ask him to bring her a parka and wool socks. But she wasn't leaving this hospital. Not yet.

"There was banana bread in the cafeteria. I'm going to get us some."

Before Elora could tell him there was no way she'd be able to eat, a woman flew into the waiting room.

No, not just a woman.

The blond.

Zain's blond.

"Helena." The woman's voice cracked as she rushed toward Zain's mother.

Edwin stiffened. "Shit."

"Oh, Mira." Helena stood from her seat, her arms opening as the two of them practically crashed together in an embrace.

Mira.

The yellow Post-it note.

The floor had opened and she was free-falling into an endless black hole. Her nightmare had morphed into a horror movie. She hated horror movies but she was stuck in this chair, a front-row seat to what would only end in death. Someone must have taped her eyes open because she was unable to look away.

She was beautiful, Zain's Mira.

When Elora had seen her at Club 27, she'd been dressed for a night out. Makeup. Hair. Heels. But today she wasn't dressed all that differently from Elora, in a pair of black leggings and an oversized green turtleneck. Her makeup was simple. Classy. She had pretty blue eyes and high cheekbones.

Elora resembled a child, but Mira was a woman. She held this grace, a poise and elegance, that was palpable.

Zain had a palpable presence too.

"Any news?" Mira asked, unwrapping her arms from Helena.

"He's stable. We can't do anything but wait."

Mira closed her eyes, taking Helena's hands in her own. "I can't believe this is happening."

"I'm sorry, I should have called you. Last night was a blur and—"

"Don't apologize." Mira gave her a sad smile. "I'm here now. What can I do?"

"I'm going to ask to see him in a bit. You'll come with me."

"I'd like that. Thank you." A tear dripped down Mira's cheek and she sniffled, brushing the drop away. The florescent lights glinted off a ring she wore on her left hand.

An engagement ring.

Even from across the room, Elora could make out the color of the center stone. It was a canary diamond, at least three carats, bracketed by two white diamonds on a golden band.

"You're wearing your ring." Helena gasped, her hand coming to her heart as she gave Mira a shaky smile. Then the tears began to fall down her cheeks as she pulled Mira into another hug. "I always hoped you two would find your way together again."

Elora's chest cracked, a jagged crevasse that bared her soul. *Engaged.* Zain was engaged. She was sitting in this waiting room, loving him from a cold seat, when he was marrying Mira.

"We've been talking," Mira said. "Sort of rekindled things. I guess . . . it's been a long time coming."

Helena nodded. "He'll be so happy to see you when he wakes up."

"Mira?" David walked into the waiting room, straight toward the women.

"Hi." She gave him a sad smile as he came to her, pulling her into a tight embrace.

"Thanks for coming, sweetheart."

"There's nowhere else I'd be," Mira whispered.

For Mira, David offered a hug.

For Elora, well . . . maybe she really had become a ghost. Her mother's ghost.

Fuck, it hurt.

She was too raw to keep up the wall to block out the pain. Between Zain and David and that canary diamond, she wanted to scream.

Like he could hear her silent heartbreak, Edwin's hold around her shoulders tightened. "Sorry."

Ivy chose that moment to return, sweeping into the waiting room with Tate on her heels. The moment she spotted Mira, she halted, her face narrowing into a glare that Elora had seen a thousand times. "What are you doing here?"

Mira stepped out of David's embrace and gave Ivy a finger wave. "Hi, Ivy."

"Why are you here?" Ivy crossed her arms.

"Hi, Tate," Mira said, ignoring Ivy's question.

"Hey, Mira." He came to stand at Ivy's side, his hand going to her shoulder like he was holding her in place.

Ivy cast him a glare, then refocused on Mira with a lip curl.

But Mira seemed immune. She offered Ivy another sweet smile, then tugged Helena to a pair of chairs. The two of them, sitting together, looked like a grieving mother and daughter.

No, a *daughter-in-law*.

Elora felt the sting of tears. Her nose burned and her throat closed.

She wasn't needed here. She wasn't welcome here.

Zain had made his decision. He'd given Mira a ring. And

when he woke up, Elora's would not be the face he sought out in the crowd.

She stood, her knees wobbling, as she slipped along the wall. Every eye was on her as she walked, their gazes burning into her skin, but she kept her shoulders straight, her spine rigid, until she was at the elevators.

"Wait," Ivy called, running down the hall to catch up.

Elora punched the down button.

"Where are you going?" Ivy came to a skidding stop at Elora's side.

"Home."

"But Zain—"

"Is engaged."

"No, he was. A long time ago. But he broke up with Mira."

Elora retraced her entire history with Zain, and not once had he mentioned being engaged.

She'd asked Zain if the blond had known his family. Apparently that wasn't just limited to his parents. Ivy knew Mira too. Maybe if Elora hadn't kept her affair with Zain a secret, Ivy would have told Elora more about his past girlfriends. Maybe Zain would have told her himself.

It didn't matter now. They'd been over for weeks.

It was time for Elora's heart to catch up with reality.

"Sounds like they're back together." Elora hit the elevator's button again, wishing it would hurry the fuck up and rescue her from this terror tower.

"Don't leave."

Elora swallowed the burn in her throat. She wasn't going to cry in front of the Clarence family, Ivy included. "It's fine."

This had always been the outcome. This had always been the final chapter.

Zain with a woman who fit his life. A woman he could cherish who had no entanglements with his family. A woman who wore yellow diamonds because they were cheerful and bright and bubbly.

A woman he could love who could say it back.

The ding of the elevator flooded Elora's body with relief. The moment the doors slid open, she stepped inside, pressing the button for the lobby.

"I'm sorry." Pity clouded Ivy's gaze.

"Don't tell him I was here," Elora said.

Ivy shook her head. "Why?"

The doors began to close.

"Don't tell him I was here," she repeated.

Then she was alone.

Then she let herself collapse.

thirty-three

. . .

IVY'S SHAKING HAD STOPPED thanks to fucking Tate in the back of his car. And with the panic attack gone, she had a plethora of emotional space available for rage.

She marched into the waiting room, her hands fisted, and stopped in front of Mira's chair. "Leave."

"Ivy," her mother hissed. "I'm sorry, Mira. We're all a bit on edge."

Dad looked up from his phone, giving Ivy a scowl.

"It's fine." Mira's smile was as fake as it had been years ago. "I understand. But I was thinking . . . on my way here, I passed a bakery a few blocks away. How about I go and grab us all something fresh?"

"That would be lovely." Mom patted Mira's hand. The hand with an engagement ring. The same engagement ring Zain had given Mira years ago. Why the hell was she wearing it again? What the fuck was happening?

"David, still love chocolate croissants?" Mira asked.

Dad gave her a soft smile. "You remember."

"Of course." Mira stood, collecting her purse. She brushed past Ivy, then stopped beside Tate, who was standing next to Edwin against the far wall. "Want anything?"

"Coffee," he said. "Need a hand?"

Ivy's vision clouded with red. Tate was cozy with Mira? *Fuck no.*

"No, I've got it." Mira looked to Edwin. "Can I bring you something?"

Edwin shook his head, his expression blank. He didn't like Mira either, he just wasn't as forthcoming with his disdain as Ivy.

She waited until Mira walked out of the room before following. Footsteps echoed behind her but she didn't turn to see who'd followed them. If it was Edwin, he could back her up. If it was Tate, well . . . he'd get a firsthand glimpse of Ivy's ugly colors.

Mira walked for the elevators, stopping in front of the doors where Elora had just disappeared.

It wasn't right. Elora should be here, not Mira. Elora should be first in line for updates, not Mira. Elora should be wearing his ring. Not. Fucking. Mira.

What the hell was Zain thinking, starting this bullshit up again? Mira was as toxic as bleach.

Ivy couldn't remember a time when Zain had brought Mira to their house for a holiday function when the two of them hadn't ended up in a room, fighting. Mira was too much like their mother, concerned with outward appearances instead of being honest and real.

Once, while Ivy had been in high school, Edwin had asked Zain what he was going to get for his next tattoo. Before he could answer, Mira had shushed him, saying that Zain's body was her temple now and there'd be no more tattoos.

"Forget the bakery," Ivy said, stopping beside Mira. "Just leave."

They were about the same height, so when Mira faced her, their glares locked. "I'm here for Zain."

"Are you sure he wants you?"

She raised her left hand, wiggling her ring finger. "What's the matter, Ivy? Worried for your friend? I know all about

Zain's fling with that little girl. But she's not wearing a ring, is she? Like it or not, I'm here."

"God, you are such a bitch."

"When necessary." Mira shrugged as the elevator dinged. "Be back soon."

"I hate her," Ivy seethed as the elevator swept Mira away. She spun, nearly colliding with Tate. "How did she even know he was here?"

Tate sighed. "I called her."

"What?" Ivy's jaw slackened.

He held up his hands. "She's been spending time with Zain. She had a right to know."

"Like hell she does."

"They have a history, Ivy. Whether you like it or not. Bottom line, it's Zain's choice."

"And Zain's making the wrong choice." She threw her arms in the air.

Tate reached for her, his fingertips brushing her arm as he tried to pull her close, but she stepped out of his grasp and stormed down the hallway. "Ivy."

She ignored him, her strides quickening, until she spotted a stairwell door. Before Tate could stop her, she threw it open and climbed. Up, up, up. She went until her legs were on fire and there were no more stairs. Then she turned and went down.

She left the stairwell on the first floor, taking a left without caring where she was going. She passed signs pointing to the emergency room and another to the cafeteria. When she came to a different stairwell, she went to the third floor and walked. Then to the fifth. Then to the fourth. Up and down and back and forth. She walked and got lost in the maze of hallways and stairwells.

But nothing about her exploration changed one simple fact.

Ivy fucking hated hospitals.

She hated the beige walls and the glossy floors. She hated

how nurses always gave you comforting smiles when they passed, like they weren't sure if you were about to get good news or bad, so they assumed the worst. She hated that the smell of death lingered beneath whatever cleaning solvents they used to mask the sick and kill the germs.

She hated every inch of this place and there was no way to escape it. Not today. Not until they learned if Zain was going to be okay.

Her stomach cramped with hunger pangs by the time she was on the seventh floor. Her phone buzzed in her pocket. She ignored them both and kept walking.

Except the shoes she'd put on yesterday weren't meant for miles. The backs rubbed at her heels, and by the time she'd retreated to the waiting room to rejoin her family, blisters were festering on her skin.

"Where have you been?" Edwin's jaw clenched when she came to stand beside him.

"Walking." The room was empty except for the two of them. "Where is everyone?"

"The doctor came in and told them they could see Zain."

Her heart lurched. "Is he all right?"

"He's improved. Considerably. If it keeps up, they'll wake him up tonight."

"Thank God." Ivy's entire body sagged.

"Edwin?" They both turned at their mother's voice. "You can go in."

He walked past her, bending to kiss Mom's cheek before striding away.

"How is he?" Ivy asked her.

"He looks awful. But better. I don't know. When your father comes out, you can go in next."

"Where are Tate and Mira?" She couldn't hide the snarl at that bitch's name.

"They left." Mom sighed, going to a chair to slump in the seat. "Where were you?"

"Just walking around. I needed to move."

Mom pinched the bridge of her nose. "I'm so sick of this room. Of this smell."

"Me too," Ivy muttered.

"I'm sick of my children landing themselves in the hospital."

Ivy stiffened. "Like this is Zain's fault?"

"I told him I didn't like that motorcycle." Mom scowled.

God, her mother. Ivy hadn't expected the peace in their family to last. But she had expected it to survive the day. Apparently not. Nothing about their solidarity would be permanent. The moment Zain turned a corner, they were back to their old ways.

Just like before.

"I suppose it's my fault for the last hospital incident too, then, right?"

Mom looked up, her eyes cold. Gone was the woman who'd been riddled with fear for her child. "Whose fault would it be if not yours?"

Ivy flinched. *Damn it.* She shouldn't have reacted but she was too raw. Too tired. Too anxious.

And her mother had always been particularly brutal when it was just the two of them. Without Dad around or Edwin or Zain, Mom wielded her tongue like a knife across Ivy's throat.

"Well, I'm sorry that your children are such a burden." Ivy sneered. "Though I guess we've chained you to Dad, so at least you've got his money."

Mom, more practiced at deflecting insults, didn't even blink. "And you think you're so free of his chains, darling?"

Damn her. Ivy was just as tied to David Clarence as his wife. They both knew it. They equally hated it. Mother and daughter, so alike in circumstance Ivy wanted to pound her fist into the wall.

Instead, she threw another verbal punch at her mom. "Having us kids didn't stop him from cheating, did it?"

"Stop it, Ivy." Mom's mouth flattened. "Today is not the day to pick a fight."

She opened her mouth, ready to object, but that was exactly what she was doing. Maybe that was why Mom had made her comments too.

So alike. So infuriating.

Her hand began to shake again. Before long, it would consume her body again. Ivy needed another outlet. Sex with Tate had been a release, but with this much upheaval, it hadn't been enough.

Mom reached for her Chanel purse beneath her seat, lifting it to her lap. She unzipped it and the rattle of pills caught Ivy's ear.

That sound was joyous. Terrifying.

Mom's hand hovered over the handbag, like she'd just realized that Ivy was sitting beside her.

"Go ahead," Ivy muttered with a flick of her wrist. "You know you need one."

It was a miracle she hadn't been popping pills for hours.

But instead of opening that bottle, Mom zipped the top of her purse shut, slamming it on the open chair at her side before storming out of the waiting room.

Leaving Ivy alone.

With that purse.

The clock on the wall ticked as she sat there, her nerves fraying with every click of the second hand. Her knees began to bounce. The shaking spread to her fingers, twiddling in her lap.

Ivy had to get the fuck out of this hospital. As soon as she saw Zain, she'd go. She'd tell her parents she needed a break. Go home. Eat something. Run ten miles on the treadmill. She'd purge this restless energy and breathe air that didn't remind her of the past.

Then she could come back refreshed and in control.

The shaking only got worse.

"Fuck." Ivy fisted her hands and shot out of her chair, rushing from the waiting room. She rounded the corner, not knowing where she was walking—and slammed into a man.

Tate.

"Easy." His hands came to her arms, steadying her. "You okay?"

"No, I'm not okay." And fuck, she was sick of his worry. It was too real. Too sincere. Too compassionate. She didn't want or deserve that compassion. She didn't want him to ask questions. To fret over the reasons she was about to pull her own damn hair out. So today, she was picking violence. "Where's Mira?"

"Downstairs. She stopped at the gift shop to get your mother something."

"Of course she did," Ivy deadpanned.

"She's trying to help."

That was the last straw. The fact that he'd defend that woman. Ivy snapped. "Leave. Take Mira with you. Neither of you belong here."

His hands planted on his hips. "Say that again."

"Leave."

"No."

God, why did he have to be so stubborn? Well, Ivy was stubborn too, so she went for the jugular. "Earlier, in your car, it was fun. But if you're sticking around hoping for a repeat, it's not happening."

Tate's nostrils flared. "What the fuck is going on, Ivy?"

She lifted a shoulder, inspecting her nails like this conversation was boring her to tears. When really, the ache in her chest made it impossible to meet his chocolate gaze. Because he'd see through her bullshit. He'd see that she was pushing as hard as possible to keep him at a distance.

He'd see that she was scared.

Scared of what would happen if she let him care. If she let him *in*.

"I needed a distraction." It took every ounce of strength to keep her tone even. Distant. "You've served your purpose. Staying is a bit pathetic, don't you think?"

A growl came from deep within his chest. He stood

unmoving. His gaze raked over her face while she continued to study her nails. Then he leaned in close, bending down until his nose brushed against hers. "Today. I'll give you today. But we're not done. Far from it. And we will be discussing this. Soon."

Her breath caught in her throat, her heart pounding, as he stalked past her for the waiting room.

She didn't let herself turn. She didn't let herself break. She didn't let herself beg him to hold her. Instead, she walked on shaking legs to the bathroom, closing herself inside.

The shaking was deep in her bones again as she stood at the sink. She couldn't breathe. She couldn't see straight. Her hand dove into her pocket, fingers fumbling, until she brought out the pill she'd stolen from her mother's purse.

An innocent little white square resting in her palm.

No, Ivy.

She'd promised herself in another bathroom she wouldn't do this again. That she wouldn't become her mother. That she wouldn't let something so small become her crutch.

That Kristopher wouldn't win.

But Kristopher wasn't here, was he? And today, she'd already lost.

Ivy turned on the water, wishing the shaking would stop.

And stared at that little pill.

It was white. But its ugly colors matched her own.

thirty-four

. . .

THE SCENTS of sage and butter and turkey lured Cassia to the kitchen in Clarence Manor, where she found Francis at the stove, whisk in a pan. Across the countertops were bowls filled with steaming food. Mashed potatoes. Stuffing. Cranberry sauce. Green beans. And in the center, a roasted turkey, its skin a perfect golden brown.

Cassia blinked, sure this was a dream. "Francis?"

The chef glanced her way, offering a kind smile. "Just in time. This gravy is ready."

"Y-you made Thanksgiving?"

"Well, of course." Francis laughed. "It's Thanksgiving."

Yes, it was. And Cassia had expected to make herself a ham sandwich.

All week, she'd been mentally preparing herself, bracing, for holidays spent alone. Meals eaten alone in front of the television weren't that bad, right? Thanksgiving was just another Thursday. She'd survive it without turkey and its trimmings. And it would still be Christmas even if there were no gifts wrapped beneath a tree—or a tree, period.

But this . . . her eyes flooded.

Cassia loathed surprises, but this was a shock she'd gladly accept. Mostly, she was grateful not to be alone.

She hadn't heard from Edwin today. Not that she'd heard from him much in the past ten days other than the occasional text.

Ivy and Elora had left the manor earlier, probably to spend time with their families. Per normal, Cassia had kept her distance from her roommates and wouldn't have had a clue about their holiday plans, except Geoff had stopped by her room yesterday.

The butler had informed her that the staff would be taking an extended holiday. He'd be gone until Monday. The weekly housekeeping would be moved to Monday. And he'd noted that both Ivy and Elora would be gone for Thanksgiving, asking Cassia if she had plans to leave the manor too.

When she'd told him no, that her plans involved a ham sandwich, he'd looked at her with utter pity. Cassia hadn't liked Geoff much before yesterday, but after that look, dislike had shifted to hatred.

So why was Francis here? Why was she bustling around the kitchen, her gray bob brushing against her shoulders?

"I thought everyone would be gone this weekend," Cassia said. "You didn't have to do this. I could have made my own meal."

"Our meal," Francis corrected, lifting two plates instead of one from the cupboard. "Would you mind eating together?"

The lump in Cassia's throat doubled in size. "Not at all."

"Good." Francis gave her another kind smile. A smile Cassia had come to look forward to each time she walked into this kitchen.

"What about your family?" Cassia asked. "Didn't you have plans?"

"No plans. My partner, Daisy, is a nurse, and she's working today. So it would have been me at home alone, making a turkey for myself. She's a vegetarian. Geoff told me that you were going to stay over the weekend, and he suggested I just cook here instead of at home. Then we could enjoy each other's company."

Cassia's jaw dropped. "This was Geoff's idea? You're kidding."

"Not kidding."

"Huh." Okay, so maybe she didn't *hate* Geoff.

Francis laughed as she filled their plates so full Cassia wasn't sure where she'd find the room for all that food—not that she wouldn't try to eat every last bite. "His motives aren't entirely pure. He made me promise to save him leftover stuffing. It's his favorite, and between you and me, his wife isn't much of a cook."

"Geoff's married?"

"For thirty years." Francis nodded. "His wife is the definition of lovely. She works at Aston in the admissions office."

"I had no idea." Probably because Cassia avoided Geoff about as much as she avoided Ivy and Elora. The only person she'd spent much time with was Francis. Even then, they didn't spend hours together talking about their private lives.

Francis picked up their heaping plates. "I've set up the dining room for us since it's a special occasion."

"That's . . . thank you." Cassia unstuck her feet, rushing to help carry a plate and follow Francis from the kitchen.

Pressed linen napkins and goblets of ice water awaited them in the dining room. A candelabra with three arms held a trio of tapered candles, their flames dancing. Above the table, the crystal chandelier cast golden beams throughout the room.

As Cassia sat down, marveling at the setting, tears welled in her eyes. This was the fanciest Thanksgiving of her life.

Francis glanced over just as a tear dripped down Cassia's cheek. "Oh no, dear. What's the matter?"

"Nothing." Cassia waved it off, wiping her face dry. "This is just so . . . nice. Thank you."

"No thanks needed. It's my pleasure." Francis picked up a fork. "Happy Thanksgiving."

"Happy Thanksgiving." Cassia's heart clenched, so she

focused on the meal. A moan escaped her throat at the first bite. "This is delicious."

Not only was the ambience stunning, the food was delectable. One of the best meals she'd ever tasted. Francis deserved a shower of compliments, but Cassia bit back the words, feeling . . . guilty.

Last year, her father had worked for hours on their Thanksgiving meal. He had never been a great cook, but the effort he'd made on holidays had compensated for his skill.

He'd tried so hard. So, so hard.

Until . . . he hadn't. Until he'd given up.

Until he'd left her alone.

Cassia shouldn't feel guilty, yet loving this meal felt like a betrayal.

"What about your family?" Francis asked. "You didn't have plans?"

"No, I, um . . ." She toyed with a green bean. "I don't have family. My mother was never really in the picture. And my father died this year."

"Cassia." Francis's fork clattered on her plate as she set it down to reach for Cassia's arm, giving it a squeeze. "I'm so, so sorry. I had no idea."

"I don't really talk about it." Just a few mentions to Edwin. And now Francis.

"Understandable."

Cassia gave her a sad smile, then changed the subject. "How long have you and Daisy been together?"

"Twelve years," Francis said, graciously leaving Cassia's history alone. "We met at a cooking class."

"You take cooking classes?"

The chef laughed, shaking her head. "No, I was the instructor. Teaching is a hobby, so I take on two or three classes a year. Daisy was my worst student of that particular course. By the end of the session—it was only two weeks—we'd gone on three dates. On date four, we decided that I'd do the cooking. She tackles the laundry."

"Harmony." Cassia giggled.

"Exactly."

Francis entertained Cassia through the meal, telling stories about other cooking students and their epic fails. Then she shared her plans for Daisy's Christmas presents and asked how Cassia's semester was going.

Finals were rapidly approaching, and Cassia's aggressive study schedule hadn't waned. Not only was she determined to maintain her perfect GPA, but the work was her companion. The work gave her something to do besides thinking about Edwin.

Besides missing him.

It had been ten days since Zain's motorcycle accident, and though he was still in the hospital, the doctors expected him to make a full recovery. That was the last update Edwin had sent, early yesterday morning.

What was he doing for Thanksgiving? She'd texted earlier and he hadn't responded. Edwin hadn't responded to quite a few of her texts in the past week.

Cassia was doing her best not to take it personally. His focus was his family, as it should be, right? And it wasn't like she was his girlfriend. They hadn't made commitments.

So why did she have this gnawing feeling in her stomach? Why did she feel like he was slipping through her fingers?

They'd only been a *something* for weeks. Yet his absence was a void.

She missed him.

And that scared the hell out of her.

"This is incredible," Cassia told Francis, shoving her worries aside. Shoving the guilt aside. The chef had earned the praise. "Everything you make is incredible, so this isn't really a surprise."

"Thank you." Francis ducked her chin. "I really love it, cooking for you girls."

"How did you come to work here?" Cassia asked.

"Geoff, actually. He's managed the manor for years. Most

of that time, it's been empty, so the staffing was minimal. But when Ivy decided to live here while she attended Aston, Geoff reached out and asked if I would be interested in being the private chef."

"Ah. And how did you meet Geoff before you started here? Another cooking class?"

"Actually, in a book club. Geoff and I bonded over our mutual dislike of every book the club picked. Until finally, we decided to leave their group and start our own."

Cassia laughed. "Do you still have the club?"

"We do." Francis grinned. "It's only the two of us and our meetings are held randomly in the kitchen."

They talked through the rest of the meal, mostly about books, until their plates were empty and their bellies full. Then Cassia insisted on helping do the dishes and clean up the kitchen.

After closing the dishwasher, she walked into Francis's space, pulling her into a tight hug. "Thank you."

Francis hugged her back. "You're welcome."

"Can I meet Daisy?"

"She'd be delighted." Francis let her go and beamed. "After you ace your finals, we'll have a celebratory dinner."

Now she had a meal to look forward to besides breakfast on Sundays. If there was still such a thing as Sunday breakfasts. This was just a hard time for Edwin, right? Soon, Zain would be home and life would go back to normal. They'd have their dates at the café and nights in Cassia's bed.

"I'm headed home for a lazy evening in front of the television," Francis said, digging her keys from a drawer in the kitchen.

"I think I'll do the same." Cassia yawned, and with one last hug, left the kitchen and meandered down the hallways.

She'd just rounded a corner, ready to cross the foyer for the staircase, when the manor's front door burst open and Ivy stormed inside.

"Fuck you," Ivy barked.

Cassia's eyes widened, her mouth opening to defend herself, but then realized Ivy wasn't speaking to her. Ivy had aimed her comment at Edwin, who came inside behind his sister, pushing the door closed.

"What the hell is your problem, Ivy?"

"You!" She whirled on him, her blond hair swishing across the back of her jade dress.

While she was dressed for a special occasion, Edwin looked rumpled and weary. His jeans bagged at the knees, like he'd worn them for so long that the denim had been stretched and restretched. His white button-down shirt was wrinkled, the sleeves rolled up his forearms. His hair was disheveled and his jaw stubbled from days of not shaving.

He was beautiful, but he looked like shit.

Cassia resisted the urge to say his name. She held her breath, her body a statue in the hopes she'd be invisible.

"You were supposed to be there today," Ivy snapped at him.

"I told you last night, I wasn't going to that fucking party."

Wait. What party? Cassia bit the inside of her cheek. If only she could blend into the walls. Maybe now that she didn't hate Geoff, he could teach her his tricks, because that butler was really good at being invisible.

"It's Thanksgiving." Ivy spoke through gritted teeth, her hands planted on her hips.

"Yeah, and you should have skipped it. Mom and Dad are pretending everything is fine. Mom's showing her friends the art she bought last week. Dad's bragging about his Ferrari. It's all bullshit. They pretend for their asshole friends while Zain is still in the hospital."

"I know that!" Ivy shouted. "Don't you think I know that?"

"Then why did you go? You could have come with me to the hospital."

Ivy seethed. "You know why I didn't go to the hospital. Why I'm not going back there."

"That is your choice. Those are your issues. So don't put the fight you had with Dad on me, okay?"

She'd had a fight with their father? Cassia hated that she was listening to a conversation clearly meant to be private. Getting tangled up with Clarence family drama would only lead to disaster, so she tried to inch away, to slip around the corner, but the moment she lifted a foot, Edwin's gaze flicked her way.

"Sorry," she mouthed.

He closed his eyes and pinched the bridge of his nose, like he knew exactly what was going to happen.

Ivy followed his gaze, turning to see Cassia—one foot in the air and an apologetic smile etched on her face.

Shit. "I didn't mean to listen. I was just—"

"Listening?" Ivy's lip curled. "Pitiful. You are pitiful."

Cassia winced.

"Ivy." Edwin raked a hand through his hair, but if Cassia had hoped he'd come to her defense, a chastising tone was all she'd get.

That stung worse than Ivy's insult.

"Whatever." With a flick of her golden hair, Ivy took the stairs, her heels accentuating every step. Her stomping faded down the hallway. Then a door slammed so loudly it would have shaken the walls of any other house.

"Fuck." Edwin sighed, his jaw clenched.

"I didn't mean to eavesdrop." Cassia walked closer, holding up her hands. "I was just leaving the kitchen."

"It's fine," Edwin muttered but nothing about him seemed fine.

"Are you okay?"

"No, I'm not fucking okay," he snapped, making her stop short. Then he turned and strode for the door, ripping it open and marching into the night.

Cassia stood in the foyer, frozen to the glossy marble floor.

For ten days, she'd missed Edwin. For ten days, she'd worried about him.

Apparently, that sentiment had been a one-way street.

Her hands fisted at her sides as she climbed the staircase. She slammed her own bedroom door, hoping that Ivy heard it from her wing. Then Cassia went to her table, putting in her earbuds and cranking up her music until it blocked out any other sound.

She dismissed the notes she'd been reviewing this morning from a lecture last week. No way she'd be able to focus on school. So instead, she rose up on her toes, her arms lifting above her head, and did a spin.

The move was graceful, though slightly off, much like the last time she'd danced around the room. Music blasted in her ears, and as she spun for a second time, she gave her emotions to the movement. Frustration streamed from her fingertips. Irritation poured from her pointed toes.

The movements flowed but with the unbalanced edge of anger. Cassia danced to take away the pain. She danced so she wouldn't scream.

She poured her wounded heart into her muscles. Her body warmed and sweat beaded at her temples by the time the first song ended. She let the next song play, followed by the next, until her lungs burned and her head had cleared. As the song changed again, she tore out her earbuds and dropped to her heels.

With her hands on her knees, she closed her eyes. "I'm not pitiful."

Cassia Collins was many things. She was lonely. She was sad. But she would never again be pitiful.

"No, you are not." The deep voice carried through the room.

"Jesus." Cassia gasped. Edwin was leaning against her doorframe. "Knock much?"

"I did." He stepped into the room, closing the door behind him. "You didn't answer when I knocked, but I heard your footsteps. I didn't know you were a dancer."

Her mouth pursed in a thin line as she crossed her hands over her chest.

"You're amazing, Red."

She shrugged. "It's just a hobby."

Edwin crossed the room, his steps slow. Predatory. "You're not pitiful."

"No, I'm not." Cassia raised her chin as he stood before her.

"I should have defended you."

"Yes, you should have."

Edwin sighed. "I'm sorry."

She made him stand before her, his eyes pleading for a few long moments, before she granted his reprieve. "You're forgiven."

Maybe she forgave too easily, not just Edwin but everyone. Usually all it took was an honest apology and the truth.

How much different would her Thanksgiving have been if her father had just given her an apology? If he had trusted her with his truths instead of hiding them?

Before she could let herself follow that train of thought, Edwin's arm banded around her back and he hauled her into his chest. His nose pressed into her hair, dragging in the scent of her shampoo. "I missed this smell. Like strawberries and vanilla."

She wrapped her arms around his waist, ready to sink into his hard chest, except he let her go too soon, walking to the wingback chair and slumping in its seat.

"You haven't told Ivy about us, have you?" Cassia asked.

"Isn't that what you wanted?"

"Yes." *No.* The idea of being his secret struck a nerve. It zapped her energy.

After months and months of secrets, she was losing the strength to keep them locked behind iron bars. The prison cell was stretched at its seams. Adding another just might cause them all to spill free.

"What happened with Ivy?" she asked.

"Drama," he muttered. "Some fight with Dad about a job she wanted that he made sure wasn't ever going to happen. I feel bad that her Thanksgiving was ruined, but I also don't. She knew what she'd be getting when she went over there. Mom and Dad have all but forgotten their son's in the hospital. While Zain's lying in a bed, they hosted a goddamn dinner party."

"Sorry."

He waved it off. "Don't be sorry for me. I didn't go."

So he'd missed his Thanksgiving too? "Francis made an entire meal. There is plenty in the fridge."

"Nah, I ate. I took dinner to Zain."

"That was nice of you." Her heart melted. As an only child, Cassia could only dream of that sort of loyalty. The unwavering love of a brother. "Do you want to stay awhile?"

"Can't." Edwin leaned forward, bracing his arms on his thighs. She'd never seen him like this, exhausted and detached.

She took a step, ready to pull him into her arms, but he stood in a flash.

"I'll see you, okay?"

"Oh." She blinked as he strode past her without so much as a glance. "Uh, sure." *When?*

She didn't let herself ask. That was something she would have asked Josh. And he would have called her clingy. So she swallowed it down as Edwin walked out the door, leaving without another word.

Cassia stood still, barely breathing, waiting until the sound of the front door opening and closing drifted upstairs. Then she wandered to her bed, plopping on its edge and rubbing the ache in her chest.

He used her when it was convenient. He tossed her aside.

Michael's warning rolled through her mind. He'd cautioned her to be careful, that Edwin had left his cousin heartbroken. But had Cassia listened? *No.*

“And I’m not going to start now.” She squared her shoulders and sat up straight.

There was nothing to worry about. Edwin had a lot happening, and after a grueling ten days, he was allowed to be in a bad mood.

He’d come here, hadn’t he? He’d held her. Told her he missed the smell of her hair.

“It’s fine,” she told herself. Everything was fine.

Except she had a sinking feeling in her stomach, and it had nothing to do with Francis’s meal.

thirty-five

. . .

"ARE YOU SICK?" Joanna Maldonado hissed.

Elora faced her mother, their chairs side by side at the dinner table. "No."

Mom bent lower, dropping her voice to barely more than a whisper. "Are you pregnant?"

"No." Elora rolled her eyes. Though if she had been pregnant, at least she'd have told the father.

"Then sit up straight and stop pushing your food around your plate. The scrape of your fork is grating on my nerves."

Bitch. Elora dragged her fork over the china, then once more for good measure. Then she raised her chin, dismissing her mother.

She'd always hated these large family gatherings.

At the head of the elaborate Thanksgiving table, Dad ate his turkey, though it was a wonder he could get anything past his clenched jaw. He'd just finished arguing with Elora's uncle—Mom's brother—about a political issue and now the two of them were no longer speaking. It happened every year.

Lucas sat sullen and slouched in his chair beside their cousin. *She* was a complete brat who'd spent fifteen minutes teasing him about his hair until finally Elora had had enough and told her to shut up.

She was young enough to still find Elora intimidating, but in a few years, that would change.

Her grandparents were here tonight too. Unfortunately they were not her father's parents, whom she actually enjoyed seeing. No, these were her mother's parents, and together, they emitted enough icy indifference toward their children and grandchildren to freeze the Hudson River.

Elora had no appetite for this charade or this meal. She hadn't felt hungry in weeks. Food had lost its taste. The only reason she ate was to keep her body and mind fueled for school. With her personal life in shambles, school had become her focus.

She'd thrown herself into her classes since the day she'd crawled—literally—out of the elevator at the hospital.

In the past ten days, she'd only stopped thinking about Zain, about his Mira, whenever she was deep into a textbook or research project. Salvation in the form of study. Maybe Cassia was onto something, given the endless hours her roommate spent studying.

But tonight, there was no reprieve. There was no escape. She had nothing to occupy her mind or steal her attention.

Was Mira with Zain in the hospital tonight? Had she brought him a Thanksgiving meal?

Elora had asked Ivy to stop giving her updates on Zain. It hurt too much. But Ivy had ignored Elora's request and stopped by with them daily.

Never in her life had Elora been so grateful for Ivy's obstinance.

He was recovering quickly. The doctors had marveled at Zain's improvement in the past week, and if everything continued on this path, he might go home as early as next week.

The majority of his injuries had been internal bleeding caused from the collision. Surgery had repaired the hemorrhaging but his organs needed time to fully mend. He had a broken leg, a broken arm and three broken ribs, one of which had punctured his lung.

Zain was moving but required crutches. And once he got home, he'd likely need some assistance. Would Mira be there to help? Would she drive him home and make his meals? Would she run his errands and stop by Treason to pick up his laptop? Would she do his laundry and take out the trash?

Elora should have been the person at his bedside these past ten days.

Except he'd let her go. He had Mira.

All because Elora was a coward. She'd let her fears drive her away. She'd let their parents' twisted affairs cloud her judgment. She'd convinced herself that one day, she'd become her mother. And after that happened, Zain would leave.

She'd let two secrets delivered in two letters consume her life.

Zain Clarence was a good man. Lucas would be lucky to call him a brother.

Their brother.

She glanced at Lucas, offering a small smile when he glanced back. Together, they'd suffered through this meal in silence, and the moment the dessert course was over, they'd retreat to his room to play video games or watch a movie.

He'd called her this morning to ask if she'd spend the night. Her aunt, uncle and cousin were staying in the guest wing like they did every Thanksgiving. *Don't leave me stuck with them by myself.* The desperation in his voice had made her decision, and she'd shown up an hour before dinner with an overnight bag.

"Elora, how is Aston?" her aunt asked.

"Fine."

"Are you still planning on graduating this spring?"

"Yes."

"But no boyfriend," her cousin said with a little smirk.

"No."

"Can you give anything but one-word answers?" her uncle snarled.

Prick.

That one-word answer she kept to herself.

Why was she sitting here? She hated this table. Besides Dad and Lucas, she hated this family. She hated turkey. It made her stomach ache and had since she was a girl, but her mother had never once requested the chef make a different option.

Elora was done being a coward. She'd lost Zain because of her fears. She'd lost Zain because she'd cowered behind blank expressions and hidden feelings.

Never again.

She would no longer be a coward.

Elora shoved away from the table and stood, waiting to speak until every gaze was aimed her way. "You're toxic. With the exception of Dad and Lucas, you're poison. If you'll excuse me, I'd rather spend my time alone than with you. Happy fucking Thanksgiving."

Gasps followed her out of the dining room.

Pulse racing, she marched to the guest room—the childhood bedroom her mother had redecorated the week after Elora had moved into Clarence Manor. God, that had felt good. There'd be consequences, a lecture from her mother, but Elora couldn't find it in herself to care. Not anymore. So with a smile toying at her mouth, she plopped on the edge of the bed.

Five heartbeats, that's all she got before the door cracked open and Dad poked his head inside. "Don't throw anything at me."

Her smile widened. "You're safe."

He walked into the room, taking the space beside her and putting an arm around her shoulders. "Hi."

"Hi." She leaned her head on his shoulder. "Sorry."

She wasn't apologizing for what she'd said. She was apologizing because he'd bear the brunt of Mom's disapproval.

"Don't be." He hugged her closer.

"Thank you for the flowers." He'd sent her a fresh bouquet yesterday. Pretty peach and orange roses mixed with greenery and golden Craspedia. The vase reminded her of a firework, an explosion of color.

"You're welcome." He hugged her closer.

For months she'd pulled away from her father. The entire time, he'd given her space. But the flowers, the *I LOVE YOU* all-caps texts and notes, had never stopped.

"Ready to finally tell me what's been bothering you, button?"

"No," she admitted. "Soon."

Soon, she'd tell him about Lucas. Soon, she'd tell him about herself. Soon, she'd decimate his world. But not today. Not yet. Because she didn't want to lose his hugs.

She wasn't ready to lose her father.

Tears pricked at her eyes. Months she'd been wrestling with these secrets and still, every time she thought about telling the truth, she convinced herself to wait. *Not yet.*

Not ever?

"I love you, Dad."

"Aww. Haven't heard that in a while." He bent to kiss the top of her hair. "I love you too."

Elora didn't say it enough.

Blood is just blood.

Zain's words popped into her head, and with them, something clicked that hadn't before. All this time, she'd wished for him to be her father. But he was.

Lawrence Maldonado was her father.

He was the man who'd taught her to ride a bike. The man who'd read her bedtime stories as a child. The man who'd let her cry on his shoulder when John Titan had called Elora a cunt at an Aston Prep basketball game.

This was her dad.

And she was going to fight to keep him.

Even after she told him about Mom's affairs, she wasn't

letting him go. She'd lost Zain because she hadn't fought. She'd been too busy standing in a fortress built on irrational, immature fears.

Elora would not make that mistake again.

Tension and stress from months unlocked in her chest, and as she breathed, her lungs were full for the first time in weeks. She sagged into his side, closing her eyes as she dragged in another inhale.

Damn, it felt good to breathe.

Dad didn't ask questions. He didn't make conversation. He simply held her, proving with every moment that he knew what she needed. Because he was her dad.

"Can I come in?" Lucas called from behind the closed door, his voice muffled.

"No," Dad teased at the same time Elora said, "Go away."

Lucas threw the door open, giving them both a flat look. "You left me out there with *them*."

Dad chuckled and patted the space on his other side. "We're hiding."

Her brother shut the door and came to sit with them, but with his addition, the silence was lost. Thirteen-year-old boys, especially this one, weren't known for sitting idle. "What should we do?"

"Movie?" Elora suggested, knowing that would be his preference.

" 'Kay." Lucas shrugged and stood. "My pick."

Elora nodded, looking up at Dad's profile. "Want to watch with us?"

"No, you kids go ahead. I'd better check in with the others." He kissed her head once more, then stood, ruffling Lucas's hair before striding out of the room.

"You go ahead," she said. "I'm going to change into my pajamas. Want to watch in the theater room or your room?"

"Mine. Definitely."

Where there was a door and a lock to keep their cousin out.

"Be there in a bit," she said.

Lucas grinned, his blue eyes sparkling as he rushed from the room, more excited than she'd seen him all night.

He was her brother. Like Dad was her father.

Elora would fight for them both.

She walked to the closet and dug out a pair of leggings and Zain's sweatshirt from her overnight bag. She'd been wearing the sweatshirt almost nightly, ensuring that if she put it in the laundry, it would be done by the time she went to bed. Then she brushed her teeth and washed the makeup from her face, tossing the heels and black dress she'd worn for dinner into a pile on the floor.

But before she retreated to Lucas's bedroom, she unlocked her phone, navigating to her favorite picture. She'd looked at this photo countless times in the past ten days.

Zain was asleep on the couch at his Martha's Vineyard cottage. His hair was a mess. His mouth was hanging open and his jaw was dusted with stubble. She could still hear him snoring.

Elora had taken the picture, not because he was beautiful and at peace. But because of his hand. Before he'd fallen asleep, he'd stretched out his arm to where she'd been sitting by his feet, reading a book.

He'd opened his hand, palm up, like he'd expected her to take it.

She hadn't.

But he'd kept his hand open anyway, even while he'd slept.

She should have taken his hand.

The urge to text him was so overwhelming that she tossed her phone on the bed and out of her reach.

He had a fiancée to text him *Happy Thanksgiving* messages. Or just tell him to his face.

Elora dragged her hands through her hair, pulling too hard at the roots. Given the number of times she'd done that lately, it was a damn miracle she had any hair left.

She turned, ready to escape this bedroom, when her phone dinged on the mattress. Her breath caught.

Was it him?

Temptation—delusion—was a powerful enemy and she caved, rushing to the mattress and swiping up her phone.

Except it wasn't a text from Zain.

"He has Mira," she reminded herself.

Did he call her Mir? A cute nickname, like he'd shortened Elora to El? Her stomach roiled. She'd make herself sick if she kept thinking about him. About them. So she shook her head, focusing on the email notification.

Sal Testa's name stood out in bold at the top of her inbox.

Elora hadn't forgotten the last email she'd sent him in October, though she'd tried. Damn if she'd tried.

For weeks, she hadn't heard a word from her investigator, and a part of her had wished he'd forgotten her too. Apparently not.

Her finger hovered over the email. Maybe he'd been unsuccessful. Because if he'd failed, then there were no answers to find. She could forget about uncovering the truth and put this quest in the grave.

Except, as she opened the message, her hopes were dashed.

I'd like to schedule a meeting to review my findings.

"Fuck." Elora's molars cracked as she ground them together.

When Sal had offered to find her biological father, she'd given him her consent because deep down, she'd suspected her mother had been lying. That her *father* wasn't really dead.

Instead of replying, she hit the icon to call Sal, holding the phone to her ear as she waited for him to answer.

"You got my email?"

"I did." She paced the length of the room. "I can't meet tonight, but I don't want to wait. Email it to me."

"I'd prefer to deliver you the report personally." So he could get paid.

"Email," she insisted. "I'll send a courier to you in the morning with your payment."

He sighed. "I'll send it now."

She ended the call, gripping the phone so tightly her knuckles turned white. She paced. She refreshed. Over and over until the whoosh of an incoming message hit her ears.

Her fingers couldn't move fast enough to open the attachment.

The first page was filled with general information. Name. Height. Weight. Age. Date of birth. Address. Phone number. Occupation.

All of the details associated with a man who was very, very much alive.

"I hate her," Elora seethed.

Of course her mother had lied. Her biological father was alive and, according to the occupation field, gainfully employed at . . .

Wait.

Aston University.

She swiped down, stopping at a series of photos on the following pages. One was a close-up, the man's face, his easy smile captured perfectly in the frame.

Elora's heart dropped.

She knew that face. She'd seen him walking around Aston's campus.

He was the dean of students.

Henry Neilson.

thirty-six

. . .

THE GLOW from Ivy's laptop was the only light in her office. Each time she tapped the touchpad, her hands caught the blue hue.

You belong in prison.

The last line of the email on the screen was the same as the previous two. Repetitive, but no less impactful.

Maybe Ivy did belong in prison. Maybe she should be locked away behind bars where she couldn't hurt anyone.

Beside her was a half-empty bottle of cabernet. Next to it, the white pill she'd stolen from her mother's purse.

Ivy hadn't taken it at the hospital. But she also hadn't flushed it down the toilet. Instead, she'd kept that pill in a drawer. Tonight, it had worked itself back into her hand.

She refilled her wineglass, took a long drink, then opened the next email, scanning the insults.

You bitch. You stole my son. Rot in hell.

This message was particularly nasty, so she moved on to the next. It was equally as painful.

It had been a while, not since Halloween and the Cooper Kennedy incident, since Ivy had gone on an email reread binge. Tonight, the words swarmed her. A thousand hornets, each delivering their sting.

Why couldn't she delete these? Why did she keep reading the newcomers when they arrived each week? All she had to do was click the block icon. One tiny tap of her finger and this would end. Delete a virtual folder and the pain would stop.

Except it wouldn't. There was no end.

Because the pain had nothing to do with the emails. The pain would linger, no matter what Ivy read in the dark of night, so she moved on to the next email, then the next.

A few vicious words from a woman across town were nothing compared to the self-loathing, the guilt, Ivy had locked inside.

One more email, and she'd go to bed. One more email, and she'd sleep. Hopefully that would help her forget about today's awful Thanksgiving dinner and the disaster that was her family.

But first, one more email.

She took a gulp of wine, then clicked the next email. She was halfway through when her phone chimed with a text.

Was it Tate? *Please be Tate.*

She hadn't heard from him in ten days. Not since she'd sent him away at the hospital.

I'll give you today. But we're not done. And we will be discussing this.

So much for that discussion.

Ivy only had herself to blame. She'd pushed, hard. But foolish as it was, she'd hoped he'd be strong enough to withstand it. That no matter how hard she shoved, he wouldn't budge.

As she opened her phone, her heart sank. A text from Michael.

No more Tate Ledger. *Damn.*

She couldn't blame him. A man like that could have any woman he desired. Why bother with a girl like Ivy? Spoiled.

Selfish. And given her obsession with these emails, obviously masochistic too.

Are you home?

She typed out her reply to Michael's text. *Yes*

Then answer your door

A year ago, hell, two months ago, that would have given Ivy a thrill. Except Michael had lost his appeal. His allure had dulled in comparison to a dark-haired man who'd invaded her heart.

With a sigh, she closed down her emails and stood, making her way downstairs to open the door. "Hi."

"Hey." He gave her a sad smile. "You left dinner in a rush."

She shrugged as he came inside.

The Bamfords had been at her parents' Thanksgiving party tonight. Michael's father and her father were probably shut in Dad's study, drinking whiskey and bragging about their latest mistress's sexual proclivities. Their mothers were likely swapping pills and discussing their latest med spa visits.

"Fight with your dad?" he asked.

"Yeah. Did you hear?"

"Kind of hard not to."

She winced. Fucking great.

So the entire dinner party had heard her call her father a manipulative asshole. Not that she'd been wrong. Except for too many years, she'd been taught—by her mother and by her own experiences—that whenever you pissed off David Clarence, he retaliated.

Tomorrow, she expected a different sort of email in her inbox. A message from her father reminding her to behave. Reminding her of what was on the line.

Clarence Manor.

She glanced around the foyer with a lump in her throat. Maybe she should start saying goodbye to this place now. "I'm doomed."

"Or . . . apologize to your dad. Grovel. Make amends."

"I can't apologize." She shook her head. "He went too far."

Tonight, after their five-course meal, her father had pulled her aside for a lecture that had ended with her storming out the door.

After he'd thwarted her career plans at the Smithsonian, Ivy had decided to try another angle. Instead of going to work for his company, she'd stick with school. After all, most history scholars had years and years of higher education under their belts before they decided to enter the workforce—or become professors themselves.

Ivy had spent a chunk of her free time in the past month researching the master's programs at Aston. She'd spoken to her favorite professors, and after receiving their enthusiastic encouragement, she'd put in her application.

Somehow, Dad had caught wind of it. Clearly, Ivy had underestimated his interest in her future.

He'd told her tonight that if she pursued any master's degree program that wasn't for an MBA, she could kiss the manor goodbye.

"I don't want the life he wants for me," she confessed.

Michael stepped closer, pulling her into a hug. "It's just a job, Ivy. Is working for him really that bad?"

Yes.

She didn't expect Michael to understand. Neither did Edwin, not really. They were each willing to work for their fathers. They were each willing to put in the time to get what waited beyond the immediate horizon.

Inheritance.

Both Michael and Edwin were poised to take over their fathers' respective empires.

Except years of corporate monotony would be torture for Ivy. Edwin wouldn't wither away under the weight of meetings and spreadsheets and financial projections and the stress that came with being a woman in a man's world.

"I think . . ." Her body sagged against Michael's. She

relaxed into him not because she craved his arms, but because tonight, they were the only ones available. That, and she was drunk. "I think I give up."

"It won't be forever. Besides, you might end up liking it."

Michael had misunderstood her. She wasn't giving up on a master's degree or a job at a museum. She was giving up this house.

Ivy stood no chance of convincing her father otherwise, so she'd say goodbye to the manor. She'd part with Francis and Geoff. She'd part with *home*.

But not yet.

Not tonight.

She'd play Dad's game for another semester, and after graduation, she'd tell him to go to hell. Maybe Zain could share a few tips on how to do it.

Guilt, slimy and thick like sludge, crept beneath her skin. She should have gone to the hospital tonight. She should have faced her own fears and had a takeout Thanksgiving dinner with her brothers.

Instead, she'd not only had a fight with Dad, but she'd yelled at Edwin too.

Edwin had been on his way home from the hospital when she'd called him, fuming. And instead of just venting about their father, she'd gone too far. She'd blamed him for the fight because he hadn't been at dinner to act as a buffer.

It was bullshit. They both knew it.

Edwin had hung up on her, but instead of going home and waiting for Ivy to apologize—she would have in the morning—he'd come to the manor. He'd rolled through the gate just seconds after she'd punched in the code to open it.

Her brother wasn't quick to anger, but he'd been irritable lately, mostly due to the situation with Zain. Their argument in the foyer might have lasted an hour, except then Ivy had caught Cassia spying.

Ivy stood taller, stepping out of Michael's arms. "Your friend Cassia pissed me off tonight."

"Did you find out about her and your brother?"

"I—" The wheels in her mind screeched to a halt. "What?"

Michael arched an eyebrow. "You didn't know?"

Cassia and Edwin.

No, she hadn't had the faintest clue. Maybe she should have for all the time both spent in the library. Was that why he'd come here tonight? Not for Ivy, but for Cassia?

Elora and Zain had hidden their relationship from her.

Now Edwin.

Another night, that might have sent Ivy into a rage. She would have blown into Cassia's bedroom and punished her roommate with a trial of sorts. Ivy had made it clear, hadn't she? Stay away from her brothers.

But as Ivy searched for that rage, a flicker of anger, she came up empty.

Her brothers had kept secrets from her too.

Fuck, but she was exhausted.

Of herself.

Ivy was so goddamn sick of herself. No wonder the only person with her tonight was Michael.

He wasn't the man she wanted, not anymore. Except maybe he was the only one she deserved.

Unless . . .

I change.

Maybe she'd deserve a man like Tate if she changed. Could she?

She had once, hadn't she? Ivy had always been self-indulgent. She was a Clarence, after all. But she hadn't been . . . cruel. Her mean streak had appeared after Kristopher. Maybe he'd nurtured what had always been hidden within her. Or maybe his own brutality had transferred to Ivy the night of the crash.

The crash. It had all started with the crash.

To end it, maybe she needed to go back. To revisit that

night. To take Michael's advice and apologize, just not to her father.

"Will you drive me somewhere?" Ivy asked. If not for the wine, she would have driven herself.

"I was thinking we could stay here." He stepped closer, his fingers brushing her collarbone to push a lock of hair out of the way. His voice dropped too, sultry and seductive.

"Later," she lied. After she did what she needed to do, she'd send him on his way. But he was here and Roy was at home, enjoying a Thanksgiving with his family. She wouldn't pull her driver away, not tonight. "Please?"

Michael sighed and nodded. "Fine."

"Be right back." She flew up the stairs, her steps uneven as she jogged down the hallway. She'd dressed for bed before she'd gone to her office to read those emails, so she hurried to her closet to trade her pajama shorts for leggings and tug a sweatshirt over her camisole. With a pair of tennis shoes on her feet and her phone in hand, she ran downstairs.

Ivy didn't linger in the foyer, instead leading the way outside and to Michael's car. She kept moving before she lost her nerve. After she buckled herself into the passenger seat, she sat on her hands to hide their trembling.

Michael's jaw clenched, his irritation as ripe as cheap cologne, as he climbed behind the wheel and pulled away from the manor. "Where are we going?"

Ivy punched in the address on her phone, then let the robotic voice give him directions.

"Across town," he muttered. "Christ."

She ignored him, focusing on what she would say when they arrived. It was late, after nine. Probably too late, and not just the hour. This visit as a whole was too late.

Sorry. If the only word she managed to choke out was *sorry*, she'd consider this trip a success. She closed her eyes, relaxing into the seat as Michael drove, and repeated her apology over and over.

Sorry. I'm sorry.

The car accelerated, too quickly, forcing her deeper into the leather at her back. She opened her eyes, leaning over to glance at the speedometer.

She didn't need to see the number to know he was well beyond the limit. Her heart dropped. "Would you slow down?"

"It's fine."

"You're speeding." *Fast. It's too fast.*

"Do you see any cops?" He nodded to the windshield and the deserted streets beyond.

Ivy felt the edge of a panic attack creeping closer, ready to pounce. "Michael, please slow down."

He shot her a glare, his foot never lifting off the gas pedal.

Turn left at the next light.

The GPS directions should have come to her rescue. Except Michael barely slowed as the green light approached, and as they careened around the corner, Ivy clutched the door's handle, holding her breath as her body began to tremble.

"Slow down," she pleaded.

Michael grumbled something. She couldn't hear it beneath the blood rushing in her ears.

"Please." She closed her eyes.

"Relax, Ivy."

"Slow down!" she screamed.

"Jesus."

The car slowed, Ivy's body heavy against the seat belt, as Michael pushed the brake. Her breath came in ragged pants. Her head throbbed and her limbs shook. But she managed a strangled, "Thank you."

"What the fuck, Ivy?"

She didn't answer. She didn't open her eyes. She let the GPS fill the silence until it signaled their arrival and Michael had eased to a halt at the curb. The moment the wheels stopped, she flew out of the passenger seat, gulping in the cold night air.

Michael opened his door but she held up her hand, stopping him. "What?"

"I need to go alone."

"Go where? What is going on? Where the fuck are we?"

They were in a beautiful, quiet neighborhood with streets and yards shrouded in trees. Even without leaves, their limbs blocked the light over her head.

Ivy turned and stared at a brick house. In the years since she'd been here, the home hadn't changed. The bushes that lined the sidewalk were thicker, but otherwise, it was like taking a step back in time.

How often had she parked in this exact spot? How often had she jogged up the porch steps? How often had she walked through that front door?

Ivy had lost her virginity in this house. She'd lost a lot behind those brick walls.

"I'll be back," she said, crossing the sidewalk and leaving Michael behind.

The lights were on inside, casting a wan glow into the darkness. The porch's feeble lanterns veiled the stoop.

By the time she reached the door, lifting a finger to press the bell, her stomach churned. Dinner threatened to make a reappearance. But she swallowed it down, waiting until footsteps sounded beyond the carved door.

A face flashed behind the inset window. Then the door flew open and she was greeted with a familiar face. Aged. Tired. But familiar.

"Get the hell off my property," the woman seethed.

"I'm sorry." The apology leapt from Ivy's tongue. Relief swirled with adrenaline and she wouldn't have to worry about Michael's driving on the return trip home. As soon as her seat belt was latched, she'd crash.

"You're sorry?" Carol Kennedy scoffed. "You killed my son, and all you have to say is you're sorry."

It was an accident. Ivy wouldn't let the excuse escape her lips. Carol didn't need excuses.

She needed her child.

"Leave." Carol stepped back and slammed the door in Ivy's face.

The air rushed from Ivy's lungs. Her head spun.

She'd done it. She'd apologized. Would Carol's emails stop now? Did Ivy want them to stop?

It took the last fragments of her strength to unglue her feet. Ivy's knees wobbled as she turned and shuffled to the stairs. Then she looked up.

And found Michael waiting on the sidewalk. Judging from the smirk on his face, he'd heard the entire encounter with Carol. "Well, that was interesting."

Fuck.

thirty-seven

. . .

THERE WAS a group next to Cassia's table on the first floor of the library. A loud group. The librarian had shushed them three times, and still, they wouldn't shush.

"Shut up. Shut up. Shut up," she muttered under her breath.

"Ha!" a guy barked. "I saw this thing once where this kid was asked to write a poem about love. All she did was turn in her best friend's phone number. What if we did something like that? Witty, you know? Creative? Easy."

"Lazy," Cassia mumbled.

She'd been listening to this project team pitch ideas to each other for an hour. At this point, given their progress, she was sure that each and every one of them was going to flunk freshman psychology.

Cassia rubbed her temples, wishing she hadn't forgotten her earbuds at home this morning. A mistake she'd never make again. She leaned closer to her book, her eyes narrowing at the text. "Focus. For fuck's sake, focus."

This was the last week of class for the semester. Next week was dead week. The following, finals. Then Aston would adjourn for winter break.

Christmas was coming.

But Cassia would worry about spending a holiday alone later. After she finished the semester with her flawless grades intact.

"How about this?" A girl in the group stood, her hands flying in the air as she explained yet another horrible idea.

Cassia groaned. "Idiots."

"Talking to yourself, Red?"

Her face whipped up from her book as Edwin pulled out the chair beside hers.

His blue eyes dazzled and her traitorous heart tumbled.

It had been two weeks since Thanksgiving. Two weeks since he'd walked out of her bedroom. Two weeks since he'd spoken to her.

And in those two weeks, she'd decided Michael's warning had been on point.

Edwin Clarence had gotten what he'd wanted from Cassia and turned into a ghost.

She was so fucking tired of ghosts.

"You're on the wrong floor," he said.

Cassia arched an eyebrow. "Seriously?"

"That spot upstairs is your study space too."

"Unbelievable." Two weeks and he wanted to talk about her study location?

She slammed her book closed, her movements rushed and angry as she stuffed her belongings into her backpack and zipped it closed. Then she stood, nearly knocking over her chair, and tugged on her coat. She rounded the table, about to march out of the library, but paused. She walked over to the project team's table instead.

"You're supposed to turn in a presentation about love, right?" she asked the freshmen. "But every idea you've come up with is shit."

Each person stared at her with wide eyes and a flapping jaw.

"Do something different. Write about when love goes

wrong. Heartbreak. Betrayal. Manipulation and lies. Tell the ugly stories of love. That's your presentation."

"Yes." The kid who'd suggested the phone number idea shot out of his chair with arms raised. "We could do like horror stories, you know? A guy cheats on his wife and she cuts him into a thousand pieces and buries him in her petunia garden."

"You've got the idea." Cassia cast a look over her shoulder at Edwin, then left the group to their brainstorm, her message delivered.

She'd had *something* with Edwin, and then he'd vanished without a word. He'd disappointed her. She'd had enough disappointment from the men in her life to last an eternity.

"Cassia." Edwin caught up to her as she pushed through the library's front doors.

She kept walking, her breaths billowing around her in the frozen December air. Snow had fallen last night, dusting the campus grounds with a pristine coat of white.

"I'm sorry." Edwin fell in step beside her. "And I realize that apology is two weeks late."

"Forgiven." She flicked her wrist. *Definitely not forgiven.* "See you around."

"Talk to me." He grabbed her elbow, forcing her to stop.

She whirled on him, tugging her arm free. "You do not get to touch me."

Edwin held up his hands, his expression wounded. "Red."

"Don't, Edwin. Just don't." Fourteen days of pent-up frustration exploded from the bottle where she'd kept it sealed. "I will not be used." *Not again.*

"I—"

"Shush." Cassia sliced a hand through the air.

At least someone listened to a *shush* today. Edwin clamped his mouth shut, his lips pursing in a thin line.

"I will not be a convenience." *Not again.* "I will not be an afterthought." *Not again.* "I will not be a toy." *Not again.*

"You are none of those things," he said.

"I don't believe you. After all the bullshit you told me, how you were going to test my limits. How you'd tell me what to think and how to feel about us. How you'd make it clear. Well, I guess you walking away has made it very, very clear."

Cassia's chest heaved as everything she'd wanted to say came bubbling to the surface. It drained from her, and with it, her willingness to fight. So she walked away.

Edwin let her go.

And that, above all else, proved their *something* had come to an end. What would it take to find a man who'd fight for her? Who'd stick by her side? Who'd choose *her*?

No one chose Cassia.

Which meant she had to choose herself.

The walk to the manor was warmer than it had been this morning and she didn't bother with her gloves. But was it an actual rise in temperature outside or anger and regret warming her blood?

When would she learn to spot a wolf in sheep's clothing? When would she stop letting charming smiles and Sunday breakfasts and coin tosses sneak past her defenses?

"Gah." She threw open the manor's door and slammed it behind her. Cassia had been slamming a lot of doors lately. Then she stomped up the stairs, pounding her irritation into each step. When she got to her bedroom, she went straight for those earbuds she'd forgotten this morning, shoving them in place.

Her coat was tossed on the floor, her backpack dropped beside it. Then she found her phone, scrolling to a playlist that fit her mad mood, ready to let it blare in her ears. Maybe she'd dance this irritation away like she had at Thanksgiving.

But before she could hit *play*, a hand plucked an earbud free.

Cassia gasped, spinning around.

Edwin towered over her, a scowl marring his handsome features as he removed the other earbud. His cheeks were flushed. The tip of his nose was red and his fingers cold.

How long had he been following her?

"What are you doing here?" she asked.

"Having the conversation I wasn't going to have on campus."

Behind him, the door was closed. A super sleuth, she was not. Seriously, how had she missed him following her home and into her room?

Another man and she might have panicked, but this was Edwin. And yeah, she was furious with him at the moment, but deep down, she knew the worst he would do was damage her heart.

She'd survived annihilation once. She could do it again.

"I fucked up," he said.

"Yep."

He raked a hand through his hair. "I don't want this to end."

She opened her mouth, ready to tell him it was too late, but he put a finger over her lips, like he knew what she was going to say.

"I'm sorry."

She had expected a litany of excuses. His brother. School. Finals. Blah. Blah. Blah. But as she waited for his justifications, they never came.

Instead, he repeated, "I'm sorry."

It was the pleading in his blue eyes that tugged at her heartstrings.

Cassia took a step away, needing some distance, and as she did, she saw what she'd missed at the library. There were dark circles beneath his eyes. His clothes were rumpled again, like they had been at Thanksgiving, but this was far worse, like he hadn't just worn them, he'd been living in them. The stubble on his jaw was so thick it was nearly a beard and he must not have shaved in, well . . . two weeks.

"I know you have a lot going on with your brother," she said. "Is he okay?"

"They released him from the hospital Sunday. I've been sleeping on his couch, helping out."

"That's nice of you."

"He's my brother." Edwin shrugged. "He's got a nurse to help during the day if he needs it, but at night, better me than a stranger in his home."

What about their parents? Weren't they around to help?

"Can we . . . can I just sit for a minute?" Edwin walked past her for his wingback chair. He slumped into the seat, much like he had the last time he'd been in her bedroom, and dropped his elbows to his knees, looking seconds from falling asleep. "I've been sleeping in chairs for weeks. Zain's couch is an improvement but I was up late trying to study before finals."

"You've been sleeping in chairs? Where?"

"The hospital."

Cassia blinked. Zain's accident had been weeks ago. "This whole time?"

"Yeah." He yawned.

"Why didn't you tell me?"

He gave her a sad smile. "Truth? I don't know."

"You don't know?"

"I have a lot of shit happening right now, and I don't know if I should put that on you."

She frowned. "Huh?"

"This is the type of heavy I'd put on a girlfriend. And I don't know if we're there."

The brutal honesty of his confession made her want to curl into a ball and hide. Because he was right. They were *something*. But on the continuum of somethings, they were firmly fixed in the middle. Neutral zone.

Not quite casual. Not quite serious.

Not quite trusting.

And Cassia couldn't blame him for this. She had been diligent about setting boundaries from the beginning. *Shit.*

"Well . . ." She sighed and walked to her bed, flopping down on the pillowy bedding. "That's fair."

Except she wanted him to trust her. She wanted him to confide in her and tell her when he was struggling. She didn't want him to shut her out.

"I have trust issues," she said, eyes locked on the ceiling.

Edwin's deep chuckle filled the room. "You don't say."

She smiled as he stood from the chair and made his way to the bed. He took the place beside her, lying on his back. His body stretched long next to hers, just inches away, but they didn't touch. The closeness was enough. For now.

"I've been talking to lawyers," he said. "About my trust funds. After Zain's accident, I thought my parents might rally. They did for about a day. But then life went back to normal for them and it was like they forgot they had a child in the hospital. Zain's an adult, but still. Wouldn't you visit your kid in the hospital?"

"Yes," she said, lacing her fingers with his.

"They just went back to normal. Donated a pile of money to the hospital. Made sure he's got the best doctors and nurses. But that's it. Dad visited twice. Mom three times. It's been nearly a month, and that's all the time they could spare him. Then on Thanksgiving, they hosted a fucking dinner party."

The argument with Ivy, Edwin's frustration that day, now made sense.

"It's not right." He shook his head. "And all I can think is that it's because Zain didn't play Dad's game. Zain's doing his own thing. Living his own life. So now in Dad's eyes, he's less."

"Sorry," she whispered.

"I'm done. Dad expects me to work for his company but he can fuck off. I want to make sure I fully understand the stipulations of my trust. That's what the lawyers are for. If I have to wait until I'm thirty to touch that money, so be it. Until then, well . . ."

"You can find a job like the rest of us peons."

The corner of his mouth turned up. "Maybe you can help

me polish my résumé."

"I'll be a character reference."

"You can attest to the number of orgasms delivered in a single night."

Cassia laughed.

And he gifted her with a megawatt smile, dimples included. "I missed you, Red."

"I missed you too." It wasn't as hard to admit as she'd thought. "Thanks for telling me."

Edwin shifted, turning sideways to tuck a lock of hair behind her ear. "I could use a girlfriend right now."

The weight of those words hit her like a sledgehammer. He was asking for a confidant. A sanctuary. A friend. And she wanted so badly to be that person.

There should have been panic at the realization. A surge of terror.

Girlfriend.

Oh, she wanted the job.

"Need a volunteer?" she asked.

In a flash he rolled her onto her back, hovering over her. Then his mouth was on hers, stealing her breath and making the disappointment of the past two weeks disappear with a delicious swirl of his tongue.

She clung to him, loving the weight of his body pressing her deeper into the mattress. She'd missed these lips. His broad shoulders. The strength in his body. She'd missed the way he sucked on her lower lip and flicked the tip of his tongue against hers.

Cassia's body ignited from a single kiss and she arched into him, craving more.

Except Edwin tore his mouth away, dropped his forehead to hers. "I wish I could spend the rest of the day here. But I have class in an hour."

"Want to take a power nap? You look like you could use it."

"Yeah, actually." He rolled them, pulling her back into his

chest. "Will you stay with me?"

She curled deeper into his arms. "I'm sorry about Zain. And your parents."

"My parents are assholes. I mean, that's not a shock. I just . . . hoped they'd be different this time."

"I can understand that. My mother is an asshole." And if she was being honest with herself, her father had become one in the end. But it was easier to focus on Jessa Neilson's faults.

"Will you tell me about her?" Edwin asked.

"She left when I was two. Came back when I was three. Left again when I was four. Came back when I was five. Left again when I was six. That was the pattern. She'd be a mother for less than a year before it was too much. Then she'd leave, completely erase us from her mind, until she remembered that she had a husband and a daughter."

"Damn." Edwin stiffened.

"I don't know what brought her back." That was the hardest part to comprehend about her mother's sporadic presence. "I understand why she left. I remember finding her in the laundry room once, sobbing over a basket of clothes, completely distraught that she had to fold them. She left not long after."

Then there was the memory of Mom in the kitchen, the smoke alarms blaring because she'd put a frozen pizza in the oven and had forgotten to set a timer, so it had burned to a crisp.

Dad had always been the cook. Jessa hadn't liked spending time in the kitchen, even less than the laundry room, but for some reason, she'd taken it upon herself to make dinner that night. After Dad had taken the charcoal pizza from the oven and calmed Mom down, she'd shut herself in the bedroom. The next day, when Cassia had come home from school, her mother had been gone.

She'd been eight. Her father had enrolled her in ballet not long after.

Maybe he'd known that Jessa wouldn't be coming back

that time around.

"She didn't want to be a mother and a wife," Cassia told Edwin. "And truthfully, the years when she was gone were better. Dad and I relied on each other and we were happy."

Or she'd thought they were happy.

"But why would she come back? That's what I don't get," Cassia said. "Why, when nothing had changed, why would she put us through that again? It feels . . . harsh. She had to know how much it hurt when she left. I would have gotten over it, especially if she'd stayed gone when I was two. I wouldn't have even known her. But because she kept coming back, it gave me hope."

And that hope was the real cruelty of Jessa's actions.

Hope that she'd return. Hope that when she did, life would be different. Hope that Cassia could be enough to make her mother stay.

"Red." Edwin hugged her tighter.

"I have no idea where she is. If she's . . . dead." If Cassia was truly alone.

"I'm so sorry." He buried his face in her hair. "To go through that. To lose your dad. And then I ghosted you too. Fuck. I'm sorry."

"I'm not telling you this so you'll feel guilty. It's just the truth."

"Thank you. For telling me." His arms loosened so he could turn her and look at her face. His thumb stroked her cheek. "I told you so."

"Told me what?"

"That I'd rip the truths free."

She smiled. "So you did."

"Was that so hard?" he teased.

She inched closer, closing her eyes as she drew in his scent. No, it hadn't been hard to talk about Jessa. But Jessa was a lesser demon in Cassia's past. The tale of her mother was an easy confession.

And Cassia had no intention of sharing the rest.

thirty-eight

. . .

HENRY NEILSON WALKED from the student union building to President's Hall at ten fifteen every morning. At noon, he ate a packed lunch at his desk, except for Fridays, when he picked up a meal from the food court. On Wednesdays, he had a standing meeting with his staff at three, and afterward, he took an afternoon walk around campus.

Aston's dean of students was nothing if not predictable.

And Sal Testa was nothing if not thorough.

Not only had Elora's private investigator tracked down her very-much-alive biological father, but he'd also supplied her with Henry's detailed schedule. Maybe Sal had gone that in-depth so Elora could avoid Henry on campus. Or maybe Sal had set her up for a confrontation.

At the moment, she was doing neither. Instead, she'd been stalking Henry on campus for two weeks.

Elora trailed behind him, keeping enough distance not to be suspicious. These Wednesday afternoon walks seemed to be the only spontaneous event in his routine. Last week, he'd weaved through the business buildings and the familiar sidewalks Elora had crossed hundreds of times. But today, they were on the opposite end of campus by the architecture, art and history halls.

She didn't pay much attention to the students they passed, but Henry did. He always nodded when he passed someone. He'd give a hello to those he recognized, and the number of names he knew surprised her.

Elora hadn't spent any time with the dean in her tenure at Aston. Granted, she stayed out of trouble, but she also wasn't interested in extracurricular volunteer work, joining clubs or participating in campus activities. Maybe if she'd been more of a joiner, Henry would have known her name too.

Maybe he would have recognized her.

Would he have recognized her? Would he have noticed the resemblance to her mother? That was, if he remembered Mom in the first place. Their affair decades ago might have been a casual tryst. A one-night stand after which neither party remembered much about the other.

At this point, she would put nothing past her mother. Without a doubt, Mom had been cheating on Dad for Elora's entire life. First Henry Neilson, then David Clarence.

Elora had spent more hours than she'd ever cared to repeat comparing her mother's lovers.

David Clarence emitted this raw power and dominance. He was cold. He was calculating. He was attractive, lethally so. And his sons, especially Zain, had inherited his striking good looks.

Lawrence Maldonado was equally as powerful. When it came to business, her father was ruthless and cunning. But Elora rarely saw that version of her father, because to her, he was simply Dad. She got his smile. She earned his hugs. It was odd to think of her father as handsome, but he was as equally arresting as David.

Then there was Henry Neilson.

He smiled easily. His demeanor was friendly, yet there was authority in the way he carried himself. Elora suspected that students who broke the university's rules would receive heavy-handed punishments from Henry. But the laugh lines around his mouth and eyes gave him a soft edge. He was handsome, with dirty-blond hair streaked with gray. He had a bit of a belly beneath his starched shirts and tweed blazers. And his wire-framed glasses relaxed him even more.

Dad and David were two sides of the same silver coin, whereas Henry was a crisp dollar bill.

"Hey."

Elora jerked as her friend fell into step beside her. "Hi."

"What are you doing on this side of campus?"

Stalking my sperm donor. "Meeting."

"Oh, for what?"

"A class," Elora lied, doing her best to sound annoyed. The last thing she needed was Ivy asking questions.

The truth was inevitable—Lucas's and her own—but the secrets would keep until after the holidays.

"What are you doing?" Elora asked.

"I have one more class this afternoon, then I'm going home to study for a bit. Maybe take a nap." Ivy looked like she could use one. There were dark circles under her eyes and her shoulders were slumped. With the heaviness in her footsteps, you'd think her backpack weighed one hundred pounds.

"Everything okay?" Elora asked.

Ivy shrugged. "Sure."

Liar. Later, Elora would find time to talk with Ivy, but today, on campus and in between classes, wasn't it.

Ivy had been off since Thanksgiving, ever since the fight with her dad about her getting a master's degree. It, along with Zain's accident, had put her friend in a funk. Ivy's spirit seemed . . . crushed. Or maybe that was Elora projecting.

"I was thinking about going to visit Zain tonight," Ivy said. "Talk to him about some stuff."

At the mention of Zain's name, Elora stiffened. Ivy hadn't spoken about him lately—or any topic. But the lack of information about Zain had begun to fester. Was he okay? When would they release him from the hospital?

She shouldn't ask. It wasn't her business. But . . .

"How is he?" Elora blurted.

"Come with me and see for yourself."

Elora shook her head, keeping her gaze locked on Dean Neilson ahead.

He turned to walk into a building and Elora frowned. Today's walk was over. So she stopped on the sidewalk.

"What?" Ivy asked.

"I think I forgot a notebook in the library," she lied.

"Okay, well, I'd better get to class. See you at home?"

Elora nodded, but before she could leave, Ivy touched her elbow.

"Zain's okay. He went home Sunday. Edwin has been sleeping on the couch every night since to help out. And Zain's got a nurse during the day in case he needs anything."

Wait. A nurse? And Edwin? It was Wednesday. If Edwin had been at Zain's for the past three nights, where was Mira? Shouldn't she be helping her fiancé recover?

There was a spark in Ivy's eyes, one Elora hadn't seen in two weeks. It was the spark that meant Ivy knew something Elora didn't. But of course, she didn't just confess. No, Ivy gave her a little finger wave and walked away. "Bye."

Elora stifled a growl as her friend ducked into a building.

Along with that spark, there'd been a smirk on Ivy's lips. That rarely boded well.

What hadn't Ivy told her? And what was happening with Edwin?

He hadn't been in many of their shared classes lately. Elora had been giving Edwin copies of her notes and collecting whatever assignments he'd missed in lecture. Each time she'd met him on campus for a quick exchange, Edwin had looked exhausted. Like a guy who'd been spending most of his time in a hospital.

A guy who'd been sleeping on a couch.

Elora hadn't asked Edwin about Zain either. She hadn't let herself.

Now, she wished she had.

Sunday. He'd been home since Sunday. Why was Edwin staying with Zain? What about Mira?

That question plagued her as she made her way across campus to the parking lot, climbing in her car and driving home. Why wasn't Mira with Zain? What did Ivy know? Curiosity was beating Elora bloody today, and instead of slowing at the normal turnoff, she kept driving straight, the manor streaking past her windshield.

Her BMW practically steered itself to Zain's neighborhood, like the car had missed it as much as Elora had. Her insides were tangled in a knot as she pulled into an empty space outside his building.

The last time she'd been here, Elora had vowed not to return. To let Zain move on. To stop the twisted little affairs between the Clarences and the Maldonados.

What a fucking coward.

Elora had made the decision to fight for her brother. Her father. Why not Zain?

If it wasn't too late . . .

"Only one way to find out," she told herself, pushing out of the car.

The lights were on at Axel's tattoo parlor and the front entrance to the building was unlocked. She slipped inside.

Axel was seated at the front counter. He glanced up from the notepad he was drawing on and gave her a roguish grin. Then he jerked his chin in the direction of the stairs. Axel had always seemed to root for Elora and Zain. Or maybe that was just her wishful thinking.

She waved at him, then headed toward the loft. Her feet got heavier with each stair. By the time she reached the landing outside of Zain's penthouse, she felt as if she'd scaled the Himalayas.

Elora froze at the door. Why hadn't she stopped at the manor to change? This morning she'd dressed for warmth, like she had every day for the past two weeks, knowing that she'd be spending extra time on campus, stalking Henry Neilson.

Her leggings were warm, the thick material fit like a second skin, but they weren't exactly stylish. She'd bought them to wear beneath her snow pants the last time she'd gone skiing in Montana.

The boots she'd chosen were Prada, but the chunky black soles weren't as sexy as the heels she preferred. Her wool coat was oversized and, though toasty, did nothing to flatter her figure.

This outfit was for comfort, not confessions. Or maybe it was perfect. At least her clothes wouldn't bind if she had to grovel on her knees.

Elora was prepared to crawl and beg if that's what it took.

No regrets. If he slammed the door in her face, if Mira was the one to answer because Elora had misunderstood Ivy, she'd have no regrets for coming today. She could at least move on with her life knowing she'd tried.

With her spine locked straight, she knocked. Her heart hammered as footsteps sounded beyond the steel door.

She'd expected a nurse—and feared it'd be Mira.

But it was Zain who answered.

He was braced on a crutch. His left leg was wrapped in a white cast from above his knee all the way down to his ankle. His sweatpants had been cut off on the casted side. His left arm had also been broken and that cast consumed his forearm. He wore a white T-shirt, the short sleeves revealing scrapes and cuts along his skin. Most had healed considerably since she'd seen him at the hospital.

Beneath his clothes she knew there were incision marks, but other than the casts and scabs, he looked like himself. Straight nose. Crystal-blue eyes. Sharp jaw and broad shoulders.

Perfect.

Tired.

Angry.

Zain's eyes held fire. His jaw was clenched. His fist tightened on the handle of the crutch. Should he be standing? How was he moving around? Where was the nurse? Where was Mira?

She swallowed those questions and settled for a whispered, "Hi."

Zain said nothing.

"How are you doing?"

He glanced at his casts. "I'll live."

Awkward tension settled between them. For a man who'd explored every inch of her body with his tongue, he stared at her like she was a stranger. His glare was unsettling, and Elora fought the urge to shift from foot to foot. "Are you alone?"

"Who else would be here?"

Mira. She'd come here to find out if he was engaged, hadn't she? There was only one way to know. "A nurse? Or your fiancée?"

"The nurse is gone," he said. "And I don't have a fiancée."

The air rushed from her lungs. "You don't? What about Mira?" *What about the canary diamond?* "She was at the hospital."

"A lot of people came to see me at the hospital. You included."

"I asked Ivy not to tell you."

"Ivy doesn't listen. Figured you'd know that by now." He shifted, adjusting his crutch. "What are you doing here, Elora?"

"I just wanted to see how you were doing. See if I could help."

"Help." He nodded, his tone dripping with sarcasm. "Right. Now that I'm out of the hospital. Now that I'm not in public. *Now* you can check on me. When no one will see you visit."

"What?" Her jaw dropped. "That's not why I came. I was at the hospital, Zain. In public. I stayed for hours and hours."

"Until Mira showed up."

"She was wearing a ring."

"Yeah, a ring I gave her years ago. A ring she kept after we broke up. So?"

Elora blinked. "So? She acted like you were getting married."

"We're not." If his expression had been cool before, it turned arctic. "Anything else? I'm busy."

"Zain," she whispered. "I thought you were engaged."

"Because you didn't ask *me*!" Zain's voice boomed through the hallway. "You could have stuck around and fucking asked me yourself about Mira. But you ran. Like always, you ran. And goddamn it, I needed you, El. I needed to wake up from that nightmare and see your face. I needed *you*. And you should have been there."

Her heart stopped. Tears welled from the pain in his voice. The pain in her chest.

He was right. He was so very right. Even if Mira had been his fiancée, even if he had moved on, Elora still should have been there.

"I'm so—"

Before she could apologize, he shuffled backward.

And slammed the door in her face.

thirty-nine

. . .

ELORA FELT LIKE A PACK MULE. Her backpack was stuffed—the seams straining—with every book, notepad and folder she'd need for the rest of this week and the following week of finals. Her two suitcases held enough clothes and toiletries to last a month.

The backpack was strapped to her shoulders. Each hand held a suitcase's handle. She'd ordered Chinese takeout for dinner, and the scent of garlic, fried rice and orange chicken wafted from the plastic sack looped over her forearm.

She'd managed to open the door without dropping anything, but as she scaled the staircase, she felt her phone slipping free from where she'd tucked it in an armpit.

Ten stairs to go. She huffed. *Nine. Eight.*

"Elora?"

She whirled at Edwin's voice, and the movement sent her phone clattering to the stairs, falling not one, but two steps behind her. Right next to Edwin's feet. "Can you get that for me?"

"Sure." He swiped it up, then took one of her suitcases. "Moving in?"

"Something like that." She hiked the rest of the stairs, depositing everything on the landing outside Zain's door.

It had been two hours since he'd slammed that door in her face, though it felt more like five minutes given how busy she'd been in that time.

After he'd yelled at her, Elora had flown home and packed. She'd stopped at a gas station to fill up her car. She'd picked up dinner. And she'd had to swing by campus to hand in an assignment that she'd planned to deliver tomorrow in class. But she'd be skipping her classes on Thursday and Friday. If she could manage it, she wouldn't be leaving Zain's loft until her first final the Monday after dead week.

That was the plan, anyway. Assuming he let her into the loft.

"What are you doing here?" she asked Edwin.

"Well, I was going to make him some dinner but looks like you've got that covered." He pointed to the Chinese.

"Yep." She nodded.

Edwin chuckled. "Guess that means I don't need to stick around."

"Nope."

His grin widened and he handed back her phone. "Call me if you need anything. He's been pushing too hard, trying to rush his recovery. So make him chill, okay?"

"I'll do my best."

"And last night, he mentioned something about getting rid of his nurse. I told him it was a bad idea, but I doubt he'll listen. Don't let him fire her."

Too late. Elora suspected the reason he'd answered the door himself earlier was because he'd already dismissed the nurse. But that suited her just fine because Zain wouldn't need a nurse. Other than the tests she had to take to wrap up her semester, she had no plans for leaving this building.

No nurse.

No Mira.

No Edwin.

Zain had Elora.

She stood a little taller, feeling a rush of pride. She was here, fighting. She was here to let her own stubborn streak shine. "Okay."

"See you at finals." Edwin waved as he started down the stairs, stopping to look back before he got too far. "He's been a miserable bastard lately. And it's more than just the accident. I'm glad you're here."

"I should have been here from the start."

He gave her a sad smile. "Bye."

Elora waited until Edwin was gone, then faced the steel door. No matter what, she wasn't leaving this building. If Zain didn't let her come inside, she'd camp out right here and sleep on the floor, for days if necessary.

"No matter what," she whispered before knocking.

"It's open," Zain shouted, probably expecting Edwin.

She sucked in a breath, then pushed inside, dragging one suitcase behind her and using it to prop open the door. Elora hauled in the second suitcase and her backpack next, setting them beside the island that separated the kitchen from the living room. She grabbed dinner last, taking it to the counter.

All while Zain watched her from a leather recliner.

That chair was a new addition to the loft, probably something he'd gotten for his recovery. On the floor beside him, within reach, was his crutch.

She felt his stare but Elora didn't let herself meet his gaze. Was he still angry? He had every right to be. Was he glad that she'd come back? Even a little bit? She wasn't ready to face him, so she didn't. Instead she opened and closed every cupboard in the kitchen, getting a feel for where he kept everything.

"What are you doing?" he asked, finally breaking the silence.

"What do you want to drink?" She took out two plates, then surveyed every drawer like she had the cabinets. When she opened the fridge, she frowned.

It was nearly empty except for a gallon of milk, a carton of eggs and a block of cheddar cheese. Elora wasn't much of a cook, but she knew balanced meals required more than dairy and eggs. After dinner, she'd be texting Francis for easy recipes. Then she'd be placing an order for grocery delivery. Leafy greens. Fruit. Protein. Yogurt. Had the hospital given him a diet to follow during his recovery?

"Milk or water?" she asked, grabbing two glasses, filling one with water for herself.

"Elora."

"Milk it is." She went for the gallon, filling his glass. Then she got to work on the food.

After Zain's plate was full, she popped it into the microwave while she tore off two paper towels to use for napkins. She took his milk and fork over, setting them on the side table beside the recliner, then went back for his meal. "Do you have a tray? Or have you just been eating on your lap?"

"Elora, look at me."

She ignored him.

"El."

Damn that nickname. He wielded it like a knight would his sword, rendering her helpless.

No matter what. She turned and met those beautiful blue eyes.

They were still angry, though not as much as they had been earlier. As far as emotions went, his exhaustion seemed to be taking the lead.

"You should go," he said.

"No."

"I don't want—"

"I love you." Elora needed her own weapon. And at the moment, honesty was her sharpest knife. She couldn't go back in time and say it years ago, like she should have. But she could say it today. "I love you very much."

Zain didn't so much as blink as he studied her. Could he

hear the truth in her words? Could he see them coming from her heart?

It unnerved her, to stand here and be this raw. Her instincts screamed to shut it down. Hide behind a mask of indifference. Erect those walls. But she resisted, standing fully clothed in the middle of his home, feeling more naked than she had in the shower this morning.

Finally, he dropped his gaze to his lap, and she remembered how to breathe.

She refocused on her task, her heart racing as she retrieved his plate from the microwave.

He didn't say a word as she carried it to his recliner and set it down on the crowded table.

"Anything else?" she asked.

He shook his head.

Elora retreated to the kitchen, dizzy and drunk on adrenaline. Could he hear her thundering pulse? Her ragged breaths? Could he see her trembling hands?

No matter what, she was here, so despite her lack of appetite, she fixed her own plate and put it in the microwave. Once it was heated, she carried it to the couch, sitting down and eating beside Zain in silence.

One piece of his chicken was too big and he pushed that to the side rather than attempt to split it with the side of his fork. She made a mental note to cut everything into bite-size pieces going forward until that cast was gone.

Elora would baby him. And when he was recovered, when he was back to normal, she'd leave if he asked her to go. But no matter what, she'd be here until he healed.

Neither finished their food. There was plenty for leftovers too, and she spent the next thirty minutes dealing with the dishes and wiping down the kitchen counters. After texting Francis, she took a suitcase to the bathroom, unpacking her toiletries. The clothes she'd brought were left in her luggage but everything was stowed against a wall so it would be out of his path.

Zain watched her flitter in and out of the living space. She'd felt his gaze on her back as she'd cleaned the kitchen too. And when there was nothing more to do, when she finally had to stop moving, his gaze was waiting.

"Elora."

The way he said her name made her heart climb into her throat. He was going to ask her to leave, wasn't he?

"I love you." It was easier to say this time. So was her apology. "I'm sorry. I'm sorry that I wasn't there when you needed me. I'm sorry that I didn't go out on that date with you months ago. I'm sorry that I didn't tell you how I felt. I'm sorry"—her throat clogged as tears flooded her eyes—"I'm sorry, Zain."

His face gave nothing away as he pulled the lever to close the recliner's footrest. Then he bent, grabbing his crutch.

Was he getting up to escort her out? Or to walk away?

"I hated being a secret," she blurted. "And I know that it was my idea, but I hated it all the same. I hated seeing that woman sit on your lap. I hated seeing a ring on her finger. I hated pretending that I didn't care."

Zain stood, finding his balance with the crutch before walking her direction.

Elora closed her eyes to keep the tears from falling. "I hate not seeing you every day. I hate sleeping alone in my bed. I hate—"

"Elora." His breath caressed her cheek. He touched her mouth. "Stop."

She opened her eyes. He towered above her. The white cast covered his forearm and most of his hand except for the fingertips he'd pressed against her lips. Another tear dripped free and he caught it.

"I can't stop. There's more I hate." About their situation. About herself. "There's more to say."

"I'd rather skip what you hate and hear you say that you love me again."

"I love you." Her voice cracked. *Damn it.* She was going to cry. Hard. There was no stopping it. No leaving to hide herself in a lonely corner. He was going to see what no one else ever had.

Elora, stripped bare.

Zain's forehead dropped to hers. "I love you."

A sob broke free and the hold she'd kept on her emotions—today, her entire life—shattered. She fell into Zain's chest, crying with her ear pressed against his heart to make sure it kept beating.

She cried and cried and cried until the tears soaked his shirt and the floodgates had closed.

"I'm sorry." She hiccupped, pressed against his chest. Here he was, leaning on a crutch, yet she couldn't seem to unwrap her arms from around his waist. "I came here to take care of you, and I'm falling apart."

He kissed her hair. "I don't need you to take care of me. I'm fine."

"You almost died." She closed her eyes, shaking her head. "I can't . . . I cannot live without you."

"You don't have to."

Not today. Not tomorrow. Maybe they'd make it.

The doubts, her irrational fears about the future, weren't gone. But they had quieted. She owed Zain a deeper explanation. She owed him a confession.

Both would wait.

"I love you," she whispered.

"I know."

They stood together, holding on to each other, until he shifted and the crutch squeaked. That noise sent Elora into a panic as she realized it couldn't be comfortable to stand for long.

"You should rest," she said, stepping out of his arms.

"I've been resting."

She pointed to his unmade bed. "You should keep resting."

He sighed. "I'd like a shower. But I've got to wrap these casts and it's a pain in the ass with one hand."

Hence the medical tape and the industrial roll of plastic wrap she'd seen in the bathroom. "I'll do it. Lead the way."

His movements were stiff as they walked down the hallway, and though he tried to hide it, she could tell he was in pain.

"Do you want to take anything?" she asked, trailing behind him.

"No. I threw out the bottle yesterday."

"Okay." Elora wouldn't press. They'd both been around when Ivy had struggled to get off her pain medications after the car crash years ago. And Zain's mother had been on pills for years.

She slipped past him once they reached the bathroom and turned on the shower. And as steam engulfed the room, she went to work wrapping his casts.

When she went to lift the hem of his T-shirt and pull it over his head, he stopped her. "Wait."

"What?"

"It's, um . . . ugly."

Nothing about this man would ever be ugly. "I want to do it. Please?"

He closed his eyes but nodded, so she dragged the cotton up his chest, careful with his cast and various scrapes.

One look at the red incision marks on his torso and she felt a brutal pinch, but she didn't let it show. She used a lifetime of experience to blank her expression so that he wouldn't see how much it hurt.

When his clothes were piled on the floor, he shuffled to the shower, tipping his head back beneath the spray.

Elora stripped out of her own clothes, then slid into the space behind him, fitting her chest to his back as she trailed kisses up and down his wet spine. She reached for his shower puff, lathering it with soap, then her hands roved over his body, tracing every line of raised flesh. Touching every wound. Tracing every scar.

They were a part of him now, like the tattoos.

And like the ink, those marks were hers.

He was hers.

Zain relaxed into her, the water and soap cascading down his skin.

His cock swelled as she cleaned his body. A low pulse bloomed in her core. But neither of them moved to take it further because this wasn't about sex. This was love.

When he was clean, he turned, pulling her deeper into the spray. Then he cupped the back of her neck with his good hand, hauling her close to seal his mouth over hers.

The stroke of his tongue was slow and languid. The slide of her hands over the rounded curve of his ass was lazy and deliberate. They devoured each other, licking and sucking, until her lips were swollen and the water had turned lukewarm.

Elora helped him with the towel and into a pair of boxers, then as he brushed his teeth, she did the same. Once he was in bed, she traded her own towel for one of his T-shirts, then climbed in beside him, curling into his right side. His good side.

Her phone dinged in the kitchen with a text, probably from Francis or maybe Ivy. But she didn't make a move to leave, laying a hand over Zain's heart.

His fingers toyed with a damp tendril of her hair that hadn't made it into her messy knot. "I'm sorry about Mira."

Elora stiffened. "We don't need to talk about it."

"Yeah, we do. She's been visiting. She might come over."

"Oh." She hated herself for what she was about to ask, but she had to know. "Did something happen with her? After you and I—"

"After you left me that fucking note?"

She winced. Not her finest moment. "Sorry."

"Once I'm recovered, you owe me for that." His hand slid

down her spine, tugging up the hem of her shirt to palm her bare ass. "And, babe, I'm gonna collect."

A shiver rolled over Elora's shoulders at the promise of a punishment she'd happily take.

"But to answer your question, no," he said. "Nothing happened. Mira and I just went out a few times."

"She was your date." The date he'd told Elora she'd ruined.

He nodded. "She wanted to try again, and I won't lie. I considered it. When Mira and I were good, we were good."

Elora did her best to keep her breathing even, but inside, she wanted to scream. He would have married her. Maybe. Probably. And if not for his accident, Elora would have been the coward who stood idly by as the love of her life married another woman.

He'd almost had to die for her to fight. It might take her entire lifetime to forgive herself for that mistake.

"El."

"It's okay." She swallowed the lump in her throat. "You don't owe me an explanation."

"Look at me."

Elora shook her head.

"It will hurt if I try to roll you over, pin you down and force you to look at me. But I'll do it if I have to."

She frowned, shoving up to an elbow.

The sun had set outside but she hadn't drawn the shades, so the glow from the streetlights lit the loft and the contours of his handsome face.

"Mira's easy to be around. We have a long history together."

God, why was he telling her this? Couldn't he hear her heart breaking?

"But there's a reason we broke up years ago," he said. "She's a damn snake when she wants to be. Like showing up at the hospital and flashing that ring because she thought it would win over my mother. Which it did. And she thought maybe it would change my mind. Which it did not. I don't want Mira."

The air rushed out of her lungs. After hearing those words, maybe now she could stop picturing them together. "Okay."

"You are a pain in my ass. Getting anything out of you is a fight. I've never met a woman so guarded and stubborn. Fuck, you are stubborn. Instead of telling me what has you spooked, you run. And then there's the bullshit you've got in your head that I'd be better off without you."

Her jaw dropped.

"Didn't think I knew that, did you?" He arched his eyebrows. "No one in this world knows me like you do. Because I haven't let them. Not even Mira. And though you might pretend to shut me out, Elora Maldonado, no one in this world knows you like I do."

She opened her mouth to say something, anything, but her head was reeling, trying to soak it all in.

"You and me, we fit," he said. "We fit so fucking perfectly it shouldn't be real. Yeah, Mira and I were good. But even when we were at our best, nothing can compare to you and me." He pressed his hand over her heart. "Two hearts."

"One beat," she finished.

Below this very bed, in Axel's tattoo parlor, he had three different tattooing rooms. Two for the artists who worked in his studio. And the third, the largest, was Axel's own personal space. He'd papered the walls with black-and-white photos of his various projects, the favorites from his career. But one tattoo he'd turned into a red, neon sign.

The script was simple and clean. *Two hearts. One beat.*

The day Elora had gone with Zain to get his eagle tattoo, Axel had told them the story about that sign.

His very first paying clients had been his grandparents. Axel had inked *Two Hearts* over his grandfather's heart. And *One Beat* over his grandmother's. They'd both been diagnosed with cancer the prior year. Chemotherapy hadn't worked in either case, so before they'd passed, they'd wanted coordinating tattoos.

Tattoos inked over their hearts by their beloved grandson.

That story had touched Elora's soul—not that she'd let it show. It must have made an impression on Zain too if he remembered those words.

"I love you." She dropped her mouth to his, kissing him with all the love she had to give. She savored his taste. She drowned in the softness of his lips. She poured her heart into the man who owned it.

Then she curled into his side once more.

And, for the first time in weeks, fell asleep.

forty

. . .

IVY'S HEAD WAS POUNDING. She'd been studying for hours and her brain felt as if she'd smashed it against a brick wall.

It was only Tuesday of dead week, and she was already dead. But she had no choice other than to press forward. If she was going to pursue the master's program, she needed impeccable grades her senior year.

So she turned the page of her textbook, yawning as she read the first paragraph, and jotted down notes from a passage about the final days of the USSR. Her professor loved to put dates in his tests and she expected the final exam to be littered with timeline questions about certain events.

She was just about finished with the chapter when a knock came at her office door. Ivy glanced up, expecting Geoff, but instead it was Michael. *Damn.* How had he slipped past her butler?

"Hey." Could he hear the fake cheer in her voice?

"Hi." Michael walked in, rounded her desk and bent his face close to hers. Not close enough to touch, but close enough that she knew what he expected.

A kiss.

She sat a little taller, pressing her lips to his. It was a struggle to maintain her smile and not grimace as she pulled away.

Whatever attraction she'd had for Michael faded a bit more with each of these forced kisses, which never went beyond a chaste brush of the lips. And thankfully, he hadn't pressed for sex. Yet. Though the clock was ticking. She still hadn't figured out what to say and how to reject him.

Was this how her mother felt about her father? Obligated? Trapped?

Because after Thanksgiving, after that stupid fucking trip to Carol Kennedy's house, Ivy had been obligated. She'd been trapped.

When Michael had asked her about the conversation he'd overheard, she'd promised to tell him the story. Just . . . not yet.

It was a damn miracle he hadn't asked about it since. Though this was Michael. On the list of people Ivy trusted, Michael wasn't even a footnote on the page. Just because he wasn't asking her didn't mean he wasn't seeking information elsewhere.

The records from the crash had been sealed. Her father had made sure to protect his daughter's name—and by extension, his own. Ivy had only been seventeen when Kristopher had died. One month and her birthday later, it might not have been as easy to keep the crash's details quiet.

But as it was, he'd been able to throw money at her problem. His fortune insulated her secrets.

Dad had paid Carol Kennedy a ridiculous amount of money to keep her from suing their family. The newspapers had reported a crash but Ivy's name had never been released; no doubt those reporters had been given an envelope of cash.

But that didn't mean she was safe. Her former high school classmates could speculate if given enough prompting.

With the exception of Elora and her family members, no one from Aston Prep knew the whole truth. Still, she didn't need Michael asking questions and digging up old graves. If she could just keep stalling—faking—Michael might eventually lose interest.

Ivy had become a wishful thinker since Thanksgiving.

She wished Michael would vanish. She wished the reprieve from Carol's emails would last forever. She wished for Tate.

Just the thought of him made her heart twist.

She'd really fucked that one up, hadn't she? First the stunt in the car, screwing him like he was a meaningless hookup. And then all the bullshit she'd spewed in the hospital.

"Ivy." Michael snapped his fingers in front of her face.

Her lip started to curl but she caught it before it could sneak free. She plastered on a saccharine smile. "What?"

"I asked what you were doing today."

"Oh. Sorry." She rubbed at her temples. "Studying. I have so much work to do and I've been fighting this raging headache. I think I'm getting my period."

He cringed.

Score.

"What are you doing?" she asked. "Want to go to dinner later?"

"Uh, not tonight."

Ivy did a mental fist pump. She'd bought herself a week by faking her period. Because if Michael knew he wasn't getting any tonight, he'd be gone in five, four, three, two . . .

"I'm heading to the library to meet up with a study group," he said. "Just wanted to stop by and see what you were doing."

"I'm glad you did," she lied, shifting to press another demure kiss to the corner of his mouth. "See you later?"

"Sure." He jerked up his chin and headed for the door.

She waited until he was gone, then wiped her lips with the back of her hand. "Fuck."

Ivy had no time for Michael. She had tests coming up, but

beyond the semester, she needed to figure out how to detach her life from her father.

A lawyer. She needed a good lawyer. But the only attorneys she knew were currently employed by Dad.

Maybe Zain could help.

She hadn't gone to visit him this past week, not because she didn't care, but because he was in good hands with Elora. But it was time to set the wheels in motion, to take control of her future, so hopefully they wouldn't mind the intrusion.

Ivy stood from her chair and went to her bedroom, stopping by the bathroom to take two Tylenol before going to her closet for a puffer coat and boots. Then she was out the door, driving to Zain's neighborhood, where she parked beside Elora's BMW.

Given the thick coat of frost on her best friend's windshield, that car hadn't left that space in a week.

The building was locked, so she hit the buzzer for the loft. Her breath billowed around her in a white cloud as she waited. Then came the click of the door unlocking as either Zain or Elora saw her on the camera system.

Elora was waiting at the top of the stairs, holding open the penthouse door. "Hi."

"Hey." Ivy smiled at Elora, glad to see color infusing her cheeks and the hollowness of her eyes gone. "You look happy."

Elora glanced over her shoulder to where Zain sat in a recliner. "I am happy."

"I should have called first."

"You never call first," her friend scoffed as they moved inside the loft. "Or knock."

"True." Ivy was dedicated to changing some bad habits. But not all.

She stripped off her coat, hanging it on a hook before taking off her boots. Then she hugged Elora. Tight. So tight it must have surprised her friend because she tensed. "I'm glad you're here."

Elora relaxed. "Me too."

Ivy let her go, then went to her brother's chair, bending to hug him just as hard. "Hi."

"Hi." Zain's good arm came around her. "You okay?"

"Not really. I, um . . ." She sighed, telling Zain something she'd never told him before. "I could use your help."

Tate had told her once that Zain didn't know what to do with her. *So show him who you are.* That concept was still fuzzy, but every step she took in the right direction, the haze lifted a little more.

"What do you need?" he asked.

She let him go and went to the couch, slumping into a corner.

"I'm going to go take a bath," Elora said, coming over to Zain for a kiss. "Need anything?"

"No, babe. I'm good."

Elora gave Ivy a smile, then slipped away, giving her time alone with her brother.

"You look like shit," he said. It wasn't an insult. There was concern in his voice. Because between the two of them, she was the person on the decline. He might have the casts, but his color was as fresh and lively as Elora's.

Ivy, on the other hand, hadn't eaten much lately. Her hair was unwashed and this headache was leeching her energy. She also hadn't bothered with makeup, another tool in her arsenal, along with a fake period to keep Michael at arm's length.

"I feel like shit," she admitted.

"Want to talk about it?"

"Yes." Then came a rush of word vomit.

She told him about Dad killing her application at the Smithsonian. About the fight at Thanksgiving over her master's degree. About the internship arrangement for the manor.

"He won't give it to you," Zain said. "He knows you want it, so there will always be a catch. One more hurdle for you to jump. And it'll never be enough."

"I was afraid of that," she muttered.

"He did the same thing to me. He had this penthouse in Manhattan. Took me a few times when I was in high school and tagging along on his business trips. It was an awesome property. Views of Central Park. Right in the middle of billionaire's row. Told me it would be mine after I graduated Aston. A gift."

"You don't have a penthouse in Manhattan."

He shook his head. "I don't have a penthouse in Manhattan."

"What did he want you to do for it?"

"Do his bidding. Work for the company. Follow in his footsteps. In Grandfather's. Become *him*."

"So it's hopeless." The manor wasn't slipping out of her grasp. It had never been there to begin with.

"It's just a manor, Ivy."

"It's my home," she whispered. "But at this point, I'm willing to give it up and tell Dad to shove it. Got any pointers?"

"A few." Zain chuckled. "You and Edwin can compare notes. He's about to do the same."

"Wait. What?" Ivy's eyes bugged out. "Edwin's not going to work for Dad?"

"No. He's as done with the Clarence manipulation as you are."

"Wow." She needed to stop by Edwin's place next. "We're supposed to get our trust funds when we turn thirty. Do you think that will really happen?"

Zain gave her a sad smile. "I don't know. Dad wasn't happy when I went behind his back. He's made a lot of changes since."

"I figured," she muttered.

"Edwin is talking to my lawyers. You should do the same. Just in case. At the very least, you both should have a team on your side to fight when—not if—Dad thinks to change the terms."

"You think he'd take our trusts away completely?"

"Have you met him?"

Ivy's nose scrunched up. *Yes.* She knew her father quite well. The asshole would pull out all the stops to screw over his own children if they slighted him. "I think I'd better get the name of your lawyer too."

"Of course."

"Why do our parents suck?"

Zain grinned. "If you want to get into that, we're going to need all night."

A smile ghosted her lips. "Thank you."

"Welcome."

The sound of the water in the bathroom turned off. "I have a feeling I lost a roommate, didn't I?"

"We haven't discussed it yet, but yeah." Zain nodded. "She's *my* roommate now."

Ivy felt a pang of sadness mixed with joy for her friend and brother. It was the end of a road. Maybe she wouldn't feel like crying if she knew which path to take next. "I'd better get going."

"You could stay for dinner."

"Another time. Tell Elora I'll call her." Ivy stood and went to his chair, giving him another hug and a kiss on his cheek. "Bye."

"See ya." He waved and watched as she put on her coat and boots, then slipped out the door.

Ivy had expected to feel lighter after that conversation, but her footsteps thudded heavily down the staircase. Though it was nice to have her brother's help, to know that Edwin was in her same position, she hadn't made any actual progress. If anything, Zain had only confirmed her fears.

Dad cared more about money and control than he did his children. She doubted that would ever change.

But it was just money, right? It was just a house.

Ivy had enough money in her bank accounts to fund an advanced degree. Maybe Zain would lease her a loft in this neighborhood after she moved out of the manor. Maybe she could reapply at the Smithsonian after graduation and they'd have a spot for her.

Wishful thinking.

She pushed outside, keys in hand, just as a woman's laugh caught her ear. A couple walked down the sidewalk. She did a double take. Her heart shriveled, like a grape withering into a raisin beneath the scorching summer sun.

Tate walked arm in arm with Allison fucking Winston.

Her cheeks were rosy. Her mouth was stretched in a smile. She was wearing a black cap but the thick, glossy strands of her long brown hair fell over her shoulders.

Tate grinned as he spoke to her, his lips much too close to her ear.

Allison laughed again, and Ivy felt the knife in her spine slide deeper.

Allison fucking Winston.

Ivy tore her eyes away and forced her feet to her Mercedes. She hit the locks and popped open the driver's side door. But she couldn't help herself. She looked over the car's roof and found a pair of devastatingly beautiful dark eyes waiting.

Tate's smile fell.

Allison followed his gaze, and when she saw Ivy, she preened. That cunt preened as she clung tighter to Tate's arm. No way this was a coincidence.

Ivy's rage came to life, fury chasing away sadness. Her spine lengthened and her bitchy attitude clicked into place. It was magnificent.

"Oh, Tate." Ivy clicked her tongue. "If you're planning on visiting Zain's apartment, you might want to consider leaving the trash on the curb. Elora is upstairs and she's a stickler about keeping garbage human beings out of her home."

Allison's mouth fell open.

Tate's jaw clenched.

Before either of them could respond, Ivy gave them a finger wave, slid into her car and drove the hell away.

"Of all the fucking women." Ivy's hands strangled the steering wheel as she made her way home.

Okay, so he'd moved on. She'd expected that. Maybe not so soon, but it was inevitable. But with Allison? What happened to that discussion they'd be having, huh?

"Bastard." She spoke the word but didn't mean it. Ivy knew who was at fault here.

Though it wouldn't save Allison from her scorn. Her molars ground together just thinking that woman's name.

Allison had seen Tate dancing with Ivy. It had been the night Ivy and Tate had met at Treason. That had to be the reason Allison was in the picture. Not that Tate wasn't a catch. Maybe if she hadn't known Allison so well, she wouldn't have suspected this was all a ruse to get her revenge on Ivy. Allison had been seeking revenge since high school.

Since Kristopher.

Her anger shifted, her emotions spilling out of their cup, and hot, furious tears streamed down Ivy's cheeks as she drove.

Tate and Allison.

Her stomach roiled.

Part of Michael's appeal had always been Allison's infatuation with him. The first time Ivy had slept with him, it had been after she'd spotted Allison fawning over him at a Sigma party. But had Allison given up her chase? Never.

Michael had slept with them both. And that hadn't hurt. It had pissed her off, but it hadn't hurt.

Except Tate . . .

A sob worked free from her chest, loud and ragged and teeming with years of frustration and pain.

Tate hurt. Seeing them together *hurt.*

Nearly as much as finding out that Kristopher had screwed Allison. He'd told her the night of the crash that he'd been fucking Allison for months, at the same time he'd been promising Ivy the world. At the same time he'd been making her life hell.

Kristopher had been with Allison.

Kristopher and Allison.

Tate and Allison.

Ivy wasn't sure which hurt worse.

Defeat settled on her shoulders. Her dad had won. And now Allison.

Maybe weeks ago, she would have fought. But today, there was nothing to do but cry. So Ivy cried, grateful that Elora wasn't at the manor when she walked through the door. Cassia was likely locked away studying, or with Edwin, so Ivy went to her office, closing the door behind her.

The desk drawer was like a magnet. She eased it open, lifting out the pill. That innocent little white square that would make all the pain go away. Ivy would be numb. All she had to do was take it.

Ivy missed being numb.

forty-one

. . .

BEYOND THE WINDOWS of Ivy's bedroom, night had fallen. She'd watched the light fade, eyes glued to the glass, as the colors had transitioned from afternoon gold to evening blue to the black of midnight.

Her stomach growled, hungry from missing dinner. But she didn't trust herself to leave her room. She was too raw. Too weak.

After seeing Tate with Allison, she's spent an hour staring at that pill on her desk. An hour spent raging an internal war. But she'd won, right? She'd swept that pill back into the drawer and walked away.

Except could she really call herself a victor if she hadn't flushed the drug? How long was she going to keep tormenting herself? Testing her own limits?

Soon, she wouldn't be able to resist. And if she broke once, she might never recover.

So she stayed draped in this chair, her shoulders against one armrest with her legs kicked over the other, and stared into the night.

Her eyelids felt heavy. She was yawning, about to call it a

night, when the echo of footsteps sounded in the hallway. Ivy sat up straighter as her guest drew closer.

Shit. It was probably Michael. She'd been such a mess when she'd come home earlier, she'd probably forgotten to lock the back door. He was getting too bold with her home if he'd invited himself inside without her permission.

Unless it was Edwin? He had his own key to the manor.

The footsteps stopped at her door and her neck prickled. There was no need to crane her neck to see her visitor. The air in the room shifted, like the electric charge before lightning touched.

Michael didn't have that sort of presence.

But Tate did.

Her breath quickened. Her skin tingled. "What are you doing here?" she asked, still refusing to turn.

"Told you we'd be discussing that stunt you pulled at the hospital." His rugged, deep voice sent shivers down her spine.

"A little late, aren't you?"

"Just giving you time to suffer."

Oh, and she'd suffered. It was equally irritating and impressive how well he had her figured out.

"I don't have time for games, Ivy."

"Then you'd better steer clear of Allison Winston. You looked awful cozy earlier."

"Jealous?"

Yes. And heartbroken. "How'd you two meet? I'm guessing it wasn't by chance."

"No, it was not."

"And who approached who?"

"She approached me."

Her teeth ground together. "If you've got her, what are you doing here? And how did you get into my house?"

"You shouldn't leave a spare key beneath a flowerpot." Tate took a step into the room, and her resolve fizzled. She turned, taking in his lazy stride. He walked right to her chair, towering above her, his cologne infusing the air and making her dizzy.

Weak. God, she was weak. Because she couldn't tear her eyes away. She tilted her head back, holding his gaze. The dim light brought out the edge to his features. That chiseled jaw. The soft pout to his lips. The sooty eyelashes and dark, chocolate eyes.

Tonight, he looked so much like the man from their first night at Treason. Dangerous. Gorgeous. Tantalizing. Tate was more tempting than that fucking pill.

"I never should have fucked you in the back of my car," he murmured, casting his gaze to the window.

"Why did you?"

He'd been so adamant about waiting. About driving her wild. But she'd asked and he'd obliged. Not that he hadn't been rewarded. But the teasing had stopped instantly.

"Because you asked me."

She swallowed hard. "I asked before."

"Then because you needed it. You were falling apart."

Yes, she'd been falling apart. He'd seen it and come to her rescue.

"You tried to push me away."

"And I guess it worked."

Tate bent, bracing his hands on the chair as his nose nearly brushed hers. "You can push me. You can push as hard as you want. But I'm not going anywhere. We're done if I say we're done. Not a minute sooner."

"Then where have you been?" She hated the vulnerability in her voice. She'd missed him and there was no hiding it.

"Like I said. Giving you time."

Her lip curled. "And while I was waiting, you passed your time with Allison? Did you fuck her in your back seat too?"

Tate's jaw clenched as they glared at each other, unmoving, until so much anger and sexual tension swirled around them she could practically see it hanging in the air.

She wanted him. Even after seeing him with Allison today, she craved Tate.

Damn him. He'd ruined her. One shallow, delicious fuck in his car, and he'd ruined her. And here he was in her bedroom.

She was seconds away from undoing the zipper on his jeans and taking him into her mouth. As long as Allison's mouth hadn't been there first.

"Did you fuck her?" she repeated. How deep was his betrayal? Was he as bad as Kristopher?

"I'm just using Allison."

Ivy felt like she'd been slapped, harder than when the man outside Club 27 had hit her. She flinched. Not as bad as Kristopher. *Worse.*

"For information, baby. Not sex."

"Information?" Her eyebrows came together. "What do you mean?"

"While Zain's been out, I've been helping out at Treason. Being there when he can't."

"Oh." Her heart melted a bit. She should have thought to volunteer to help at the club. Not that she had any experience. Tate was the right guy to help her brother, but still, she should have asked. "How does Allison fit into this?"

"She found me last weekend. Flirted. Made it pretty obvious she was into me. Then she asked me how I knew you. If I've known you for long. If we were together."

"Me?" She swung her legs from the chair, sitting straight.

Fuck. Ivy had suspected Allison's interest in Tate hadn't just been for his gorgeous face and sculpted body. Was Allison making moves on Tate because Ivy wanted him? Or was Allison trying to dig into Ivy's past? Had Michael enlisted Allison's help?

Her heart raced. It had to be the past. It had to be about Kristopher.

Allison had always wanted to know more about the night of the crash. She was just as in the dark as everyone else. She'd heard the rumors floating around Aston Prep too. But

Allison had always taken it further. She'd gone so far as to hunt Cooper down and beg for information about his brother's death.

Money was the only reason Cooper hadn't spilled the horrid details. Because that life Cooper lived in San Francisco had been funded by the same settlement that kept Carol Kennedy quiet. The only time Carol broke her silence was to send Ivy a Sunday email.

"What did you tell her?" Ivy asked.

"That I was friends with your brother. And that I knew you . . . intimately." A smirk spread across his mouth. "That got her attention. She went from curious to jealous so fast I almost got whiplash. She offered to fuck me in the parking lot behind the club."

Ivy's lip curled. "Slut."

"She hates you with a passion."

"The feeling is mutual," Ivy muttered.

"Gathered that earlier." He leaned closer, his lips just a breath from hers. "God, you are gorgeous when you're jealous."

Ivy opened her mouth to deny it, but there was no point. "What other questions did she ask about me?"

"None yet. But that was why I was with her today. It didn't sit right with me. There was a desperation to her curiosity. Like she was grasping. That's why you saw me with her today. I turned her down for a hookup in the alley. Asked her on a date instead. Thought I'd take her to that little café in Zain's neighborhood, let her ask more questions."

"And did she?"

"She was rather forthcoming after that encounter on the sidewalk. She told me how you went to Aston Prep together. How you think you're so above other people. How you get away with anything. How your boyfriend in high school died in a car crash after a party. How everyone saw you leave with him but no one knows what actually happened."

Ivy felt the color drain from her face.

"The crash. That ties to those emails I saw, doesn't it?"

She managed a nod.

"The crash is the reason you lost it at the hospital."

She nodded again. There were plenty of gaps to fill in, an entire story to share, but she couldn't. Not tonight.

"Hey." Tate took her chin, tilting up her face so she had no choice but to look at him. His eyes softened. Whatever he saw in her face made him shake his head. "I shouldn't have fucked you in my car."

"But you did," she whispered. Because she'd asked him to.

"That was yours. Tonight is mine." He came closer, never loosening his grip on her face as his lips brushed hers.

She lifted, seeking more, but before she could deepen the kiss, he moved away.

He trailed his mouth along her jaw, moving to whisper in her ear. "What do you want?"

"You." More than her next breath.

Those lips left a trail of tingles along her cheekbone. "No more games. Say it."

"No more games," she whispered.

Then Tate's mouth claimed hers.

One stroke of his tongue against hers and they were all over each other, gripping and petting and touching and rocking. Her legs fell open as he pressed her into the chair, his strong body trapping her in place while his mouth devoured.

Tate's grip on her chin never faltered. The other threaded into her hair, his palm molding to the shape of her skull, tilting her exactly the way he wanted so that his tongue could make these incredible swirls against her own. He bit her bottom lip, hard enough to make her gasp. Then just as she was about to return the favor, he picked her up, arms banded around her body, and carried her to the bed.

Ivy hit the mattress and he was on top of her, solid and warm and wearing too many clothes. She fumbled with his coat, shoving it over his shoulders and trying to push it to the floor. But Tate was too intent on kissing her, on tasting her, to break his mouth free.

Instead he gave her more of his weight, settling into the cradle of her hips. His arousal pressed into her core, jolting desire through her body. Every time she pressed for more—tugging on his clothes or arching her hips—he'd just give another flutter of his tongue and prolong the kiss.

Tate was in command.

Tonight was his.

And Ivy was helpless to resist. So she kissed him, sinking deeper and deeper into his taste. Their tongues dueled, wet and sloppy. He left no corner of her mouth untouched.

The throb in her core bloomed, thrumming harder. Faster. Just this kiss and she was on the verge of quaking. More. She needed more. So she tilted her hips, seeking a sliver of friction to satisfy her ache. Except the moment she moved, he was gone, standing up and wiping his mouth dry.

Damn him, was he going to *leave*? He'd worked her up into a frenzy and now he would become a ghost. More suffering for her behavior at the hospital.

But then his coat hit the floor and her sigh of relief filled the room. He reached behind his neck, fisting his sweater and yanking it over his head.

Ivy's mouth went dry at the sight of his naked torso.

She hadn't appreciated his body enough that day in his car. Taut skin stretched over rippled muscle. Defined, sinewed arms. A strong chest and—God—when had a man had such perfect nipples? She reached for him, desperate to feel the heat of his skin against her own.

Tate grabbed her outstretched wrist, stepping closer to take the other. Then he raised both arms above her head. "Don't move."

She gulped.

Ivy liked control with sex. She liked control period. And this was too much like the last time with Kristopher. The night he'd pinned her hands above her head and fucked her against the hood of his car. The car where he'd died.

Panic mingled with memory and she bent her elbows, bringing them to her sides.

Tate frowned, taking her wrists again. But he paused instead of lifting them to the headboard. "Do you trust me?"

"Yes." It was the truth.

He leaned down, kissing the inside of both wrists, then raised her arms once more. "Breathe, baby."

She sucked in a sharp inhale as his fingers drifted down the underside of her forearms, past her shoulders and to her ribs.

He plucked the hem of her sage sweatshirt, tugging it up just enough to get to the waistband of her jeans. One flick and the button was undone. The zipper's click was as loud as her heartbeat as he inched it free.

He eased the pants off her hips, stripping them from her legs until they dropped to the floor with a muffled thud.

As the cool air caressed her skin, Tate moved on top of her once more, the bed sinking with his weight.

His lips found her navel. His tongue tasted her skin as he explored. Up and down, he peppered her belly with kisses. Whenever he got close to the edge of her panties, he moved away.

Torture. Exquisite torture.

She fought the urge to thread her fingers through his hair, to steer him where she needed his mouth. It went against everything in her experience to let him play. To let him set the pace.

But she closed her eyes, and when he finally slid his hands beneath her sweater, gliding them along her flesh until they touched her bra, she moaned.

Tate's mouth followed as he pushed up her shirt, stripping it free of her arms. When her hands left the headboard, more out of habit than fear, he didn't say a word as he took her wrists once more and placed them back against the headboard.

Another shaky breath. Another hint of fear. Both vanished when he took a nipple in his mouth, sucking it through the lace of her bra. The material gave his mouth a rougher edge but she needed more. She needed to feel the slickness of his tongue without a barrier.

"Tate," she whimpered.

He read her thoughts, pulling the cups of her bra down. Then his hot mouth circled a nipple and her back arched off the bed.

"Yes," she hissed.

He sucked. He lapped. He tormented her breasts until she was sure she'd orgasm from his mouth alone. Her body was engulfed in flames.

"Mine," he murmured against her skin as he shifted, moving down her belly, letting his tongue taste her along the way.

His fingers hooked into her panties, drawing them free and tossing them to the floor. Then he pushed her knees aside, kissing the sensitive flesh on the inside of her thighs.

She trembled. She pulsed. And her hands never left the headboard because the fear of him stopping was worse than her fears from the past.

Tate blew a stream of air on her soaked folds, following it with a slow lick.

Ivy gasped, her gaze dropping to where he was perched between her legs.

Tate's dark gaze was waiting. "Mine. Understood?"

She nodded.

"Say it, Ivy."

"Yours."

That was all he needed to latch on to her clit, giving it a suck that ripped a cry from her throat. Then he feasted on her, his magnificent tongue showcasing its talents as an equally skilled finger plunged inside, finding that perfect spot.

Ivy shattered. Before she'd even known she was coming, she flew apart into a million pieces that would never fit together the same way again. And as she came down, her hands were still safe against the headboard.

He'd taken her hands. He'd taken her control. So that she had no choice but to surrender.

And she'd never felt so free.

Aftershocks racked her body as Tate moved off the bed, stripping out of his jeans. His thick cock bobbed, and a new rush of heat blazed through Ivy's skin. More.

He returned to the bed, hovering above her. "Do I need a condom?"

"No." She was on birth control and she hadn't been with anyone in months. Not since before Tate had danced with her at Treason.

He reached between them, a hand fisting his shaft to drag the head of his cock through her folds. It was as delicious as his tongue. But he didn't press forward. He didn't plunge inside or rush to capture his own release. He stilled, his eyes closing, like he was on the edge and needed a moment to pause. To find his own control.

It was the most sensual sight of her life, seeing him like this. Beautifully, barely restrained. His muscles were bunched, his brow furrowed. And when he finally opened his eyes, those stunning pools were brimming with lust. He took her breath away.

Ruined.

Tate rocked them together, inch by inch, sliding deep until her breath hitched. His features tensed. "Fuck, but you feel good."

She stretched around him, savoring the fullness. Then she angled her hips, pressing her clit against the root of his shaft. "Oh, God."

He pulled out only to thrust inside. Fast. Her breasts bounced between them. Her whimper of surprise made him grin.

She gave him her own wicked grin and clenched her inner muscles.

He groaned, and the teasing stopped. Playtime was over. He fucked her hard and rough and exactly as she wanted. He worked her up until she was a writhing mess, lost to anything but the sensation of them together.

Ivy detonated again. Her release triggered Tate's and he came on a roar of her name, pouring inside her body.

They collapsed together, boneless and spent. Tate rolled to his back, pulling Ivy across his chest as they regained their breaths. And then he held her. Those strong arms held her as she drowned in the rhythm of his steady heart.

She felt . . . numb.

No, not numb.

Bliss. This was bliss. Reality didn't exist. There were no Allisons or Michaels or Kristophers or Coopers. Here, in Tate's arms, she was his.

And he is mine.

She was ruined.

Everything good in Ivy's life was eventually ruined. But she was a wishful thinker now, wasn't she? So she closed her eyes and made a wish. That when this relationship crashed, it would be her life lost this time.

Not Tate's.

forty-two

. . .

TIME'S UP, *Red*

Cassia laughed at Edwin's text. He'd sent her a picture of her empty chair at the library. On the table in front of it was a Mike and Ike box.

He'd begged her to come and study at the library today, but she'd told him no, staying at the manor instead. As much as she wanted to spend time with him, she couldn't afford any distractions. And Edwin was the perfect distraction.

So she'd told him to give her five hours. Five hours to soak in as much information from her notes and textbooks as possible before he came over and stole the rest of her day—and night.

It had been a week since their *something* had become serious. Since she'd become Edwin Clarence's *girlfriend.* In just seven days, that label had become so familiar and comfortable that it was as soft and cozy as the tag on the vintage tee she'd put on today.

On my way

She smiled as his text appeared, quickly typing out a reply.

Hurry

Then she packed away her books, having finished studying

for the day. What she hadn't accomplished would be there tomorrow. For the remainder of the day, she planned to do nothing but, well . . . Edwin.

Cassia had studied him as intently as she had economics this week.

She'd memorized the contours of his face with her fingertips. She'd kissed every inch of his chest and shoulders. Her favorite pastime was taking him in her mouth just so she could watch the handsome face he made as he came on her tongue.

Her core clenched. Whatever hunger she had for him, he seemed as ravenous. They couldn't keep their hands off each other, which was why they couldn't study together, even in the library. They'd tried yesterday, and not an hour into their work, he'd dragged her out of her chair and into a storage closet to fuck her against the wall.

That man was as addicting as candy and as sinfully sweet.

A blush spread across her cheeks as she left her bedroom, needing a quick snack before he arrived. She'd skipped lunch, and no doubt Edwin would keep her occupied until well past dinner.

She hurried downstairs and breezed into the kitchen, hoping to find Francis. But the room was empty and a note was on the counter.

Went to the grocery store

Cassia sighed. Besides her time spent with Edwin, the best part of her day was talking to Francis. "We'll have to catch up tomorrow," she told herself.

She hurried to make a quick ham sandwich, then scarfed it down standing next to the counter. She'd just put her plate in the dishwasher when she heard footsteps at her back. She turned—had Francis returned from the store?—and froze.

"Oh. Hi," she muttered.

"Hi." Ivy walked to the fridge, taking out a bottle of coconut water. "How are you?"

Cassia blinked. Was that a trick question? "Um, good."

"Studying today?" There was no malice in Ivy's tone. No narrowed eyes or evil grin.

"Yes," Cassia drawled. Okay, what was going on?

Ivy hadn't spoken to Cassia since Thanksgiving. The day Ivy had called her pitiful. And now they were making small talk?

Cassia didn't trust her roommate and that wasn't going to change today.

"Is Edwin coming over later?" Ivy asked as she twisted off the cap to her water, then took a drink.

Cassia nodded.

"Maybe we could all have dinner together or something."

Yep. Definitely a trick. It had to be. "Seriously?"

Ivy shrugged. "Or not. It was just an idea."

Cassia opened her mouth, not totally sure of what to say, but before she could speak, a voice called from the hallway.

"Ivy?"

"Think I could hide in the pantry?" Ivy grumbled.

"Huh?" Unless Cassia was mistaken, that was Michael's voice. Why would Ivy want to hide from him? Weren't they friends? Or fuck buddies? Except the look on Ivy's face was anything but welcoming as Michael strolled into the kitchen.

"Hey." He jerked up his chin. "Geoff said you went this way. Hi, Cassia."

"Hi." She looked between the two of them, feeling like she was missing, well . . . a lot.

"You still on to meet with the study group tomorrow?" Michael asked, either oblivious to the waves of annoyance rolling off Ivy or ignoring them.

Whatever. "Three o'clock, right?" Cassia didn't really want to study with the group, but they'd all endured an Aston finals week before, and if they had tips, she wanted them.

"I'm going to head to the library early if you want to meet up," Michael said.

"Okay. I'll see how my morning goes. Maybe I'll come by early." With one last look at Ivy and the blank expression on her face, Cassia decided it was time to retreat to her room. "See you tomorrow."

She walked out of the kitchen just as the chime of the doorbell rang from the foyer. There were rarely visitors who used the doorbell, mostly because people first had to get through the gate, and by then, Geoff would be waiting at the door. Michael had probably come through the gate and someone had followed him inside.

The butler emerged from a hallway ahead of her, walking to the door.

Cassia trailed behind him, heading for the staircase. Edwin wouldn't ring the doorbell and whoever was here was certainly not visiting her.

Geoff opened the door as she reached the bottom stair. "Can I help you?"

"I'm looking for Cassie Neilson. I heard she lives here."

That name. *Her name.*

That voice. *His voice.*

Why? How? The world shifted out from beneath her feet. Her heart plummeted. Her vision blurred. He'd found her.

"Do you mean Cassia?" Geoff asked.

The visitor didn't answer. Because his gaze must have drifted past Geoff's shoulder to where Cassia stood frozen at the base of the staircase.

"Cassie."

She didn't move. Why hadn't she used the back staircase? They were for the staff mostly, but she should have been using them too. The ugly, gray stairs that weren't beautiful or grand and were purely intended for function. Those were the stairs for Cassia.

"Cassie," he repeated her name.

Her heart thundered as she turned, slowly. She reached for the railing, gripping it tight to keep her balance as she locked eyes with him.

Josh.

His brown hair was shorter than it had been when she'd

seen him last at Hughes. The beard he'd grown last winter was gone. He looked like the version of Josh from when they'd first met. The clean-cut, sexy, sweet guy she'd loved once.

Cassie—foolish and naive—had fallen for that attractive face.

But Cassia wanted to slap it.

"What are you doing here?" she snarled.

Josh pushed past Geoff, stepping into the foyer.

The butler tensed, his eyes widening, and Cassia had no doubt that if she asked, he'd toss Josh out on his ass. Oh, but it was tempting.

"I've been trying to find you." Josh took one step toward her and Cassia's hand shot out, palm out.

"Don't." She didn't trust herself around him. She didn't trust him period.

"Cassie. Please." Josh pressed a hand to his chest, like she'd wounded him. The gall of this bastard. Like any pain she could inflict could compare to the agony he'd brought to her life.

"How did you find me?"

Josh cast a glance toward Geoff. "Can we go somewhere private?"

"How did you find me, Josh?" She raised her voice, the sound almost booming through the foyer.

Geoff tensed, and she could have hugged him for the worry on his face. "Sir, you need to leave."

"I'm not leaving." Josh took another step, ignoring Cassia's hand, still outstretched. "I tried to call but you changed your number. You didn't leave a forwarding address. I've been worried about you."

"Worried," she deadpanned. "Answer the question. How did you find me? Was it my uncle?"

"No." Josh shook his head. "He wouldn't return my calls."

Well, that was something. She'd have to thank Uncle Henry for that later.

"I got a call from your roommate," Josh said.

Cassia shouldn't have been shocked. It shouldn't have made her knees buckle. If not for her grip on the railing, she might have fallen.

Ivy.

Like she'd planned it, like she'd stalled Cassia in the kitchen on purpose, Ivy came walking through the foyer with Michael on her heels.

Red coated Cassia's vision.

This was the boiling point. For months, Cassia had minded her own business. She'd gone out of her way to avoid Ivy and just live her own damn life. But this? Cassia could get over the invasions of her privacy. The name-calling and shaming. But by bringing Josh here, Ivy had gone too far.

"You fucking bitch."

Ivy's steps faltered. "Excuse me?"

"You are a fucking bitch," Cassia repeated, enunciating each word. "What is your problem? Are you really so miserable that you can't leave other people alone? You have nothing left but to bully those you find beneath you?"

"What are you talking about?" Ivy asked, glancing around the room.

"Fuck you." Cassia raised her chin. Damn, that felt good. Too good. So she turned her glare to Josh. "And fuck you too."

His mouth fell open.

The door was still open, Geoff standing at its side, and because apparently the universe wanted everyone to see Cassia lose her shit, Edwin strolled inside. The concern on his face meant he must have heard her curse.

"What's going on?" He walked straight to Cassia, glancing at his sister.

"Ask her." Cassia tossed a hand at Ivy.

"I have no idea." Ivy had that clueless, innocent look down to perfection.

And every man in this room bought it. Including Edwin.

"I hate you." Cassia's entire body vibrated as the words spewed out. "I fucking hate you."

"Red." Edwin put his hand on her arm. "What is going on?"

"Cassie," Josh said.

Her hands balled into fists. "Leave, Josh. Get. Out."

"No, I came all this way—"

"Then you wasted a trip!" she yelled. "I don't want to see you. I don't want to talk to you. I will never forgive you for what you did. Never. And I never want to see your face again. Leave."

"I just . . ." Josh swallowed hard. "I'm sorry."

Too late. His apology rang hollow because he was too late.

A part of her, the part who'd loved him once, felt a pang of guilt. He'd lost someone he'd loved too, hadn't he? But her overwhelming emotion was anger. Josh's loss was nothing compared to her own.

She leveled him with a glare, ignoring the tears in his hazel eyes. "Goodbye, Josh."

His frame slumped as he turned and walked out the door.

Geoff closed it behind Josh, clearing his throat. Then he made his own escape.

Smart man. Whatever anger Cassia had sent toward Josh was nothing compared to the rage she had toward Ivy. Months and months of pent-up emotion came bursting free.

"You're a loathsome cunt," Cassia said, glare locked on Ivy.

"Whoa, Red." Edwin brushed her arm. "Easy."

Cassia flung off his touch, her eyes still aimed at Ivy. Her jaw was slack too. No one had probably risked calling her a cunt recently. Cassia was beyond caring about the risks. "Fuck you for bringing him here. Fuck you for these trials and games. Just fuck you."

Ivy held up her hands. "I didn't do anything."

"Oh, bullshit," Cassia barked. There was only one person who'd gone through her belongings. Who'd found the photo of Josh. Who even knew he existed. The day Cassia had come home to find her suitcases packed, there was no doubt that Ivy had seen the photo Cassia should have left behind at Hughes.

"If you're going to be cruel, at least own it. Admit that you brought him here to mess with me. What, were you bored? Being rich and spoiled isn't enough to keep you entertained?"

"Ivy, did you do this?" Edwin asked.

"No. I don't know what she's talking about. I swear, Edwin."

"Stop lying!" The scream tore from Cassia's throat. "Stop fucking *lying*."

"I'm not." Ivy took one step forward, her eyes glued to her brother. "I did not do this."

Cassia saw Edwin's face change. She spotted it the moment he believed Ivy. The moment he took his sister's side over hers. "You believe her."

"Let's just talk." Edwin sighed and reached for her again, but she took a step away.

No, there'd be no talking.

Edwin had no idea how excruciating it was for Cassia to see Josh's face. Maybe that was her own fault. Maybe if she'd told him the whole truth, he'd realize just how lethal a move this was on Ivy's part.

But even if he didn't know the whole story, she needed him on her side. And yet once again, she was alone on this beautiful, sweeping staircase.

A tear dripped down her cheek, followed by another. Scalding, heartbroken tears.

"Red," Edwin murmured, but she spun and bolted for the second floor, sprinting to her bedroom, where she locked the door.

Cassia went straight for the closet, doing what she should have done months ago. She packed a suitcase, stowing her favorite clothes with haste. She crammed her books and school supplies into her backpack.

"Cassia." Edwin knocked on the door. He wiggled the handle. "Talk to me."

She ignored him and rushed to the bathroom, putting her toiletries in a case. Then she pulled on her coat and shoes, taking her bags to the door, where she waited. Where she listened.

Once his footsteps moved away from the door, she counted to ten and made her escape.

Down the gray, staff staircase.

Out the back door.

To her car.

To put Clarence Manor in her rearview mirror.

forty-three

. . .

"STOP LYING!"

Elora's gaze whipped to her bedroom door as Cassia's scream carried down the hallway. She dropped the shirt in her hand and jogged through the manor toward the foyer. She rounded the corner in time to see Cassia fly up the staircase with Edwin trailing not far behind.

"What's going on?" Elora asked Ivy.

Her friend stood perfectly still, her shoulders rigid.

Elora's eyes darted to Michael. "What's wrong with Cassia?"

"No idea." He shrugged. "I just got here."

Ivy shot him a glare. It was subtle, and had Michael been looking at Ivy, he would have caught it. But before he noticed the sneer on her face, Ivy masked it with a sigh. "Well, that didn't go like I'd planned."

Michael's head cocked to the side. "You planned it?"

"I told you I'd learn her story, didn't I?"

He studied her, his eyes narrowing. "Yeah, I guess so."

Ivy stared right back, like they were having a silent conversation—or a silent feud. Those two were seasoned soldiers and neither would admit defeat until every drop of blood had been spilled.

Elora frowned, having no desire to get caught up in drama today. But before she could turn and retreat to her rooms, Edwin came jogging down the stairs.

"I need to talk to my sister," he told Michael. "Alone."

Michael arched his eyebrows, then a smirk spread across his lips. He stepped closer to Ivy, lifting a hand to trace a line across her cheek. "Later."

Ivy didn't move. She didn't so much as breathe as Michael strode for the door. Only when it closed did Ivy's shoulders fall.

"Goddamn it," she muttered, wiping the place on her face that Michael had touched.

"What is going on?" Elora asked. "Why was Cassia yelling? And what about a plan?"

Elora had been living in a Zain bubble for the past week. She'd only come to the manor today because in her rush to pack, she'd forgotten a phone charger. She'd been using Zain's, but then her dad had texted this morning that he'd sent flowers, so Elora had decided to pop home to bring the bouquet back to Zain's loft along with a few more items from her closet.

"Did you do it?" Edwin asked Ivy, his hands braced on his hips.

Do what?

"Michael." Ivy pinched the bridge of her nose. "It was Michael."

"You just said it didn't go as planned," Elora said.

"That's because I wanted Michael to think I did it. Or would have done it. That he beat me to it." Ivy sighed. "Shit."

Yes, exactly. Elora was so tired of this shit.

The smart thing for her to do would be to turn and walk away. For any other roommate, she would have. But she liked Cassia. Even though they had spent hardly any time together, Elora respected Cassia.

"Who was that?" Edwin asked. "Josh?"

Elora had missed *Josh*, whoever the hell Josh was.

"I'm pretty sure he's Cassia's ex," Ivy told him.

Edwin stiffened. "Why would Michael call him here?"

"I don't know." Ivy tossed up her hands. "Because Cassia didn't fall at his feet. Or he's jealous because she is smarter than he is. Or he has no reason other than he's an asshole. What are Michael's reasons for doing anything? All I know is that he wanted to know her story. And when she moved in here, I, um . . . I sort of goaded him. I gloated that I'd find out about her first."

Edwin's nostrils flared. "Can't you mind your own fucking business?"

"I did," Ivy muttered. "Sort of."

"You're telling me you didn't hire that PI of yours to dig into Cassia's past?" Edwin asked.

Guilty. It was all over Ivy's face.

"I mean . . . I did," Ivy said. "But I didn't do anything with his report. And I haven't even read it, okay? I swear."

"Un-fucking-believable." Edwin scoffed. "You invaded her privacy. You went too far. Goddamn it. That's my girlfriend."

"I'm sorry. Okay? I'm sorry. It was weeks ago. Before you got together. Or . . . before I knew you were together."

"And if I hadn't gotten together with her?" Edwin challenged. "Then what?"

"I don't know," Ivy admitted. The hurt on Ivy's face, the self-loathing, made Elora's heart clench. "I really am sorry."

"Don't apologize to me." Edwin pointed to the ceiling. "Apologize to Cassia."

Ivy strode past Edwin and took the stairs. She didn't even hesitate.

For that, Elora was proud of her friend. Ivy was going to make this right. And knowing Ivy, making it right would include her revenge against Michael too.

"Christ," Edwin mumbled. "I'm so sick of this."

"You and me both. Is Cassia okay?"

"I don't know. She locked me out of her bedroom." Edwin rubbed a hand over his jaw. "I believe Ivy. That she was telling the truth. Do you?"

Elora nodded. "Yes, I do."

When Ivy made a mess, she did it intentionally. When she'd put past roommates through trials, she'd owned every single minute. There'd been no question about who was pulling the strings. Ivy proudly wore the puppet master's badge. So if Ivy claimed she hadn't done this, hadn't called Cassia's ex, then Elora believed her.

"What do you think Michael's problem is?" Elora asked.

"He's a cruel motherfucker? He thought this would get to me? I don't know." Edwin dragged a hand through his hair. "But he's not getting away with this."

Ivy wasn't the only Clarence who understood vengeance.

"Edwin." Ivy's voice was panicked as she jogged downstairs. "She's gone."

"What do you mean?" Edwin straightened, running for the stairs. But Ivy put a hand on his arm.

"She's not in her room."

"Yes, she is. I was just up there."

"Well, I opened the door and she's gone."

"Her car." Elora spun and rushed through the manor with Ivy and Edwin close behind. They made it to the back door just in time to see Cassia's taillights disappear from the driveway.

"Fuck." Edwin pounded a fist against the wall. Then he dug out his phone, scrolling over the screen before pressing it to his ear. "Straight to voicemail. You try calling her."

"Uh . . ." Elora gave him an exaggerated frown. "I will. But you'll have to give me her number."

If Edwin was pissed before, he was furious now. "You've been living with her for months."

Ivy and Elora shared a look.

"I could dig it up," Ivy mumbled. "I'm sure it's in my phone or email somewhere."

They'd both stopped saving their roommates' phone numbers after Ivy had chased the first few away. Elora should have gotten Cassia's number.

"You two are unreal." Edwin backed away. "Cassia's done here. The minute I find her, we're coming back to get her stuff, and she's done with this house."

Without another word, he stomped away, his shoulders bunched. Then the slam of the front door rang through the manor.

"Maybe we should all be done with this house," Ivy whispered.

Elora's first instinct was to object. This was their home, right? Especially Ivy's. Elora knew how much these walls—Francis and Geoff—meant to her friend.

But this wasn't home anymore. Elora was ready to move on.

With Zain.

"Maybe you're right," she said.

Ivy's eyes flooded. "What a fucking cluster."

"You had Sal investigate Cassia." Elora didn't phrase it as a question.

"Yes," Ivy said.

"Why?"

"Because I'm cruel."

It was the same word Edwin had used for Michael. But where it fit him, it didn't Ivy.

Yes, Ivy had few boundaries. She was shallow and often spoiled. She said things she almost certainly didn't mean. But it was mostly an act. Ivy and Elora had been playing roles for far, far too long.

Except it wasn't who they really were.

"You're not cruel," Elora said.

Ivy scoffed. "Our roommates would beg to differ."

"Those bitches deserved it."

"And Cassia? I should have called off Sal weeks ago. But I didn't. Because I wanted to know her secrets. So I took them.

They weren't mine, but I took them anyway. For what? So I could hurt her if I wanted to? So I had ammunition? What is that if not cruel?"

Elora wished she had an answer. But it was Ivy's to find. "I don't know."

"Neither do I." Ivy's chin quivered. "But I'm tired. I'm so fucking tired. There are just . . . too many secrets."

Too many secrets.

Elora watched as Ivy retreated through the house, not pursuing because her friend needed space.

She had her charger in her pocket. The items Elora had come to take home, flowers included, were still in her rooms. But she had her charger in her pocket, and she had no desire to linger.

It was time to move on.

From the manor. From the past. The only way to make that happen was with the truth.

Too many secrets.

Elora slipped out the door, walked to her car and found an odd calm on her drive to Zain's. It was time to tell the whole story. Every truth, no matter how painful.

Her decision to keep Lucas's paternity to herself until after the holidays had been an excuse. If Elora kept delaying, she'd find other reasons to put it off—birthdays, sports, more holidays—until so much time had passed that the secrets would eat her alive.

Was that how her mother had become so cold? Had she detached from the world, her family, her husband, her children, because of the secrets she kept hidden?

Elora was not Joanna.

Elora would not become her mother.

Zain was in his recliner when she walked through the penthouse door, his laptop resting on his thighs. The smile he gave her was effortless. Comforting. "Hey, babe."

"Hi." She unzipped her coat and pulled off her boots, a few clumps of snow falling to the doormat.

"I meant to get you an opener for the garage so you don't have to park on the street."

She waved it off. "I'll move the car in later."

"Or you can drive the Rover. I'd rather have you in something bigger this winter."

"Okay."

She'd drive his SUV if that made him feel better. She'd let him worry over her safety just like she'd worry over his. She'd been fretting over his upcoming doctor's appointment and had compiled a list of concerns on her phone to run past the nurse.

Assuming she'd be going to his appointment. Assuming what she was about to tell him didn't ignite a stick of dynamite under the peace they'd found inside these brick walls.

This past week together, Zain and Elora hadn't had many serious conversations. They hadn't talked about the future or the past. They'd just settled into this serene present.

Together.

They'd navigate these secrets together. Just because they hadn't discussed a future didn't mean it wasn't laid beneath their feet. Their paths were intertwined. And sharing her secrets wasn't going to change the outcome.

Together. They'd find a way to the other side.

She went to his chair, bending to brush a kiss to his lips. "I need to tell you something."

Zain's forehead furrowed. "Did something happen at the manor? Are you okay?"

"I'm okay." Elora nodded. Later, she'd tell him about the drama with Ivy and Cassia. After they talked about Lucas. After he had time to adjust to the shock of her news. "But I've been keeping something from you for a while."

Worry flashed in his blue eyes. "El, I'm not liking this."

"Trust me?"

"Yes."

She took his laptop and set it on the coffee table. "I love you."

"Elora." His tone held a warning that she'd better not delay. But it was important for her to say those three words. Every day. Multiple times a day. Not just so he'd hear her.

But so she would too.

The only way she'd be able to open up to people was with practice. And Zain deserved her unguarded heart.

She went to the couch, sitting on its edge and turning so that she could face him. Then she took a deep breath and let it pour free.

"This summer, I hired a private investigator to do a paternity test on Lucas. I told you my dad isn't my biological father. He's not Lucas's either. That's how it all started. I had these suspicions about Lucas. And when my PI started digging, well . . . he dug into me too."

Zain opened his mouth, but she held up a hand.

"Just let me get this out."

The hardest part was coming. She'd been holding it so tightly for so long that Elora had to take another breath before coaxing the confession loose.

"Lucas is your half brother. David—your father—is his father too." Whoosh. It was gone. Elora felt the weight lift off her shoulders.

And watched as it settled on Zain's.

His handsome face turned to granite. His jaw ticked.

"You told me you were tired of the twisted little affairs," she said. "Then I found this out about Lucas and all I could think was that it would never end. That my mother, your father. Your mother, my father. I was worried that their sins would plague us. Taint us."

She swallowed hard, dropping her gaze to her lap. "It's part of why I walked away. Because I just didn't want to bring this to you. To continue this sick cycle. That's not all of it. I was a coward. I'm so terrified of becoming my mother that I did become her. I pushed everyone I love away, especially you."

Elora would regret it. For years, she would regret her decision. Because maybe if she'd been here, where she was supposed to be, he wouldn't have gotten in that motorcycle accident.

"I'm sorry I didn't tell you sooner. I just . . . Lucas is my brother. He's this incredible, tender kid with a big heart. I love him. I don't want to see him hurt."

"I would never hurt him," Zain said.

"It's not you I'm worried about." Elora knew enough about David Clarence to know that man was not averse to inflicting pain, even on his children.

Strange how such a massive secret that had consumed her had taken just a minute to share.

The room went quiet as the new reality hung in the air, the truth soaking in for them both. They were connected by more than love. They were tied by Lucas. Blood. Everything was different now, and there was no going back.

Next, her father would have to learn the truth.

Then, Lucas.

"El." Zain's voice was steady. Composed.

She lifted her chin and met his gaze.

Maybe she'd expected to see conflict on his features. She'd definitely expected more of a reaction. But he looked at her with . . . pity. Like he felt bad that she'd discovered the truth this way.

Like he'd wanted to be the one to tell her.

She sucked in a breath. "You already knew."

forty-four

. . .

IVY WAS ON THE PHONE, pacing the length of her bedroom, when Tate walked through the door. She focused on the call, needing to finish this conversation with Sal. "Anything you can give me. The dirtier the better."

"With the last name Bamford, dirt won't be easy to find. They've probably got their skeletons locked in iron coffins and buried at the bottom of the ocean."

Not unlike the Clarence family. Especially considering how close her dad was with Michael's.

"Well, Sal. I hope you're a good swimmer. Whatever the cost. Get me leverage."

He sighed. "I'll be in touch."

"And Cassia."

"I'm on it."

She ended the call and her stomach churned. She was going to puke or cry or scream. She hadn't landed on which yet.

"Want to tell me what that's about?" Tate asked.

Ivy lifted a shoulder as her nose began to sting. Cry. She was going to cry. Because here she was again, ordering Sal to invade the privacy of yet another person in her life. Hadn't Edwin just scolded her for doing exactly this?

She'd had Cassia investigated out of curiosity. Mostly. Today's request was driven purely by the need for revenge. But she'd used that motive before too, hadn't she? Here she was again, being . . .

"Cruel," she whispered.

"What?" Tate closed the distance between them. "What's going on, baby?"

Ivy swallowed the lump in the back of her throat. "I messed up. That's the short of it."

"And the long of it?"

"I'm not a good person."

Maybe Ivy hadn't read Sal's report on Cassia, but to Edwin's point, she still had it. It was on her computer, waiting for the opportune moment. She should have deleted it.

She should have cut her ties with Sal and walked away.

Instead, she'd come to her room after Edwin had stormed out of the manor and Sal had been Ivy's first phone call. Michael had to pay for manipulating her. For manipulating Cassia.

Plotting revenge was her first instinct.

It was the same cycle, over and over again. When was it going to stop? When was she going to stop?

Tears welled in her eyes.

"Hey." Tate cupped her cheek. "Talk to me."

Ivy almost made an excuse. She nearly changed the subject. But when she met his gaze, her confession tumbled free.

She told Tate everything. About the other roommates. About her silly trials. About Cassia and their argument earlier. About Michael. The admission burst forward, and when she finally came up for air, she expected to watch Tate leave.

Ivy was a fucking train wreck.

"Aren't you glad you asked?" she muttered on a dry laugh. "I'm the worst."

"You're not the worst." He tucked a lock of hair behind her ear, then clasped her hand. "Come on. Let's go somewhere."

"Where?" she sniffled.

"Out of this house."

That was the best idea she'd heard in months.

Ivy snagged a coat from her closet, tucking her phone in her pocket in case Edwin called, then let Tate lead her downstairs.

Geoff was in the foyer when they reached the first floor, probably having waited after letting Tate inside. "I'll be leaving soon for the evening, Miss Ivy. Can I get you anything before I go?"

"I've got her." Tate winked at the butler before towing her outside to his car.

Ivy melted against the warm leather. A faint smile tugged at her mouth, thinking of the last time they'd been in this vehicle together.

Tate closed his door, following her gaze to the back seat. The corner of his mouth turned up too as he started the ignition. As he headed down the lane toward the gate, he took Ivy's hand, lacing their fingers together and lifting her knuckles to his lips.

She'd seen that sort of kiss in movies. Watched couples on campus be sweet to each other. Never, not once, had a man done that for Ivy, including Kristopher.

"Don't be sweet to me," she said. Not because she didn't love it. Not because she didn't want it every single day. But because today of all days, Ivy didn't deserve sweet.

"Don't tell me what to do." His grip on her hand tightened and he kissed it again.

Yep, she was going to freaking cry.

The way he kept her hand was the way he'd held her last night. Firm. Steadfast. She'd woken this morning in Tate's arms and had been so hopeful for the day.

After he'd showered and kissed her goodbye, promising to

be back later, she'd had breakfast with Francis. She'd studied through lunch, then she'd gone to the kitchen for a coconut water. When she'd spotted Cassia, she'd been nice. Hadn't she been nice?

Michael had interrupted them. He'd ruined their short conversation, much like he'd ruined the afternoon.

What if Sal couldn't find anything on Michael? Could she let this go? No. Never. Because if Michael had gone this far with Cassia, there was no doubt in Ivy's mind that he would stop at nothing to figure out Ivy's tie to Carol Kennedy.

She never should have let him drive her on Thanksgiving. *Damn it.* Her only hope was finding leverage. Discovering Michael's weakness in the hopes that it meant keeping him quiet.

The afternoon sun was setting, dipping closer and closer to the horizon. Good. Ivy was ready for this day to be over.

"Where are we going?" she asked as Tate eased through the gate and onto the road.

"Nowhere. Thought we could just drive."

Tension crept into her shoulders. Her hand immediately found the door, gripping it tight. Ivy didn't spend time driving. If she had a place to go, she'd go, either on her own or with Roy. But she had no desire to simply drive around. "We could go out to eat."

Tate hummed, heading straight down the street.

"What about a movie?" she suggested.

"Another night."

A knot of nerves wound tight in her stomach as they reached an intersection to an arterial and he turned, picking up speed as he joined the flow of traffic.

If Tate drove wildly, if he was reckless, Ivy wouldn't look at him the same way again. Considering he had no idea that she needed extra care when it came to driving, it would be entirely unfair. Yet it would change everything. Tarnish everything.

At the moment, the only promise of good in her life was Tate.

It wasn't like she could fire him like her other drivers. Would he get mad at her like Michael had if she asked him to slow down?

Ivy had learned through her various drivers that one of the quickest ways for a woman to bruise a man's ego was to critique his driving.

She braced, waiting for Tate to go faster. To zoom past a car ahead who was clearly going under the limit. Instead, he settled into the slower pace, his hand linked with hers never loosening.

Tate slowed for every yellow light. He let other cars pass him if they were in a hurry while he stayed strictly at or under the speed limit.

The only other person who drove like this was Roy.

And that was because someone, probably Geoff, had warned him to be safe if he wanted to keep his job.

Tate's driving was so similar it was uncanny.

Meaning . . . he'd been warned too.

"Zain told you about the accident," she said.

He glanced over, his brown eyes softening. Then he brought her knuckles to his mouth once more.

"That wasn't his story to tell." She tried to wiggle her fingers free, to put some distance between them, but he just clamped down harder. "Let me go."

"No."

"Tate, let me go."

He glanced over, letting her see the determination in his gaze, before returning his eyes to the road. "What did I tell you last night?"

"A lot." She frowned but stopped fighting his grip. He was driving and she needed him to focus on that task, not struggling with her physically.

"I said you could push me as hard as you want. And I'm

not going anywhere." His voice gentled. "I'm not going anywhere, baby."

"The way you use *baby* to make me not be mad at you is entirely unfair."

His smile made her heart skip. Tate had the most breathtaking smile, another of his unfair advantages.

She relaxed into the seat, studying his profile. "What did Zain tell you?"

"After I moved to Vegas, we'd touch base every month or so. One day, I called to see how he was doing. It happened to be the day after your accident."

"Oh." *Shit.* "What else?"

"Zain's been my friend for years. He'd make comments about you, and I'd pick up on them."

"Like what?" Exactly how much had her brother shared?

"Like how you go through drivers like water. How you wouldn't even think about getting behind the wheel after a drink. How he always makes sure the bouncers at Treason have your driver's number so you have a safe ride home."

Ivy wasn't sure what made her heart swell most. That Zain had always looked out for her. Worried for her. Or that Tate had paid attention when Zain talked about her.

And they hadn't even met yet.

"I don't talk about the accident," she said.

"I'm not asking."

"But what if you did?" she whispered.

Why had she said that? She hadn't spoken of the accident in years, not since high school, when she'd told Elora. But what if Tate knew? Shouldn't he be warned about the demons in her past? If Tate really was going to stick around, shouldn't he know what he was getting into with Ivy?

He kissed her knuckles again and touched the brake, signaling to turn off the road and into a parking lot outside of a commercial complex. He drove past a row of cars until they rounded the building and parked in a secluded corner. Then he put the SUV in park and shifted, giving her his fullest attention.

"Okay, I'll ask. What happened?"

Ivy filled her lungs. And told him her secret. "My boyfriend in high school, Kristopher, was my first everything. My first date. My first kiss. My first lover. He was also the first man to hit me."

Tate's anger was instant and palpable. "What the fuck?"

Ivy dropped her gaze, studying her knees. "It was playful at first. He'd push the physical boundaries by biting me during sex or pinching me hard enough to leave a welt. Always in places that would be hidden, like at my hips where my panties covered the bruise. My ribs beneath a bra strap. The insides of my thighs. He'd joke and say it was his way of marking me. Making me his forever."

And Ivy had convinced herself it was love, even when it had hurt.

"Kristopher was . . . addictive. He was the guy at school everyone wanted to be around. Confident. Smart. Controlled. He had a mean streak that gave him an edge, but he wasn't so horrible that it drove people away. He had a sharp tongue, but he was funny. And I loved him. I loved him to the point that he was my entire world."

Fake love.

Shallow love.

"He hit you." Tate's molars ground together. "Zain told me your boyfriend died in that crash. He didn't tell me that the son of a bitch fucking hit you."

"It's . . ." No, of course Zain hadn't told Tate that detail. She hadn't even had to ask anyone in her family not to share the whole truth. "It's humiliating."

"That's not on you."

"No, it isn't." It had taken Ivy a long time to realize that she wasn't to blame for Kristopher's abuse. "But that still doesn't make it any less embarrassing."

Mostly she was ashamed she'd covered it up. She was ashamed that she'd stayed, especially after it had escalated.

Kristopher had taken her on a spring break vacation their junior year to a house in the Hamptons. They'd gotten drunk that first night and it was the first time he'd hit her in the face. He'd apologized. Worshipped her the rest of the week. And the evidence had faded by the time they'd gone home.

The other times, well . . . Ivy had learned how to hide almost everything with makeup and clothes. All because she'd loved him. Or thought that she'd loved him.

"The night of the crash, there was a house party at a friend's house. My parents were hosting a Christmas holiday event at an art gallery that Edwin and I were expected to attend. So Kristopher went to the house party, and I met him late."

Kristopher had probably been fucking Allison while Ivy had been wandering the gallery, watching the clock and waiting for her parents to release her.

"When I got there, he was drunk and high. He'd been doing cocaine a lot. Those were the bad nights. The party was rowdy and loud and I didn't want to stay. I was sober and told him I'd drive us home."

Ivy wished she had stayed at the party. That she had endured the noise for just a few more hours until Kristopher was so drunk he would have passed out in the car.

"He was mad at me for making him leave but he came with me. About a mile from the house party, he told me to pull over."

"Why?" Tate asked.

"Sex." Ivy left out the details. She didn't tell Tate how Kristopher had slapped her hard enough that one eye had swollen shut. How he'd bitten her nipples until she'd bled. She didn't tell Tate that Kristopher had pinned her hands above her head against the car and fucked her so roughly that it had hurt to walk for a few days.

"Afterward, he wanted to drive." There was a weight on

Ivy's chest and speaking became difficult. Her knees bounced. "I told him no. I tried to keep the keys away from him and he, well . . . he didn't like that much."

Tate's nostrils flared. "What did he do?"

"It doesn't matter."

"Tell me, Ivy." Waves of fury radiated off Tate's body, but it was a different kind of fury than Kristopher's had been. Tate's rage was *for* her, not against.

She swallowed hard and told him the ugly truth. "He punched me in the belly. And while I was trying to catch my breath, he took the keys. He told me he'd been cheating on me with Allison Winston for months."

To this day she wasn't sure what had hurt worse. That punch, delivered with all of Kristopher's strength, or the fact that he'd had sex with another woman.

Understanding flashed in Tate's gaze. "Allison."

Ivy nodded.

Allison embodied her once-broken heart. Allison was the living face of Kristopher's betrayal.

"I was pretty much done fighting after that. I let him drive."

And that was how she'd killed him.

"When we got in the car, he was going so fast. I told him to slow down. Instead he just went faster. Faster and faster. He ran a few red lights. There were horns blaring. Told me he'd slow down if I sucked his cock."

Tate stiffened.

"I didn't," she told him. "He kept reaching for me. Tried to grab my hair and pull my mouth over. I slapped him. And he backhanded me. I can't even remember how the crash happened. I remember crying out. I remember the screech of tires and spinning out of control. He was yelling something. I don't remember what. But those were his last words and I can't remember them. He swerved and slammed us sideways into a tree. He wasn't wearing his seat belt."

And even though the airbags had been deployed, it hadn't stopped his body from being crushed.

"He died on impact."

Ivy cast her gaze out her window, staring at the parking lot and blinking away the tears.

"Ivy, look at me."

She shook her head.

"That's not your fault."

"Yes, it is. I could have fought harder. Walked away. Taken the keys and thrown them into a bush. Anything but let him drive. His mother likes to tell me what I should have done in some of her emails."

"She's the one who emails you?"

"My father paid her a lot of money to keep quiet. He paid a lot of people money so that my name wasn't linked to the crash. The official records were sealed. I'm not sure exactly how he made that happen but he is good friends with a judge. So Carol emails me because it's her only outlet."

"That's not right."

"It's just some emails." She'd take those over Cooper's phone calls any day of the week.

Cooper hadn't wanted to take the money. He'd loved Kristopher and they were so alike. Charming and violent and unpredictable. He'd wanted Ivy to suffer publicly. He'd wanted the crash to haunt her until the end of time. But Carol had insisted.

Since public shame hadn't been an option, Cooper had inflicted his punishment through death threats. After the crash, Cooper had called Ivy every day for three months, telling her exactly how he was going to kill her.

She wasn't sure why the calls had stopped. Still, Cooper's threats would stick with her for years, which was why Ivy paid Sal Testa to track Cooper's whereabouts. She wouldn't put it past Cooper, even all these years later, to take his revenge.

There was more to the story. Ivy had walked a destructive

path in the aftermath of the accident. But she was drained. Story time was over.

"Everything changed after the crash," she said. "Mostly . . . me."

"Baby."

Why was he with her? Why would someone like Tate want her? It didn't make sense. "Will you take me home now?"

He studied her for a long moment, then unlaced their fingers. He let her go. "All right."

She choked down a sob.

This was always going to be the end result. They'd been doomed from the start.

But when he reached the road, he didn't retrace the way they'd come from the manor. He turned the opposite way.

"Where are we going?" she asked.

He steered the Rover toward Back Bay. Toward his neighborhood. "Home."

"But . . . why? After all I just told you, don't you want to get away from me?"

"What did I say last night?"

"That I could push."

He nodded. "What else?"

"I don't know." She searched her memory, trying to remember what else he'd said in the haze of lust.

"I said that we're done when I say we're done. Did I say we were done?"

"No?"

He took her hand again. "No."

Ivy's heart swelled. There was just too much inside and it came out as a cry. Laughter. Tears. Relief. Maybe even love. Maybe right then, she fell in love with Tate Ledger.

Real love.

Or maybe she'd fallen months ago.

On the dance floor at Treason.

forty-five

. . .

CASSIA STARED at the eight fifty-dollar bills she'd spread out on the mattress. Four hundred dollars. The rent she'd planned to pay on January first for her room at the manor.

Except Ivy wouldn't be getting a penny. Cassia would be using this money to fund a few more nights in this hotel room.

A shitty hotel room for her shitty life.

Thud. Thud. Thud. The couple in the room next door deserved an award for stamina.

"Not again." She closed her eyes and groaned.

Her neighbors had been having sex on and off for hours. And with every thud, Cassia wanted nothing more than to leave. Maybe if she'd had somewhere else to go, but tonight's room was paid in full and she wouldn't waste the funds.

She'd hardly slept last night. After leaving the manor yesterday, she'd driven aimlessly, not sure what to think. The scene from the manor had replayed in her mind countless times. Her emotions had swayed in every direction. Anger. Shock. Hurt.

Disappointment.

She was just so disappointed. Mostly in herself.

Cassia had thought Edwin would take her side, not believe his sister's bullshit. Nope.

She'd assumed Ivy had forgotten about making her life hell. Nope.

She'd hoped to finish out her year at Aston while living at the manor. Nope. Nope. Nope.

So fucking disappointing.

Where was she going to go? The money in front of her would keep her in this room through finals week. Part of the reason she'd chosen this hotel was because of the low nightly price advertised on the neon sign outside.

Except even if this was her cheapest option at the moment, after she spent her cash, she'd be even shorter on funds with another semester to go. It would be difficult to pay for a deposit on a new rental. That was if she could even find a room for the next semester.

Thud. Thud.

She clenched her teeth, pressing her hands to her temples.

Between the neighbors and the musty smell in this room, Cassia's headache was becoming unbearable. She'd slept on top of the bedding last night, fully clothed. She didn't trust the sheets. She hadn't eaten much in the past day either. Breakfast, lunch and dinner had come from the hotel's vending machine.

All she wanted was one of Francis's delicious meals, a hot shower and a quilt to sleep under that wouldn't give her lice. Cassia had tried to sleep earlier this afternoon, except the moment she closed her eyes, she'd pictured Josh's face. She'd heard Ivy's lies. She'd seen Edwin's doubts.

Cassia took her phone from her pocket and stared at the black screen. She'd shut it off yesterday as she rushed to her car. She'd left it off as she'd driven around. And when she'd finally settled into this exact spot—legs crossed on the bed with her back pressed against the thin pillows—she'd turned it on.

Edwin had left her message after message. He'd flooded her with texts. He'd sounded worried in the voicemails. Last night, she'd been so tempted to call him that she'd shut off her phone before crying herself to sleep.

Should she call him? What would she even say? Until she figured that out, she was stuck.

Thud. Thud. Thud.

"Stuck with the sexual dynamo next door," she muttered. Her backpack slumped on the foot of the bed, the textbooks spilling out.

She'd spent most of the day studying. Even if her life was in shambles, she refused to ruin her future. A degree was her ticket to freedom. Her ticket to a new life. Her uncle had pulled plenty of strings to get her into Aston and she wouldn't waste this chance.

What if she called Uncle Henry? He'd done everything she'd asked of him. He'd kept her identity a secret. He'd let her come to his university and had kept his distance. And when Josh had contacted him, Henry hadn't told him about Cassia's whereabouts.

Could she stay with her uncle for a few months?

"Last resort. I'll call him if I can't find something else."

Behind her, the thumping stopped. She tensed, waiting for it to restart. But the silence stayed.

"Oh, thank God," she breathed. Then she twisted to talk to the wall. "Please be done screwing. I'm begging you."

Cassia unfolded her legs and stood from the bed, collecting her money and stowing it in her wallet. Then she reached for the remote. Maybe she could find something mindless to watch before falling asleep.

She'd just hit the power button when a knock sounded at her door. She gasped. Either the couple next door was here to invite her to join their naked escapades or a serial killer was about to turn her coral hair into his own personal wig.

The knock came again, more like pounding this time.

"Shit," she hissed, her heart racing as she tiptoed across

the room, holding her breath as she peeked through the peephole.

Not a serial killer. Not her neighbors.

How had he found her?

"Open this door, Cassia."

She gulped, then slid the chain free and flipped the deadbolt, stepping back to let a fuming Edwin storm inside.

"Where is your goddamn phone?" He marched to the bed and picked it up. "When I call, you fucking answer."

Cassia stared unblinking, drinking him in. She'd never seen him like this, not even after Zain's accident.

Oh, he was mad. And he looked like hell. The purple rings beneath his bloodshot eyes looked more like bruises than dark circles. His hair was sticking up at all angles and he was in the same clothes he'd been wearing yesterday—a pair of jeans and a black hoodie. He wasn't even wearing a coat.

He was a mess.

A stunning mess.

Edwin fisted his hands on his narrow hips, staring at her for a long moment, his chest heaving.

Thud. Thud.

Her neighbors were back at it again.

Edwin looked to the ceiling, his nostrils flaring. Then he moved to the bed, pounding his fist against the wall.

The thudding stopped. A woman's muffled laugh came next. Then *thud, thud, thud.*

"For fuck's sake." Edwin flew into action, picking up Cassia's backpack, shoving everything inside before zipping it closed. He moved to her suitcase on the table next, stuffing the few dirty items she'd folded beside it inside. Once it was zipped, he marched to the bathroom, returning moments later with her toiletry case in one hand.

All while she stood frozen, mouth agape.

"What else?" he asked, scanning the room. When she didn't answer, he took a step closer. "Cassia, what else?"

"How did you find me?"

"Really?" He gave her a flat look, then set the toiletry case on the bed and crossed his arms over his chest. "That's your question? Christ. I love you, Red, but if you don't get your stuff together so we can get the fuck out of this hotel, I'm going to lose my shit. Pack. Now."

Wait. Did he just say he loved her?

"Cassia! Let's go!" he bellowed. "I saw a cockroach in the hallway the size of my shoe. We're leaving. Now. Get your coat on."

She flew into action, rushing to slide on her coat and sling her backpack over a shoulder. Then she hurried to the bathroom to make sure he'd gotten everything. When she returned to the main room, he had her suitcase in one hand and her car keys in the other.

Without a word, he ripped the door open and stormed down the hallway.

Cassia surveyed the room one last time. Hopefully she'd never set foot in this building again. Then she jogged to follow Edwin.

She caught up to him in the stairwell winding to the first floor, where he shoved out the exit and walked straight to her Honda. "Where's your car?" she asked.

This wasn't the type of hotel where you left a Bentley parked in the lot for long.

"It's being driven to my place."

"By who?"

"His name is Sal." Edwin took the backpack off her arm and tossed it in the trunk beside her suitcase. Then he slammed the lid closed. "He's Ivy's private investigator."

"Oh." So that was how he'd found her. Sal probably knew a lot about Cassia, didn't he?

"Yeah. Oh." Edwin's mouth pursed in a thin line. "Get in." He rounded the Civic to the driver's side door.

"I could have just followed—"

He shut the door before she could finish talking. Clearly, Edwin wasn't willing to leave her alone. So she went to the passenger seat and slid inside. The air was cold and her breath billowed as he turned the key. But he didn't race to leave the hotel. Instead he blasted the defrost to thaw the windshield.

"Are you all right?" he asked.

She lifted a shoulder. "No."

Could they go back in time to yesterday morning? She'd go with him to the library. Maybe she would have missed Josh entirely if she'd just gone with Edwin.

Edwin sighed, his anger deflating. He reached over, sliding his hand to the back of her neck, fitting it beneath her hair. Then his thumb stroked the column of her throat. "Don't ever do that to me again. Please. You need space, fine. I'll give it to you. But don't you ever hide from me."

Tears flooded her eyes. "Sorry."

"If anything had happened to you . . ." He tugged her closer, pressing his forehead to hers. "Promise, Red. Never run from me."

That was what she'd been doing for months. Running.

Just like her mother.

It was time to stop.

"Okay."

Edwin kissed her forehead, his lips warm despite the frigid winter air outside. They lingered there, soft and still, until he let her go and put the car in reverse.

There were only two thawed circles on the glass, but Edwin drove anyway, ducking low until the glass cleared. By the time they'd made it close to Aston, the chill had left her bones. It returned the moment Edwin turned down a familiar road.

"I'm not going back to the manor," she told him.

"No, you're not."

Out her window, Clarence Manor came into view. Beautiful. Glowing. Evil. "Then where are you taking me?"

"My place." He didn't so much as slow as he passed the iron gate.

Then four short blocks later, he turned into a narrow

driveway, also blocked by a gate. He rolled down the Honda's window, punching in the code, and as the gate opened, he steered them past a row of hedges to a courtyard shrouded with evergreens.

Ahead of them were two garage stalls. He parked the Honda in front of the left door.

When he'd told her he'd bought a place nearby, she'd expected a condo or a townhouse. But this was . . . huge. Of course, Edwin Clarence wouldn't live in a dive like any normal student.

The three-story home stretched tall above the garages. The exterior lights illuminated the courtyard and a red-painted door. The brick façade was covered with leafless vines that crept all the way from the foundation to the roof.

"Stay here." Edwin got out of the car and walked to the garage, opening a keypad she hadn't noticed. He punched in a code, the garage door lifting, and then moments later, he eased the Honda inside and parked it beside the Bentley.

Without a word, he popped the trunk and began hauling her things across the spotless garage to the door that opened into the house.

"Are you coming?" he called.

Cassia sprang into action, hurrying to follow him inside.

The house stretched long, like it was the length of the entire block. It probably was. Edwin passed a sitting area, dropping her backpack on a round table, before taking the stairs against the far wall.

From the exterior, Cassia had expected a more traditional style inside, similar to the manor, with crown molding and intricately carved accents in the trim and doors. Outside, this house shared that historical look with the other properties in this area. But inside, it was all clean lines and modern touches.

Cables and steel posts formed the staircase's railing. The hardwood floors were gray-washed. The walls were painted a stark white.

Edwin climbed past the second floor, rounding a landing and continuing straight to the third level. And when he flipped on the light, her jaw dropped.

This was his bedroom suite. The floor was open, stretching the entire length of the building. On the opposite end were floor-to-ceiling windows, and beams ran from one side to the other.

His massive bed rested in the center of the room. The gray covers were neatly made with a pile of pillows resting against the headboard. Two doors bracketed the bed, likely leading to a closet and en suite. Bookshelves framed a wide entertainment center.

It was larger than any bedroom she'd ever seen, including any at the manor. But it wasn't the bed or the shelves or the artwork hung along the walls that captured Cassia's attention.

It was the pile of suitcases in the center of the room.

Her suitcases.

"Those are my things."

"Yep." Edwin dropped her suitcase to the floor. "I didn't have time to make room in the closet. I was too busy driving all over, trying to find you."

She blinked. "Those are my things."

"Yes, and after we talk, you can unpack them." He dragged a hand through his hair. "If I missed something, I'll go get it tomorrow."

"You moved me out of the manor."

"Did you want to live there?"

"No."

"Didn't think so." Edwin's irritation was still seeping through his tone. Or maybe he was just sleep deprived.

"You believed Ivy." She wrapped her arms around her waist. As much as she wanted to take a shower and climb into that bed beside him, they had to talk. About yesterday. About Ivy. About Josh.

About everything.

"Is that why you didn't answer my calls? Because you thought I picked Ivy's side over yours?"

"Yes." She lifted her chin, hoping to appear confident, when really, her doubts were eating her alive. What if Ivy had been telling the truth?

"I believe my sister." Edwin went to the bed, slumping on its edge. "I'm not going to apologize for trusting her. Though I am sorry if you feel like I don't have your back. Because I do. I always will."

"You really believe her?"

He nodded. "I know she did some things that she shouldn't have. I'm not defending her. But I know Ivy. If she'd done it, she'd have owned it. That's her style. She likes to take credit. She owned up to having you investigated."

Cassia tensed. "She had no right."

"Agreed." He nodded. "Though she promised me she didn't read the investigator's report."

"Josh said one of my roommates called him. I highly doubt it was Elora. So how else would he have known where to find me? If it wasn't your sister, then who?"

"Michael."

"What? Michael?" Cassia shook her head. "That makes no sense. Why would Michael do something to hurt me? He's my friend."

"No, he is not. He probably did it to fuck with you. Maybe to drive a wedge between us. Maybe to piss off Ivy. Who the hell knows? But it wasn't Ivy and she's pretty sure it was Michael."

"Or she's saying that to deflect her guilt."

"I can't . . ." Edwin pinched the bridge of his nose. "Do you trust me?"

Cassia could have lied and told him no, if only to prove to herself that she'd managed to keep up the walls she'd worked so hard to build. But lying was pointless. Despite her efforts to guard her heart, Edwin held it in her hands.

"Yes," she whispered.

"Then please believe me. I don't know exactly why he did it, but Michael is just like my ex. He manipulates and lies."

"So does your sister."

He nodded. "Yeah, she does. But I would never hurt you. And I would not let my sister hurt you either."

"What if you're wrong? What if Ivy did this?"

Edwin locked his gaze with hers. "Then she's dead to me."

Maybe she still didn't believe Ivy was innocent. But she did believe the absolute sincerity in Edwin's voice.

"I'm sorry I ran," she said. "That fight with Ivy. Seeing Josh. I didn't know what else to do."

"Next time, ask me." Edwin stood and crossed the room, walking straight into her space. Then he wrapped his arms around her, holding her tight. "Just talk to me."

"Okay." She wrapped her arms around his waist, sinking into his embrace.

They clung to each other for minutes until any lingering frustration had melted away.

"I stink like that hotel room," she murmured.

Edwin took her hand and led her into the bathroom, turning on the shower and giving her some time alone. Steam billowed from the bathroom when she returned to the bedroom, wrapped in a thick white towel.

She found Edwin in the closet, making space for her clothes.

Cassia wouldn't claim the empty hangers and drawers. Not yet. First, they had to talk.

So she pulled on a clean pair of panties and one of Edwin's T-shirts while he took his own shower. Then they settled into his bed, warm beneath the covers. Cassia hugged her pillow close as she lay sideways to face him.

Tired as she was, there would be no sleep. Not until she told him the truth.

"I haven't seen Josh since I left Hughes."

"Hughes. That's where you went to school before?" he asked.

"Yes. That's where I grew up. My father was a professor there."

"And Josh?"

"Josh is my ex." She swallowed hard. "And my father's lover."

forty-six

. . .

CASSIA STUDIED Edwin's expression as her words sank in. Disbelief. Shock. Confusion.

Josh is my ex. And my father's lover.

"What?" Edwin lifted off his pillow.

"I suppose the place to start is the beginning," she said. "Josh and I dated for about two years. We met at a fraternity party. His fraternity. It was . . . normal. I don't know how else to describe it. We had what I thought was a normal relationship. We hung out all the time. Normal boyfriend-girlfriend stuff. He introduced me to his parents. And I took him home to meet Dad. Everything was good. Then it wasn't."

Cassia had spent countless hours examining her relationship with Josh. Searching her memory for clues that she'd missed. Signs that she'd ignored. She still wasn't sure when they'd started lying to her. Maybe from the start.

"I could feel our breakup coming. The last couple of months were awful. Josh and I fought a lot. He pulled away. I tried to talk to him about it but he called me clingy. He blamed his moods on school. He told me he needed some space to focus. I understood."

It had been the spring semester of their junior year and Josh hadn't been the only one busy with classes.

"I knew something was wrong but I pretended everything was fine. That once the semester was over, Josh and I could have some downtime over the summer and get back to the place where we were happy again."

Or maybe they'd never really been happy. When Cassia compared her years with Josh to the short time she'd been with Edwin, it was no contest. She was lighter with Edwin. They fit more naturally. Their chemistry was undeniable, and she craved more.

With Josh, she hadn't even known what she'd been missing.

Until it was too late.

"Hughes was like a second home," she said. "When I was a little girl, I'd go to campus with my dad. I'd help him carry books. I'd color on the dry-erase board while he was working at his desk. We'd go to special lunch dates at the student union."

Cassia had memorized the paths around campus before she was ten.

"Our house was about a half a mile from campus," she told Edwin. "I moved out for my freshman year. Dad thought I should live in the dorms to have that experience and make friends. But it was expensive, and I didn't have great friends, so I moved back home my sophomore year to save money."

Dad hadn't let her pay rent, but Cassia had always done her best to contribute. She'd cleaned and done laundry, much like she had as a teenager. Hughes wasn't nearly as expensive as Aston but it still cost money and she hadn't wanted to walk away with her degree, buried in debt.

"I didn't mind living at home. Dad and I were close. And he was always cool about my life experiences. He knew Josh and I were dating and that some nights I stayed at the fraternity in Josh's room. As long as I texted, Dad never cared. Maybe that was because he'd spent so much time around college students. Mostly, I think he just liked having me there. And by living at home, I could . . . be close to watch him."

"Watch him?" Edwin asked. "What do you mean?"

She took a moment to breathe, to summon added courage. Sharing Dad's story was always going to be hard. Not only because of how it had ended, but because of the way it made him seem.

Wrong or right, Cassia had spent her entire life loyal to her father.

"Dad was brilliant. I'm not just saying that because he was my dad. He was widely admired. He'd been trying to write a book for what felt like my whole life. There were mornings when I'd find him asleep at his desk. I remember waking up in the middle of the night when I was in high school and finding him at his typewriter."

Dad had wanted to type his book the old-fashioned way. He'd always told her that there was a deeper connection to the words when you felt the press of a key and heard the clunk of a typebar. He'd told her that there was something magical about watching the letters get stamped onto a piece of white paper.

"He finished his book when I was a freshman at Hughes. And I wish . . ." Cassia's throat closed. It was so hard to pinpoint where everything had gone wrong. But the start of it had been that fucking book.

Edwin's hand came to her cheek, his thumb stroking her skin, as her eyes flooded. "You don't have to talk about this."

"Yes, I do." She sniffled. "I don't want you to find out from Ivy or Michael or anyone else. I want to tell you."

"How about tomorrow? You're exhausted. Let's just—"

"I'm okay." She had to do this. Now that it was coming loose, she wouldn't be able to stop it. And she wouldn't be able to sleep. So she sucked in a shaky breath and shifted, sitting up and against the pillows.

Edwin mirrored her position, scooting closer so their

shoulders touched. Then he took her hand, threading their fingers together.

"Dad never talked about Mom after she'd leave. Never. He'd tell me she was gone and then we'd immediately go back to the routine we'd had before she'd ever come home. But just because he didn't talk about her didn't mean she wasn't there. Even when she was gone, she was there. It was like this cloud always hanging over our heads."

It would take them months to get used to her living in the house with them again. Awkward was too gentle of a word. That tension didn't vanish, even after she left.

"I honestly don't know why Dad let her come home," she said. "I wish he had just told her to stay away. But he let her come back, time and time again. Maybe he was doing it for me. I don't know. We never talked about it."

As much as her father had loved to examine history, their own life, their own pasts, had been off-limits.

"It was a roller coaster. Ups and downs. Even after the last time she left, when we should have leveled out, the ride just kept on going. And for a long, long time, I thought it was Mom. But now, after this past year, I can see it was him too. Dad had mood swings. And to give him credit, when I was younger, he did a great job at hiding them. At hiding the depression."

Edwin's hand tightened on hers. "Shit, Cassia."

Maybe he'd guessed where she was leading them, but she still had to say it aloud. She had to speak the words, for them both.

"He queried his book to some agents. It was fiction and most of his colleagues were publishing nonfiction. But he had this story and he loved it. So he sent it into the world. And the world was harsh."

For years, he received rejection after rejection. He'd poured his heart into that book and no one had been kind in their rebuffs.

"It crushed his spirit. He went spiraling. And I should

have done more," Cassia said. "I should have gotten him some help earlier on. Told him to forget the book. I don't know. By the summer before my junior year, he was drinking a lot. He had to take pills to sleep. I was worried, so I confronted him about it. And he cried. He cried so hard it broke my heart. I'd never seen him cry before. Not once, after all the times my mother hurt us, can I remember him crying."

Each time her mother had left, the tears had always been Cassia's. Dad had been there to catch them for her.

"He promised to get help. He started seeing a therapist. And he was happier. But it wasn't because of counseling. It was Josh."

And that was the crux of Cassia's conflict.

Because while she hadn't been able to help her dad, Josh had.

"I had no idea. None." She closed her eyes and the image of them together popped into her mind. "I was supposed to be in class, but the professor got sick, and instead of sticking around campus, I walked home. I walked in on them . . . together."

"Together," Edwin repeated.

"Together." She closed her eyes but it didn't stop the tears from leaking out of the edges. "Why didn't they just tell me? Why didn't Dad talk to me? Why wouldn't he share that part of himself? I never would have cared. I just wanted him to be happy."

Even if that meant losing Josh.

"It was a shock. To be hit with not just my dad in that situation but also Josh. I, um, didn't react well."

Edwin nodded. "Understandable."

"I yelled. I said some things I didn't mean about never wanting to see either of them again. And then I left. I did what I did yesterday, I drove around for hours. I rented a motel room and cried myself to sleep. It hurt. That they'd lie to me. That they'd hide from me. Especially Dad. Why hadn't he just told me? Why go that far? When they could have told me first. Why?"

And she'd never get the chance to ask.

Tears streaked down her face and she couldn't catch them fast enough.

"I came home the next morning. I had to get my stuff for class. The house was quiet and I thought maybe Dad had gone to campus. But his briefcase was on the dining room table and he never went anywhere without that briefcase."

She'd bought it for him as a congratulations the day he'd finished his book.

"I found him in his room." Her throat felt like sandpaper but there was no stopping. "With a bottle of vodka and a bottle of sleeping pills. They said it was an accidental overdose."

"Cassia." Edwin let her hand go to wrap her in his arms, pulling her against his chest. "Fuck, I'm sorry. I'm so sorry."

"Me too."

Would the images from that day ever fade? The wrong color of her dad's cheeks, ashen and translucent. His chest unmoving, even when she'd pressed her ear against his heart, knowing she'd be met with silence. His eyes, hazel like hers, closed forever.

"Why?" A sob worked loose. "Why would he leave me?"

"Red." Edwin held her closer as another sob came from her mouth. And then any hope of keeping her emotions in check fizzled.

"I can't even remember what I said to them," she choked out, her words muffled against his chest. "When I caught Dad and Josh. I know I was angry. I was hurt. And I just keep trying to remember but it's like that moment is gone from my memory. And I don't know if I said something to make Dad—"

"Stop." Edwin shook her. "You can't take responsibility for this. It's not your fault."

Maybe it wasn't. But that didn't make the reality any easier. "I miss my dad."

She missed his laugh. She missed his cheesy jokes. She missed how excited he'd get about history. She missed the way he'd hug her and how his eyes would light up when she walked into a room.

And this longing to see him again, to apologize and tell him that no matter what, she loved him, would never go away.

Only tonight, she didn't have to carry the burden alone. So she leaned into Edwin, letting him comfort her, as she cried. Cassia wasn't sure how long her breakdown lasted, but when she pulled away, Edwin's shirt was soaked. "Sorry."

"Don't apologize." He ran his hand through her hair, still damp from her shower. "All this happened just this past spring?"

"Yeah." She nodded, wiping her face dry. "When Dad died, I inherited everything. Our house was in a great location and he'd paid it off. I sold it and everything else. I left Hughes because it was just too hard. Too many people knew about what had happened. I was sick of getting looks. Hearing whispers behind my back. Around every corner, there was a memory. Plus Josh."

"You haven't spoken to him."

"He came over about a month after I buried Dad. He wanted to explain. He told me they were in love. That neither was sure how to tell me. That it would be best to keep it between us. It felt . . . shallow. Like he was more concerned about me not telling anyone than the fact that I'd lost my father. So I told him never to speak to me again. And the next day, I called my uncle about transferring to Aston."

"Your uncle? Who's your uncle?" Edwin asked.

"Henry Neilson."

His eyes widened. "*Dean* Neilson?"

"Yep. My dad's brother. They weren't close."

Cassia could only remember seeing her uncle a handful of times as a kid. But he was Dad's only family, and to Uncle

Henry's credit, he'd stepped up at the funeral, helping her make arrangements. He'd also helped her navigate the process for selling the house and settling Dad's estate.

"That's why you came to Aston," Edwin said. "Your uncle."

"He was able to get me transferred in. I used my inheritance to pay tuition and fees. When I found Ivy's classified ad for a room, I jumped. I can't afford much more. Everything I have went into school."

Her future.

"Neilson." It was strange to hear her last name—or former last name—in Edwin's voice. "Do you ever talk to him?"

"No. I changed my name before I got here because I just . . . I didn't want to be Cassie Neilson anymore."

"Until Ivy and Michael," Edwin muttered.

"I hate that they know." Or that Michael knew. Maybe Ivy had told Edwin the truth and she hadn't read her investigator's report. Regardless, it was only a matter of time before her secrets were out in the open.

"People are going to find out, aren't they?" she grumbled.

"Who fucking cares what people say?"

She gave him a sad smile. "Me."

His face softened. "You have a beautiful heart, Cassia. We'll get through it."

"Do you regret coming up to me that day at the water fountain?"

"Never." He dropped a kiss to her forehead. "And I get why you didn't tell me. It's heavy."

It was heavy. Though as she leaned into him, listening to his breath, some of the weight lifted.

Cassia was exhausted but her insides felt like they were on the outside, her entire being turned wrong and raw. "This feels strange."

"Confessions usually do," Edwin said. "What other secrets do you have?"

A smile tugged at the corner of her mouth. "None for tonight. Guess you'll have to stick around and see what comes up next."

"Oh, I intend to." He chuckled, kissing her hair.

She smiled, then realized in their rush to get here and through her story, she'd missed something from earlier. She pushed away from his chest, meeting his blue gaze. "You said you loved me. At the hotel room."

"I did."

"Did you mean it?" *Please, don't take it back. Please, don't blame it on the heat of the moment.*

"Have I ever said anything to you that I didn't mean?"

"No?" It came out as a question.

"No." He kissed her, his lips lingering against her own before his tongue swept inside, and for a few moments, she forgot. About the hotel room. About the fight. About the past.

"Better?" he asked as he pulled away.

She nodded. Then she opened her mouth because he'd told her he loved her and she hadn't said it back. She wanted to say it back.

Except, before she could speak, he pressed his fingers to her lips. "Tell me tomorrow."

Right there in that moment, Cassia knew there'd be no other man in her life but Edwin Clarence. Because he knew what she needed when she hadn't even been sure of it herself.

Tomorrow. She would start fresh tomorrow. Start over.

With Edwin.

"You really got all my things from the manor?" she asked.

"Yep. But we'll deal with keys and moving you in tomorrow." He shifted, dragging her beneath the covers and curling her back against his chest. "After we sleep for twelve hours."

She groaned. "I probably have to talk to Ivy, don't I?"

"At some point."

"I don't know how to feel about her."

Edwin chuckled and buried his nose in her hair. "She's not even the worst. Wait until you meet my father."

"Well, that's comforting."

He laughed again. "Welcome to the Clarence family."

Maybe that should have scared her away. But if dealing with his family meant keeping Edwin, she'd handle whatever the Clarences threw her way.

"Want me to start calling you Cassie?" he asked.

"No."

"Good. Because I like Cassia better than Cassie."

She smiled. "Me too."

"Or maybe I'll just stick to Red. My Red."

forty-seven

. . .

IVY'S PHONE buzzed on Tate's nightstand. She stretched across his bare chest, unlocking the screen to read Edwin's text.

Got her last night. Thanks for calling Sal

She sighed and dashed out a reply. *Is she okay? Can we meet up later? Please?*

Ivy expected a firm no. But the three dots on the screen blinked at her for a few long moments until Edwin's response came through.

She's good. Wants to see Francis. We'll come to the manor for lunch

The breath rushed from Ivy's lungs. Phew. Maybe she had a chance to make this right with Edwin. And Cassia.

See you then

It was only seven in the morning. That gave her a few more hours with Tate before she'd head home and face reality.

"All good?" Tate asked.

She put her phone aside and burrowed into his chest. "Yeah. Edwin found Cassia. I need to be back at the manor before lunch."

" 'Kay." He kissed her hair. "We'll go over in a bit."

"I can call my driver."

"That would be a waste of his time since I'm taking you."

The corner of her mouth turned up. "Do you always get your way?"

"Baby."

Meaning yes.

She propped her hands on his chest and met his gaze, swimming in those chocolate pools. Since Tate had brought her to his place on Wednesday, they'd barely left his bed. The few times they'd donned clothes had been for short trips to the kitchen. Refueling before he'd ravage her body once more.

If Ivy could have a wish come true, it would be to stay here, hidden away for another week. Another year. But this escape from reality was coming to an end. After she met with Edwin and apologized to Cassia, she had to get back to work.

"I need to study," she said. "My finals start Monday."

"We'll get your stuff. Bring it here for the weekend."

"What if I need to spend the weekend at the manor? Alone?"

Tate chuckled.

"Was that a no?" she teased.

"That was a fuck no." He fused their mouths together, rolling her until she was pinned beneath his strong body.

His tongue tangled with hers in a slow, languid slide. Damn, but he had a wicked tongue. When he reached between them, his hand dipped to her sex, toying through her wet folds. Talented tongue. Talented fingers. Talented cock.

His arousal hardened between them with every stroke of his tongue. Every slide of his fingers. She gasped when he flicked her clit.

They came together effortlessly, like lovers who'd spent years, not hours, perfecting sex. Ivy had lost count of the orgasms he'd given her in the past day. But with each and every one, she fell a little deeper. She craved him a little more. Hoped that the promise of *them* would come true.

She wished for Tate.

He rocked them together, stroke after stroke. The coil in her belly curled tighter. The hitch in her breath came as he slammed inside. A flush crept along her skin, her every nerve ending awake and alight, before stars broke across her vision.

She wished on those stars.

And then she shattered. "Tate."

"Fuck, Ivy." He groaned and gave into his own release as she pulsed around him, milking him dry.

They collapsed in a heap, sticky and boneless. Their legs were tangled together. The sheets had been kicked free of the bed. Her pillow was gone, so she used Tate's shoulder when he stretched out on his stomach.

These naked moments, when there was nothing but mingled heartbeats and tender touches, had become Ivy's salvation. She was losing herself in Tate.

Once, after Kristopher, the idea of losing her identity would have sent her into a panic. Except Ivy didn't care much for who she was at the moment. Becoming someone new, someone worthy of a man like Tate, seemed like a brilliant idea.

And the sex was, well . . . life-changing.

"Has it ever been like this for you before?" she asked.

"No."

And they were only getting started.

She needed to get in the shower, but she closed her eyes to take a short nap first. But before she could drift off, Tate's phone rang.

He shifted to check the screen and frowned as he brought it to his ear.

She couldn't make out the words on the other end of the line, just the murmur of a deep voice.

"Damn," Tate grumbled. "Then we'll have to shut down. I'd rather take a hit for the closure than risk a weekend when we don't have the right staff."

He listened for another moment, then said, "Sounds good. See you in a bit."

Ivy waited until he'd ended the call and returned the phone to the nightstand. "Everything okay?"

"That was my manager at the club." He sighed into the pillow. "Two other bouncers refused to take drug tests. I'm going to have to head over there later. Meet with the remaining staff. Tell them we're closing for a while."

"Sorry." She dropped a kiss to his spine. "How long will you close?"

"I don't know yet. Hopefully not long."

Not only had they spent yesterday having sex, Tate and Ivy had talked for hours.

She'd told him about school and the fight she'd had with her father. She'd told him about her decision to walk away from his expectations, even if they cost her the manor. And she'd told him about Michael and how she feared he'd discover the truth about the crash.

Her problems seemed trivial compared to Tate's. He was in the throes of restructuring Club 27. From the day he'd taken it over from the previous owner, he'd had nothing but problems. As promised, he'd cleaned house to ensure that anyone who'd been selling drugs for the previous owner was gone. A few of the original staff members had stayed, including Ivy's favorite bartender, the one who knew how to make her a Ramos gin fizz. But for the most part, his staff was as new to Club 27 as Tate.

Applicants had to pass a background check. Everyone was required to undergo random drug tests. No one was allowed to drink while on shift. Zain had the same expectations at Treason. Yet hiring was proving to be difficult. Finding bartenders hadn't been too bad. There were only two open positions on Tate's waitstaff. But bouncers were hard to find at the moment.

A guy they'd hired two weeks ago had gotten handsy with a female customer, so he'd been let go. Another had decided not to show up for his shift last Saturday night. And now two of them had refused their drug tests.

Tate, Ivy was learning, did everything with precision. He wouldn't leave the club open if there wasn't enough security to ensure his patrons and employees were safe.

She had no doubt that Club 27 would soon have the reputation of Treason. The guest list would be just as impressive. But he had some hurdles to leap first.

"My dad thinks I should close down through Christmas," he said. "Reopen on New Year's Eve with an elite party. Make a splash."

"That's a good idea. It would give you a couple weeks to hire staff and get them trained."

"Exactly." He blew out a long breath. "I hate closing. I really do. It feels like losing. But . . . it's the right move."

"Sorry." There were a few faint freckles on his shoulder. She traced them, connecting the dots into different patterns. She'd learn everything there was to know about his body before they were done. And if by that point he still wanted her, she'd start all over again. "You're close with your dad, aren't you?"

"I'm close to both of my parents."

"What's that like?" There was no jealousy or animosity in her question, just genuine curiosity. Most people she knew were trying so hard not to become their parents.

"I can't lie. It's pretty great." He laughed. "They respect me. I value their opinion. They value mine. And they challenge me."

"How so?"

"They push me to be a better person. To make sure I put people before money. I make sure my staff are well paid and feel safe in their environment. I give to charity not so it will secure me invites to fundraising galas or mentions in the media, but because I'm fortunate and my parents taught me to help those less fortunate."

She fell a little deeper. She craved him a little more. How the hell had Ivy landed in this man's bed? He was too good for her, but she was going to keep him anyway.

Who made Ivy better? It certainly wasn't her parents. It wasn't her brothers or her friends. In the absence of someone to challenge her, maybe she'd have to push herself.

"I'd better get ready." She pressed a kiss to those freckles, then climbed out of his bed, retreating to the bathroom for a shower.

Tate, as insatiable for her body as she was for his, didn't leave her alone for long. He joined her under the spray, and by the time they emerged, she was late to meet Edwin and Cassia.

Ivy dressed in clothes from earlier in the week while Tate hurried to pull on a pair of jeans and a long-sleeved T-shirt from his closet. Then they left the haven of his bedroom and hustled to the main floor.

He'd just picked up his keys from the kitchen counter when the doorbell rang. "Let me just see who it is. I'll be fast."

While he strode for the front door, she wandered to the living room, surveying the space. The house had clearly been updated recently but whoever had done the remodel, maybe Tate, had kept some of the original touches.

The fireplace had a hand-carved scroll detail that antique lovers would drool over. The largest window in the room was decorated with a stained glass inset. The thin-planked floors held a few dings and dents that meant they'd probably been walked on for decades.

This house had history.

It was like the manor in that regard. The similarities gave her hope that even after she lost Clarence Manor, she'd find a home she loved. A home that her father could never wrench from her grasp.

As Ivy touched the smooth leather of Tate's couch, a woman's voice carried down the hallway from the front door. Something about the pitch caught Ivy's ear and raised the hairs on the back of her neck.

It was familiar. Not a good familiar. So she weaved past the furniture, padding toward the entryway.

"You need to leave." Tate's voice was a growl.

"Tate, please."

Ivy's stomach sank and her footsteps picked up speed. She walked straight to Tate's side, pushing past him. Allison Winston was on his doorstep.

Allison's face was splotchy. Her eyes were red rimmed and tears coated her cheeks. She didn't even glance at Ivy. She was entirely focused on Tate as she extended a white stick.

A pregnancy test.

With a tiny plus in the window.

forty-eight

. . .

ELORA STOOD OUTSIDE HER PARENTS' house, staring at the front door. "Tell me this will be okay."

"It will be okay." Zain dropped a kiss to her hair.

"Thank you for coming with me." If—when—this conversation went sideways, she had Zain.

"You've said thanks ten times since we left the loft." He nudged her elbow with his. "Time to open the door, babe."

"One more minute," she whispered.

One more minute for her father to be a father.

Zain didn't argue. He stood beside her as their breaths billowed around them in the cold December air. He gave her his unwavering support, without question, just like he had over the past two days.

Just like he had since the beginning.

He'd known about Lucas for years. He'd known the first night she'd walked into his club.

Elora had been so worried that their parents' drama, that sharing a half-sibling, would cause Zain to walk away. She should have known better.

Zain Clarence wasn't the kind of man who walked away from what he wanted.

And he wanted Elora.

Nothing else mattered.

They'd spent the past two days talking, mostly about how Elora would tell her dad the truth, but also about how Zain had learned of David and Joanna's affair.

When Zain had been in high school, Helena Clarence had moved out of their home. She'd taken Edwin and Ivy with her to live at the manor, but because Zain had been older, he'd opted to stay with David. Not because he had much loyalty to his father, but because he'd been happy in his house and his routine. He'd been old enough to do his own thing while the twins had needed more supervision.

Zain had never expected his mother to move home again, so one night, he'd walked into his father's office to ask if they were getting divorced. David had been drunk.

Zain assumed it was the scotch that had led to David's slurred confession that he'd gotten another woman pregnant.

Was it David and Joanna's affair that had pushed Helena to sleep with Elora's dad? Revenge against her former friend? Whatever the reason, the entire situation made Elora's stomach churn.

When David had admitted to his affair that night, it had been a turning point for Zain. The last threads tying him to his dad had broken. He'd vowed never to become David's mirror, but to forge his own path.

Helena had eventually returned to David. Even Zain wasn't sure why. His mother could have walked away with plenty of money in a divorce. But she'd returned with Ivy and Edwin in tow, and not once had anyone mentioned a baby. And during his drunken stupor, David hadn't told Zain that the woman was Joanna.

Zain had assumed for a long time that there had been no baby. That his father's lover had gotten an abortion and that had appeased Helena enough to come home.

Except as time had gone on, Zain's curiosity had gotten the best of him and he'd done his own investigation.

It hadn't taken much effort. Zain had tracked down David's assistant at the time of the affair. David had fired her, claiming she was underperforming in her duties. The assistant had a different theory, that Helena had insisted his next assistant be male. She hadn't been sad to see the job go, especially because she'd been paid well to stay silent about everything she'd witnessed. But Zain was a convincing man, and he'd promised never to reveal her breach. He'd just wanted to know the truth about his father.

There had always been other women in David's life. His marriage vows were guidelines at best. And his assistant remembered clearly that David had been particularly infatuated with a dark-haired woman who would come to the office every Thursday afternoon.

The assistant had given Zain Joanna's name. Because one day she'd arrived at the office not on her typical Thursday, but on a Monday morning. Tears had streaked her face and she'd demanded to see David immediately.

Zain had put it together easily enough. He'd found Lucas. But he hadn't had the heart to break up the Maldonado family.

So he'd kept the truth to himself.

And when Elora had walked into Treason years ago, he'd taken one look at her and known he was fucked. Because even though their parents had created a goddamn mess, he'd wanted Elora anyway.

"I love you," he said, breaking the silence, like he knew she needed to hear it.

"I love you too." She met his striking blue gaze. "Should we walk away?"

"Your call."

She knew he'd keep the secret if she asked. That if it saved Elora this pain, he'd take it to the grave.

"No." She sighed. This wasn't something she could carry for her entire life. She wouldn't ask Zain to bear it either. And Lucas deserved to know the truth.

So she turned the door's handle and stepped inside with Zain following close behind.

The new butler—she really needed to learn his name—rushed to greet them, probably annoyed she hadn't knocked. "Miss Maldonado."

"Can you please tell my father I'm here?"

"He is in his study and expecting you."

"Okay." She blew out a long breath.

Yesterday, Elora had called Dad to ask if he could meet today. Normally he'd be working at the office on a Friday morning, but she didn't want to do this while he was at work or while Lucas was home. So she'd asked if he could be here instead.

Dad rarely denied her.

She shrugged off her coat, handing it to the butler, and turned to help Zain out of his. She'd just given it over when footsteps sounded from the hallway.

"Hey."

Elora's head whipped around. Lucas, dressed in baggy maroon sweats, was coming their way. "W-what are you doing here? Why aren't you at school?"

"I got sick last night, something I ate I guess, but I was puking my guts out. So Dad said I had to stay home."

No. No, he couldn't be here. This wasn't the plan. First, she'd tell Dad. Then together, they'd decide how to tell Lucas. Now what? Should she wait? Oh, God. The idea of doing this morning all over again, pumping herself up to do this . . .

Lucas gave her a strange look but his attention quickly darted over her shoulder to Zain. "Uh, hi. Who are you?"

Elora was too busy freaking out to introduce them.

Zain used his crutch and shuffled closer, extending his unbroken arm. "Zain Clarence."

Lucas shook his hand, glancing between them. "Are you guys like together or whatever?"

"Yeah," Zain said. "We're together."

"Oh." Lucas turned to Elora. "Is that why you're here? To introduce us?"

"I, uh, actually came to talk to Dad."

"He's in his office." Lucas took a step in that direction, like he was going to go with them.

"Alone, Lucas. I need to talk to him alone."

"Why don't we hang out while they're talking?" Zain asked Lucas. "Get to know each other."

"Yeah. Okay." Lucas shrugged. "Cool. Feel like watching TV or something?"

"TV would be great." Zain gave Elora a small smile, then followed Lucas down the hallway.

"What happened?" Lucas asked, waving to Zain's broken leg.

"Motorcycle accident."

"Whoa." Lucas hissed. "Sorry."

"I got lucky. Your sister kept telling me to wear my helmet. It saved my life."

Lucas smiled back at her, then they were gone.

Brothers.

She'd lost half of Lucas. But that half would go to Zain and Ivy and Edwin. Watching Lucas and Zain together, it didn't hurt like she'd thought it would.

A wave of nerves rocked Elora on her heels, but this was her chance. There was no more delaying. So she unglued her feet and found her father in his office, sitting at his desk and sipping a cup of coffee as he read something on his monitor.

His eyes flicked to the door as she walked into the room and he smiled. "Hi, button."

"Hi, Dad." She closed the door behind her.

"Uh-oh. It's one of those conversations, huh?"

She nodded and went to give him a hug.

"When you called, I had a feeling this wasn't going to be good. Everything okay? Are you okay?"

"Not really," she admitted. "Can we sit on the couch?"

"Of course." He sprang out of his chair and escorted her

to the leather couch, settling against one arm while she sat next to the other.

She'd rehearsed how to tell him, what exactly to say. But in her heart, she must have known that there was no way she'd be able to speak the words, so she reached into the pocket of the jacket she'd worn today and pulled out the papers folded inside.

Two letters.

Elora handed them to her father.

"What's this?" he asked, unfolding the pages.

She didn't answer. The moment he tensed, she braced for whatever came next. Tears. Shouting. Denial. Maybe he'd accuse her of lying. Or maybe he'd march out the door and strangle her mother.

Instead, he set the letters on the coffee table and dropped his elbows to his knees.

Elora was ready to console him. To hug him through his heartbreak. But for the second time in two days, she realized that she was ten steps behind.

"You already know," she said.

"I do."

"How? When? Why didn't you tell me you weren't my father?"

Dad leveled her with a glare. "I am your father, Elora Maldonado. From the moment you took your first breath until the moment I take my last. Understood?"

She swallowed the lump in her throat. Yes, he was her father. That should have filled her heart. That was the answer she'd wanted, right? To walk out of this room and know that he still wanted to claim her? But that didn't make the pit in her stomach go away. Because now it wasn't just her mother's lies. It was his too.

"How long have you known?"

"You are my daughter, Elora. Lucas is my son."

"But—"

"No. That is the end of it."

The end of it? No, this was only the beginning. "I deserve to know the truth. So does Lucas."

Dad blew out a long breath, shaking his head. "I never wanted you to find out."

"You wouldn't have told me?"

"No." He shook his head. "Your mother and I agreed it was better left in the past. I'm your father. Nothing will change that. Not even your DNA."

"Then, as my dad, I'm asking you to tell me everything. Please don't make me go search for the story." There was a warning in her unspoken words. Either he told her or she'd find out another way. "Please, Dad."

"Why? So you can go find your bio—" He shot off the couch. "I can't even say it."

"This isn't about me finding . . . him." She couldn't say it either. "I don't want another father. You are my dad. But I have a right to know."

His shoulders slumped.

"Dad, please be honest with me."

He looked at her with so much regret etched on his face that it cracked her heart. Then he returned to the couch, sinking into his seat. "I can't have children. I'm sterile."

"Sterile." That wasn't at all what she'd expected him to say.

"Your mother wanted kids. She wanted to be pregnant and feel you grow inside her. We talked about options. A donor. We went to a doctor. Got a list of potentials. The whole thing, choosing some other man's sperm, was too much. I told your mom we'd adopt. She didn't want to adopt. So one night, she went out with some girlfriends. I knew what she was planning. She timed it right. Two weeks later, she told me she was pregnant. With you."

"I—" Elora was stunned speechless, trying to let that all sink in. So Mom had hooked up with Henry Neilson at a bar? Elora was the product of a one-night stand? And Dad had known about it? "You didn't try to stop her?"

"No."

"You didn't care?"

"That my wife had sex with another man? Of course I cared. But she wasn't the only one who wanted a baby."

"What if it hadn't worked?"

"I don't know," he muttered.

Elora's mind was spinning. "And Lucas? Was that the same?"

"No." There was a razor-sharp edge to Dad's voice. "Your mother and David had an affair."

"Not unlike your affair with Helena."

His molars ground together.

She didn't really care about the affairs. That wasn't what this was about. Elora was here to ensure Lucas came out of this intact. "Does everyone know? David and Helena?"

"Yes. We all came to an . . . agreement."

"What kind of agreement?"

"Lucas is my son."

"And that's the end of it, right?" She threw his earlier words at him.

"Yes, it is."

David wouldn't be coming to claim Lucas. He'd had thirteen years to make that move and hadn't. That was a consolation at least, wasn't it? Dad was ten times the father that David was. Yet it still didn't sit right in her heart.

"Lucas has the right to know."

"Elora—"

"Don't make him find out the way I found out." She pointed to the letters. "He deserves to hear it from you. And if you won't tell him, then I will."

Dad pinched the bridge of his nose. "How long have you known?"

"Months."

"Months? And you kept it to yourself?" He reached his hand across the couch to take hers. "I'm sorry."

"Yet you still wouldn't have told me." Maybe if she were

in his place, she wouldn't have been forthcoming about it either.

"Lucas is only thirteen," Dad said. "This is . . . he's only thirteen."

"I'm not asking that we march out and tell him today. I don't want this to derail his youth. But, Dad. Someday, he has to know."

His gaze shifted to the letters. He stared at them, the minutes passing in agonizing silence, until finally, he nodded. "I promise that I will tell him. When the time is right. Can you live with that?"

"Yes." Her dad didn't make promises to his children lightly. If he promised to tell Lucas, he would. For today, that was good enough. So Elora stood and started for the door, leaving those two letters behind.

She'd carried them long enough.

"Elora," he called before she could slip away. "I love you. What I have done, right or wrong, has always been because I love you."

"I know, Dad." She left his office and walked down the hall in a haze. Like she was outside of her body, still on the couch with Dad, trying to process everything he'd told her.

What next? Would it be strained between them? What would she say to her mother?

Nothing. Elora would let Dad deal with Mom. She'd done what she'd needed to do today. And it was time to go home.

Her feet carried her to the theater room, where Zain lounged in one recliner and Lucas in another. The movie on the screen was the latest streaming hit. Lucas had the volume so loud, neither of them heard her as she walked to the chairs and put her hand on Zain's shoulder.

"How'd it go?"

She shrugged and felt a sting in her nose. No doubt on the drive home, she'd be in tears.

"Are you gonna cry?" Lucas hit pause, the room going quiet, and flew out of his chair. "What's wrong?"

"Oh, it's nothing," she lied. "School stuff I needed to talk about with Dad."

"Are you flunking out?" Lucas asked.

"No, I'm not flunking."

Zain stood, slower with his crutch, but once he was on his feet, he raised an arm, making space for her at his side. "Proud of you."

She was proud of herself too. "Can we go home?"

"Wait. Home?" Lucas looked between the two of them. "You live together?"

"We do," Zain said before Elora could say no. "El just moved in."

"That was just a temporary solution while you're healing," she said.

"Then I'm making it permanent."

Elora wasn't going to argue.

"Once you're feeling better, you should come over," Zain told Lucas.

"Maybe." Lucas shrugged, doing his best to appear nonchalant, but his smile was peeking through. "I guess that could be cool."

Zain chuckled as he studied Lucas's face. Anyone else might have missed the flash of wonder in his gaze, but Elora didn't. And she didn't miss the admiration in Lucas's either. They were already enamored with each other, Lucas simply because Zain was Elora's. And Zain because Lucas was his.

Brothers.

And she got to keep them both.

With one last goodbye, Elora led the way outside after collecting their coats. She made sure Zain was settled into the passenger seat of his SUV, and then she climbed behind the wheel.

"Well? What did he say?" Zain asked.

She put the car in drive and, as she took them to the loft, told him everything.

"How do you feel?"

"I don't know." She shrugged. They were parked in the garage but neither had made a move to leave the car. "Strange."

"Are you up for something?"

"What something?"

"Something happy." He leaned across the console and planted a kiss on her mouth. "Follow me."

Instead of heading for the elevator to go upstairs, Zain headed for the tattoo parlor, where Axel was waiting. The shop was closed and there weren't any other artists around.

"Hey." Zain shook Axel's hand. "Thanks for doing this."

"My honor, man. Come on back." Axel winked at Elora, then led the way to his tattoo room.

"You're getting a tattoo?" Elora asked Zain as he settled into a chair.

"We are. I was hoping you'd get one too." Zain pointed to the neon sign on the wall.

Two hearts. One beat.

An hour later, Zain had the first part of that script inked over his heart.

And Elora had the second half inked over hers.

forty-nine

. . .

IVY DIDN'T WAIT for Roy to open her door when they pulled up to the manor. The moment the car's tires stopped rolling, she flew outside and hurried through the cold to sneak inside.

Her teeth chattered as she slipped through the back door, trying to keep her footsteps quiet as she walked down the hallway. Voices drifted from the kitchen. Edwin and Cassia were probably here with Francis.

It had been noon when Roy had collected her from Tate's neighborhood. She'd have to apologize to her brother and roommate—or ex-roommate, since Edwin had hauled Cassia's belongings to his place—later.

She needed to change clothes. Dry her frozen hair. Cry. Scream.

All of the above.

Maybe she should hop on an airplane. Leaving Boston, leaving the manor and Aston, seemed like a fantastic idea at the moment. After her finals. She'd make it through one more week and then she was gone. She would go anywhere as long as it wasn't here.

Her steps were stiff as she climbed the stairs. Roy had

cranked the heat on the drive home but it hadn't chased away the chill that had seeped into her bones. That was her fault for going outside without a coat.

The moment Allison's pregnancy test had landed in Tate's hand, Ivy had shoved out the door and stormed away. Her anger had kept her warm for a few blocks. But then her ears had started to freeze, and so had her fingers. Thankfully she'd had her phone to call Roy for a ride home, but it had taken him a while to get to her. By the time he'd arrived to pick her up, she'd been an icicle.

Her fingers were beginning to thaw and the tingles were so sharp they pricked. The smart decision would be a hot shower and her thickest wool socks. Except Ivy didn't go straight to her bedroom. She walked into her office, rushing for her desk drawer and that little pill inside.

Was this why she hadn't taken the pill yet? Had she known, deep down, that life would get worse? That Tate would hurt her so much she'd need this escape?

How could he? She'd told him everything. She'd trusted him. She'd fallen for him. How could he have fucking lied to her about Allison? Unless . . .

Unless Allison was lying about being pregnant. She could be lying. Ivy wouldn't put anything past that bitch.

Or maybe Allison was telling the truth. She'd looked devastated, and Ivy didn't think she was that good of an actress.

Tate had told Ivy that Allison had approached him just a week ago at Treason. Maybe he'd taken her up on that offer for a fuck in the parking lot behind the club. Was a week or two long enough to know you were pregnant?

Allison had known where Tate lived. That was something, right? Allison had obviously been to his place before. Maybe they'd been fucking for weeks. Maybe he'd taken her to his bed just like he had Ivy.

Or maybe Allison had her own investigator on staff. Finding Tate wouldn't have been that hard.

"Damn it." Ivy slammed her fist on the desk's surface. The doubts were making her head spin. Her heart was beating so hard it hurt. Her entire body was vibrating.

Water. She needed some water to swallow this pill and block out the world.

Ivy tore out of her office, going to her bathroom to turn on the faucet. Her hand trembled as she filled the glass at the sink.

She lifted the pill, ready to place it on her tongue, but caught her reflection in the mirror. Her face was pale. Her lips had a blue tint. The tip of her nose was as red as her eyes.

She looked like death.

An image of her in this very bathroom, looking nearly the same, popped into her mind. A different pill had been in her hand then, though the effects would be the same. She'd take this and be numb. She'd take this and the pain would stop, at least for a little while.

Except she'd been down that road.

The pain didn't stop.

In exactly four days, it would be the four-year anniversary of the crash. Of Kristopher's death.

Four years ago, Ivy had started taking pain pills. They'd been prescribed to her after the accident because of neck pain. She'd walked away with her life—and her own bumps and bruises. But even after those injuries had healed, she'd kept taking the pills to dull her senses.

Her mother had been doing the same for years and Helena had taught her daughter well. For a time, the pills had worked beautifully.

Until . . . they hadn't.

Until Ivy had woken up on this very bathroom floor without any recollection of how she'd gotten there, scared to death.

It was Geoff who'd confronted her about the pills. Geoff had been the one to notice her addiction. Not her parents. Not her brothers. Not her friends.

Her butler.

Geoff had gotten her help. He'd enlisted Francis, and together, they'd found a counselor who'd come to the manor every day for three months.

Ivy hadn't wanted to go to a rehab facility for fear of the gossip it would spur. So the counselor had gone with her to the doctor and they'd tapered her dosage until she'd been able to quit entirely.

She'd had to tell Elora about the pills and the counselor because it was hard to hide a woman coming to your home every day. And Edwin had found out about it too, so he'd told Zain. Their brotherly intervention had led to a full-fledged confession about Kristopher and the crash.

The story she'd told them wasn't all that different than her confession to Tate. And like Tate, her brothers had been livid. They'd made her promise no more pills. So had Geoff.

Geoff had made her swear to quit so that one day he wouldn't walk into this room and find her lifeless body on the floor.

She'd made that promise.

And she was seconds away from breaking it.

Her hand shook, water sloshing over the glass's rim.

Ivy stared at the pill, so close to her tongue she could taste it. She hadn't looked at the bottle closely when she'd stolen it from her mother's purse. It was probably a Xanax. Maybe a Valium. Not nearly as strong as the opioids Ivy had once craved.

Did it matter?

This pill, mild as it was, would break her promises.

Flush it.

Take it.

"What the fuck are you doing?"

The glass in her hand slipped, crashing to the counter and clattering into the sink. By some miracle it didn't break.

Ivy's gaze met Tate's in the mirror as he stepped into the room.

While she felt like an ice cube, he was the opposite. Hot, molten lava. His cheeks were flushed and his eyes blazed.

"What are you doing here?" she asked.

He grabbed her wrist, tearing the pill from her fingertips. "What is this?"

"A broken promise," she whispered. To her family. To Geoff. To herself.

He held her gaze, like he was trying to see into her soul. See the other pieces that she'd omitted when she'd told him about the crash. "This will not fix what is broken."

"Then what will?"

His jaw clenched as he set the pill on the countertop. "You left."

"You lied."

"Did I?"

"You fucked Allison." She crossed her arms across her chest, trying to hide the shaking in her hands. "How could you?"

Tate's expression turned to stone. "You know . . . Zain talked about you and Edwin. He'd tell me about his younger brother and sister occasionally, mostly milestones or when shit with your family went sideways. Like with the accident. And when you started at Aston. He told me when you asked to come to Treason. He was worried that it was a mistake, letting you in when you were that young."

Ivy didn't risk a word. She had no idea where he was going with this, and as mad as she was, as hurt as she was, she still clung to his every word.

"He always wondered if your parents had completely fucked you and Edwin up. He worried about it. That's why he let you come to Treason. Because he wanted to know who you were."

"And I bet he was disappointed."

"No." Tate shook his head. "He wasn't. He told me you had spirit. That you were a brat but he suspected you'd grow out of it. He said you reminded him of himself. Bold and stubborn. Fearless. That between you and Edwin, you might be the one to break free from your dad's plans, like he had."

Ivy didn't even know who that woman was anymore. She'd lost her somewhere along the way.

"To me, you were just his sister," Tate said. "A faceless girl we'd talk about sometimes. And then I walked into Treason, and the second I saw you, the moment you threw that attitude of yours in my face, everything changed. You weren't Zain's sister. You were mine."

A whimper escaped her throat. Tears welled in her eyes because behind Tate's anger, there was pain. Heartbreaking anguish and she was the person who'd put it there.

"From the moment I saw you in that club, you were mine. To touch. To hold. To kiss. To protect. You were mine. But that means fuck all if you can't trust me. If I'm not yours too. Decide, Ivy. You're either in or out."

Without another word, he walked away, leaving her in silence. His words ringing in her ears.

She reached out and picked up the pill, setting it into her palm. Her fingers closed around it, squeezing tight.

Decide, Ivy.

Flush it.

Or take it.

She walked to the toilet and opened her hand. Then she turned over her palm.

That little white square slipped from her skin, falling with the faintest of plops into the water. Then it was gone, swirling, vanishing, as she flushed.

Decide.

Lose him.

Or fight.

fifty

. . .

IVY WAITED IN THE FOYER, sitting on the staircase and wringing her hands. When she heard a car door slam, followed by another, she shot to her feet, meeting Edwin and Cassia at the door. "Hi."

"Hey." Edwin nodded, his hand clasped with Cassia's as they stepped inside.

"Sorry I didn't meet you yesterday." Ivy forced a smile. "Something came up."

Cassia's expression was blank. So blank Ivy wondered if she'd been taking lessons from Elora.

Okay, then. Time to get on with it. Ivy had somewhere to be this morning and she didn't have time to waste with small talk. "I'm sorry. About everything."

Cassia gave her a sideways glance. "Everything?"

"Everything. If you'd like your room—"

"She doesn't," Edwin answered for her.

"I figured as much," Ivy said. "But the offer stands."

Cassia stood taller. "Did you call Josh?"

"No."

"I don't know if I can believe you."

"Fair enough." Ivy nodded. "Maybe someday you will."

After Ivy earned her trust. And damn it, she would. The way Edwin looked at her, Cassia would be around for a long, long time.

"Francis adores you," Ivy told Cassia. "I think she secretly hopes your good influence will rub off on me. Even though you're not living here, I hope you'll visit her often."

"I'd like that."

"Good." Ivy smiled. "Then you'd better keep your key."

Cassia studied her for a long moment, then gave a little headshake like she couldn't believe this was happening.

Edwin chuckled, tugging her into his side. "We'd better go. I left the car running. We're heading to the library to study."

"Bye." Ivy walked them to the door. "Oh, and Edwin?"

"Yeah?"

"I'm not going to Mom and Dad's for Christmas. I was thinking of inviting Elora and Zain over for dinner here." The idea was forming in her mind as she spoke. "Maybe Francis and Daisy could come. We could hire a caterer or something. I don't know. Would you guys come?"

Edwin looked to Cassia. She lifted a shoulder. Was that a yes?

"Depends." Edwin smirked. "What are you getting me this year?"

"Guess you'll have to show up to find out."

He chuckled. "Good luck with finals."

"You too." She waved, waiting in the threshold until they were in the Bentley. Then she retreated to the foyer, only to stop short as Michael came down the rear hallway.

Was there a revolving door at the manor she wasn't aware of?

"Hey." Michael moved with that confident swagger she'd once found so appealing. Today, she hoped that swagger would lead him the hell out of her house. For good.

"What are you doing here?" She didn't mask the irritation in her tone. And how had he come in? She'd be having a conversation with Geoff once Michael was gone. The back door was usually left unlocked, but if Michael was using it at will, that would change.

"Thought I'd see what you were doing tonight," he said. "Feel like dinner?"

"No."

"No?"

"No, I don't want to go to dinner with you."

His eyes narrowed.

"You need to knock before you come into my house." She strode past him, but he grabbed her elbow a little too tight. Ivy dropped her gaze to his hand, then lifted her chin. "Today is not the day to provoke me, Michael."

Michael let her go but sneered. "Heard your guy cheated on you with Allison."

"No, he didn't."

After Ivy had flushed that pill yesterday and thawed, both physically and mentally, she'd thought about Allison. How she'd come to Tate's doorstep. How she'd handed him that pregnancy test. Somehow, Allison had known Ivy would be there to overhear. And somehow, Michael had known to bring it up today.

Was Allison even pregnant?

She should have realized it sooner. She should have stood by Tate's side.

She'd assumed the worst. Shame on her. She wouldn't make that mistake again.

"You sure about that?" Michael asked.

"Oh, I'm sure. But if we're sharing rumors, I heard that Allison is pregnant. Should I be saying congratulations, Daddy?"

There was a flash of shock in his gaze.

Okay, so he hadn't known. Which meant Allison's play had been hers alone. Chances were, that pregnancy test had been bogus. Or maybe she was pregnant with Michael's kid. If Ivy planted a few doubts in his head, she'd call today a win.

"Bye." Ivy left the foyer and walked through the manor, collecting her coat before going outside to meet Roy.

He was waiting for her in the rear driveway, per her request earlier. He smiled at her through the rearview mirror as she settled into the back seat. "Where to?"

Ivy gave him the address, earning a wary glance, but he kept his mouth shut and drove.

"Should I wait here?" he asked as he parked against the sidewalk.

"Probably not a bad idea." Her stomach twisted in a knot as she stared at the building out her window.

Given her track record, she'd screw this up sooner or later. But if she truly wanted her life to be her own, to be happy, it was time to act. So she pushed out of the car and walked to the front door, her heart pounding as she raised a finger to ring the doorbell.

It didn't take long before the lock flipped. The door swung open.

And Tate filled its frame.

He crossed his arms over his chest, his biceps straining at the sleeves of his shirt. His scowl was firmly fixed in place, but even angry he was beautiful.

"You told me to decide," she said.

"I did. And?"

"And I don't like who I am. But I'd like to change."

"Good."

She waited for more—a crack in his expression or an invitation inside. But he just stared at her, blocking the doorway. "I should have trusted you."

"Yep."

"I'm sorry."

"Good." Another good. Nothing more.

What was he waiting for her to say? It was like trying to finish a puzzle when three of the pieces were missing. "May I—"

"No." Tate stepped out of the way and closed the door.

"Uh, okay." Ouch.

Her heart, her pride, crumbled into tiny, brittle pieces at her feet.

This had always been a possibility, right? She'd spent last night tossing and turning in her bed, knowing that he might be done with her. She'd gone too far this time, believing Allison's bullshit.

Even a man like Tate would have his limits, and clearly, Ivy had found the edge.

But damn it, she wanted him. She wanted one more chance. Just one more chance to do better.

As she stared at the door's wooden face, her stomach sank. There'd be no more chances. "Damn."

Roy spotted her returning to the car and climbed out, rushing to meet her at the back. "Let's get you home. I knew this was a bad idea after picking you up yesterday, frozen on the sidewalk. What kind of man would send you out of his house without a coat?"

"It's not him, Roy." Ivy gave her driver a sad smile. "It's me. I screwed this up. And I left without my coat. I failed him."

Roy studied her, his eyebrows knitting together. "Well, if that's the case. You don't strike me as someone who fails, Miss Clarence."

"I've been failing a lot lately," she admitted. As a roommate. As a sister. As . . . what was she to Tate? A lover? Girlfriend?

Those labels sounded so trivial, even in her head. She wanted to be more. She wanted to be his entire world. She wanted to be so wrapped up in his life that no one would be able to tell where he ended and she began.

This couldn't be over. She wouldn't allow it. What if this was all a test? What if this was a trial of her own to pass?

"You know what, Roy? You're right." She was Ivy Clarence, for fuck's sake. "You can go. I'll be staying."

"Are you sure?"

"Very."

"If you change your mind, I'm just a phone call away."

"Thank you." Ivy waited until the car's taillights were out of sight, then she steeled her spine and returned to Tate's, pressing the doorbell again.

That stunning scowl was still on his face when he answered.

Ivy planted a hand on his chest and pushed. Hard. Until they were both inside and she closed the door behind them. "I don't have many people in my life who challenge me."

Tate planted his hands on his hips. "Ivy—"

She held up a hand. "You make me better. So you can't be done with me. Not yet. I want you. But mostly, I *need* you."

Tate sighed. "I'm pissed at you. You should have trusted me."

"I know."

"What did you do with that pill?"

"Flushed it."

"Good."

"Stop saying good."

"Great."

She rolled her eyes. "I'm sorry."

His shoulders relaxed and his arms fell to his sides.

"Can I have one more chance? Please?" Ivy would beg if needed.

Tate took a step forward to tuck a lock of hair behind her ear. "Did I say we were done?"

"No."

"No, I didn't. And what did I tell you?"

Her heart skipped when his eyes gentled. The scowl on his handsome face disappeared. "We're done when you say we're done."

"Exactly. And we're not done. But stop acting like a fucking brat, okay? I don't like it."

"No promises." It probably wasn't what he wanted to hear.

Ivy wouldn't change overnight. "Though I'll try to tone it down."

Tate chuckled, framing her face with his hands. "Good."

"What's with you and *good* today?"

"Just calling it like it is." His lips coasted against hers, his tongue dragging along the seam of her smile. "Because, baby, this is going to be so fucking good."

No, this was going to be great.

This was going to be the love of her life.

fifty-one

. . .

"HOW'D THE TEST GO?" Edwin asked Cassia.

"Fine." Her gloved hand was locked in his own as they walked across campus. "There was only one question I'm worried about."

But missing one out of a hundred wouldn't break her grade.

"It feels good to be done." There was a weight off her shoulders. The semester was finished. A final term remained, then she'd bid farewell to Boston. Though she didn't feel the urgency she had just a week ago to move across the world. As it turned out, Boston wasn't so bad. Living with Edwin for a week had been a dream.

And though she still wanted to leave for a year or two, Cassia had a feeling she'd return. That *they* would return.

After an adventure.

Edwin was lobbying for a move to Australia. Just last night, he'd read her the list of pros he'd been making to living in Melbourne. Item number one? Kangaroos. He really wanted to live where there were kangaroos.

So much so that he'd given her an early Christmas gift.

Last night, he'd surprised her with two first-class tickets to Australia for spring break.

Now that she had a break from classes for a few weeks, she planned to start researching job opportunities. Maybe even line up an interview or two for their trip.

"Are you going to hang out?" he asked as they approached the building where he had his last final exam. "Or walk home?"

"How long do you think this test will take?"

"Twenty minutes. Thirty max."

"Then I'll wait. We can go home together." It was cold but she was dressed for winter in a coat, hat and gloves. The fresh air was invigorating and she wouldn't mind a little extra time outside. Edwin had insisted on driving together today, and Cassia missed her daily walks around campus.

" 'Kay." He kissed her, a little too long and a little too deep to be considered anything but blatant PDA. But she didn't care.

Cassia wanted the world to know that Edwin Clarence was hers. "Love you. Good luck."

"Love you too, Red." He smiled, then headed inside while she wandered to a bench beneath a tree, brushing off the snow before taking a seat.

Campus was quiet today. Being the Thursday afternoon of finals week, there were plenty of students who had finished their last tests and were on their way home for the holidays.

This would be the first Christmas without Dad. Finals had been a welcome distraction, but now that they were over, dread was seeping in. Edwin would probably go over the top to make her smile. She'd let him.

Cassia hugged her backpack to her lap, the bag almost empty now that she'd sold back her textbooks. The money she'd gotten today was going toward Edwin's Christmas present—AirPods, since he'd lost his somewhere at home, and a black lace teddy she'd bought at a lingerie shop. She'd let him shred the latter off her body on Christmas Eve.

"Hey."

Cassia's head whipped around as Elora took a seat beside her on the bench. "Hey."

"All done with finals?" Elora asked.

"Yeah. You?"

"Just finished. How are you?"

"I'm good." Cassia hadn't seen Elora for weeks. Not since before the fight with Ivy at the manor. "How are you?"

"Good." A smile stretched across Elora's face. A smile so bright and vibrant, Cassia barely recognized her former roommate. "You moved in with Edwin, right?"

"I did. And you're living with Zain?"

Elora nodded. "I still have some things at the manor. I'll probably get them at Christmas. You're going, right?"

"Yes, she is." Ivy strode to the bench and sat on Cassia's other side. "Hi."

"Um, hi?" Cassia still wasn't sure what to say to Ivy.

They weren't friends. But were they still enemies? After a week away from the manor, she'd had plenty of time to think. As much as she wanted to doubt Ivy and stay on guard, Cassia believed that Ivy hadn't called Josh.

And when Michael had approached her on Monday after a test, Cassia had ignored him completely.

"How did finals go?" Ivy was bundled in a thick green parka. The color was practically neon against the snowy backdrop and a sharp contrast to both Elora's and Cassia's black coats. But it suited Ivy. Green of any shade really was her color.

"I probably should have studied more." Elora's mouth curved into another smile. "Zain's doctor cleared him for sex, so . . ."

"Eww." Ivy feigned a gag. "We need to put some boundaries in place. The fewer details I know about my brothers' sex lives, the better."

Elora laughed, a sound so carefree and happy once again Cassia stared at her like she was an entirely different person.

"This is weird," Cassia blurted. "Are we acquaintances? Or . . ."

"Friends," Ivy declared. "We're friends. You'll get used to it."

"How's the manor?" Elora asked.

"I don't know," Ivy said. "I haven't been there in a week. I'm staying at Tate's. But Geoff will have it all ready for Christmas. The decorators came today with a tree."

"I—" Whatever Elora was going to say was cut short when a man walked past on the sidewalk.

He slowed, doing a double take at Cassia. Then he dropped his gaze to his feet, ready to keep on walking. He would pretend she didn't exist, simply because that's what she'd asked him to do.

"Hi, Henry," she blurted. Apparently today words were just spewing from her lips.

He stopped walking, turning to give her a small smile. "Hi, Cassie."

"Happy holidays."

"Happy holidays," he repeated, then dipped his chin before carrying on his way.

"You know Dean Neilson?" Ivy asked.

Cassia nodded. "He's my uncle."

"He's my biological father," Elora said, and if Cassia hadn't been sitting, she might have fallen on her ass.

Her biological father? Henry hadn't even glanced at her. Did he know? Did that make them cousins?

Ivy's jaw dropped. "What?"

"He doesn't know about me," Elora said. "And I'd like to keep it that way. It was more of a sperm donor situation. But Zain knows. You might as well too."

"You're confiding this secret in me?" Cassia asked. Maybe she'd fallen asleep on the bench. Maybe this was a dream.

Elora shrugged. "We're friends."

"Exactly," Ivy said.

A giggle broke free from Cassia's mouth. It started small,

then grew and grew until she was laughing. Why was she laughing? Maybe because of all the people at Aston, the last two she'd expected to be sharing secrets with were her roommates—former roommates. Whatever the reason, she couldn't stop.

Ivy joined in next. Then Elora. Until the three of them were making such noise that they were getting looks from the few people walking by.

Minutes passed until they finally pulled themselves together. Cassia had to wipe tears from the corners of her eyes. There was an ache in her side. She hadn't laughed like that in, well . . . in a really long time.

"Sounds like we have stories to share. How about we celebrate the semester being over at Treason tonight?" Ivy asked.

This little encounter had been surprising. It was enough for one day. Best not to push it.

Ivy stood. "Let's meet at nine."

Before Cassia could say no, Ivy was gone.

"Zain wanted to go to the club tonight anyway. He's slowly working his way back to normal." Elora stood and waved. "See you tonight."

Cassia was still sitting dumbfounded when Edwin found her on the bench.

"What's that look?" he asked.

"I, uh"—she shook her head—"I guess we're going to Treason tonight."

"Cheers!" Ivy raised her champagne.

Everyone clinked their glasses together, a chorus of cheers sounding through their group.

Cassia took a sip from her flute, then laughed. How was this fun? A night at Treason with Ivy and Elora shouldn't have been enjoyable. But since the moment she'd set foot in the club, she'd had a blast.

"What's funny?" Edwin asked, his arm draped around her shoulders.

"Nothing." She leaned in to plant a kiss on his mouth. "Just surprised this is fun."

"Save some energy for extra fun later," he murmured, pulling her closer into his side. His other hand was splayed on her thigh and he inched it higher.

They'd already had a post-semester celebration in bed before they'd come to the club. Since they'd been here, his hands hadn't once left her body, and the foreplay was beginning to make her ache.

"Your cheeks are flushed, Red," he whispered in her ear. "One more hour. Then we're out."

She nodded, taking another sip of her champagne.

Elora was sitting in a similar position with Zain, tucked into his side as he reclined on the couch in his lounge. The bouncers hadn't let many people onto this tier tonight, wanting to make sure Zain had space and it didn't get so crowded that someone accidentally bumped his broken leg.

Beside them, Ivy was sitting on Tate's lap. While Elora was wearing a pair of black pants and Cassia had chosen jeans and a sexy top, Ivy was in a flowy green, strapless dress. The slit in the skirt ran to her hip and Tate's hand trailed up and down her bare leg.

Cassia credited the men for making the conversation tonight easy. Comfortable and unexpected. Tate and Zain had shared stories from their own days at Aston. Elora and Edwin had commiserated about their shared classes and what they'd registered for in the next semester. Ivy had told them she'd be applying to the Aston history master's program soon.

And Cassia had listened, content to simply feel included.

Maybe someday she'd share more of her past. Maybe not. Tonight, she was just enjoying expensive champagne and cuddling close to Edwin.

The noise from the main floor grew loud enough to draw attention. Cassia sat a little taller just as Michael strode through the front entrance with a cluster of men. Probably his fraternity brothers.

"Well, well, well." The glint in Ivy's eyes was terrifying.

"Oh, I know that look." Elora laughed. "What are you planning, Ivy?"

"He had Allison fake a pregnancy to fuck up my relationship with Tate. I made a few calls and found out that one of the girls in her sorority is pregnant, not Allison. There's no question that Michael is involved. That, and he called Cassia's ex to hurt her." Ivy took a sip of her champagne. "So obviously, I'll be getting revenge."

"I'm going to need something stronger for this." Tate signaled the waitress and ordered a round of tequila shots.

"What exactly are you planning?" Elora asked Ivy.

Ivy shot a glare at the dance floor, where Michael was showing off. "Turns out that our friend Michael has been screwing this cute little girl. My investigator sent me some interesting photos this evening."

"You're basically funding Sal's retirement at this point, aren't you?" Edwin asked.

"Pretty much. It's worth it. The girl Michael has been fucking really is just a girl. She goes to a local high school. Sneaks out of her parents' house at night, puts on a bunch of makeup and pretends to be in college. Goes to the fraternity parties. But the sweet little thing is only fifteen."

Cassia's jaw dropped. "And Michael doesn't know?"

"He will soon." Ivy grinned. "Michael Bamford will no longer be a problem. He messed with the wrong people."

"Asshole," Elora muttered.

"Agreed." Ivy thrust her champagne flute into the center of their circle. "Let's do another toast."

"Again?" Zain teased. "What are we toasting this time?"

"To secrets." Ivy smirked. "And the friends we trust to keep them."

Cassia and Edwin shared a look. Then they both laughed with the others, everyone clinking glasses once more.

"To secrets."

epilogue

. . .

TWO YEARS LATER . . .

"I don't like this blindfold, Tate." Ivy would have sent him a glare if she could have. Not that it would have made him take it off. Her husband had a surprise, hence the black cloth he'd wrapped around her eyes the moment they'd gotten into the car. "It's going to ruin my makeup."

"Not if you hold still."

She frowned because that, he would see.

"We're almost there." He took her hand off her lap, weaving their fingers together before kissing the knuckle on her ring finger. That was one of his favorite places on her body to touch his lips, the spot just below the four-carat diamond ring he'd given her a year ago and the diamond-studded wedding band he'd added six months later.

"Give me a clue," she said.

He chuckled. "Baby."

Meaning no.

"You look beautiful," he said.

"Don't try to flatter me into a good mood."

"Why? It's working."

She curled her lip. Yes, it was. He'd pulled out all the stops tonight for whatever they were doing and wherever they were going.

She'd walked in the door tonight after her last class and had found him dressed in a black suit. He wore suits to the club on occasion, so she'd assumed he was heading to work. But then he'd handed her a garment bag with this stunning juniper dress inside. The green was so dark it was nearly as black as her long wool coat. The bodice was a fitted corset with a tulle overlay that swept over one shoulder. Then the skirt billowed wide, hitting her midcalf.

It was exactly the dress she would have chosen for herself.

"The blindfold is not the accessory I would have chosen."

"Oh, I like the blindfold." Tate's voice dipped low, a gravelly tone that he usually reserved for their bedroom. "We'll be keeping it for later."

A shiver rolled down her spine.

He chuckled, then the car slowed. After they'd left the brownstone, Ivy had tried to keep track of the turns. She'd tried to visualize where they were going, but after about five minutes, she'd gotten lost and given up.

"Are we going to the club?" she asked.

"No."

"Treason?"

"No."

"Are you at least going to feed me? I'm hungry. I didn't get lunch today."

The master's program at Aston was demanding, though she loved every moment of it. Her thesis project was exhilarating, and today, she'd been so caught up in her research that when she'd finally pulled her head out of the book she'd been reading to look at the clock, she'd almost been late for a class.

Her focus as of late had been cartography. Maps were the written proof of someone's curiosity. The class she'd taken her senior year had left an impression and her thesis supervisor had encouraged her to follow her passions. She still had time to decide exactly what she'd be writing in her thesis, but for now, she was brainstorming ideas and ran her latest past Tate every night.

"Yes, we're having dinner," he said. "And I'll be asking Francis to start packing you a lunch."

Francis would be all over that. She'd grumbled for years about Ivy eating *campus* food.

Tate had asked Ivy to move into his place in Back Bay after they'd been together for a few months. She'd spent every night there anyway. But she'd been resistant to leave the manor because of Francis.

Geoff would always have a position there, maintaining the house. But if no one lived there, her father would eliminate Francis's position.

So Tate had solved that problem. The morning after Ivy had told him she didn't want her chef to lose her job, she'd walked into Tate's kitchen to find Francis unloading groceries.

It wasn't the same as the manor, not without Geoff, but he came over once a week to say hello. His friendship with Francis was as close as ever. Their two-person book club was still going strong. Though Geoff liked to lament that the manor was too quiet.

Her father had done exactly as Ivy had expected. When he'd found out that she'd applied to the master's program at Aston, he'd ordered her to meet him at his office. She'd stopped him in the middle of his reprimand and told him exactly what she'd be doing with her life—whatever the hell she wanted.

She'd never seen her father's expression so cold as when he'd told her she could forget the manor.

Ivy had taken a bit of delight in seeing the shock on his face when she'd informed him that she'd already moved out.

It had been a bittersweet day. Clarence Manor would always hold a piece of her heart. But the rest belonged to Tate, and with every passing month, the brownstone was becoming home.

His new Jaguar slowed and Tate unwound their hands.

Her body jostled in the seat as they made a couple of turns. Then he shoved the car in park. "Stay put."

Would he divorce her if she peeked? Probably not. But he was excited about this. And as much as she wanted to rip this blindfold off, she left it alone.

Tate opened her door and took her hand, helping her out. Then he locked his arm with hers and guided her forward. "Careful, it's a little slippery. Here's a step. And another."

They climbed, her heels clicking, until she felt the warmth of being inside. A door clicked shut behind her. She drew in a breath and the familiar scent gave away Tate's secret.

White roses and lilies.

Geoff's preferred flowers for the bouquet he kept on the late-seventeenth-century table in the foyer.

"You know where we are, don't you?" There was a frown in Tate's voice.

"The manor," she breathed as he untied the blindfold. It took a moment for her eyes to adjust, then she took in every unchanged inch.

The chandelier's crystal drops and beaded chains sparkled over their heads. The Italian marble floor gleamed beneath the golden light. The baroque banister on the staircase shined from a fresh polish.

Home.

She spun around, and there was Geoff waiting by the door.

He gave her a slight bow, his eyes crinkling with his smile. "Miss Ivy."

"Hi, Geoff." She smiled back, then turned to Tate. "Why are we here?"

"You miss it."

Yes, she did. How did he know? She'd never told him that she missed the summer flower garden or the massive bathtub in her old rooms. She'd loved these walls since she was a little girl.

He stepped closer, tracing the line of her cheek with his finger. "You know I'll do anything to make you happy."

"Yes."

"You know I love you."

She soaked in the sparkle in his dazzling eyes. "I love you too."

The corner of his mouth turned up. "Good."

Ivy waited for an explanation but he just grinned. "You didn't answer my question."

"Didn't I?"

"Tate," she warned. "Why are we here?"

Voices came from the upstairs hallway, and before she could pester Tate for an answer, Edwin and Cassia stood at the top of the staircase.

"What?" Ivy gasped, then looked to Tate. "This is my surprise?" She hadn't seen Edwin or Cassia in months. Not since they'd flown home last summer.

"No."

"Then what is my surprise?" Because if it wasn't having Edwin and Cassia home from Melbourne, what else was there?

"You'll see."

She rolled her eyes, then left his side to hug her brother after he came down the stairs. "Hi."

"Hi." Edwin held her tight. "Missed you."

"I missed you too." She let him go to embrace Cassia. "I missed you more than Edwin."

Cassia laughed.

"I heard that." Edwin chuckled.

"Because I said it so you'd hear me."

It had taken the rest of their senior year at Aston, but Ivy and Cassia had made it to a place where the awkwardness from the past was gone. Now they were just . . . sisters.

Sisters-in-law.

Edwin had taken Cassia to Las Vegas after graduation to celebrate. He'd invited Ivy, Tate, Elora and Zain along. Their second night in Vegas, after staying up too late and spending too much money in a casino, they'd all found themselves at a little chapel.

Edwin had wanted to marry Cassia but hadn't wanted an elaborate affair. A reminder that her father wouldn't be there to walk her down the aisle. And though she had developed a closer relationship with her uncle that last semester of senior year, Cassia had still mourned her dad.

Her brother's plan had been as obvious as Sin City's neon lights. He'd had an appointment and a diamond ring in his pocket.

"How long are you here?" Ivy asked Cassia. "Can you stay through Christmas?"

Cassia and Edwin shared a look before her smile widened. "We are actually going to stay for a while. We're moving back."

"What?" Ivy's face turned to Tate, who was shaking Edwin's hand. "Is that my surprise?"

"No."

Ivy poked him in the side. "Tell me."

He ignored her, brushing past to hug Cassia. "Glad you're back."

"Me too," she said. "Australia was fun. But we're ready to be closer."

"Much closer." Edwin grinned at Tate, like they were in on something.

Cassia suddenly found her shoes very interesting.

"Okay, what is—"

The door opened, cutting her off, and Geoff welcomed Elora and Zain inside.

Zain was dressed similarly to Tate and Edwin, each in tailored suits with a crisp white shirt. Cassia had opted for trousers and a pale pink top that was the perfect complement to her coral hair. But Elora was in a dress like Ivy, and as her best friend let Zain help her out of her coat, the material hugged her growing belly.

Ivy's nephew.

Elora and Zain didn't seem at all surprised to see Edwin and Cassia. As everyone exchanged hugs, Francis came into the foyer, clapping her hands.

"We are just about ready. Wine is poured in the dining room."

"Ready for what? Francis, will you tell me what is going on?" Ivy asked.

Her chef zipped her lips shut and turned on a heel, taking Geoff with her to the kitchen.

"Tate." Ivy's nostrils flared. "I don't like surprises."

Zain coughed to hide a laugh. "I take it you haven't told her."

"Nah." Tate laughed. "I'm waiting to see how long it takes her to figure it out."

"Figure out what?" Ivy looked to Elora. "Do you know?"

"Yes." Elora splayed a hand on her baby bump. The light reflecting on her wedding rings was nearly as bright as her smile.

"Will you tell me?"

"No. You're always the one who knows the secrets. It's nice to be on this side of it for a change."

Ivy harrumphed, which only made Elora laugh.

Elora smiled more often than not these days. Ivy credited it to Zain and their baby, but also to the sheer lack of drama in Elora's life. She was as close with Lawrence as ever. She tolerated her mother, and the two rarely crossed paths. And she and Zain made a point to see Lucas at least once a week.

Lucas still didn't know he wasn't Lawrence's biological child, but Elora had confided with Edwin and Ivy the truth. If —when—the day came that they welcomed Lucas into their lives as a half brother, they'd have his back. Elora's too.

That was what sisters were for.

They'd found happy lives these past two years, mostly thanks to the fact that they'd cut ties with toxic people like

Michael Bamford and Allison Winston. But they'd also cut some closer ties too.

The last time Ivy had spoken to her father had been as he'd walked her down the aisle to marry Tate. It hurt that he'd dismissed her so completely from his life when he still kept in touch with Edwin and Zain. And her mother, well . . . Helena didn't reach out often.

It was for the best—that's what Tate said.

But why were they at the manor? This was her father's property. He'd made it inescapably clear that this was no longer her home.

Ivy studied Tate's face, searching for a clue to her surprise. To why he'd brought her here. There was no way her father would let them come here for this reunion. Sure, Ivy's trust fund was still in her name, and she hadn't heard of any changes, so at least she hadn't been disinherited. But she wasn't holding her breath that she'd get her inheritance when she turned thirty. Dad might deny her, just like he had this manor.

"Why are we here?" she asked Tate again.

Zain took Elora's hand. "We're going to sit down."

"We'll join you." Edwin tucked Cassia into his side, kissing her as they left Tate and Ivy alone.

"Tell me." Because her hopes were soaring and she wasn't sure her heart could take it if she'd guessed wrong.

"I made a call a few months ago."

"To my dad?"

Tate nodded. "I told him I wanted the manor."

"And he let you have it?" No way. Was this real?

"It took some negotiating." He stepped closer, towering above her as his arm banded around her back.

"What was the negotiation? What did he want?"

"Some photos."

Ivy gave him a sideways glance. "What photos?"

"Just some photos that Sal took. You see, a long time ago I

learned that my wife had this handy connection to a guy who was great at getting her leverage."

Ivy's eyes widened. "You had Sal follow Dad."

Tate nodded. "It took me two years, but I finally got him. Turns out your dad's latest affair has been with the city commissioner's wife. David is trying to get past a few zoning regulations for this development he's funding. He's been careful to hide the affair, but not careful enough. Those photos would mean the end to a multimillion-dollar project. I promised they'd never see the light of day, just as long as I could have the keys to my wife's house. So we made a trade. He sold me the manor at a fair price and I handed over the pictures."

Her mind was reeling. A giggle escaped. Then she threw her arms around Tate, holding him close. "Oh my God."

"Welcome home, baby."

Home. They were home. And just in time. She wanted to turn one of the upstairs bedrooms into a nursery.

Was this a good time to tell Tate she was pregnant? No. She'd keep that secret to herself for a few more days.

Ivy would play with him a bit. Torture him like he'd tortured her.

After all, secrets were Ivy's specialty. And oh, what fun those secrets could be.

acknowledgments

Thank you for reading *Ivy*! Talk about a passion project. This book consumed me from start to finish.

Special thanks to my editing and proofreading team. Judy Zweifel, you are a rock star and I can't thank you enough for squeezing this in every week for months. Julie Deaton, thank you for fitting this into your jam-packed schedule and for the sweet comments you'd leave me each week. Elizabeth Nover, a huge shoutout to you for tackling this beast. And thanks to Sarah Hansen for the cover I love so much.

Thank you to all the members of Perry & Nash and the wonderful bloggers who help promote my stories. I truly have the best readers in the world.

And lastly, to my incredible family and friends. Thank you!